John E. Lee

   In the murky and rancid front room of the Hero of
Waterloo, where patrons served themselves from open
barrels of whiskey, per Sydney custom, Nat Gane
drank to forget his treachery. He sat at a table with
three of Honey Fitz's men, hating them and hating
himself for what he had done to Michael Bourke
Irons. Around Gane drunken men and women argued,
struck each other, shouted and continued to drink
while dancers shuffled endlessly to the speedy notes
of trumpet and violin, both played with more ambition
than ability. The harsh rum warmed Gane, but could
not cleanse his mind and soul. He needed money with
a desperation he had not believed possible. Without
money he would be disgraced, impoverished and
imprisoned.

THE UNVANQUISHED

by
Terry Nelsen Bonner

DELL PUBLISHING * * * NEW YORK

Published by
Dell Publishing Co., Inc.
1 Dag Hammarskjold Plaza
New York, New York 10017

Dell ® TM 681510, Dell Publishing Co., Inc.

ISBN: 0-440-09257-4

Printed in the United States of America

First printing—October 1983

No country was ever saved by good men
because good men will not go to the
lengths that may be necessary.

Horace Walpole
4th Earl of Orford
(1717–1797)
English writer and
historian

BOOK I
Michael Bourke Irons
1890 . . . And The Beginning

1 _____

SYDNEY
October 1890

AN angry Michael Bourke Irons, his wife on his arm,
stepped from the ballroom of Government House and onto
a terrace, leaving behind a crush of dancers waltzing under
flickering gaslight. He had almost killed Redmond Glass
and the remembered hostility still drove Irons like an
engine, making it almost impossible for Camilla to keep
up with his long infuriated strides.

Tonight Sydney's rich and powerful, its social climbers
and celebrity collectors, its politicians, bankers, sheep
ranchers, mine owners, journalists and madames had
crowded into the official residence of the Governor of New
South Wales to honor the visiting American author and
journalist Mark Twain. The fifty-five-year-old Twain, whose
recent lecture tour of Europe had been well received, was
now being given the same sort of celebrity's welcome in
Sydney.

From the terrace Irons breathed deeply to calm himself
and looked past acres of gardens and rolling lawns towards
the oil lamps that danced in the distance, dangling from

clipper ships anchored in the harbor. On the morning tide the long and narrow clippers, each with three masts of wide sails, would carry tightly wrapped bales of wool, barrels of tallow, carcasses of frozen mutton and prime beef and stacks of gold ingots to England, America and Europe. The ships, meat, tallow and gold belonged to Michael Bourke Irons.

He was a giant of a man, with a black patch over the empty socket of his left eye and a face that had endured untold conflicts. His black frock coat, with gold sovereigns for buttons, his tight black trousers, ruffled white shirt and sealskin boots had been made in London's Jermyn Street by the Prince of Wales' tailor. A blue diamond stickpin decorated one lapel. He was forty-eight, and clean shaven, with dark hair graying at the temples. His remaining eye was a startling blue.

His nemesis, Redmond Glass, was one of the perhaps too colorful characters of the time. Glass was the 300 pound, balding and red bearded publisher of a scandalous newspaper called OPUS DEI; GOD'S WORK, which specialized in reporting murders, rapes, incest, corruption, thefts and the dark secrets of people's private lives. Glass was a drunkard, seducer, gambler, wife beater and blackmailer, who often enriched himself by extorting money from people who paid rather than see their indiscretions in print. He was ruthless, witty, debauched and a cynical demagogue skilled at stirring up the public. Twice he had failed in his attempts to blackmail Michael Irons. The two were implacable enemies.

Earlier in the evening the fifty piece orchestra had begun the gala for Twain by playing American dances—the Virginia Reel, barn dance, clog dance, cake walk, Paul Jones and the latest United States import, the Two Step. The men were all dressed in the somber conformity of black frock coats, pants, ruffled shirts and boots. Almost all were bearded, many with the florid complexions of heavy drinkers and those who lived on beef with the run still in it. But the women, with their rich Victorian plumage, gave the round, white pillared ballroom a glittering warmth and beauty. Their floor length gowns were narrow waisted with bustles and were made of Ottoman satin embroidered with flowers; of Algerine, a twilled shot-silk of blue and gold; of Sultane, a mixture of silk and mohair with alternate satin strips. There was Pekin point, a rich white silk painted with bouquets of flowers and containing a light mixture of gold. There was the latest sensation, Victoria silk, which produced that sound so enticing to Victorian imaginations, the rustle of ladies' underwear.

Twain had declined to dance, preferring to sit in a rocker near a tall window, drink brandy and hold court for the admirers who encircled him on all sides.

"Your Australian history is full of surprises and adventures," he said to Irons, who yesterday had been his host at a private luncheon. "And incongruities, and contradictions, and incredibilities, but they are all true, they all happened."

"But the chapter that matters most," said Irons, "has yet to be written. It will tell the story of how we ceased to be six colonies in opposition to one another and became the United States of Australia. It is a great pity that there are still those who do not wish this to come to pass."

There were several "here, here's" and grunts of approval.

Twain stopped rocking long enough to bite off the end of a cigar and spit it into a spitoon. "What of your ties to the British monarchy?"

Irons stared down into his empty champagne glass. "The last British troops left Australia twenty years ago. To speak bluntly, on that very day all of Australia became defenseless. Oh, we attempted to raise our own local militia, but without much success. Matters did not improve when France moved into New Caledonia and Germany planted its boots in New Guinea. New Caledonia is but ten sailing days from here and New Guinea is close enough that it should belong to Australia or Britain and no one else. The crown courts German favor and occupies itself with subduing Egypt and we, I fear, are ignored. I am saying, Mr.

Twain, that only the Union Jack should fly over these South Pacific islands.''

"Here, here," *"He speaks for me,"* *"Australia forever,"* the gathered crowd murmured approvingly.

Glasses were lifted in impromptu toasts and quickly drained.

"I am told you fear Russia and America as well," said Twain.

Irons smiled, and a scar near his eye patch momentarily disappeared into his gray sideburns. "Ah, the Russian bear. Most carnivorous. Five years ago it moved into Afghanistan, then threatened India. The Russian fleet can reach Australia from Vladivostock in a mere fourteen days. As for your American eagle, with all due respect, sir, it appears to have its own appetite for land in the South Pacific.''

Twain chuckled. "Oh, indeed, Mr. Irons. In sixty-nine, I think it was, we reached out for the Fijis and your Brits snatched them right from under us. So do you think your gracious Queen Victoria has turned her back on you? That too many concessions are being made to Germany in Pacific waters without consulting you?''

Before Irons could reply Redmond Glass cleared his throat. "You seem to forget yourself this evening, Mr. Irons. You know, of course, that it is treason to speak ill of the Queen, that a man can go to jail merely for refusing to drink to her health. Germany is far from a favored nation these days, with England or anyone else. I detect slurs, sir, slurs against the ancestry of Her Majesty, who has Teutonic blood in her veins.''

Irons' voice was suddenly soft. "It is the case that the royal children are first taught to speak German and that seven of her Majesty's nine children have married German princes and princesses. And pitiful specimens at that.''

Glass, who had been drinking heavily, hooked a thumb in a bright red vest that gave his awesome belly the appearance of a small crimson mountain. Like Irons, he was Irish, but spoke with a stronger brogue. "A disrespect for things sacred is not unknown to Mr. Irons. Why don't you point out that Australia, despite its lack of a standing army, enjoys the protection of the British fleet, the strongest navy in world history?''

"To be independent," said Irons, "a people must be able to defend themselves."

"But since we cannot defend ourselves is it not far better to remain attached to a mighty state? There are heavy burdens and risks attached to your precious independence."

"I will take those risks."

"But not alone. You never do." Glass fingered his heavy watch chain and grinned malevolently. Suddenly he threw up both hands, commanding the floor. "Mr. Twain, indulge me. For your delectation, sir. A month ago there occured here in our fair city a happening of some consequence and no small excitement. There was a downing of tools, a general strike which saw shearers, miners, maritime workers and dock workers leave their positions and press the rich of this wonderous colony for a living wage. Mr. Irons opposed that, as did most if not all of the gentlemen immediately surrounding you.

"A decision was made, Mr. Twain," he continued, "to attack those common, decent, honorable strikers, to drive them into the sea by use of force, by use of the constabulary, troopers and police. Mr. Irons led that oppressive coalition. He drove one of ten wagonloads of wool, accompanied by certain gentlemen here, in a nefarious journey from the rail station to the harbor. Ten wagons with gentlemen in top hats, lemon colored gloves, frock coats, trembling hearts and with whisky flasks on their hips. All surrounded by the armed might of New South Wales. This juggernaut was designed to crush the underdog and to show that the good men, so-called, of Sydney are an establishment that could not be intimidated. The poor lost that day, Mr. Twain, as they do so often in life. They were mowed down, clubbed to the earth and trampled, and their blood covered the cobblestones. Mr. Irons safeguarded himself admirably. He had a virtual army of support in his bullying assault.''

The silence was deafening. Glass continued to grin drunkenly and rock back and forth on his heels.

As Irons took a step towards him, the grin disappeared. Visibly straining to control himself, Irons hissed through clenched teeth, ''You shame me in front of this illustrious man. I shall not forget that. You lie, distort, twist the truth, and you continue to walk in the company of men better than you. I will not forget this day, Mr. Glass, take my word for it.''

He looked at Twain. ''Glass does not tell you what others here are aware of, that he and I are sworn enemies, that the unionists he praises did me and others here much harm.''

There were sounds of approval.

''The unionists killed three of my men,'' said Irons. ''One of the dead was a second father to me. They burned carloads of my wool and burned one of my prized ships. Other men had their wagons overturned, harnesses cut and horses set free. The strikers blacked our wool, decreed that none of it would be loaded—and without wool Australia does not live. When other men sought work loading ships the strikers beat them, maimed them and threatened their families as well. Mr. Glass speaks of violence. I speak of justice.''

Applause drowned out anything else that Irons might have said.

The mammoth Glass, however, only sneered. ''Somehow, Mr. Irons, you always managed to shine like a good deed in a naughty world. Justice, you say. Justice, sir, is any decision in your favor.''

Irons' voice became a stage whisper. ''They say that dying men always tell the truth. As you stand here, Glass, you are closer to death than you have ever been.''

''I am well aware that you are a life taker,'' Glass rejoined, undaunted. ''Fortunes such as yours are not compiled by vicars and choir masters. Isn't that how you made the acquaintance of your new young wife, your very young wife? Didn't you murder a man—"

At that, Michael Irons lunged at Glass, but several men stepped between them. Glass yelled, "You have enemies to go with your riches, too many enemies to see with your one eye, and one day they will bring you down. Down, down, down! You want a united Australia so that you can tuck it in your pocket like a snuff box. Well, here is one man who is too big to fit in your pocket, sir. Too big!"

Someone said, "We bloody well know you're shaped like an elephant's behind, Glass. No need to remind us."

The laughter eased the tension and even Twain joined in. "Australian irreverence," he said. "A national treasure. Mr. Irons, it appears the drums speak correctly. You are a legend in this 'The Lucky Country'."

Sir John Robertson, five times Premier of New South Wales and an attractive, husky voiced politician whose expert use of profanity made him popular in the legislature and at public meetings, took two brandies from a thick, silver tray held by a liveried servant. He drained one in a single gulp, returned it to the tray and swallowed half of the other before saying, "Mr. Irons is our very own icon, which is only fitting, since both are made of gold and brass."

Even Irons was able to chuckle at this crack, and some of the tension in the room dissipated. Australians were immune to hero worship—distrust of authority or of those who had achieved too much was a basic fact of Australian life. Even as one of Australia's wealthiest and most powerful men, Irons could take a ribbing with the best of them. It was one of the keys to his success.

"Is it true about your horse, Mr. Irons?" asked Twain, relieved that the ugly edge seemed to have worn off the gathering.

"It is, sir."

Irons owned a champion race horse, named Finn McCool after the legendary Irish hero known for his remarkable strength and fearlessness. The horse had a golden bit for its mouth, a saddle edged in gilt and four golden shoes. As one of the fastest thoroughbreds on the continent, Finn was favored to win next month's Melbourne Cup with its prize of twenty thousand guineas. It was Australia's most important race, in a land where horse racing was a passion and gambling, like drinking, a compulsion.

Irons smiled with half his mouth, his eyes never leaving Redmond Glass. "What one hears of Sir John's horsemanship is also true."

The handsome Robertson joined in the laughter at his expense. True or not, Sydneysiders prefered to believe that before Robertson made the six mile ride from town to his home in Watson's Bay he stopped at an Elizabeth Street hostel and ordered three pints of rum. He drank one, poured the second into his boots to protect his feet from chills and fed the third to his horse. Heavy drinkers, foul language and violence, were the rule in the New South Wales parliament on Macquarie Street. Fistfights and drunken legislators falling off the bench during major debates aroused amusement rather than disgust.

Irons felt Camilla's hand in his. "Let us go outside, Michael." She knew him well enough to realize that despite the laughter and the men standing between him and Redmond Glass her husband was far from letting Glass's insult ride.

Camilla was his second wife, a slender and beautiful child-woman with green eyes. Tonight she wore a dress of Levantine *folicé*, a soft, rich silk with Arabesque patterns. A tiara of diamonds, rubies and sapphires crowned her waist length auburn hair. She was as gentle as a kitten, deeply in love with Irons and at twenty-two years, younger than his three children. Two of them, a daughter Morag and a son Dai, were at the Mark Twain gala. Heath, the oldest, had ridden out to meet the armed escort accompanying the gold wagon heading to Sydney from Irons' claim in Braidwood 200 miles south.

"Please, dearest," said Camilla, her eyes pleading with him to leave the ballroom. "Do not let Mr. Glass spoil this lovely evening for us.'' In gaslight her green eyes were as radiant as the glittering stones in the tiara that Irons had purchased for her in Paris from a former mistress of the Emperor Napoleon III. Yielding to her words and her small hand on his elbow Irons reluctantly turned his back on a smirking Redmond Glass.

Outside Camilla drew a shawl around her bare shoulders and stared up at the sandstone keep and turrets of Government House, as Irons watched three New South Wales troopers in white helmets and dark blue uniforms slowly patrol the wide lawn below the terrace. Each trooper carried the new British Lee-Metford repeating rifle and an American pistol, the Smith & Wesson Schofield, popular because it had once been the favorite of the American outlaw Jesse James.

Irons wondered if these particular troopers had been with him and other businessmen and police last month when they had clashed with strikers at Circular Quay harbor. No shots had been fired, but the conflict had been a bloody one nonetheless. The Riot Act had been read and after that batons, rifle butts and charging horses had been used. Boatloads of wool had already been burned and ''scabs'' murdered; the unionists had forced Michael Irons and others to act.

Wool. Australia had made its way to prosperity on the sheep's back. *Put everything into four legs,* had been the advice to new immigrants. So huge was the demand for Australian wool, clipped from the Australian merino, a breed unmatched in America or Europe, that exporters such as Irons could absorb huge shipping costs and still outsell all international competition.

Sheep ranching, however, was a risky trade. One deadly Australian drought, bushfire, flash flood or epidemic of disease could threaten or destroy a good year's wool clip. Rabbits or kangaroos were another menace; by eating acres of much needed grass they doomed herds of sheep to starvation. Without the sale of his wool a squatter, or land owner, lost his land to bankers holding his mortgage or to biger ranchers; wool was a precious commodity and the greatest event in the lives of these men was the once a year wool sales.

Four years ago wool prices had dropped by twenty-five percent and continued to fall by one or two percent points each succeeding year. The reason: improved productivity, the gold standard with its tight money policy and revolutionized transportation, that found expanding railroads and faster ships bringing increased amounts of wool to market. Squatters understood none of this; they only saw their profits shrinking. The fabulous prosperity of mid-century was gone and to bring it back wool growers took a first step: they reduced wages. When unions fought back, squatters turned to the large pool of non-union labor. The shearers, supported by miners and maritime workers, chose to strike, resulting in confrontations at Sydney's Circular Quay and in the port of Melbourne, where a Colonel Price, commanding troopers facing the strikers, told his men that if they had to open fire on the unionists to, "Fire low and lay 'em out!"

Irons lit a cigar and drew Camilla closer to him. Three rail cars of his wool had been burned, along with one of his prized clippers. Two of his warehouses had been damaged and men who worked for him intimidated and beaten. Davy Pease had been his greatest loss. Pease had been his partner in the Braidwood gold claim, and a second father to Irons and the unionists had murdered him. After that no one had to ask Irons to lead prominent businessmen, troopers and police against strikers.

The governor, the mayor and most Sydneysiders wanted to see the strikers punished and cleared from the streets and docks. The majority of Australians had either poorly paying jobs or were unemployed and believed that any free white man had the right to a job abandoned by a striker. By opposing non-union labor the strikers lost the sympathy of most people.

My enemies continue to multiply, thought Irons. "They come with the gold, lad," Davy Pease had said. "The

envy of both your friends and enemies is a sure sign that
you have reached the top of the mountain. But take care,
Michael, for it is your enemies who will show you your
mistakes.''

Irons' enemies could be found in the posh suburbs of
Darling Point and Elizabeth Bay and in the rowdy slums of
Wooloomooloo and *The Rocks*, Sydney's oldest and most
dangerous quarter. They could be found in the other five
colonies as well. He felt the warmth of Camilla beside him
and smelled her scent of crushed roses and was reminded
that his deadliest foe in Australia was her father, Lord
Edward a' Becket, and his son Denis. Lord a'Becket was a
banker in Melbourne, the capital and major port of Victoria,
the colony to the south of New South Wales. The a'Beckets
had made a great deal of money by unscrupulous means
and business practices which Irons openly opposed.

The enmity between Irons and the banking family had
increased when he had married Camilla, for she was their
prized possession, reserved for a titled Englishman, with
wealth and prestige that would have enhanced the status of
the a'Beckets. Worse, Irons had killed a man to get her. In
the eyes of the a'Beckets, Michael Irons was a social
inferior, the son of convicts and Irish potato farmers, the
spawn of superstitious Catholics slavishly obedient to Rome.
Irons saw them as rapacious and cunning, grasping and
treacherous.

He had said of them, ''They would pick a farthing out
of a dog's turd.''

Above all he despised them for their snobbishness, a
particular trait of Melbourne's upper class, which followed
British customs, manners, goods and fashions and turned
its back on anything Australian save its riches.

Inside the ballroom the orchestra finished one Strauss
waltz and immediately launched unto another. Irons considered returning and dancing with Camilla. Then suddenly
he was alert, pausing with the cigar in front of his mouth,
sensing the man behind him. The big, one-eyed Irishman

grinned, still keeping his back to the stocky figure who had stepped from the shadows ringing the terrace.

"You make a fine tracker, mate," said Irons, "but a ratbag of a coachman. You are supposed to stay with the carriage tonight."

He turned slowly, the cigar between his teeth. There was humor in his voice when he spoke. "How did you get inside? No Abos allowed, they tell me."

"Did not come inside," said the Aborigine, who was called Johnny-Johnny. "There are steps at the end of the terrace. Someone sent me to fetch you. He is waiting by the carriage."

Irons frowned. Something was wrong. He and the Aborigine had been together long enough to read each other well. Johnny-Johnny was keeping something from him.

The Aborigine was of medium height and muscular, in his mid-twenties, with black curly hair, a flat nose and a wide mouth. Because his father had been white, he had tan skin instead of dark brown. He wore the black frock coat, trousers, boots and collarless white shirt of the coachman, minus the tall black hat which he refused to put on. He had worked for Irons most of his life, as everything from stable boy to stockman or cowboy. As a tracker Johnny-Johnny was without equal; he could follow a man's trail across hard rock, fiery desert and snake filled marshes and never lose the man's sign or scent. He was an expert with boomerang, bow, knife and *woomera*, a wooden device used by Aborigines to give a bullet-like spin to a spear, increasing its power, accuracy and range, and he had been the one to teach Irons' sons to shoot a rifle and pistol.

Johnny-Johnny and Irons were not master and man; for despite the brutality of whites to his people it was not in this Aborigine to submit to anyone. The two were *mates*, and in Australia this loyalty between two friends was absolute. There was a mystic element in the life of Aborigines which few white men could understand, a life that was full of supernatural forces, rituals, legends and mythology.

Irons, however, understood more than most and was one of the few whites who did not treat these native Australians with contempt.

"This man says he wants to talk to you about Heath," said Johnny-Johnny.

Irons' mouth hardened and he stared at the Aborigine for a long time. Then he turned to Camilla. "I must leave. Tell Dai that I place you in his charge until I return. He is to see you safely home."

He silenced her with a gentle touch, his fingertips brushing her lips. "Trust me, dearest." She remained silent. Women obeyed men, served them and, as her husband had just ordered, trusted them. Her gloved hand came up to take his and she kissed it and then he was gone.

Irons and Johnny-Johnny walked across the darkened lawn towards the road where coaches and carriages, drivers and saddled horses waited. The chilled night air smelled of azaleas, roses and spider orchids and in the air over the harbor gulls called to one another in long squeals.

"If it's Heath he's wanting to speak of, then we have trouble with the gold," said Irons.

"Perhaps," said Johnny-Johnny. He touched Irons' arm, halting him. "The man who waits for you is a *larrikin*. He is from Sydney and that could mean that Heath is still here, that he never left the city. The *larrikin* has two horses. I think he means for you to go with him."

Larrikins were street thugs, brawling hoodlums prone to hunting in packs and using broken bottles, chunks of steel, knives and boots as weapons. They dressed alike, in tight fitting black bell-bottomed trousers and high heeled boots, large round hats and purple scarves. Flogging and hanging did not discourage them from attacking police, picnickers, innocent night strollers and rival gangs. Sydney's notorious slums bred them year after year, spilling them like slops into a dirty street. The *larrikin* had his apologists and sympathizers, those who claimed that society forced him into criminality. Irons, who had once been a half-starved immigrant, rejected such rubbish.

The *larrikin* who had summoned him was both arrogant and nervous. He leaned against Iron's carriage, a bone-thin, sharp faced man with only a few rotting teeth remaining in his head. He was bearded, aged before his time and could have been twenty-five or fifty. His black clothes were shabby and worn and he chewed tobacco rapidly, spitting its dark juices deliberately on the carriage wheels.

He eyed Irons up and down. "Well now, ain't you Jack the Lad. Tarted up like Christmas, you are, and don't that make me heart beat faster. My name is Rust but you can call me Mr. Rust if you like. I be doin' most of the talkin', but first I sees that I must be gettin' your attention."

He reached inside his shirt and Johnny-Johnny took a step forward before Irons held a hand against his chest, restraining him. A suddenly alarmed Rust stepped backwards, lost his balance and fell against the carriage. The horses, a matching pair of gray Morgans, shied and whinnied, lifting their heads.

From the ground Rust aimed a finger at Johnny-Johnny. "You keep that nigger away from me, Mr. Irons or you'll be sorry. If anything happens to me, it will go crook with your son, you mark my words. It be crook for him. Here, be takin' a look at this, say I. Here, go on."

Removing a crumpled, dirty rag from inside his shirt Rust offered it in a trembling hand. Irons nodded once and Johnny-Johnny stepped forward, took the rag and handed it back to the big Irishman, never once removing his glance from the fallen Rust.

"I said it be bad for the lad," said the *larrikin*, "and I mean it. No harm is to come to me, for if I do not return soon the lad is done for and he dies hard. Go on, Mr. Irons, see what you hold in your hand."

Irons unravelled the soiled, stained rag, feeling a small, hard object hidden inside. The object fell to the dew-wet grass and he squatted down to pick it up and stiffened. It was a human finger. There was a gold ring on it, with a black onyx stone in the center. A gilt H covered the face of the stone. The finger and ring belonged to Heath.

For a moment; Irons was paralyzed with horror and fury. When he finally did look up, though, the *larrikin* felt the Irishman's rage and swallowed hard. "I know what you be thinkin', Mr. Irons. Make me tell the lad's whereabouts, then murder me. Aye, in your boots I be thinkin' the same. But you see the two of us has only minutes to get to where we are goin'. In that time you cannot do for me and gather your men and make it to where your son is. If you and me is not walkin' arm in arm through a certain door very shortly, them as have Master Heath are going to commence more removals. Could be another finger or maybe a foot. Could be one of his eggs hangin' 'twixt his legs or maybe an eye like what happened to you.

"So I say," he went on, struggling to keep his voice level, "you put aside any thoughts you might have of harmin' Gertie Rust, because Gertie Rust is the only chance you have of ever seein' your first born alive and in one piece ag'in. You come with me, sir, and you do so *now*. You was to have no time to prepare. You comes alone your Abo stays behind. One thing more. I am to see if you are armed."

"I carry no gun on this night."

"I will be the judge of that, your worship. Be takin' off your boots. Known many a gent with a hide out in his boot top. A derringer can send you to your maker as quickly as a cannon, says I."

Irons said, "Who has my son?"

Rust, feeling more courageous, spat tobacco juice on the Irishman's boots. "You may be Moses-in-the-mountain when you are at home, but tonight I be doin' most of the talkin'. You and your curly haired ape just hop it like I say. Off with them fuckin' boots and be quick about it."

He jerked his head at Johnny-Johnny. "Give him a

hand—and no muckin' about. If you two think you can make me talk, just try, says I. If I am dead or delayed where will Master Heath be? In hell lickin' the devil's arse, that's where. Now move, the both of you!''

Johnny-Johnny knelt in front of Irons, removed his boots, then stood up and stepped aside. Rust stepped forward and began patting the Irishman's body. ''Mother of us all,'' said the *larrikin*, ''what have we here?''

He removed Irons' watch and chain, held them up in the moonlight and grinned. ''Never thought I would be holdin' such a fine watch. The Lord does provide, says I. Let us see what other treasures are weighin' you down. A cigar case. We'll have that, your worship, if you please.''

He found Irons' wallet, whistled at the wad of pound notes inside, then folded the wallet once more and tucked it inside his shirt. But it was the blue diamond and gold stickpin in Irons' lapel that stopped Rust dead and made his eyes bulge. ''Jesus, Mary and Joseph. What a beauty!''

He was awestruck. ''Is she the goods? Is she real?''

''Yes,'' Irons answered, trying to keep the loathing and contempt from his voice.

''I approve, Mr. Irons. Yes sir, I approve muchly.'' Bending over, Rust pulled up his right trouser leg and carefully attached the stickpin just inside the top of his bot. ''No need to share this little treasure now is there?''

Still stooped he looked up at Johnny-Johnny. ''Well, you bloody heathen, don't just stand there. Help the white man on with his boots.'' He watched as Irons sat on a carriage step and the Aborigine knelt once more, a boot in his hands, his back to Rust. The *larrikin* turned from them to again look down at the stickpin. He had never owned anything so lovely in his life. He definitely wasn't going to share this with his mates.

On his feet the *larrikin* became more nervous. ''I want to be away from you bloody rich swine in your fine silks and carpeted floors. Mr. Irons, you take the horse with the broken saddle horn, the one on the left. And you, Abo, climb into the carriage and do not let me see your monkey face again.''

Irons, seeing Johnny-Johnny clench both fists and hesitate, said, ''Do as he says.''

Other drivers had ignored the three men; they slept inside their vehicles or huddled in groups at a distance, passing around bottles of cheap gin and rum. Sydney coachmen, particularly those in hansom cabs, were known for their speedy and reckless driving, much of it caused by heavy drinking.

Rust caught Irons' elbow. ''Be doin' me a favor, if you please, and return that finger. Ring's mine. Payment for services rendered, for seeking you out and being the bearer of these here glad tidings. Gertie Rust likes a full pay packet, he does. And now, guv, let us hasten to our destination and to those what badly wants to make your acquaintance.''

Irons pulled his arm away with deliberate slowness. ''Is my son alive?''

Rust looked up at the stars, his sharp face hawklike against the night sky. A pale yellow half moon slipped behind gray clouds. ''On my oath I want you and your lot knocked down and ground into dust. Yes, he is alive, but for how long I cannot say. That will depend on how fast we ride. Unless you have decided to remain here and thereby murder the lad yourself. Can you live with that, Mr. Irons?''

Rust giggled. With icy calm Irons turned his back on the *larrikin* and walked towards the two horses tied to a carriage wheel.

Untying the reins he placed a booted foot in a stirrup and with practiced ease swung into the saddle, wheeled the horse about and waited for Rust to mount.

They rode in silence, Rust leading the way on a brown mare and never once looking over his shoulder to see if Irons followed. From Government House they rode through the Royal Botanic Gardens, past fountains, statues and hothouses filled with orchids and ferns. Leaving the giant park they rode east, past rows of eucalyptus gums, with their sharp, medicinal smell and blossoms of deep scarlet and coral pink. To their right the harbor remained in view as they rode through a stretch of elegant homes in the Italian and French Renaissance styles. Shortly afterwards the quality of homes and buildings declined.

There were brick buildings built by convict labor fifty years ago and then older suburbs, stretches of beige cottages roofed in red tiles, designed by London architectural firms and cheaply built by real estate speculators to the satisfaction of English and Irish immigrants eager for these reminders of the British Isles they had left behind. From Alfred Street, paved in wood because asphalt could not stand up to the Australian sun, they turned into Circular Quay, the horseshoe shaped pier that embraced Sydney Cove, "the cradle of Australian history."

Here England's Captain Arthur Philips had landed in 1788 with 1500 men and women, 703 of them convicts, to begin building the first colony on the continent. And it was here a month ago that Irons and Sydney businessmen, backed by the armed might of the state, had clashed with strikers. In all fifty thousand strikers had downed tools; all knew of Michael Irons and would gladly have done him harm. Were they using Heath to lure Irons to his death? One thing was certain: the Irishman now knew where Rust was taking him.

They were in *The Rocks*, Sydney's oldest and most dangerous quarter, an unholy ground drawing thieves, murderers, military deserters, whores, whalers, thugs, convicts and *larrikins*. On Argyle Street the two men, their horses now at a trot, turned right and went uphill through the Argyle Cut, the dark, 300-foot tunnel hollowed out of solid stone by convict labor almost fifty years ago. In daylight one could see the prisoners' names, marks and messages of despair scratched on the granite walls. Tonight Irons and Gertie Rust, their horses' hooves echoing in the Argyle

Cut, rode past drunken prostitutes and sailors, past half-case children of Aborigines, Chinese and whites, who pawed through mud and garbage for food; past *larrikins* standing over a blood-stained victim; past men blinded in gold mine explosions and now reduced to begging for a penny. The tunnel was the gateway to the hell that was *The Rocks.*

From here they made their way through the slum's winding dirt streets, past cafes, brothels, oyster shops, rundown hotels and pubs, past groups of loud, brawling, drunken men and women and child thieves before stopping at the Hero of Waterloo Hotel, Sydney's oldest and most notorious pub. Irons knew it as a hangout for crimps, those who drugged then kidnapped men for sea duty aboard merchant ships. Since entering *The Rocks* the big Irishman, because of his elegant clothes, had been the subject of insults and ribald remarks from *The Rocks'* inhabitants.

As they dismounted Rust cackled and spoke for the first time since leaving Government House. "Take no notice of what they say, Mr. Irons. Me old mum used to tell me that insults are written on sand."

Irons remained silent. Insults are carved in stone, he thought. Never to be forgotten, forever to be avenged.

He followed Rust into the pub.

In a dark and putrid smelling back room on the ground floor, lit only by a pair of sperm whale lamps, Irons sat on the edge of a sagging bed, a hand on the perspiring brow of his son. With great effort Heath Irons opened his eyes and rolled his head towards his father. He opened his mouth to speak but could only croak; the alcohol and drugs forced on him by his kidnappers were still having their effect. At twenty-three he was tall and lean, with dark blond hair and a long, handsome red bearded face. While women had always found him attractive and amusing Heath had yet to command the respect from men that his father did.

There were blood stains on his shirt and dungarees and

he was barefoot. On entering the room Irons had noticed that one of the men holding his son prisoner was now wearing the boy's boots. Irons' eyes went to the dark stained green rag around Heath's right hand and a vein throbbed on the big Irishman's temple. He tightened his right fist until the knuckles were white under the skin.

"You have stared at him long enough," rasped a voice behind him. "He is alive, so let us get on with it, then."

Leaving the bed the Irishman walked over to a small wooden table covered in the remains of food and empty liquor bottles. The room was small, low ceilinged and faced a group of tin-roofed, wooden and canvas shanties behind the pub. On the walls were pictures of Queen Victoria and Henry Parkes, Australia's best known politician, along with framed newspaper pages dealing with the career of Ned Kelly, Australia's most notorious outlaw. Since his hanging ten years ago at the age of twenty-five Kelly had become a folk hero, his career of bank robbery, horse stealing and cold blooded murder now invested with romance and chivalry. Five men were in the room, two at the table with Irons. One was the leader, Honey Fitz Clare, a barrel chested man with a large head and a mangled right ear. With him was the largest man in the room, a surly Scot named Pedy, who drank rum from a bottle, and took bites from a large raw onion and kept his murderous gaze on Irons. The Irishman knew Pedy. The Scot had once worked for him as a stockman before turning *gullyraker*, Australian parlance for sheep stealer. Irons had personally flogged him, lashing his back raw before turning him over to the police. The huge Pedy, who had vowed to kill Irons, had managed to escape prison to disappear in *The Rocks*.

Two men leaned against the room's front door, while Gertie drank gin and looked through an open back window at the shanties around him. All of them were armed with pistols and knives. Pedy had a knife and his strength while Gertie had a knife. In the large front room of the pub a violin and trumpet played a spirited polka for shouting men and women who clutched each other and shuffled around a sand-covered, wooden floor in the quick walk that was dancing to most Sydneysiders. Eleven o'clock closing had been the law since 1882, but all night drinking could be found citywide and police turned a blind eye to it, especially in *The Rocks*.

Honey Fitz used his long-blade knife to poke at the remains of a half-cooked John Dory, an Australian fish. "You pay," he said without looking at Irons. "One hundred thousand pounds in gold sovereigns." A scar across his throat told Irons why Honey Fitz's voice was a dry rasp.

Pushing aside an empty rum bottle Irons folded his hands on the table. "If all you wanted was gold you could have contacted me at my home. Perhaps I would have sent it."

Honey Fitz's eyes hardened. "Perhaps, says he. What you would have sent was a bullet for us all. You would have tracked us down, you bloody cyclops. No man offends you and lives for very long. No, your eminence. Whilst we have you we live."

"And how long will my son and I live when you have what you want?"

Honey Fitz glanced quickly at Gertie, who shook his head in denial.

Irons said, "So you mean to kill us both, as I figured. Now tell me this: you are not unionists and you are not businessmen I have bested in a deal. So whose bidding do you do? Who's behind this?"

"Why do you ask that? Who says we're not on our own?"

"Because you are too stupid."

Pedy spat a paste of onion and rum into Irons' face and as the Irishman slowly wiped it away with a handkerchief the Scot leaned forward, the point of his knife against Irons' ruffled shirt front. "Ain't with the tall poppies now, Jocko. Down here Jack is as good as his master and the man on the ground speaks to the man with his feet in the stirrups. Show some respect, mate, or I will gut you like a bloody hog.''

Irons was over six feet tall and muscular, but Pedy was bigger, broader, heavier. Yet, Irons held his gaze until Honey Fitz touched Pedy's shoulder, pushing him back into his chair.

As Gertie giggled Honey Fitz rasped, ''We mean to have our way. One hundred thousand in gold for the three of you.'' When he saw Irons frown he grinned.

''That is the correct tally, Mr. Irons. Three. Friend of yours its tucked away next door and his life depends on you doin' what you are told. Gertie.''

The thin *larrikin* left the room and seconds later returned with the third man. Irons leaped from his chair. ''Nat. Nat Gane.''

The portly man, his gray hair askew and clothing torn, his hands tied behind his back, took a step towards Irons but Gertie cruelly yanked him back. Gane was a leading Sydney lawyer representing Irons and other wealthy businessmen. He also sat in the Legislative Council, the upper house of New South Wales' parliament, which functioned along the lines of England's House of Lords. In addition he found time to serve as Sydney representative of the Ferdinand Brothers, London's leading investment firm, which over the years had invested over forty million pounds in Australia. On Gane's advice, Irons had recently purchased a fifty percent interest in a Sydney bank, in which Gane was a director and investor. He was Irons' closest friend, a godfather to Heath and Dai.

''Michael,'' said Gane, ''I am truly sorry. They came to my home and brought me here.''

Irons placed his hands on Gane's shoulders. ''I understand, dear friend. Have they harmed you?''

''Just a blow or two, nothing worse than that. I want to live, Michael. I have a wife, a son. I want to live.''

Irons turned to look at Honey Fitz, who had been watching the two men with hooded eyes. ''Three, your eminence,'' said the thug. ''Father, son and Holy Ghost. So no muckin' about, then. We propose to send Mr. Gane for the money. You will sign a paper givin' your banker complete power of attorney, allowin' him to do as he pleases. He brings the lolly back here and we, well, we will deal with you fine folk when we come to that part of it. If you refuse to sign the proper paper, Pedy here will murder Mr. Gane dead where he stands. I will then shoot your son and turn you over to Pedy, who has a score to settle with you.''

Irons looked at the unconscious Heath and at the frightened Nat Gane. His shoulders slumped. ''I will do as you say.''

Three men now guarded Irons; two had joined with others from the front room to accompany Nat Gane to his home and Irons' banks. Gang members would stay with Gane's wife and son until the lawyer returned with the gold. If the gold was not in Honey Fitz's hands within twenty-four hours all hostages, including Gane's family, would be killed.

Honey Fitz moved his lips as he slowly counted the money in Iron's wallet. Pedy held Iron's watch and chain in his huge hands, eyeing them as though they were alive. At the open back window Gertie continued to drink and stare at a shanty where two prostitutes were arguing loudly. The music, dancing and shouting from the front room had gotten more raucous.

Irons said softly, ''What would you do to a mate who did not share with you?''

Honey Fitz narrowed his eyes.

Irons jerked his head towards Gertie's back and whispered, ''There is more than you have there in your hands.''

''I say you're a liar,'' Pedy snapped. ''Tonight Mr. Almighty Irons is a big nobody, and he's trying to make trouble. He is not one of us, remember that.''

Irons leaned forward, hands under the table. ''I was once lower than you, a starvin' Mick brat who lifted himself up by his bootstraps and with no man to thank for it. This much I know: a man must be true to his mates or he is no man at all. I can prove to you that what I am sayin' is the truth. In the front room there is a whore, a half-caste, an Abo girl no more than twelve.''

Honey Fitz frowned. ''That would be Donna, Gertie's sheila. So what about her?''

Irons whispered, ''He gave her the lolly. Five thousand pounds that I had brought to the affair for Mr. Twain tonight, money to bet on me horse Finn. Now before you be callin' me a liar why don't you have a peek inside Gertie's boot.''

Pedy sneered. ''Why? You just told us he gave the money to his bloody whore.''

''That he did, oh that he did. What he did not give her was a lovely diamond stickpin, blue stone, encased in gold. He took it from me and he has taken it from you as well and one is as true as the other. I am speakin' of the money. You have heard of me horse Finn, of course. Flies like the wind, he does and there's none faster.''

In a country where two pounds a week was considered a living wage, five thousand pounds was a fortune.

Honey Fitz was silent. Irons grinned. ''If I am lying about the blue diamond, then I am lying about the money. But if I am telling the truth about the diamond, what then?''

''And what do you hope to gain?'' said Honey Fitz.

''Your word that you will at least spare the life of me son.''

Honey Fitz stroked his beard with a meaty hand, carefully studying Irons. Then, ''Gertie? Come away from that window, please.''

Gertie did as ordered.

''Take off your boots,'' said Honey Fitz.

''My boots? Why?''

''Because I said so.''

Gertie looked at Irons. ''What's he been tellin' you? I have nothing in me boots.''

''Then take them off.''

Gertie chewed his lip, his eyes going from Irons to Honey Fitz. Then he shrugged, forcing a smile. "I did not mean to cheat you, mate. It was just that I never seen such a bauble in me life—"

Pedy was out of his chair, shouting, "One is true as the other, I'm thinking. Where's the five thousand quid?"

Gertie's eyes bulged and he began to back away.

Honey Fitz, pistol in his hand, joined the huge Scot in stalking Gertie. Irons, hands still below the table, gripped the knife Johnny-Johnny had tucked into his boot when Gertie had been admiring the stickpin back at Government House. On his feet the Irishman silently crossed the floor and because he was closest to Honey Fitz he killed him first.

From behind he slipped his knife hand around Honey Fitz's throat, placed the blade hard against the left side of the thug's neck and drew it swiftly and savagely around in a semi-circle ending just under the right ear. Blood spurted in a high arc and Honey Fitz fell to his knees, his pistol slattering to the floor and sliding under Heath's bed. Gertie had now gone as far as he could, his back to the open window. That's when Johnny-Johnny leaned in, tossed a horse's bridle over the *larrikin's* face and around his neck, yanking him off his feet and outside.

Pedy clawed for the knife in his belt as Irons, coming at him from behind, kicked him in the left knee, spinning him around and sending the knife flying across the room. With a lunge Irons leaped forward, driving his knife deep into the Scot's right side, feeling the blade scrape bone, then go forward and stay there. Pedy, on his feet, drove a pile driver of a blow into Iron's temple. A painful, red blackness raced through the Irishman's skull; he had never been hit so hard in his life.

Johnny-Johnny, now in the room, slashed at Pedy with Gertie's knife, cutting him on the left shoulder; the Scot however, never backed up. He drove his fist into the Abo's jaw, sending him crashing to the floor. Irons, on his feet, grabbed a chair and lifted it high, bringing it down on

Pedy's head and shoulders. The Scot staggered backwards, dropped to one knee, breathing loudly through his bloodied mouth. "I will have you, you shit eatin' Mick. I will have you."

He charged Irons, who stood his ground and punched him twice in the face, blows that would have stopped any other man. Pedy, however, still came, hands reaching for Iron's face, thumbs seeking his eyes. From behind Johnny-Johnny grabbed the Scots' arm, but was tossed across the room, hitting the table and knocking it over, scattering bottles and dishes. And that's when Pedy remembered Irons' knife still stuck in his side. He yanked it out, sending blood spurting down along his ribs and leg. Eyes bright with a lust to kill, he shuffled towards Irons, who slowly backed away.

Johnny-Johnny, bleeding from the nose, was again behind Pedy, and this time he smashed him in the head with a full bottle of rum, raising a spray of glass bits, alcohol and blood that made Irons crouch, arms crossed in front of his face. Now Pedy went down, but he crawled, forward, still reaching for Irons with the knife. Without hesitating the Irishman kicked him in the head and the Scot flopped over on his back and moaned. Bending down Irons pried the knife from Pedy, and using two hands drove the blade into the Scot's heart up to the hilt. Pedy stiffened, then went limp and still.

The Irishman and the Aborigine, on their feet and swaying, breathed loudly. Gingerly feeling his face Johnny-Johnny winced, then spat a tooth to the floor.

"You are out one horse," he said. "I stop in front of a Chinee restaurant up the street and gave him the Morgan for letting me go through his place and out the back to the shanties, no questions asked. I think maybe them Celestials they cook your horse and eat it."

Irons touched his shoulder. "They can eat the bloody carriage for all I care, mate. No trouble tracking us, I see."

"Your horse, the one Rust gave you, is missing a shoe.

His horse, the mare, is starting to go lame in a hind foot. Nothing serious and I do not think Rust noticed it.''

Irons walked over to his unconscious son. "Mr. Rust. What of him?''

"Hanged sooner rather than later. I used the bridle of the Morgan. It remains wrapped tightly around his neck. And Heath?''

"He is my son and there is strength in him. He lives and will continue to live for many years, praise God. There is another thing we must do. We must ride to save Nat Gane. The *larrikins* forced him into this dirty business and now they have taken him away. We will have to ride hard.''

"I do not think so.''

Something in the Aborigine's voice made Irons look at him. "Nat Gane is here,'' said Johnny-Johnny. "He sits in the front room at a table with the *larrikins*. He drinks with them, talks with them and they laugh together.''

Irons shook his head, unable to absorb what he had just heard. "Nat Gane is their prisoner, a hostage to them. They have taken him away.''

Johnny-Johnny took a blood stained rag away from his nose. "Nat Gane is but a few feet from here and he is hostage to no man.''

It was a truth that Irons did not want to believe. But he knew that the Aborigine would never lie. When the Irishman spoke his voice was hoarse with betrayal. "Let us be gathering the pistols scattered in this room. Then I would be grateful if you would help me get Heath on his feet.''

Irons, his eyes shimmering behind tears, looked at Johnny-Johnny. "Then let us go into the next room and talk with Nat Gane.''

In the murky and rancid front room of the Hero of Waterloo, where patrons served themselves from open barrels of whiskey, per Sydney custom, Nat Gane drank to forget his treachery. He sat at a table with three of Honey Fitz's men, hating them and hating himself for what he had done to Michael Bourke Irons. Around Gane drunken

men and women argued, struck each other, shouted and
continued to drink while dancers shuffled endlessly to the
speedy notes of trumpet and violin, both played with more
ambition than ability. The harsh rum warmed Gane, but
could not cleanse his mind and soul. He needed money
with a desperation he had not believed possible. Without
money he would be disgraced, impoverished and imprisoned.

The men at the table with him were vulgar, brutish, a
foul lot whose bearded chins were wet with saliva and
spilled drink. Malignant specimens all of them. The kind
who would rape a child and blind a woman for a shilling.
And Nat Gane had done a deal with them to rob and
murder his closest mate.

Gane's investments had betrayed him, and so he had
betrayed Irons. How many times had the lawyer heard that
Australia's streets were paved with gold, that there was
unlimited land for the asking, that sheep grew fat and
yielded mountains of wool overnight? How had he come to
believe that a man could go to bed poor in this country and
wake up richer than Croesus? All it took was luck.

But it seemed that Australia was running out of luck.
Dark shadows had begun to fall across the continent,
growing longer and more ominous with each passing day.
There had been strikes and bank failures, along with droughts
and a drop in the price of wool and wheat. Almost all the
fertile land was located on the east coast, and what there
was of it could not produce crops or support livestock
during a damaging dry spell. Three quarters of Australia,
particularly the center, was desert land and uninhabitable.
"The Dead Heart" many called it.

Like others with access to privileged business information,
Nat Gane had used it in an attempt to better himself. He
speculated in stocks, land, and banks, and he lost heavily.
To get even he had begun borrowing from his clients
without their knowledge, taking money from one account
to cover shortages in others, a common enough practice in
Australian banking circles. Before he knew it he had lost
the stolen money as well. Even the bank which he had

helped form and talked Irons and others into investing in
was about to fold. All over Australia men like Nat Gane
were speculating in the economy, gambling that they could
become rich overnight no matter how shady their business
methods. Few knew or cared about a worldwide economic
slowdown whose ripples would soon touch Australia.

In 1882 the Union General in France had collapsed. The
South American failure of the long established and reputa-
ble London firm of the Baring Brothers had been even
more tragic, with repercussions in Sydney and Melbourne.
Suddenly there was a loss of confidence by investors
worldwide. England cut back its investments in Australia
but still Australians refused to stop being optimistic, to
cease speculating and reaching for instant wealth. Australia was the magic land, the wealthiest country in the
world. It was worth taking chances to become a million-
aire overnight.

Gane knew that in the past ten years more than 175
million pounds had been invested in Australia by outside
interests. But this year had seen only a fraction of that
amount come into the country. All indications were that
less and less outside money would find its way to these
shores in future. Lawyers, legislators, bankers, even colony
premiers and governors were speculating, sometimes
winning, often losing. For Gane it had been all losses;
fortune had turned out to be the cruelest of gods. His
house of cards was collapsing. He had embezzled the most
money from Irons, and he had also taken a large amount
from the Ferdinand Brothers, the London investment house
he represented.

And now the investment house was sending someone
from London to run the Sydney office. Did they suspect
Gane of theft? He wasn't sure. He only knew that they had
never been too happy with his being in politics and banking while working for them. Sir D'Arcy Corder would
arrive soon to look over the accounts.

Gane's worst move had been to listen to the a'Beckets,
Irons' enemies. They had misled him, selling him Mel-

bourne land with the assurance that it would rise in price.
Instead had dropped horribly. Gane had been forced to sell
the land for a tenth of what he had paid for it, having used
stolen money. The ball was bouncing downstairs, heading
inexorably toward the bottom. Unable to confront Irons
with the thefts, a desperate Gane had decided to murder
his best friend and loot his accounts to at least cover the
Ferdinand losses before Sir Corder arrived in Sydney.

Somewhere along the line Gane should have learned
from strikes that were occuring with more frequency, from
price drops, international financial failures, droughts and
bank failures. He should have paid attention to the gathering storm. A united Australia might have saved him. A
central government with control over banking and the
stock market might have prevented him and others from
getting in so deep. Bankers like the a'Beckets, however,
opposed federation, preferring to do business as usual,
without close scrutiny from anyone. They prefered six
bickering colonies going their own way, each with their
own slipshod banking laws, their own customs duties,
taxes, railroad gauges, postage stamps, militias and educa-
tional systems.

Of course, Gane, too, was against federation. He could
not afford anyone looking over his shoulder as he sought
money to sustain his desperate juggling act. He lifted
another glass of rum; he had lost count of how much of
this swill he had swallowed tonight, but he needed it. Lord
Jesus, he needed to drink.

''*Nat.*''

The one word was agonizing, a cry of pain, an accusa-
tion and a warning of vengeance to come.

Nat started to turn and rise from his chair at the same
time, but the pressure of the pistol barrel on his shoulder
kept him in place.

''I do not want to look on your face again,'' said Irons.
''You gentlemen sitting here with him kindly place your
hands flat down on the table. Some of you know me. For

those of you who do not I am Michael Bourke Irons and I
have left three dead men in the room behind me.''

Johnny-Johnny, a pistol in one hand and supporting a
semi-conscious Heath with his other arm, stayed close to
Irons, eyes sweeping the room. Most of the dancers continued to move and some people didn't notice anything out of
the ordinary. Men always carried guns in *The Rocks* and
no one paid attention. Only those near Nat Gane's table
knew that trouble was close to breaking out. Chairs scraped
the floor as onlookers scrambled to give Irons room.

The Irishman said, ''I want one man from this table to
go into the backroom, then come out here and report what
he has seen. You. Stand please.''

The man across from Nat stood, eyes on Irons' pistol.

''Leave your knife on the table,'' said the Irishman.
''Go into the backroom, look on what is there and return
here. Do not make me come searching for you.''

''Please, Michael,'' said Gane brokenly, wanting to beg
for forgiveness even more than for his life.

''No, Nat. Do not look upon me again. Sit where you
are and gaze forward. When your mate has returned, we
shall talk.''

''God above, he is not my mate.''

''Then let God forgive you, for I never shall.''

They waited. And as they did more people became
aware of what was happening. They saw blood stained
Irons and Johnny-Johnny, saw the pistols in their hands,
saw the semi-conscious Heath, and the terror on the faces
of Nat Gane and the *larrikins* at his table. And slowly the
room became quiet. Dancers ceased to move and stood
watching Irons. The music faded.

Then the *larrikin* was at the doorway connecting the two
rooms and he was shaken, his face pale, his voice shrill.
''He's done 'em. Three of 'em. He's done, 'em.'' He
aimed a finger at Irons, who calmly brought his pistol up
until it was even with the *larrikin's* head.

''Close your stupid mouth and come over here.''

The man did as he was told, but a woman burst from the dance floor and disappeared into the backroom. Seconds later she screamed, "Fitz! Darlin' Fitz! Oh my God, he has killed you!"

Irons felt all eyes on him. And he gloried in their fear of him. To the silent room he said, "Tonight I have sent three of you to hell. If necessary I will send more. Understand me, all of you. Anyone who strikes at me and mine will not find me wanting when it comes to evening the score."

To Gane he said, "I want you gone from Australia by tomorrow. Leave this land as quickly as you can. If I see you again I shall kill you without hesitation, without so much as a single word between us. The rest of you here who were involved with him, who did this to my son, leave New South Wales and never return so long as I and my son live. Do not let the sun go down on you in this colony. If you know me then you know I will do as I say. If there is a single man left in this colony who had a role in this business I will find him and deal with him."

Gane leaped from his chair, face wet with tears. "For pity's sake, Michael, we are friends, mates."

"We are not."

"Where will I go? Australia is my home. I know no other country. I shall die if I leave."

"You shall die if you stay. Johnny-Johnny, I will take Heath. Go to the door and guard my back."

Pistol held belt high and covering the room Irons backed towards the door, half-dragging, half-carrying his son. "I have no wish to be followed. I shall borrow three horses from outside this establishment. If anyone wants to reclaim them you will find your animals at my home in Elizabeth Bay. I shouldn't advise any of you to try to stop me."

At the door he hesitated only long enough to say, "Leave Australia, Nat. For both our sakes leave this country."

2 _____

CONOR Irons had been born to a family of Dublin shipbuilders, men who bloodied their hands sewing huge canvas sails and who went to their graves smelling of hemp and tar. He was a small, dark man who grew up with a love of books and skills as a *shanikee*, or story teller, and as a musician who could play the *uilleann*, the Irish pipes, the *bodhran*, a goatskin drum, the fiddle and tin whistle. His sweet tenor brought tears to the eyes of many who heard him sing centuries old airs and ballads. Only his irreverence for the Catholic Church was looked askance at by a devout family, to whom religion was a matter of grim and unquestioning allegiance.

The Irons, however, never questioned Conor's desire to turn his back on the docks and pursue learning as no one among them ever had before. At Trinity College he spent whole days in the high, wood vaulted reading room, pouring over Greek, Latin and Gaelic manuscripts and losing himself in Racine, Shakespeare, Moliere, Dante and Jonathan Swift. It was a proud day for his family when 19-year-old Conor graduated first in his class from this school, where the majority of student were Protestants and a boy from a Catholic home had to be both highly intelligent and good with his fists.

In that same year Conor married Dylana Rees, daughter of a dairy farmer in Dun Laoghaire, the outport seven miles south of Dublin. She was a tiny, red headed woman with violet eyes and a fiery spirit that gave beauty to her round, freckled face. She had fallen in love with Conor on hearing him sing and was carrying his child on their wedding day. She bore him two sons and a daughter in quick succession and never tired of hearing him sing to them and tell them stories of the ancient Irish warrior-kings and legendary heroes. They lived on land given to her by her father, a man ill at ease with Conor's intelligence and biting wit. Nor did Frank Rees hesitate to remind his daughter that she had married a man who taught school for only shillings a week and who could not afford to purchase the land on which he lived.

Worse, felt Rees, was Conor Irons' involvement with politics, with Irishmen who hated the British and would drive them out of Ireland if they could. "I say of Conor Irons," Rees told his daughter, "that with this political business he has taken to, he is a man standing on the edge of a cliff and about to take one step forward. You mark my words, girl, if I am not correct."

Dylana, who loved her husband with a passion that made her hands shake, listened calmly to her father, then kissed his cheek. "Conor is for me until I die. In truth I cannot tell you why. I only know that it is so."

Rees, who knew how obstinate his daughter could be, shook his head. "Why could not Conor be like the bishop? Then my heart would rest when I think of you with him. The bishop knows how to get along in this world without irking anyone, a trick Conor shows no ability to master."

Bishop Andrew Weeks was not only admired by Frank Rees, but by the entire Irons family, with the single exception of Conor. The bishop lived in a large Dublin house near the Bank of Ireland on College Green, rode in a carriage behind well-cared for horses and appeared destined to rise even higher in the church. He was a distant cousin of Liam Irons, Conor's father, but had had no contact with him or any of the Irons in years. They were forced to admire Cousin Bishop, as Conor called him, from afar, seeing him only at church services on high holy days and never from the front row.

Bishop Weeks spent his time solely with ranking church officials and Dublin's ruling elite. Conor alone saw him for what he was, an ambitious social climber in clerical robes, guided more by self interest than by any spiritual purpose. The rest of the Irons spoke of him with pride, bragging of their tenuous connection to a man sure to wear the red hat of a cardinal one day.

"He may well receive the red hat," said Conor to his father, "but it will not cover a venerable head. Cousin Bishop seems to have succeeded in securing God as an accomplice and nothing else."

"Praise the ripe field not the green corn," said Liam Irons. "Bishop Weeks is our own and he has certainly achieved enough to earn your respect."

"Cousin Bishop is a man who loves the smell of his own farts."

"When your eyes close in death you will wish that he were by your bedside holding your hand and pointing your way towards the feet of the Lord. Aye, that you will. He has power, our cousin, both in this world and the world to come. Remember that. Certainly more power than those rebels you consort with. And they may be the ones to humble you in future. Indeed they may."

Conor had supported all Irish causes opposing the English, particularly any movement led by Daniel O'Connell, the Irish nationalist, lawyer and statesman who had long championed his people's fight against England's abuses. In particular O'Connell had fought discrimination against Catholics, founding the Catholic Association which pursued its goals by peaceful and often effective means. In 1825 the English had suppressed the organization, but the tenacious O'Connell had found other ways to make his fight. He got himself elected to Parliament in London, but refused to take his seat until that body passed the Catholic Emancipation Act.

When Conor first met him in 1841, O'Connell had just been elected Lord Mayor of Dublin.

The sixty-six-year-old Irish nationalist took to the young college student, inviting him to his home and walking Dublin streets with him in long private talks about politics, religion and Ireland's future. He attended Conor's wedding, the christening of his first child and eventually got him away from teaching by giving him the position of a city hall clerk, which brought with it a much needed rise in pay.

And then in 1845 Ireland's potato crop was destroyed by blight, a disaster that was to be repeated during the next four years and which history would call one of the major catastrophes of all time. Hundreds of thousands starved to death, with more dying from resultant diseases. The death toll reached one million, with twice that number emigrating to America and Canada. Ireland's population loss was immense, never to be regained.

A plan by England to import foreign grain and begin a program of public works to give employment to the Irish was started, then abandoned. In the chaos that followed Irish nationalism reached a fever pitch, as the Irish agitated for home rule and the right to sell their own land, for protection of tenant farmers from eviction and increased freedom for Catholics. English response to these and other demands was woefully unadequate. Ireland's agony continued.

O'Connell once more established his Catholic Association and again England declared it illegal, this time trying him and convicting him on a charge of conspiracy. The conviction, however, was overturned and O'Connell was freed. But prison had ruined his health and at the age of seventy-two, on his way to Italy to recover, he died.

Conor grieved for weeks and while some of the lightness disappeared from him there was a new fire in his eyes. Ireland had just lost one of its greatest men and was in the grip of starvation. Conor had lost his clerkship, Dylana's father had died, with what little estate he had acquired in life being split among three sons and none of it going to his widow or daughter. Conor's own three children were going hungry too often and he had borrowed all he could from family and friends, who had little enough to spare. These were desperate times and they called for desperate measures.

A new and radical group, *Young Ireland*, had come out of the Catholic Association. It was militant and anti-English and committed to violence, something O'Connell had always opposed. The leaders were William Smith O'Brien and Thomas Meagher, both of whom had pressed Conor to join, a move he had not even considered while O'Connell was alive.

One day Conor returned home dizzy with hunger. The pain of not having eaten in too long gnawed at his belly and his soul was sick from the shame of begging and receiving nothing in the dying city that was Dublin. Until now he, Dylana and the three little ones had lived on turnips, oats and barley. Even for the wealthy meat was unattainable, for there was no grain or fodder to feed animals. Men ate food once reserved for feeding livestock, and even zoo animals had long since been slaughtered to feed the starving. Men also ate grass, plaster scraped from walls and wood chips carved from furniture. Some had turned to cannibalism, digging up corpses and pulling the worms from the putrifying flesh before eating it.

Conor's small, bare cottage was quiet. In the corner of one room two of the children, a boy and a girl, lay quietly in hand carved, wooden cradles and Conor praised God for blessed sleep, the opiate that could eliminate hunger for a time. The door leading to the back yard was open and through it he saw Dylana, the other boy at her heels, hunched over something lying on the ground. Moving closer Conor saw the blood stained knife in her hand.

He watched as she sliced again into the haunch of a

scrawny cow, a pitiful, unkempt animal whose eyes were glazed with approaching death. As blood began to ooze she caught it in a cracked wooden bowl and when the bowl was half filled she held it to her son's mouth. "Drink, boy. Drink."

He did, swallowing the warm liquid slowly, crimson drops dribbling down his chin. Setting the bowl on the ground she took a chunk of raw turnip from an apron pocket, bit off a small piece, chewed then removed the soft slivers from her mouth and fed them to her son.

Conor squatted beside her, took her into his arms and wept into her hair. She felt him shiver.

"I found the poor beastie in the road," she said of the cow. "God knows how she had the strength to get as far as she did. Stealin's wrong, I know, but so is this terrible blight that God has sent down upon us. Let us kill the animal quickly and hide the meat."

Conor nodded his head yes. "I'll bring the wee ones out here. They must be awake now."

"No. Leave them be."

The way she said those few words sent a chill through Conor. He was suddenly sick with fear.

"They are dead," said Dylana. "The cow came too late for them. Only one lives."

At his mother's feet three-year-old Michael Bourke Irons, face and hands smeared with cow's blood, chewed on turnip bits and stared into a blue and gold sunset.

That same night Conor found the leaders of *Young Ireland* and said that he would do whatever they asked of him.

In a chilling night rain Conor leaned against the Customs House to catch his breath and look at his bleeding arm. A flash of lightning made him look up at the stocky figure of *Hope* perched atop the building. Little hope for you tonight, Conor lad. If that soldier had been a better marksman you'd be in heaven now, eating manna and plucking your harp.

He pressed a torn piece of his shirt against the wound in

his left bicep, the result of a bullet from a British Baker rifle. The pain in his arm was white-hot, burning his side from foot to brain and he was soaked with rain and his own blood. His lungs ached with fatigue, from running across rooftops and through streets crawling with English soldiers, now between Conor and any escape from Dublin. His home and that of his parents were outside the city. He would have to go to ground within Dublin and soon.

When he heard horsemen draw near it was fear alone that gave him the strength to push himself away from the Customs House wall and stagger down Abbey Street. After tonight *Young Ireland* would not exist, crushed before it ever had the chance to spill English blood. Tonight English soldiers had come for them, surrounding the pub on Eden Quay where the rebels had been meeting. When he heard the uproar downstairs in the pub Conor, on the second floor, had gone to the window, looked out into the street, and a bullet had whizzed near his cheek, embedding itself in a wooden beam running across the ceiling. A second bullet ripped into and through his left arm, throwing him back against a shutter. English soldiers had the pub surrounded and the entire area cordoned off.

Scrambling to his feet a bleeding Conor found himself pushed and shoved into the hall, where shouting men scattered in a frantic attempt to escape. Those who rushed to the staircase met soldiers racing up to meet them. Conor and others ran away from the stairs, along a dark, narrow hall and up a small staircase leading to an attic which was used as a storeroom. Inside the low ceilinged, musty room they blocked the door with broken chairs, cracked barrels and cases of the *Dark Fantastic*, the popular Guinness ale.

On the roof and in a heavy rain they went their separate ways. Two men raced across rooftops leading to the River Liffey, to hide in a warehouse, under a pier or in a ship anchored at one of the ports. Conor, in pain, knew he could not run for long. Hunger and his wound had left him too weak to go without resting soon.

He was alone, running across rooftops, dodging smoking chimneys, slipping on rain slicked red tiles and scattering clumps of sleeping pigeons, sending them flying high into the night. And then he tripped over a pair of chamber pots and went flying, landing on his wounded arm in a puddle of water and laying there, glad to rest and never wanting to run again.

Ahead of him a door opened and a dark figure in a nightshirt stood holding a lantern in one hand and a club in the other.

"Who's out there? Speak up, I say."

Conor crawled to his feet. "I have been shot. The English—"

"Yes, yes, I know. Over here and be quick about it."

The man, Irish, old and almost toothless, looked at Conor for long seconds before stepping aside and letting him into his attic. When he had closed the door the old man held the lantern close to Conor's face. "Havin' a bit of trouble lately with footpads on me roof. Young men larkin' about on other people's property. You look a right mess, you do. I take it you're one of the new-fangled warriors stirrin' up trouble, Young Ireland you call yourselves?"

Eyes closed, Conor nodded.

"Well, you cannot stay here, that's for certain. The English are up and down this street, which is what woke me in the first place. I'd hide you if I could, but they'd only find ye and we would both be transported to bloody Australia or have our necks stretched in Kilmainham jail. Best I can do is let you out through the back. Get to your own, son, if ye can. Or try to get sanctuary in the church up the street. St. Michan's."

"I know it."

"Reassurin' it is that some of you new warriors do go to mass once in awhile. Now follow me and take care ye leave no blood behind, for if the Brits see a drop it could mean me death. If ye should spill, I'll clean up after ye. Mind the stairs."

Now Conor was at St. Michan's, the two hundred-year-

old church where last century Handel had played the organ
for the first public performance of the Messiah. With his
last strength Conor pushed open the great door, stepped
inside and dropped to his knees. His own loud breathing
reached his ears as though coming from someone else who
was far away. He felt a hand on his shoulder and he
looked up to see a shrunken, tonsured priest frowning
down at him. The priest began to speak and Conor passed
out.

When he opened his eyes he screamed. The priest had
hidden him downstairs in St. Michan's crypt, among corpses,
which because of the dry atmosphere, had not decomposed,
but whose skin remained brown and leatherish, retaining a
lifelike softness. Shadows cast by a flaming torch made
the dead seem to quiver. Conor's screams echoed along
the damp stone walls while the flaxen haired woman in the
sky-blue gown, who lay to his left, stared at him with
unseeing jewel-like eyes that refused to turn away.

At sunup Liam Irons looked from his sleeping son to
Dylana. "He cannot stay in Dublin. They are searchin' for
him in every nook and cranny of the city. Young Ireland is
no more, I tell you that. And there is a price to pay for
bein' one of them. The British will see to collectin'."

"You will get him out," said Dylana, drawing her
shawl around her.

"And would you be tellin' me how? Yes, he is my son,
but if you're sayin' smuggle him aboard a ship in my port,
I say you're daft. Every ship is being watched—"

"And you're afraid."

He folded his arms, keeping her at bay. "You're a
meddler, I've said that before. Forever scalding your tongue
in other people's broth."

"I've a mind of me own. And I have two dead children,
Mr. Irons, with no intention of havin' a dead husband to
lay beside them."

Her eyes, red rimmed from lack of sleep and weeping, bore into his.

He looked at a nearby torch which had almost burned down. "You do love Conor, I grant you that, and it's him who needs helpin' now. The English came to me home just hours ago and drove us out into the cold at gunpoint. They tore me home apart like wild dogs worryin' a single piece of meat. Broke precious things, they did. Threatened us and promised to come back." He looked at her and almost pleaded. "I cannot bring Conor back there. I cannot."

"You know someone who can help him."

"Who?"

"The Bishop. You've asked nothin' of him 'til now. Go to him. For Conor, go to him."

Liam wanted to say no, to tell her that the Bishop was too important to approach with a favor that would only benefit Conor and not the rest of the family. But the look in Dylana's eyes was overpowering, hypnotic, threatening. He resented this woman's strength and he was worried about his son and he didn't want to annoy the Bishop. In the end he did as Dylana asked and in doing so he betrayed Conor.

Bishop Andrew Weeks, round faced and fleshy, with thinning blond hair, leaned back in a black oak chair, steepling thick fingers under a pair of smooth, pink, hairless chins. Sun poured through a stained glass window of his book lined study, causing Liam Irons, who had not been ased to sit, to duck his head and shade his eyes.

"What you ask of me," said the Bishop, "violates both the laws of God and man."

Fear had almost constricted Liam's throat. "Eminence, I did not want to approach you, but I was pressured by a shrieking madwoman."

"Conor's wife."

"Yes."

"Conor joins Young Ireland in its treason and his wife

falls in step. Judas in skirts. She presumes to order me about, it would seem.''

That's when Liam knew that despite any concern he might have for Conor it would be wise to distance himself from this favor being requested of the Bishop. This one was Dylana's horse and let her ride it alone.

"There was no reasoning with her, eminence. Quite out of mind, she was. Would not have done for her to have brought this business to you herself, which she is certainly most capable of doin'. She is not as aware of your position as she should be, her livin' with Conor and all.''

Bishop Weeks' face hardened and he gazed up at the ceiling in thought. After a full minute of silence he reached for a thin, delicate glass half filled with brandy, taking it between two sausage-like fingers, his pinky extended. Liam found the gesture upsettingly feminine.

"I wish no more interruptions of this sort,'' said the Bishop. "I cannot allow my position in the church and with the English to be adversely affected. The sooner Conor Irons and his wife are removed from Dublin, the better for us all.''

The following night Conor, supported by Dylana and the old priest who had found him in St. Michan's two nights ago, slipped from a side door of the church and stepped into a quiet, empty street. Awaiting them was a cart and driver sent by Bishop Weeks. Trailing his parents was little Michael Irons, who dragged a bundle containing the few belongings the Irons had chosen to bring with them. At the cart Conor clung to it to keep from falling. He was about to say farewell to the priest when the driver, sitting in front, stood up, took off his ragged cap and pulled an Allen six-shot pepperbox revolver from under shabby clothing.

"Captain Russell, Irish Guards. Stand where you are.'' His voice was English elite and commanding.

There was a flurry under the straw and two uniformed soldiers pushed their way clear of it and stood in the street, rifles tipped with bayonets and aimed at the Irons and the old priest.

Captain Russell leaped to the cobblestones. "Bishop's compliments, but he will not be dining with you tonight."

Along with Young Ireland leaders Thomas Meagher and William Smith O'Brien, Conor was sentenced to hang. And because they had been found with him, Dylana and the old priest were also given the same fate. The sentences, however, were not carried out. Instead all received a commutation of transportation to Australia. Conor, Dylana and the old priest were held in Kilmainham jail for almost two years; Michael was allowed to live with his mother. Conor provided most of his education and because his own musical and story telling skills made him one of the most popular prisoners, the murderers, whores and check forgers around them took to Michael. They were as sympathetic to him as their dark natures allowed and the boy came to love them, for they were his first friends.

On the day that the old priest died in his sleep it was a cadaverous, sore encrusted pickpocket who told Michael, "Ain't death what's 'orrible, lad. 'Tis the dyin' what ain't so good. The friar ain't worryin' no more. It's us what's weepin'. Remember that when somebody you love crosses over."

1850.

The prison ship carrying eight year old Michael Irons, his parents and 642 convicts from England to Australia was the *H.M.S. Isle of Wight*, a clipper with a raked bow and masses of snapping canvas sails. Men and women, filthy and in rags, were packed into the ship's holds, with the most dangerous chained in pairs to the walls. Flogging was the penalty for one word of insolence to the crew or the theft of a crust of bread. Children, providing they were not murderers, were occasionally allowed unchained on the upper deck, a privilege which the captain, more humane than most, extended to less violent convicts. Most, however, spent the three month voyage below deck, beneath hatchways covered in iron bars, in a foul smelling darkness broken only by sunlight coming through holes cut in the walls to allow rifle fire on the rebellious.

Prison had taken an unholy toll on Michael's parents. At thirty his father was sickly, with white hair and a lined face. His mother had also aged unmercifully, but her strong spirit had not been broken, and her unflagging love warmed both her husband and son. Conor Irons was still a first rate story teller; his tales of the legendary Finn McCool and his singing of Shakespearean sonnets raised the spirits of the despondent convicts and for a few moments took their minds off their destination.

The ship was heading to Western Australia, a colony so vast that it took up a third of the continent and was as large as all of western Europe. It had been founded by private Australian interests who, to attract immigrants, gave away land to anyone who would settle on it. The land, unfortunately, was not fertile, nor did the early arrivals have any agricultural skills. Almost overnight what little manpower the colony did attract disappeared; the immigrants came, then left to follow the sun elsewhere, a frequent practice in "The Lucky Country." Faced with a labor shortage, Western Australia petitioned London for convicts. And because transportation had been abolished in the east, England, in need of a new penal colony, granted the request. In 1849 Western Australia began receiving what were euphemistically called *government workers*, or canaries, after the yellow prison uniforms convicts were forced to wear in their new home.

On board the prison ship Michael's parents cared for him as best they could. His father told stories, sang songs and made him a toy drum from rags and a tin can. His mother shared her food with him and somehow managed to find a bit extra; a piece of rotten fruit, raw fish or a cup of stagnant water. When the ship was rocked by violent storms she held him in her arms and there were nights when she stayed awake with a stick in her hand, to beat off the bright-eyed, rust-colored rats that boldly attacked sleeping children or the dead.

Conor and Dylana Irons loved their son deeply. Long after their deaths the memory of this love sustained him, making Michael the boldest of men. It was as though evrything he achieved was but a monument to them.

"You're our immortality, lad," said his father. "Gain more from this world than we have and trust your hopes, boy. Aye, a man does that. Remember, too, that there is only one way of fightin' in this world and that's to win. Right now you've nothin' but yourself, for I've little to give you. But a man with nothin' to lose can be dangerous. Never forget that and make the world know it as well."

The convict women lived not only half starved and under constant threat of the lash, but in fear of rape by the crew. Some gave themselves voluntarily in exchange for a piece of tainted meat or a stale bun, but others, some as young as twelve, were taken on deck by crew members and attacked, often savagely. The man most feared by the women was Bob Swain, ship's first mate and a bearded, burly man with a gold earring in one ear and quick to use his boots, fists or a belaying pin or anyone—crew or convict, who disobeyed him. Swain, called swine behind his back, preferred young or small women and had so brutalized one teenager that the young girl was to remain forever speechless, too horrified by what he had done to her to ever utter a sound again.

At sundown one evening Michael was on deck to search for his mother, who had gone foraging for extra food. The ship was docked in Teneriffe, largest of the Canary Islands and one of three stops to take on food and fresh water. Near the bow, in darkness under tarpaulin covered rowboats the boy saw a man and woman coupled on the deck and he knew what they were doing, for he had seen men and women do that in prison and even below deck and had heard them moan and cry out with the joy of it. Sex neither shocked nor surprised him, for there had been no illusions of his world for as long as he could remember.

He was about to turn away when he heard the man say, "Bitch, I don't have to give you food or anything else. I can have you when and where I please."

"You promised me," said the woman. "I need the food for my son, for my husband."

"Aye, of that I am sure. None of your lot stays alive for long on the swill we feeds 'em. One in three of you will die before this voyage ends. But Bob Swain does not like being obligated to the likes of you. So there will be no food for you, whore. You hear me? From now on, you gives me pleasure when I wants and you gets nothin' in return but me spunk."

The woman again pleaded for the food and Swain slapped her in the face. Michael stood rooted to the spot. The woman with Swain was Dylana Irons.

When the first mate struck his mother again Michael ran at them, throwing himself on the couple, punching and clawing at the man, who easily threw him to the deck. "Damn me, if it isn't your miserable little spawn."

Quickly sitting up a tearful and shamed Dylana drew her ragged clothes around her thin body. "Dear God." She touched Swain. "Please do not hurt the boy. I beg you. His father must not know."

A leering Swain turned to her. "Well, well, says I. Daddy musn't know, eh? Well, I think it's time daddy knew his wife is nothing but a bloody harlot, happy to spread her legs for a cup of beans. Yes, indeed. Thinks I will go below and tell him about his cheap baggage of a wife."

He shoved her in the face and Michael attacked him once more, scratching Swain around the eye and drawing blood. The first mate touched his face, saw his blood smeared hand and said, "You're dead, you mick brat. You are dead."

He reached for Michael and Dylana threw herself on the

burly sailor, clinging to his neck, clawing for his eyes. "Run, Michael, run!"

Instead the boy kicked Swain, who slapped him hard, knocking him dazed to the deck. Then turning he caught Dylana's neck between his thick hands and strangled her to death. When he had finished he looked down at the unconscious Michael. "Not the end for you, mick brat. Bob Swain has more to put on your plate. For certain, he does."

Striking a member of the crew was punishable by fifty lashes of the cat, to be administered with the entire ship looking on.

"It will kill him," a distraught Conor said to the ship's captain. "He's only a boy who tried to protect his mother."

"I'm well aware of what occurred. But I cannot run my ship if convicts feel they can break my laws and go unpunished."

"My wife—"

"Lured my first mate to the rowboats, where an argument ensued over payment regarding particular services. During said argument the ship suddenly rolled and your wife, sir, slipped, accidentally striking her head on a rowboat. I believe she was also quite ill, which undoubtedly contributed to her accidental passing."

Without Swain's brutality the captain could not hope to control the crew, let alone the convicts. As much as he despised the first mate the captain had no choice but to back him up. However, there was one small victory that could be scored over *Swine*.

The captain looked at Michael, who had a discolored face and blackened eye. "Fifteen lashes. Best I can do. Swain!"

"Sir."

"Proceed to carry out the sentence."

Michael was stripped naked, tied to a mast and his back whipped into bloody strips by Bob Swain. A silent ship watched, waiting for the boy to cry out, but he didn't. Not until the end, when Swain threw a bucket of salt water into the wounds. It was days before the boy could walk again and then Swain saw to it that he was not allowed on deck until the ship docked in Perth, Western Australia. The beating, a lack of exercise and poor food left Michael unable to walk and his father had to carry him ashore.

He was in his father's arms as they walked down the gangplank. "You have a sacred duty," Conor said to Michael, "to remember that your mother acted out of love. That is why she died, boy. See only the good in her. Promise me that."

Huddled against his father's chest Michael, who had not wept during or after the beating, wept now. "Yes, daddy. I will always love mummy. And you."

Perth, the capital of Western Australia, was a small, isolated town occupying both shores along the Swan River. Its nearest neighbor, Adelaide in Southern Australia, was 1300 miles away. Housing consisted of tents, huts, lean-tos and shanties made from canvas, branches, bark and wood. A few buildings—the Old Mill, Court House, Town Hall—were made from bricks and wood by convict labor. Windows lacked glass; the sandgropers, as the town inhabitants were called, were under permanent attack by swarms of flies and numerous other bugs.

None of the streets were paved and the monsoonal rains often left behind knee high mud that could pull a man's boots off. A whaling fleet was the town's primary source of income, along with a small fishing fleet, timber, sheep and the barest minimum of farming. There was talk of gold and silver in the ground, of iron, oil and bauxite, but so far no one had found any of it.

Conor Irons was that rarity in Australia, an educated man, and so he taught school and worked as a clerk for the governor. He drank and dreamt of Ireland and Dylana; the tents and lean-tos that were pubs and grog shops got to know him well.

Michael, left to his own devices and forced to survive

by his wits, went to work immediately. He served an apprenticeship to a tanner, then to a blacksmith and took jobs as a messenger boy and sweeper in stables and saloons. He seized every opportunity to earn a penny and learned to fight in order to protect his earnings from older boys who would rob him. He used fist, knife and club to hold on to what was his and in time town bullies and young thieves left him alone.

At fifteen he divided his time between cutting down clumbs of jarrah trees, a beautiful dark-red hardwood with brown stringy bark, and working with kangaroo hunters, who slaughtered herds of the animals for meat to sell to the whaling fleet. Because he was not a convict Michael grew up a free man, not subject to the rigid rules that governed prisoners. His father eventually became an *emancipist*, a convict who received an unconditional pardon before he served out his sentence. Both Michael and Conor Irons felt the scorn of the "pure merinos", the Australians who had no convict blood in their veins and who discriminated against those who did. They were also known as *exclusives*, because they snobbishly tried to keep anyone sentenced to transportation out of public service and away from polite society.

"The higher climbs the baboon," said Conor to Michael, "the more one sees of his hairy arse. That's what you see in a man who snobs you. His hairy arse."

Of the convicts who had come to Australia with Michael and his father many had died, weakened by English jails, the difficult voyage and the harsh treatment they received after landing. They were ill suited to Australia; convicts, after all, were England's undesirables, not its skilled labor or willing workers. Flogging and hanging failed to turn them into the work force the colony had envisioned. Slaves, Michael learned early, were no substitute for free men.

At eighteen he was tall and broad shouldered, an accomplished shot and horseman, a veteran of the rugged land and at ease in it. He grew up knowing that he had more freedom and future than his father or any man in Ireland.

In those years he wore the uniform of the outdoor Australian male: dungarees, high boots, denim shirt and a leather belt, from which hung a pistol, knife and tobacco pouch. Unlike other Australian men his drinking and gambling were controlled and while no spendthrift, he did insist on having the best in horses, guns and food, winning the nickname ''Prince'' from his mates.

When prison ships from England landed at Fremantle, Perth's outport, Michael could be found on dock, seemingly one of the casual onlookers. But he stayed in shadows or where he could not be seen, eyes picking out the crew among the chained convicts being herded down the gangplank. Then he would scrutinize the sailors lining the ship's rail before he disappeared, to silently move from brothel to pub, following the crew. He spoke to no one and stayed on the edge of crowds, a hunter anxious not to scare away his prey.

He was almost nineteen when his father died after a lingering illness. Conor had developed a brain tumor, which caused him untold agony and twisted his mouth into a permanent smile. Michael cared for him until the end, washing the shrunken man, spoon feeding him and reading to him from treasured books, feeling the pressure of his father's hand in his when a passage particularly pleased him. The available doctors were helpless to treat the dying man, who often called out his wife's name in the middle of the night, waking Michael, who slept on the floor beside his father's bed.

On the day of Conor Irons' funeral, the *H.M.S. Isle of Wight* was scheduled to dock in Perth with another load of convicts. No one could understand why Michael, pistol and knife in his belt, rode furiously to be there when it landed, leaving others to bury his father. When the ship was unloaded and the crew had gone ashore, Michael began his search of the pubs and whorehouses but did not find what he was seeking.

When he returned to Perth, his father was in his grave and Michael stood alone looking down at the hand-carved redwood tombstone marking Conor Irons' final resting place.

"I haven't forgotten," he whispered. "I haven't forgotten."

On his nineteenth birthday Michael killed his first man. With this act he crossed a line; he became an object of fear and respect. On a Saturday night he was one of seven players at a poker table in a crowded, noisy tent. One of the players, a Frenchman, had lost heavily. He had taken an instant dislike to Michael and bet heavily whenever he was dealing. Michael said nothing and continued to take the man's money, thinking that if the Frenchman wanted to be a fool, let him pay for it.

When the Frenchman had lost twenty pounds in gold, the heaviest bet of the night, he said to Michael, "Is that why they ran you out of Ireland? Cheating at cards?"

The sudden silence at the table took on a dangerous expectancy. Both of the Frenchman's hands slid off the table to rest in his lap. When either hand reappeared, Michael knew it would be holding a pistol.

Gathering the cards he reassembled the deck and casually offered it to the Frenchman. There was an edge to his grin. "Examine them yourself, my friend. The 'Devil's Handbook' our Irish priests call them."

Leaning forward Michael held out the cards, then quickly tossed them in the Frenchman's face. Both of the Frenchman's hands came up as a protective reflex and one held a derringer. Instantly he thrust his arm forward and fired across the table where Michael sat. The bullet struck an empty chair. On his feet and off to the side Michael fired his pistol once, tearing away the top of the Frenchman's skull. After holstering his pistol Michael righted his chair and sat down. The silence was broken when one of the card players said, "Let's have a new deck. Somebody's been bleedin' all over this one."

Weeks later on the docks at Fremantle, where Michael had gone to watch the late night unloading of an incoming prison ship, two drunken members of a whaling fleet tried to rob him. One grabbed him around the neck from behind, as the other shuffled closer, a skinning knife held low in his hand. Without hesitating Michael drove his boot heel into the foot of the man attempting to strangle him. Cursing, the attacker released him and Michael, wanting no noise, wanting no one to know he had been hiding in the shadows, ignored his own pistol and drew his knife.

The two knife fighters clashed, each grabbing the other's knife hand at the wrist, pushing, grunting, desperate to survive. Michael, a veteran of the violence in raw frontier towns like Perth, expected no mercy and gave none. He brought up his knee, striking the second attacker in the stomach, driving him back. The attacker dropped his knife and before the man could regain his balance Michael had closed with him, a hand over the man's mouth to silence him as he drove his own long bladed knife into his stomach. The man's scream was smothered against Michael's palm and became a soft, muffled moan.

Whirling, he kicked the first attacker in the knee and in close he smashed an elbow across the man's face, crushing his nose. When the attacker dropped at Michael's feet he kicked him in the head three times.

After wiping the blade of his knife on one of his victims' trousers he walked away, leaving them on the darkened pier. Once again, no one knew that he had hidden in the shadows and watched every men to come off *H.M.S. Isle of Wight*. Once more he had been disappointed. Bob Swain had not been on board.

With a reputation as a man who was both tough and *fair dinkum*, honest, Michael went to work as the youngest peace keeper in Perth. The owner of the town's largest gambling tent hired him to maintain order in the premises and to escort him whenever he carried large amounts of cash to the bank. It was a dangerous job, involving fights or tense arguments with card cheats, drunks, bushrangers, sailors and other menacing characters with too much to drink and uncontrollable tempers.

The handful of police in Perth were unpaid, ignorant and corrupt, existing on bribes, fines and what they could steal. Law, justice and survival belonged to those strong enough to enforce their will.

Brutalizing living conditions, a forbidding terrain, and too much liquor combined to bring out the worst in the hard working, lonely men of Western Australia. Perth prepared Michael Irons for the worst that life had to offer anywhere.

In the eleven years he had been in Western Australia he had managed to save three hundred pounds, an enormous sum for the time. His plan was to buy the best land available and raise sheep and wheat. So far he had not been able to raise enough to buy the property he wanted, but he held onto his dream of being his own master. He would own land and bow his head to no one. However, a man he met in the gambling tent was to change Michael's life forever. Within a week of that meeting the two would leave Western Australia to forge an exciting destiny together in New South Wales.

A heavy rain beat down upon the tent. Inside, Michael circulated among bearded, unwashed men and painted whores, who surrounded poker, roulette and keno tables. At one table, he paused. Watched by others, two men were playing *Swy* or *Two Up*, a wildly popular gambling game.

Swy, from the German 'Zwei' for two, was fast, simple and honest. A man bet whether two spun pennies would land heads or tails. Tonight a small, round faced Englishman with high-glasses and strands of thin blond hair across his pink scalp, was on a winning streak. He had cleaned out several men and was in the process of doing the same to two more, both of whom disliked losing. The Englishman was a newcomer to Perth, one Michael hadn't seen before tonight. As for the pair of losers Michael recognized one as Edward Low, an Australian bushranger wanted for sheep stealing, robbery and murder. Others, too, knew who Low was, but Australians, remembering their convict heritage, would not betray any man to the authorities.

When the Englishman had won Low's last money he swept all of the pound notes and gold coins off the table into a tall beaver hat, then placed it squarely on his head. Low was mean when he was drunk and he was drunk now. He squinted at the Englishman who sat to his right. Michael knew the signs; he stepped between a pair of onlookers until he was standing behind Low. As the small Englishman pushed away from the table, Low slid a knife from his boot. The blade had cleared the cracked leather when Michael slammed the barrel of his pistol into Low's temple, then quickly cocked the hammer and pressed the end of the barrel into the neck of Low's companion.

Low collapsed in his chair, head flopping back, hat falling to the earthern floor. Leaning forward Michael whispered to Low's companion, "I keep the peace here. Now remove yourself and your ugly companion from these premises. Don't let me see either one of you in here again. I will have your weapons and his."

When the bushrangers had left, the small Englishman peered over his half glasses at Michael and grinned. "Your servant, sir. Pease is my name. Davy Pease, late of London and points west. Allow me to shake your hand and share a cup with you, if I may."

"Thank you, Mr. Pease, but I do not indulge during working hours. It is not a habit to acquire in employment such as mine."

A smiling Pease nodded. "Indeed. Your foresight did keep me alive and may it continue to do as much for you. Be ever vigilant, sayeth the prophet, for such is the price of freedom."

Michael immediately warmed to him. "You remind me of my father. You seem an educated man, as was he."

"I am honored by the comparison. In truth, such men seem rare in Australia. Neither my daughter nor I have

seen a one, as a matter of fact. No offense intended
Mr—''

''Irons. Michael Bourke Irons. You have not brought
your daughter to this tent, have you?''

Pease tapped his tall hat and Michael heard the chink of
gold coins. ''I have not, sir. She remains with a respectable woman here in Perth, while I attempt to gain our
passage money. Respectable women are another commodity in short supply here, I must say.''

''Where are you bound for?''

''Sydney. We almost lost our lives on a hell ship. Only
the mercy of God himself prevented that. May we continue
our talk at the bar? My throat is parched and in need of the
soothing touch of demon rum, an old and cherished friend.''

With a pint of rum in his hand Pease continued his
story. Three months ago, he and his sixteen-year-old daughter
Elizabeth had sailed from London on board the *Prince
Albert*, bound for Sydney and the goldfields of New South
Wales. The voyage was trouble from the beginning; the
ship was barely sea worthy, provisions were poor and the
captain was abusive. He had even molested the women.
Knowing he couldn't keep the captain away from Elizabeth,
Pease and his daughter jumped ship in Rio de Janeiro,
leaving their belongings behind. Somehow Pease had man-
aged to earn their passage money to Perth on another ship.
Now he had to get them to Sydney. And the goldfields.

''But I fear our beast of a captain awaits us there,'' he
said. ''Whenever he was drunk, which was frequently, he
would brag of his plans to sell his ship in Sydney and use
the money in pursuit of the glory hole, that gold strike we
all dream of. By all that's holy, may he find only scorpions,
spiders and snakes and may they feast on his eyes and
privates. A swine, indeed. Fitting name for the bastard.
Captain Robert Swine.''

The scars on Michael's back seemed to burn anew and he
tensed, in his mind hearing the lash whistle in the air
before it tore at his flesh.

''Swine?''

Pease signalled for another rum. "Swain the swine. If any man belongs in hell with a broken back, it is he. May our paths never cross. I fear what may happen should he see Elizabeth and me again. We cheated him, you know. My taking Elizabeth away in the dead of night, I mean."

He looked at Michael. "Mr. Irons, suddenly you seem ill at ease. Have I offended you in any way? If so, I apologize most abjectly. I am not always a master of caution and prudence. Accountancy is my area of expertise and I possess some knowledge of mining and engineering. Words, sadly, oft times lead me astray."

"You have given no offense, Mr. Pease. You say that Robert Swain is in Sydney?"

"Unfortunately. I say unfortunately because Sydney still remains my destination."

"It is now mine as well."

Michael saw his mother's face as she pleaded with Swain for food, pleaded with him not to hurt her son or expose her to her husband. He saw her corpse covered by her ragged clothes and saw his grief stricken father cradle the lifeless corpse in his arms.

"Bob Swain and I have a long delayed meeting," he said.

Pease blinked and hastily brought his pint to his mouth. Did he imagine a deadly intent in those words that wasn't there? A second look at Michael's face told him that he hadn't. The strapping young Irishman planned to do serious harm to Captain Swine. An excited Pease lifted his rum in a silent toast to those gods who had unleashed the wrath of this young stranger on Robert Swain.

With the toast went a silent prayer that those same gods protect Michael Bourke Irons, future husband of Elizabeth Macklin Emma Pease.

Sydney. Michael had never seen such an exciting city. Its harbor was breathtaking, its two main branches enclosing an area of twenty-two miles. Built on coastal hills Sydney had golden beaches and white surf at its feet, blue sky and sunshine overhead. The entire city was within sight of walking distance of the ocean. Swimmers crowded its beaches, while women in hoop skirts and bonnets glided through broad streets, past fine shops, telegraph lines and buildings made of brick and stone.

But there was another Sydney, this one with its unemployed sleeping in parks; with narrow muddy streets and shanties; with prostitutes, Chinese opium dens, mass drunkeness and yellow dust storms that stung the face and burned the eyes. More than a hundred thousand people lived here, a figure Michael could not begin to comprehend. The magic of this lusty, sprawling and uncouth seaport touched him on sight, but he could not remain here. Not while Swain lived.

On shore Davy Pease found the ships registry office and learned that the *Prince Albert* had indeed been sold, with former owner Robert Swain loudly telling one and all that he was off to seek his fortune in the Braidwood goldfields, two hundred miles south of Sydney. For the first time since their meeting Elizabeth Pease feared for Michael Irons. She did not care if Swain lived or died, but Michael had to survive.

At sixteen she was tall with green eyes and wide cheekbones set in a freckled face moving from girlish prettiness to womanly beauty. She was strong, warm and outspoken. On the voyage from Perth she had learned what had happened to Michael and his family at the hands of Bob Swain and her sympathy for Michael was instant and wholehearted.

In accordance with Davy Pease's most fervent hope, the youngsters had become close. This time there had been no shipboard danger for Elizabeth; Michael had quickly assumed a protective posture, escorting her to and from her cabin and glaring at any sailor who so much as looked at her. Elizabeth had responded just as quickly, taking his arm as they strolled the deck, taking her meals with her father and Michael, or sometimes with Michael alone.

Even with Swain on her mind Michael still found time to enjoy being with one of the few women he had ever met who was near his own age. Elizabeth Pease was no drunken and hard-faced whore, old before her time, or dark skinned Aborigine woman with mustache and beard. She was young, attractive, alive and he was drawn to her.

Which was why he did not want her to accompany him and her father to the goldfields. Michael had heard stories of how primitive and dangerous it was there, of how men were made treacherous and brutal by the craving for overnight riches. Women were a rare sight in any mining camp, save for an occasional wife and a handful of prostitutes. Davy Pease, however, refused to be parted from his daughter.

And so in the week they spent in Sydney obtaining a wagon, horses, food and mining supplies Michael purchased a pistol for Elizabeth and taught her how to use it. "The largest target," he said, "is between a man's shoulders and knees. Aim there. Squeeze the trigger. Do not jerk it. Keep your weapon dry, free of mud and near to hand. It is wise to learn to care for it and when you point a gun at a man, do so in earnest. No larkin' about. Aiming a gun at someone makes him desperate and sometimes he will risk all to save himself, thus endangering you. Aim and be ready to kill."

Michael's business was how Pease and Elizabeth referred to the matter between him and Swain. "You go about your business," Pease said to him, "but know this: you and I are partners. We are mates. When I am poking about in the earth I'm doing so for you too, and no arguin'. You helped me and my daughter with passage money and with supplies. It's a comfort to us to have you on the trip to Braidwood and that is a fact. So, laddo, like it or not, you are my partner."

Each man spat in his palm and they shook hands, the Irish way of sealing a bargain. But that night Davy Pease lay in his room and listened to his daughter weep next door. She wept for Michael and for fear of what might happen to him when he and Swain met. Bringing the young Irons into her life had given her happiness, but had also brought her misery and Pease stayed awake for a long time, wondering if he had done the right thing.

The Australian goldfields drew men from America, Europe, Africa, Canada, South America and China. In Australian ports entire crews jumped ship, while in the six colonies soldiers deserted their units and joined clerks, policemen, school teachers and outlaws in succumbing to gold fever. Some Australian towns were abandoned as men, on fire with a craving for the yellow metal, raced down the road they hoped led to wealth.

Too often there was no road on which to travel. Michael, Davy Pease and Elizabeth joined many in a grueling trip made without roads or even a crude path. The column of men, wagons, horses and carts followed the barely visible tracks of those who proceded them, lone riders or families pushing wheelbarrows or bearded, hairy men in drays pulled by teams of bullocks.

The New South Wales sun, which had seemed so attractive at first, soon became a curse. It was torrid and fiery, searing a man's skull as he travelled mile after mile into the bush, sometimes in knee high mud and always hounded by masses of insects. Michael had wondered if Elizabeth could survive the rigors of the journey; the sun browned her face and peeled her skin and her hands were rubbed raw by the horse's reins. But the young English girl proved sturdy and resilient, a willing worker and most cheerful. In years to come Michael would remember that it was during this trip that he fell in love with her.

The Braidwood goldfields consisted of tents, along with shacks made from bark, tin and gum branches, a collection of crude dwellings sprawled over miles of low hills, valleys, streams and rivers. There was no law save that enforced by the men themselves. None of the diggers, as the miners were called, had beds. Few could afford blankets. Straw was a luxury, but Michael, once he and Davy had staked a claim, spent two shillings to buy some to make a bed for

Elizabeth. The men had not seen a woman in months, and they stared at Elizabeth openly. A few called to her, mostly in good humor, but an obscenity from one digger brought Michael's whip slicing into his face. The enraged miner's hand dropped to his pistol butt.

But that's when he froze, not daring to move, not wanting to die. The click he had heard had come from Michael's pistol now aimed at his head, the hammer cocked. Terrified, the digger waited for death. "Speak to her in that fashion once more," hissed Michael, "and I shall kill you." The cold savagery in his words and manners silenced onlookers; they recognized a killer when they saw one. Disrespect to this young woman, it was clear, could be fatal. The tall Irishman at her side was no one to cross.

Gold mining was pitiless work. For the first few days Michael had no time to spare for Bob Swain; he, Davy and Elizabeth labored from sunrise to sunset, establishing their claim, obtaining a license and digging. Freshly spaded earth was washed in a nearby stream, then sifted for nuggets and gold dust. Being late arrivals the three were forced to take the leftovers, those claims no one else wanted, claims thought to be played out and likely to yield little if anything at all. But Davy, with his mining experience in Wales and England's midlands, felt that the soil could yield some "color" and he was right. Hours of backbreaking effort brought forth a handful of nuggets, which Michael insisted they keep secret. Diggers were a desperate lot; many, after untold disappointments, would kill for a spoon of gold dust.

And so Michael and Davy, like others, quietly handed their gold to a New South Wales government representative, who gave them a receipt. The gold escort, a heavily guarded stage coach, would bring the gold to refineries in Sydney.

As for Swain, there was no need to search for him. The brutish seaman came to Michael.

* * *

Not far from Michael and Davy's claim was the Chinese encampment. Called 'celestials,' the orientals were the most hated people in the goldfields. Their mining areas had already been picked clean by others and had little chance of being profitable. They worked the longest hours, sending what money and gold they came by back to their families in China. It was their willingness to toil for lower wages than white Australians that made them victims of a racial hatred that was frequently maniacal.

By 1860 Australian unions had already achieved the unbelievable goal of the eight hour day, with an eight shilling minimum daily wage to go with it. Anyone undercutting this, as colored immigrant labor usually did, became the enemy, to be opposed with the ferocity of a people who remembered the abuse and poor working conditions their convict ancestors had endured. It was this fear of losing hard won gains that would cause trade unions and most Australians to systematically oppose all immigration, colored in particular.

Near the end of his first week in camp Michael rode away from the ramshackle lean-to that served as a general store. It was sundown and he wanted to return to his own tent before dark. In his saddlebags were tea, sugar, salt and wheat flour used in making *damper*, the unleavened bread which along with mutton, formed the diggers' diet. In his shirt pocket was a yellow ribbon for Elizabeth's hair. He smiled, remembering the touch of her hand on his when she had taken his gift of a perfectly formed autumn leaf and placed it inside her blouse, against her bare breast. She had not meant the gesture to be sexual but Michael's response was. The look on his face, his breathing, his obvious longing for her.

A blushing Elizabeth had placed a hand on his chest and he had reached for her and then they remembered where they were, in a tent shared by her father, who was due to return any second. They drew apart, eyes still locked, body and soul linked by a desire which needed no words.

The attraction between the two was growing stronger daily and becoming harder to ignore.

Michael touched the pocket containing the ribbon. He loved her, wanted her and by God, no man but he would ever possess Elizabeth Pease. Bob Swain, however, was never out of his mind and it was Swain that his thoughts had turned to when he smelled smoke. It came from the Chinese encampment, from tents now aflame. Michael reined his horse to a stop and stood up in the stirrups, a hand shading his eyes. An animal instinct told him something was wrong. The fire and smoke were too near *his* tent. Cursing himself for leaving Elizabeth, he spurred his horse forward, using the reins to whip the animal into a gallop.

The trouble had reached his tent in the form of four drunken miners who had broken away from a larger group attacking the Chinese. Now they menaced Elizabeth. The tent Michael shared with her and Davy was flattened, its stakes pulled up and scattered. An unmoving Davy lay face down in the mud, while the miners, drinking from bottles and carrying ax handles and rifles, had surrounded a terrified Elizabeth, whose clothing was being ripped from her. Nearby, a young Chinese boy, naked and no older than twelve, cowered near the miner's horses, his round face puffed and discolored from a beating.

"Damn bitch, you are," shouted one of the miners, a hand reaching for Elizabeth's clothing. "We'll teach you to hide a bloody heathen from honest white men. Goin' to peel you like an orange, we will, then take our fun in turns. Heard about you bein' here. Nice bit of crumpet, we was told and so you are, missy. When you are buck naked, I'll give you the first ride meself."

Swain. The hated rasp of his voice was etched in Michael's brain forever. It triggered a hot rage that washed over him in waves that threatened to overwhelm him.

Michael drew his pistol and that's when one of the miners, an American with a red beard worn in braids, spotted him. With a drunken leer, he held up a bottle and beckoned Michael over, mistaking him for one of them.

"Goddam, hoss, you're just in time. Got us the only filly round here worth plowin' and we—"

Michael shot him between the eyes. His next two shots went into the chest of the man standing next to him. The gunfire, however, spooked Michael's horse; it reared up on its hind legs, tossing him over from the saddle, and when he landed in the mud, the gun had flown from his hand. Still on its hind legs and between Michael and Swain, the horse continued to whinny and paw the air, as Michael, on his hands and knees, threw himself at his pistol, fell short of the weapon and frantically scrambled for it.

He heard a booming noise, the powerful roar of a shotgun and there was a burning pain on the left side of his face, in his left shoulder, arm and down his side. He was on his back, staring up at a sky streaked blue and gold by a setting sun, the salt taste of his own blood in his mouth. His horse cried out in pain and so did Elizabeth, and it was her cry that gave Michael the will to fight, to survive for the both of them.

Rolling over, he pushed himself to a sitting position. His vision was blurred, but he saw his horse hobbling, its right front leg shattered by the shotgun blast. Elizabeth and Swain fought, the two clinging to the seaman's shotgun. A bleeding Michael, racked by agony and barely able to see, summoned his remaining willpower and crawled towards his pistol. He reached it, and brought it up with both hands just as Swai.. shoved Elizabeth to the ground and whirled to face him.

From a sitting position Michael turned his head to the left, the better to see out of his right eye, the only vision left to him. Aiming deliberately he shot Swain twice in the stomach. The hulking, bearded man staggered backwards, tripped over the naked Chinese boy and fell to the ground. The boy scurried towards Elizabeth, who took him in her arms. Michael tried to stand, failed, and so began crawling past his crippled horse, past Davy Pease, until he reached Swain.

Swain was still alive and Michael rejoiced. He wanted Swain to know. And he wanted to see the seaman's eyes when he died.

Michael pulled Swain's shotgun towards him, then paused to rest, wipe blood from his eyes and rub the stained hand against his thigh. For long seconds he and Swain stared at each other, until Michael placed both barrels of the shotgun against Swain's jaw.

"Michael Irons, I am, and this is for my mother and father." He pulled one trigger. Click. The chamber was empty. Swain had fired it at Michael. The second, however, was loaded and its report was loud enough to temporarily deafen Michael. Swain's eyes bulged; he tried to beg for his life and sit up at the same time, but his fleshy, bearded face disappeared in a blood red explosion of pulp, brain bits and bone fragments.

Michael wasn't through. He had waited too long and his vengeance demanded more. Seized by an uncontrollable frenzy, he raised himself to his knees, gripped the shotgun by the barrel with both hands and held it high overhead before bringing the butt down again and again on Swain's lifeless body.

Only when his arms tired and the pain of his wounds bit deeper did a dazed Michael allow a weeping Elizabeth to take the shotgun from him. And then he began to tremble and weep and heard his parents call to him from a distant golden mountain. He saw them and tried to stand, to go to them. Instead he fell back into the deepest blackness he had ever known.

He awoke to find his eyes bandaged and a bitter, unfamiliar smell about him. There was another smell, too, and his mind fought to identify it. Davy's pipe. *Davy*.

Michael's hands went to the bandage, but Davy stopped him from removing it. "Must keep covered for a time, lad. Doctor feels it's best. Says in a day or two we can take it off.''

There was an uncomfortable silence, as though Davy was keeping something back.

"I may be a thick-headed mick," said Michael, "but I know there are no doctors in the goldfields. Leastwise, none that I would trust.''

"The Chinese. Helped you for what you did for the little boy. Saved him, you did. Swain and the others chased him to our tent. Elizabeth and I tried to protect the boy from certain death. Saved my life again, you did. Not to mention Elizabeth. Took a nasty knock on the head but I'm fit and ready to proceed, as it were.''

"Elizabeth?''

"Here, Michael," she said.

Davy chuckled. "Hasn't been anywhere else, that girl. Tending to you and ignoring her poor father.''

Elizabeth touched Michael's cheek. "The Chinese tended your wounds. They used salves and roots and powders and many things I have neither heard of nor seen before. With all my heart I thank them for saving you.''

"Wise race, the celestials," said Davy. "They were writing and reading when our ancestors swung from trees and painted their arses blue. That foul smell at which you are wrinkling your nose is a salve that is nothing less than miraculous. Well, I will be leaving you two alone for a wee bit. You know, of course, that few tears were shed in the camp at the demise of the late Mr. Swain or his two companions. Nasty piece of work the lot of them.''

"Three?'' said Michael. "I saw four.''

"One ran, the bugger. He's in hiding. Terrified of you, I hear. That business of beating Swain's corpse into a bloody pudding, which he reported to one and all, seems to have given you a reputation for being the devil incarnate. It appears we three will be let alone to prosper or not, as the Lord so wills. Claim jumpers and would-be seducers, I'm told, plan to walk easy around you. Delightful, old boy. It's absolutely delightful.''

When Davy had gone, Michael listened to the awkward silence.

"Tell me," he finally asked Elizabeth. "I have to know."

She brought his hand to her lips and kissed it. He felt her tears trickle into his palm. "We will not know for two days," she said.

"Know?"

"Whether or not you are blind."

Michael stiffened, his hand catching both of hers.

"The shotgun," said Elizabeth softly. "Only a portion of the charge hit you, but it, it—"

"Tell me."

She could barely be heard. "Tore your left eye from the socket. And maybe damaged the nerve on the right one."

Only when he heard her wince with pain did Michael realize he was squeezing her hands with the grip of a tormented man standing at the mouth of hell.

"Sorry," he said.

"Oh, Michael, Michael." She threw herself on him and held him tight. "There's a chance, love. Believe, please believe. The Chinese said there is a chance."

He snorted. "Lyin' in mud, I am, and in darkness and waitin' for the Chinese to save me bloody eyesight. Dear Elizabeth, will I never see your face again? I do love you so."

She kissed the tears that came from beneath the rag covering his eyes, then a corner of his mouth and his lips and his arms went around her and they kissed for the first time, with a hunger so desperate that it left the two of them weak. She felt him warming to her, felt his need for her, his wordless insistence igniting a passion she no longer wanted to fight. She wanted him desperately. And it was right, it was right.

She pulled her skirt up around her hips and he whispered her name with a need that made her weep. His hands shook as he fumbled with his pants, but she, calmly, deliberately, pushed his hand aside and undid his pants for him. She wanted to say *your wounds*, but he wanted her so much and he had almost died, so she pulled him onto her and there on the earthen floor they became lovers.

Michael's right eye survived undamaged. His face, near the empty socket of his left eye, was scarred. In time most of the scars faded, save for two thin, criss-crossing white lines on the left cheekbone. He owed his life as well as his eyesight to the Chinese miner's ministrations—the boy he'd saved was the man's only son. A large part of the Chinese encampment was destroyed by Swain and other white diggers, who also killed a half dozen Orientals.

Less than two weeks after being wounded and almost blinded for life Michael married Elizabeth in a ceremony performed by an English curate, who had fled life at Westminster Abbey in London for the New South Wales goldfields.

While giving Michael time to recover from his wounds Davy, rather than work the claim alone, went gambling. He was shrewd at it, a hard headed player who never pursued whims. He won big—gaining the deeds to several gold claims as well as other property and some cash.

A grog shop was part of his winnings; the shabby tent, with a full supply of liquor, was quickly sold for profit. Other men lost their wagons to him, along with teams of horses and bullocks and fair amounts of mining equipment. Wagons, animals, and equipment were sold profitably, as were the obviously useless claims, which newcomers insisted on buying even after being told the claims had run dry. Any bit of ground that might yield gold was in heavy demand.

A recovered Michael, feared and respected for the manner in which he had disposed of Swain and his friends, took charge of those claims won by Davy that were worth exploring. Men were hired to work them, with a bonus going to anyone who sighted gold. Those who had run out of money and hope were glad to work for fair wages, the payment of which Michael regarded as simply a good business practice.

A modest strike was made at one claim, yielding enough color to send Davy to Sydney for equipment that included diamond drills and explosives. Michael moved Elizabeth into a sturdy wooden shack. She no longer handled pick and shovel; she kept records of men hired, wages paid and receipts given to Irons/Pease by the New South Wales representative. When word reached the mining camp that bushrangers had attacked a gold escort and made off with the gold, it was Michael who led mounted and armed diggers in a hunt for the outlaws. And when the bushrangers were captured it was Michael who said that they must hang and Michael who fitted the noose around their leader's neck.

Elizabeth lost their first child in a bloody miscarriage that almost killed her as well, and despite her tearful pleas to be allowed to remain in the goldfields, Michael decided she would be better off in Sydney.

In the third year of their marriage she gave birth to a son, Heath Conor. A year later he was followed by a second son Dai David, and two years after that a daughter christened Morag was born. By then both Michael and Davy were wealthy men, no longer rooting about in mud and living on half cooked mutton, but residing in Sydney and enjoying the best that city had to offer.

Bigger strikes were made on their claims, including the discovery of a single gold nugget weighing over one hundred pounds. Michael placed it on display in Sydney, guarding it with one of the world's deadliest snakes, the Australian *taipan*, a reptile whose bite injected more venom than a cobra. Newspapers around the world carried the story of the massive nugget, and the frightening viper that watched over it, and Michael Bourke Irons, the tall Irishman with the black eyepatch, who had brought gold and serpent together.

The discovery of gold changed Australia forever. In just ten years its population doubled, the industrialization of the continent began, and millions of pounds in investment capital poured into the country from overseas, particularly from England. Land speculation was rife while the high quality of Australian wool, combined with an insatiable demand for it in the mills of England, brought riches to those who dealt in wool. The lack of refrigeration in ships prevented mutton and beef from being exported, but grain was sent to the rest of the world in record amounts. Prosperity had arrived. Almost all of Australia believed it would never end, turning a blind eye to any possibility that it could be precarious or temporary. Nor did anyone see the liability in an unstable political system that found six colonies determined to remain independent from each other at all costs.

As his wealth increased Michael became an even bolder businessman. Those he bested in business saw him as arrogant and ruthless, a pirate complete with black eyepatch, a matching lack of scruples, and a hunger for vengeance that would not let him stop until the one who had offended him was destroyed.

"I am an impatient man," he said to Elizabeth, "and cannot wait until the Last Judgment. I give each his due in this life, in this world, in my way."

Others found him honest, a man of his word, fiercely loyal to his mates and secretly helpful to the unlucky and even the irresponsible to whom he felt a sense of responsibility. Any man permanently crippled in a mine owned by Michael Irons and Davy Pease was supported for life. Friends who lost sheep to drought or brushfires were offered financial help. Widows of men who had worked for them, and their children, were looked after.

Davy and Michael were not only partners, they were friends. "Only got three eyes between us, lad," said Davy, "so we must be as clever as six foxes in a sack. I know you be watching my back. I just want to say I shall do the same for you. If I don't, I'll never hear the end of it from my daughter."

It was Elizabeth who said, "We have so much now, Michael, you and I. Riches, servants, a fine home and lovely children. But if God were to take it all away I would bless his name if he would only leave me you, my darling.''

They did indeed have riches, and all because in business Michael had become the gambler, quick to accept a challenge that one day might prove lucrative. He was not intimidated by determined competitors or the thought of failure. The spirit of Australia—risky, free-wheeling, unfettered—spurred him on. Known as 'The Irons Pirate,' because of his name and eye-patch, Michael invested in *Thirds*, a common business arrangement which saw a backer put up money for investments in sheep, land and other business, in return for a third of all profits. He foresaw increased Australian exports and talked Davy into agreeing to a heavy investment in ship building. Within months of launching, their fleet of six clippers had paid for themselves completely.

More investments followed: warehouses on Sydney's docks; real estate in and out of the expanding city: the formation of a major brokerage dealing in wool, mutton, grain and beef; *Thirds* in an iron foundry, a coal mine and one of the few private railroads to show a profit. Money was Aladdin's lamp, said Davy, quoting Lord Bryon. To best manage the money flowing into their company Michael and his partner purchased a building near the Stock Exchange on Pitt Street, refurnished it and had a grand opening attended by the Governor of New South Wales, the Premier, Sydney's Mayor and Members of Parliament.

Attracted by the name and its beautiful view of the harbor Michael moved his family to the posh suburb of Elizabeth Bay, where his hillside mansion had stables, rare birds and an artificial lake complete with black swans. Davy's gift to him at the new house was a complete library of books, enough to line three walls. ''Education is an ornament in prosperity and a refuge in adversity,'' he said to Michael. ''That is the wisdom of Aristotle, whose works you will find here, along with other fine thinkers. Your father started you off with a wee bit of reading and

knowing your letters. 'Tis wise to remember that education
is the difference between man and man.''

As it did in every society, social snobbery found its way
into Australia. Here, where two-thirds of the population
came from England, that country remained the standard of
excellence, representing the best in everything from fashion and education, to food and speech. Prominent in Sydney as well as in Melbourne, Sydney's rival for the country's
leadership, anglophiles held all things Australian to be
inferior. Melbourne, perhaps, was the most class conscious city on the continent, striving hard to resemble the
most Victorian metropolis in the United Kingdom. It was
the prosperous capital of Victoria, the colony named for
the British sovereign, that had broken away from New
South Wales rather than be associated with that state's
convict past.

In both cities, those people with titles bestowed by the
British crown, and who could prove they had no convict
ancestors, stood atop the social ladder. It was they who
constituted Australian nobility and usually included the
Governor, his military and civil staff and middle to upper
class Englishmen who had come to Australia seeking their
fortunes. Many of them made no secret of the fact that
they considered Australia to be a primitive backwater.
They did everything possible to live a life reminiscent of
Britain.

Michael Irons was twice damned in their eyes. He was
the son of convicts and he was Irish, permanent drawbacks
to any social acceptance. Irons had worked with his hands. He
had killed men. Women might gush over him, but gentlemen of quality did not want his company. His money,
perhaps, but nothing more.

Michael applied for membership in the Empire Club, the
club for merchant princes and rich businessmen. Led by
Walter Gibbon, an English banker with whom Michael did
business, the club rejected the application, making sure
that all of Sydney knew of the rejection. Angered, Michael

purchased the building, evicted the members on short notice and turned the building into a hotel. The Empire Club became the laughing stock of Sydney and the subject of several tongue in cheek newspaper accounts.

When the Empire apologized and Gibbon, a notorious snob, suggested that Michael re-apply for membership, a suspicious Davy said, "Lad, I worked among these foppish swine in England and I tell you they never forgive a slight to their grand sense of pride."

"Father's right," said Elizabeth. "They are twenty thousand miles away from England and that is why they must be more English than ever. Gibbon's wife refuses to speak to me because I told her that our children will not be sent to England to be educated as she and the others have done with their children. What a silly cow she is."

"It's another mountain for you to climb," said Davy, "and we both know it. Another world to conquer. You don't need them, lad. You're a better man than the lot of them put together."

Michael, however, did not listen. His pride said he had to win. He accepted Gibbon's invitation and apology and was told that there would be a club dinner in his honor in two weeks. On the night of the dinner Michael appeared at the men's club to find it deserted. There were no members present and there was no dinner. There was only an empty dining room, with a small, plain wooden table set for one. A cracked plate and single crude spoon, the kind used in prisons, were on the table, along with bowls of animal feces and urine. Enraged, Michael strode from the club, not knowing that a hidden Sydney reporter had observed his every move and reaction. When the story appeared in print it was Irons' turn to be an object of ridicule.

"They will never accept you, lad," said Davy. "You are not the right sort to the English and never will be. That is one reason why we Australians, and I now consider myself an Australian, are talking of federation. Unite and break off from England, I say. Christ, who wants to spend his life imitating people who aren't worth imitating in the first place?

"Michael, listen," he continued almost pleadingly. "If you want to play amongst fools like this sort, you never chase them. You make them come to you. Bucko, you do not need them to tell you what a fine man you are. You *are*. Hear me, Michael, you are a fine man. Look at me. English I am, but without the proper parents, the proper accent, the proper school. I am clever enough, indeed, but that did not get me the money to start me own business or prevent me from being cheated by proper Englishman. And when I went to court to fight back what happened? I will tell you. What happened is that in a land where property is all that matters, I was denied justice because I was not a man of property. Australia does not need England, Michael, and neither do you."

He returned to a water color he was painting of Georgina Flatly, a middle-aged Irish woman who was his housekeeper and Michael suspected his bedmate as well. Davy never spoke of their relationship, but it was obvious that he cared for her more than most masters cared for their servants. Swallowing the rest of his brandy Michael said, "Well now, I suppose I had best be settin' about proving that we Australians have our own place in the sun."

Davy looked over the top of his half glasses at his partner. "You are beginning to sound like the wild boyo who can bring Sydney to its knees if he so chooses. That is the Michael I know. Planning a reply to Mr. Gibbon, are we?"

Michael fingered the gold watch chain stretching across his vest. "Mr. Gibbon has become my abiding interest for the time being. It's a distinction he will not find pleasing."

A month later Michael had his revenge. Walter Gibbon, like other bankers, joined ambitious businessmen in land and wool speculation, often with great success. Lately, Gibbon had been buying land for the sole purpose of reselling it as quickly as possible for a profit. Most land was purchased from the New South Wales government and Gibbon, to gain an advantage, had bribed a clerk to inform him in advance of the time and place of those sales featuring the best property. Before anyone knew the land was for sale Gibbon owned it and was preparing to deal it to his own customers at a huge markup.

After learning the identity of Gibbon's man in the property office, Michael made his own secret arrangement with him and only when Gibbon was in pursuit of the biggest land deal of his life did Michael strike.

It was a warm, sunny afternoon as a calm Michael stood at a window in his office and looked down on a Pitt Street jammed with stage coaches, wagons, hansom cabs, traps, drays pulled by teams of bullocks and horsedrawn buses with straw on the floor. When he saw a black coach pull up and Gibbon step out and disappear into the Irons & Pease Building, Michael smiled. You have brewed the mixture, Mr. Gibbon. Now prepare to drink.

When one of the fifteen clerks on the other side of the door knocked on the thick, frosted glass Michael said, "Show Mr. Gibbon in."

Gibbon, a small, fastidious man, with a trim gray beard and rimless spectacles, refused Michael's offer of a chair. He remained standing, his eyes boring into the Irishman, who sat with hands folded on his stomach. Gibbon's gripped an enamel cane in one hand and held his left over his heart.

Gibbon sneered. "How much?"

Michael remained silent.

"I will write you a check," said Gibbon with a precise arrogance. A hand was already inside his jacket.

"No you won't," said Michael. "It's not for sale. Not at any price."

Gibbon smiled. "Social rejection suits you. It allows you to see yourself in true relationship to your betters."

Michael showed no reaction. "Good day, Mr. Gibbon. Our business is concluded."

Gibbon's composure began to crack. He frowned. "Very well, then. You name a figure."

"Good day, sir."

Clutching his walking stick in both hands a nervous Gibbon stepped forward. "I need that piece of land you own. I need it immediately."

"I know you do. It has the only water near your acreage. Without it, you cannot sell the land you purchased yesterday."

In buying more land at one time than he had ever bought before, Gibbon had borrowed heavily. He had gone into debt believing that the newly purchased land could be sold twenty-four hours later for ten times his purchase price. He had a buyer. What he did not have was the only water for miles around. Michael Irons had that.

"The clerk assured me I had water, plenty of water," said a nearly distraught Gibbon.

"Did he now." Michael had arranged for the clerk to lie to the English banker, bribing the man with gold and the promise of a job with Irons & Pease at twice his current salary.

Gibbon's eyes narrowed. "You bloody bugger. You wretched sod. You had Danforth deceive me, while you purchased the water rights yourself, didn't you? That bastard Danforth. I shall have him flogged."

"Danforth is now in my employ and I will personally kill the man who lays a hand on him."

"You know damn well that land is useless to me without water."

"Useless to any sensible man, I would say. Appears to me that no one will buy from you without water."

"I have borrowed much beyond my means, and if I do not sell the run I have purchased I face ruin."

Michael said nothing.

"Damn your eyes," said Gibbon. "You were not worth the pig shit we served you."

An icy Michael replied, "I hope you saved that pig shit, sir, because soon it will be your turn to make a meal of it.

I believe we have nothing more to say to one another. Good day.''

Minutes later he again stood at the window looking down, watching Gibbon step into his coach. The driver whirled his long whip overhead before bringing it down on a team of matching grays. But Michael was to see Gibbon once more and it would be the saddest day of Michael's life.

A week later Michael and Elizabeth exited Fuller's Theatre, where a sold out house had enjoyed the performances of Albert the Dancing Steed, a female rope dancer from England, a four hundred pound French organist and the most popular act in Sydney, a troupe of 'nigger minstrals,' eight white Sydneysiders in blackface who called themselves 'The Ethiopian Serenaders.' The minstrals had sung two songs while facing the box where Michael and Elizabeth sat. It had been one of his gifts to her in what was a week long celebration of their fifteenth wedding anniversary.

Tonight as they made their way to their carriage Michael looked at her in the gaslight. She wore diamonds and furs, and handmade high boots and carried a painted fan that cost more than most men earned in a year. The two of them had come a long way from the shabby tent they had shared in the goldfields. For all of the credit given him by the world, Michael knew that he could never have achieved his success without Elizabeth. He consulted her on everything, valued and trusted her opinion and often refused to proceed with a project if she disapproved.

And yet she was neither a nag nor a scold. She remained kind, loving, giving, a good wife and mother and quick to take the mickey out of him, to bring him down to earth when he became too full of himself. The gaslight and shadows muted the crows' feet at the corners of her eyes and the lines that were half circles from her nose to the edges of her mouth. She looked mysteriously beautiful and he loved her immensely. His infidelities were occasional and discreet, short-lived and tinged with the remnants of Irish Catholic guilt, though he no longer attended church regularly. None of his momentary sexual adventures meant anything to him. They were a matter of glands—nothing more. He blessed the day Elizabeth had entered his life and she was the only woman in the world for him.

At the carriage, on impulse, he placed a hand on her arm, stopping her in place. When she turned, a half smile on her face, his heart melted with love, with memories of their years together. "My dearest," he whispered, holding her hands and drawing her towards him. She was against his chest when a pistol cracked from a doorway, flame spurting from its barrel. Elizabeth stiffened, and breathing her husband's name once, she died in his arms.

The killer ran for his life, footsteps echoing in an awkward gait, his left hand held over his heart. A stunned Michael, clinging to his dead wife, saw the killer only as a small, top hatted silhouette hurrying to the corner, then disappearing. His brain registered the information *I know who he is*, but his conscious mind stayed on Elizabeth and he willed her to live. The part of him that knew she was dead refused to accept it and pushed him into repeating her name again and again.

He did not remember her being taken away or the long hours he sat beside her cold, still body in a room that would forever be a blank to him. Only when a tearful Davy arrived, summoned by a rider, did Michael leave and go looking for Walter Gibbon.

He found the English banker lying dead on the floor of his study, his small, bearded face contorted by the poison he had taken in brandy. On his desk was the gun he had used to kill Elizabeth. Gibbon had lost everything and faced total ruin, social disgrace and poverty. He no longer had his good name, for that had been shredded in the scandal precipitated by his failure to repay borrowed money on time. Destroying himself and the man who had brought him low was all that Gibbon had left. Drained and numb,

Michael looked down at Gibbon's corpse, worked spit into his dry mouth and spat on the dead banker. In that moment, Michael had never hated God more, for God had cheated him out of killing Gibbon. Feeling a pain he had never thought possible, Michael fell to the floor and wept for Elizabeth and for himself.

He drank, gambled, lost himself in the flesh of women he did not care about, and still there was the agony of his loss. A housekeeper helped with the children and Davy ran their companies. Michael cared about nothing and nobody, least of all himself, and when Davy had once more taken him out of a seedy hotel room, leaving behind a hard looking whore, the little Englishman's anger could no longer be held back.

"You are a profligate ass," he said to a disheveled Michael. "You shame my daughter. Would you do these things if she were here?"

There were tears in Davy's eyes and a chastened Michael, unwashed, unshaven and in clothing he had worn for days, took his partner's round face in his hands.

"Sydney laughs at you," whispered Davy. "Men of Gibbon's ilk and the Empire Club are waiting for you to fall. The vultures circle overhead, Michael, and they wait for you to collapse so that they can take away what we have. Be strong again. For me, for yourself, for your children, for Elizabeth."

Michael dropped his head. "Help me to try, dear friend. I beg you, help me."

At Davy's suggestion Michael went to Braidwood for several weeks, to their gold claims and away from Sydney, family and familiar surroundings. The harsh existence in the mining camp would be a tonic, Davy thought. If the camp reminded Michael of happy, carefree days with Elizabeth, it allowed him no time for self pity and the slow suicide of self indulgence. Here, he had to be alert, strong and at his best. Here, he had no choice but to work hard.

His presence at the camp brought out the best in others as well. Spurred by his watchful eye and increased bonuses, his men worked harder. Even those who didn't work for him knew of his wife's murder and that 'leather eye,' once a digger himself, had come back here to regain the best part of himself. And so some tipped their hats to him, a rare tribute among fiercely independent Australian workers.

Evenings Michael spent alone, riding into the bush among wildflowers and eucalyptus gum trees that sometimes grew over 300 feet tall. He rode past the hulking Great Grey kangaroo, which was almost as tall as he and strong enough to kick his horse to death; past the slow moving and small koala bear that spent most of its life living in trees and chewing gum leaves. The howl of the dingo was never far away, along with the hoarse trumpet voice of the graceful brolga, the crane-like bird capable of performing surprisingly graceful dances. He smiled when the kookaburra, the bird known as the laughing jackass, fearlessly came near him when he stopped, looked up and giggled. The sights and sounds of Australia were a tonic to him and so was the silence that went with them, the quiet that could only be found in the bush.

It was here that he met Johnny-Johnny, the Aborigine. On one late evening ride, Michael heard a pack of dingos snarling and yelping and by the sound he knew that they had cornered a prey who was not yet ready to die. Out of curiosity he rode closer and saw that several of the wild dogs had surrounded a teenage Aborigine boy who was on the ground in a sitting position, a knife in one hand, a boomerang in the other. Obviously hurt and unable to stand, the boy swung his weapons wildly, desperate to keep the dingos at bay. Not far from him lay the bleeding bodies of two of the wild dogs.

Reining his horse to a stop, Michael drew his rifle from its scabbard, brought it to his cheek, sighted and squeezed the trigger. A dingo leaped in the air, then fell to earth, its spine shattered. A second shot sent another rolling in the dirt, to come to rest in a bloody heap. A third bullet tore into the head of another, throwing him onto the legs of the Aborigine boy, who kicked the dead animal away. In seconds the remainder of the pack had scurried away, to disappear into the bush and growing dusk.

Riding closer, Michael looked down at the Aborigine. Half white, he was stocky and muscular, with a square shaped face topped by black curls. The pain on the boy's face said he had broken bones. Michael noted with some amusement that the Aborigine did not seem grateful.

"Can you stand?" he said to the boy.

"If I could, I would not be sitting here."

Proud, thought Michael, with the bravado found in only the young or the foolish. He pointed to the boy's weapons. "Isn't enough to know how to use those. You have to know who to use them against."

The Aborigine stared up at him, then looked away. His eyes were on the setting sun. "I thank you." The words were bitter.

Michael dismounted. "You have a name?"

"Johnny-Johnny."

"Well, Johnny-Johnny, let us see what is wrong with you."

"Broken leg. And ribs, I think."

"How did it happen?"

The boy hesitated. "My horse threw me, then ran off."

Michael smiled. "You were searching for dingo pups to rear, to be used one day in stealing white men's sheep."

The boy remained silent.

"I appreciate enterprise meself," said Michael with a wink. "Except that most white men would either hang you for that or put a bullet in you and forget the whole business. I observe that you do not like whites, for which I cannot fault you in the least."

"You take our land, defile our women. You get us drunk and force us to fight one another for your amusement. You slaughter us like kangaroos."

"Yes. I cannot deny that. None of this is my doin'

personally, but I do see your point. Your father was white.
I notice.''

Defiantly, Johnny-Johnny said, ''I killed him.''

Michael raised his eyebrows. ''Did you now? And did
that make your skin black?''

Johnny-Johnny looked surprised, as if a secret long
kept had finally been exposed. His face relaxed, not with
trust, but with curiosity. He listened closely as Michael
said, ''We're alike, you and I. Couple of tough boyos.
That is until life deals us a wicked blow and then we
wonder why we are no longer masters of this world. Now
then, it's back to camp for you.''

''Cannot. Miners will kill me.''

''And what did you do to incur their wrath, may I ask?''

''Stole sheep. Stole cloth. Stole horse, killed it and sold
meat back to man I stole horse from.''

Michael roared, his laughter echoed in the calm twilight.
There were tears of joy in his eyes when he said, ''Oh, I
do admire enterprise. You will return to camp with me. I
guarantee your safety.''

Johnny-Johnny snorted. ''An Abo protected by the 'Iron
Pirate,' by 'Leather Eye.' Yes, I know who you are. I had
planned to steal something from you one day.''

''Your plans are changed. You will not steal from me.
You will work for me and I will stop the diggers from
putting a rope around your neck and forcing you to dance
on air.''

''I will be no servant.''

''As you wish. But work you shall. As a man.''

The Aborigine frowned. But he allowed the white man
to help him to his feet.

When the two of them were mounted on Michael's
horse, the Irishman looked over his shoulder at Johnny-
Johnny and said, ''Enterprise,'' and as the horse began its
trot back to camp, both men burst out laughing.

Sydney, 1888.
From a semi-dark wing of the Royal Theatre a proud

Michael Irons stared at Louisa Heller, who in white ermine trimmed with red and orange silks, was alone onstage, arms raised as she curtsied to a packed house that had been on its feet cheering and applauding her for two full minutes. Her Gilbert and Sullivan medley had excited the audience, Michael included, to the point where roses and orchids were now being tossed onstage, along with bank notes and small bags containing gold coins or gold dust. The thirty-year old Louisa Heller, a tall, buxom, American singer, was Sydney's reigning star. She had arrived in Australia over a year ago and remained ever since. For most of that time she had been Michael's mistress.

Gliding off stage to an applause which seemed to grow louder, she reached Michael in the darkness, embraced him and kissed a corner of his mouth. And then she clung to him for a long time, ignoring the thirteen hundred people who screamed her name and clamoured for the sight of her once more. Michael was leaving Sydney tomorrow, for an important trip to London and she would not see him again for months.

"They want you," he said.

"I want you."

"Sorry, lass, but it's me Catholic upbringing. No fornicating in public no matter how loud the applause."

An assistant stage manager gestured for her to disengage herself from Michael and take another bow. Lou Heller, born with a strong streak of independence and known to be profane at times, spoke to the theatre employee almost seductively. "Little, little man. Be gone and may the drippings of your cock rot your shoelaces."

The assistant howled with glee. "Bloody cheek you've got. Bloody cheek." Still laughing, he waved her away and left.

"Dear God, what a bawdy sheila you are," said a smiling Michael.

"And you love it. Tell me: will it be rough for you in London?"

"I fear so, yes."

Michael was to be the spokesman for a group of Sydney bankers and businessmen seeking a five million pound loan from Whitehall to build a private railway and new roads leading from New South Wales to Victoria. The planned construction would provide work for a growing labor force and increase the colony's wealth by increasing exports and supporting bond issues. There were those in London who opposed the granting of the loan; a prosperous colony could only want more political independence from the mother country.

In addition to the London opposition Michael had Australian enemies; the a'Beckets, the powerful father and son banking team from Melbourne, were already on their way to England, anxious to stop Michael at all costs. English born and unscrupulous, the a'Beckets were sworn enemies of Michael and Davy Pease, who had come out openly against their shady business practices. The Melbourne bankers themselves sought eight million pounds for similar construction ventures by Victoria companies and businessmen with whom they were involved. Some of that money, Michael knew, was destined to stick to the hands of Lord Edward and Denis, his portly, lisping son. Not long ago the two had sold Melbourne land they did not own to a friend of Michael's and when Irons learned about it, he had threatened swift and sure retribution unless the money was returned. It was, but neither willingly nor gracefully.

Michael's thoroughbreds had raced against those of the a'Beckets for the prestigious Melbourne Cup, winning twice to the chagrin of the Englishmen. The Irons & Pease group of companies did business in Melbourne, a lovely and very British city, but one in which Michael never felt comfortable. It was too attached to the British crown, too proud of its titled citizens and royal parks. And while Michael was accepted into the Victoria Racing Club, the a'Beckets had seen to it that he was never accepted among the *right people*. The *right people*, however, did not hesitate to seek out Michael's advice on investments for a quick profit.

"Hypocritical buggers," said Davy. "Hiding behind masks, all of them. Frogs attempting to be elephants."

"False coins all of them," said Nat Gane, the charming and brilliant lawyer-politician now helping Davy and Michael with their finances.

And now in Louisa Heller's dressing room Irons watched the half naked singer as she sat before a dressing table mirror, painting her lips a bright scarlet. She had violet eyes, the most striking color he had ever seen on a woman and hair as black as a bat's wing. Her mouth was full—a meal in itself he had once called it—and her breasts were God's gift, ample, high and firm, demanding to be worshipped, caressed, consumed.

Irons was forty-six now—rich, notorious and attractive. He had been with more than his share of women, but Lou Heller was the best. She was exciting and satisfying to be with—in bed and out. Even now, when their eyes met in the mirror, she was both humorously lascivious and overpoweringly sensual. Sitting behind her, he felt his erection rise and crossed his legs to hide it. Lou pointed to his groin. "Aha! You can't fool me. It wants to come out and play."

Every man in Sydney, including Michael's sons Heath and Dai, both now in their twenties, lusted after her. Australians loved her down to earth manner, her generosity and American energy. The theatrical community, ordinarily a hot bed of envy, adored Lou Heller, whose kindness to other performers was almost legendary and whose golden voice could bring the most hardened critic to tears. She was from New York, had worked hard for a career, had performed in the White House and before the crowned heads of Europe and was said to have stabbed a drunken, brutish husband who beat her once too often. She was also said to have successfully defended her honor, while on tour in Egypt, by using a hatpin on the testicles of a descendant of the pharoahs.

If Michael was fond of her, she loved him. Her biggest rival for his affections had been Morag, his daughter and the apple of Michael's eye. But on meeting Lou, Morag had succumbed on the spot. The American became the only woman to win Morag's approval, a fact not lost on Michael, who knew his daughter was not one to suffer fools gladly. Morag had been brought up differently than most Australian women. Recognizing her superior intellect early on, Michael gave her a first rate education and encouraged her to use his extensive library. Heath and Dai, while older, often sought her advice when their father was not around.

Lou stood up and faced him, her breasts still bared. "I will miss you, you one-eyed bastard. Our last night together and you want to spend it having supper."

"We won't be eatin' supper the entire night, you hellion."

She fell on her knees before him, both hands on his erection, warming his now painfully swollen member. Her eyes were a startling shade of purple and he could not tear himself away from them. London and the intrigues in store for him could wait. And so could the champagne supper laid on for them in the presidential suite of the Hotel Dylana, formerly the Empire Club and currently Sydney's most popular hotel. He began removing his clothes.

"Our food will be cold when we arrive," he said.

"Well, sweet Cyclops, allow me to do my best to get your mind off sauces and meat pies."

Grinning, Michael turned to lock the door. As he did so, thoughts of another woman, a woman he was to meet in London, came, unbidden and undeniable, to his mind. He was drawn to her, too, irresistibly so. But when he turned to face a nude, voluptuous Lou Heller, the white heat of desire blinded him to everything else, including guilt, and with fierce passion he took the singer on her dressing room floor.

London.
The meeting was of vital importance. Ordinarily, it

would have taken place in Whitehall, or some other suitably official setting, but the meeting with the one man who spelled success or failure for Michael and his Australians was being held away from the city's centers of power, away from prying eyes, loose tongues and overly curious natures.

The five men met in the elegance and glamor of Mayfair, in a white mansion that was a cross between an Italian palazzo and Greek temple. It sat opposite the church of St. George, scene of the weddings of Percy Shelley, Benjamin Disraeli and George Eliot.

In a long room of huge leather chairs, oak panelled walls and endless shelves of hand bound books with gold embossed titles, Michael Irons sat to the left of the mansion's owner, Sir Norris Held, the man who had allowed the Australians one hour to plead their case for the five million pound loan. By seven-thirty this evening Sir Norris, chairman of the board of one of London's leading banks, was due at the Lord Mayor's mansion for dinner with fellow board members, major investment bankers, members of Parliament, the Foreign Office and the Colonial Office. His own bank would follow the recommendation of the tall, patrician looking Held, who would also carry weight with the others, "the men in black," as London's power brokers were called.

Sir Norris, however, had already made a decision in favor of the a'Beckets, a decision facilitated by a bribe of one hundred thousand pounds. It was Michael who passed on this news to his fellow Australians, refusing to tell how he had come by the information.

"Christ Jesus, we are beaten men," said a devastated Nat Gane. "We cannot top that bit of benevolence and even if we could, the a'Beckets would only come back and outbid us for Sir Norris' wretched soul. Palms have been crossed with silver in the past, but this beats everything. Why in God's name did you insist on our meeting with Sir Norris tomorrow?"

"Because, dear friends, once bought is twice bought."

And now in his study Sir Norris sipped gin and tonic and prepared to be amused by these sons of convict sods who spoke with a nasal twang that was all but unintelligible. At least the one-eyed Irishman's brogue did not attack the ear, which was a small blessing, since he appeared to be their leader. But how laughable it was that these oafs thought they stood even the ghost of a chance against Lord a'Becket and his son! He could dine out on tales of these boorishness for days.

A relaxed and condescending Sir Norris acquainted Michael and the Australians with what he called the ugly realities of life by noting recent bank and investment house failures in several countries, along with such recent disappointments in Australia as a drop in wool and mutton prices, droughts, and strikes by unionists.

Drake Setty, an Australian banker, heatedly interrupted. "Beg pardon, Sir Norris, but if what you say is true, then why—"and here he chose his words carefully, "has Lord a'Becket been so well received in these here parts, meanin' all over London."

Sir Norris swallowed more gin, and spoke without bothering to mask his disdain. "Because he is English, because he does not believe in federation, because he feels that what is best for England is best for Australia."

An angry Drake Setty was about to reply when Michael interrupted him. "Let me get this straight, Sir Norris; Lord a'Becket is against a united Australia?"

"As strongly, Mr. Irons, as you are for it. You, sir, are Irish and a fomenter of the strong anti-British feeling that exists in New South Wales."

"That I do not deny. England has allowed France and Germany to colonize the islands around Australia. We see this as a threat to our survival even if you do not. If England does not care enough for Australia to protect her by annexing these islands, we will resent that neglect and remember it."

Sir Norris put his empty glass down on a small end table. "We are one empire and intend to remain so."

"Twenty years ago Disraeli called the colonies mill-
stones around England's neck. The empire, sir, exists so
long as your country needs colonies to buy her goods. You
will hang onto us so long as it is profitable and not a
minute longer."

Sir Norris smiled. "Indeed. Empires and markets are
synonymous. The fact remains, however, that those people
who oppose Australian unity feel that any investment in
your country at this point would be futile if *your* country
plans to be independent."

"Did you know, sir, that Britain's trade with her American colonies increased after the war of independence?"

Both men smiled as Sir Norris nodded his head. The
Irishman was no imbecile, he noted, and his attitude towards the proceedings, shifted subtly.

"What is your opinion of the Colonial Office?" asked
Sir Norris. This Whitehall department created policy for
all of Britain's colonies, and was bitterly resented by
militant Australians for interfering too often in their country's
affairs.

"They are men capable of drowning on dry land and
like all fools, to quote Goethe, they rob you of time and
peace of mind."

"Whores and politicians. We loathe both, but impatiently seek out their services."

" 'It is folly for a man to pray to the gods for that
which he has the power to obtain himself.' "

Sir Norris cocked an eyebrow and Michael said,
"Epicurus."

Both men smiled as though sharing a secret. It was the
custom of the directors in Sir Norris' bank to write long
erudite letters to a major London newspaper, with the
writer using the name of a Greek or Roman philosopher.
Epicurus, a Greek philosopher, who lived almost three
centuries before Christ, and who taught in Athens, was Sir
Norris' classical nom de plume. The English banker could
not have been more shocked at Michael's intelligence—or
more pleasantly surprised.

"More brandy, Mr. Irons," he said, getting up to pour it himself. The other Australians were open mouthed at the sight of a man of Held's stature on his feet and waiting on a bloody Irishman, of all things, and an Australian one at that. Perhaps those books in The Iron Pirate's mansion weren't there just gathering dust after all.

"I do wish we had more time," said Sir Norris. "Perhaps when you are in London again, Mr. Irons, we can have dinner at my club."

"It would be my pleasure, Sir Norris."

The Englishman frowned. "I do wish I could be more helpful to you, but alas I have already committed myself. Perhaps in future you and I can do business together."

"Very kind of you. Incidentally, you have heard of my new refrigeration ship."

Impressed, the banker raised both eyebrows. The introduction of refrigeration ships by Australians in 1880 had meant the export of mutton and dairy products all over the world. Michael and Davy had taken a risk when others had backed off, investing heavily in such ships and prospering. The a'Beckets, among others, had thought the enterprise doomed and by the time they had learned differently it was too late. Recently, Irons & Pease had commissioned the building of the largest refrigeration ship in Australia.

"Such a ship is a sure success," said Michael. "We have businessmen waiting to ship their perishables to this country, America, Europe, the Orient, South America. I expect that ship to be a floating gold mine."

"I quite agree. It's a marvelous venture, sir. I congratulate you."

Michael stood up. "Gentlemen, let us not delay Sir Norris any longer. He had been very generous with his time and most helpful. By the way, Sir Norris, do you know of anyone who would care to buy a one percent interest in my new refrigeration ship? Modest cost and one bound to pay huge dividends."

Sir Norris' eyes narrowed. "One percent?"

"In perpetuity. It will be a steady moneymaker over the

years. That one percent will be worth many thousands of pounds. Many, many thousand of pounds.''

''And the cost to the investor?''

''As I said, modest, sir.'' Michael paused dramatically, calmly pulling on his deerskin gloves and reaching for his walking stick. ''Ten pounds.''

The Australians' eyes widened. Their heads snapped towards Michael, then back to Sir Norris, who frowned in deep thought.

''Mr. Irons,'' he said. ''You are staying where?''

''Russell Square. The Eagle.''

''Quite. Please do me the kindness, should you be away from your quarters for any length of time, of keeping the desk clerk informed of your whereabouts. I may have some interesting news for you.''

Outside on the quiet street in front of Held's mansion, the four Australians lifted Michael Irons to their shoulders and carried him along the spotless pavement, cheering him and waving their hats. None of them gave a tinker's damn for the somber looking, well dressed gentlemen and their ladies forced to step aside for this rabble who could only inspire disdain.

Camilla a'Becket, Lord a'Becket's beautiful twenty-one year old daughter, was the other woman in Michael's life. She had accompanied her father and brother to London and it was she who had told Michael of the bribe to Sir Norris Held. Now it was she who told him of her father's bitterness at having been refused the loan he had counted on. In a turnaround that shocked the a'Beckets and the entire London financial community, Sir Norris had strongly urged a long term loan for Michael Irons and the Sydneysiders.

''Michael, father has never despised anyone as he despises you. I am terrified of what will happen to both of us if he learns that—''

Michael's embrace silenced her. Standing behind Camilla, he wrapped her in his arms and from the flat near

Westminster Abbey they stared out into the fog at the craggy silhouette of the House of Parliament and listened to Big Ben, the thirteen and a half ton bell in the famed clock tower, strike the half hour. To keep their affair secret he had rented this small flat on a side street for their meetings. Michael felt her warmth, breathed deeply of her scent and woman smell and closed his one eye in silent pleasure at the feel of her hair brushing lightly against his chin. Camilla was so young, so fresh, so reminiscent of Elizabeth in their first days together. Not as strong as Elizabeth, but like her somehow, and she made Michael feel young and protective once more, as he had felt twenty-five years ago in the Braidwood gold fields.

They had met in Melbourne, at the annual cup race, a fleeting contact that had ignited a mutual attraction in them both. Their paths had crossed again, at Government House in Sydney, where she and her father had attended a reception for the Prince of Wales. After that, urgently drawn to each other, their meetings had become deliberate—a "chance encounter" while riding or when Michael was in Melbourne on business, at social gatherings of mutual friends and always behind her father's back. The greatest risk and challenge had been to find time alone. Their passion offered the excitement of forbidden fruit and for Michael, an added triumph over Lord a'Becket, who made no secret of his desire that his daughter marry a titled Englishman. That's why she was in London, to be paraded before the *haute monde* in hopes of snaring a husband who would satisfy her father's voracious appetite for social aggrandizement.

Camilla had grown up with all that a wealthy daughter could want. The sole thing she lacked was freedom, for Lord a'Becket was tyrannical and uncompromising, a stern and unbending Victorian father. But however much she feared him, she loved Michael Irons more and dreamed of the day when he would free her from a father and brother who had oppressed her from the day she had entered the world. It did not disturb Michael that her love for him carried with it no small desire to get back at her family.

London was not a city Michael could take to his heart. It was too big and inhuman, too dark, and dreary, too blackened by smoke and dirt and dampened by fog and rain. There were too many people clogging its streets, too many carriages and wagons on its avenues and everywhere the taint of complacent chicanery and corruption. He missed Australia—its warming sun, its roguish, laughing people, its schooners of strong beer and meat pies, its beaches, open spaces and mobs of kangaroos. Camilla was part of that "wide, brown land" and he clung to her now in a longing for home.

She hesitated before saying, "Michael, my father has found a husband for me."

He froze. "Who?"

"Lord Gerard Bond-Cocking."

"Dear God."

The short, fat Lord Bond-Cocking, who could trace his lineage back five hundred years, was a doddering sadist, gambler and epileptic, who attempted to cure his illnesses by swallowing liquid gold. He had been married four times, abusing his wives while exhausting their fortunes and was known for cruel practical jokes, the least offensive of which was placing corpses in the beds of his houseguests.

"You'll not marry that whoreson," snapped Michael. "I will see him and your father in hell first."

"Lord Bond-Cocking is of the nobility and prominent in London society. Father will achieve much by this marriage and is determined that it take place."

"And I am determined that it won't."

Weeping with relief, she turned and clung to him with all her strength and Michael, remembering how Elizabeth had looked to him as her savior years ago, vowed that Camilla would never belong to the animalistic Bond-Cocking or to any other man save Michael Irons.

*   *   *

Lord Edward Alphonse a'Becket looked at his watch, then angrily snapped it shut and returned it to his vest pocket. He abhorred a lack of punctuality in anyone, particularly in members of his own family, who were subject to his rule and preferences. Camilla was to have returned from shopping in time for afternoon tea which was held promptly at five, whether in Melbourne or London. It was now almost six and Lord a'Becket was becoming increasingly irritated by this show of disrespect. When Camilla appeared he would reprimand her severely for this slight to his dignity. Then he would tell her that the wedding plans had been finalized. She was to be married to Lord Bond-Cocking in the fall, in a London ceremony to be held on Bond-Cocking's fifty thousand acre estate in Surrey.

Lord a'Becket was slim, with white mutton chop whiskers, waxed mustache, a long nose, and a complexion made florid by too much liquor, tobacco and rare roast beef. He was as rigid and demanding in his personal habits as he was cold and ruthless in business. Servants attending him had to first wash their hands in rose water, then wear white gloves before drawing his bath or setting his table. He epitomized every thing distasteful implied in the term "Victorian"—from high domestic tyranny to his ruthless grasping for wealth and social position.

His son Denis, despite the severity with which his father treated him, admired and sought to emulate him. And to the extent that he, too, had become a shrewd and unscrupulous businessman, he had succeeded. Corpulent and lisping Denis still managed to attract women by his money, power and animal sensuality.

This evening father and son stood before the marble mantlepiece of a large fireplace in the leathery study of their rented Belgravia townhouse and listened as a grandfather clock struck six o'clock. Camilla was now an hour late, which Denis knew his father regarded as a capital offense. The old man would have her guts for garters and rightly so, since women were to be obedient to God, father, husbands and brothers without deviation or question. Denis poured more port for his father and himself, then recapped the decanter, dismissing any qualms about his sister's punishment. He cared little for her, anyway, considering her to be nothing more than an ornament to be peddled to the highest bidder, which had turned out to be Lord Bond-Cocking, a lecherous, drunken sod with a twisted mind and a taste for deviancy that went beyond anything Denis himself had ever tried.

Bond-Cocking would bring his title and social position to the marriage. The a'Beckets would pay a dowry of a hundred and fifty thousand pounds, along with shares in their Melbourne bank. A hefty price for a boost up the ladder of London society, but Lord a'Becket considered it a fair trade. The wedding would be *the* social event of the season, attended by the elite of England and all of Europe. Denis cared little for such frivolity, but if his father wanted it, so be it. After the refusal of Sir Norris Held to remain bought and paid for, Lord a'Becket had turned positively foul, making Denis' life a hell on earth. The wedding represented a badly needed triumph and the culmination of a lifelong dream.

Two hours later, Camilla had not returned. A by now worried Edward a'Becket was just about to summon the police when a messenger delivered a note addressed to him in Camilla's handwriting. He read it carefully, then without a word handed it to Denis and walked away. Seconds later the study door slammed and Denis knew his father wanted to be alone. The air seemed to crackle with his displeasure. With trepidation, Denis read:

Dearest Father:
I know this will disappoint you and blacken me in your eyes, perhaps forever, but I must follow my heart. By the time you read this Michael Irons and I will have married. I am of age, having achieved my majority and I know what I must do to be happy. Please do not hate me, nor turn from me. You are my father and will

always have my love. Please wish me happiness. I pray
that in time I may come to have your blessing.
Your most loving daughter, Camilla.

Stunned, Denis re-read the note several times. That
bloody twit, that insane, ungrateful little fool. Wretched,
wretched woman. She should be thrashed within an inch of
her life and sent packing barefoot in the snow. How dare
she so brazenly defy their father? Whatever grudging admi-
ration he might have felt for his sister's daring he struggled
to suppress.

As the son stood in front of the study, fist poised to
knock on the door, his father's voice bellowed his name.

He had witnessed his father's ill-temper many times, but
never in his life had he heard him so enraged, so frenzied,
so infuriated.

Apprehensive and edgy, his stomach churning with past
memories of his father's fury, Denis entered the room and
stood still, waiting until he was spoken to. His father faced
the fire and spoke in a small, trembling voice. "Irish
slime. Fiendish and diabolical and forever mocking me.
He is my hell here on earth, my torment unending. Well,
no more, I say. Let there be an end to it, I say."

He turned, his face older and wet with tears of anger.
"He will best me no more. You will see to it."

A puzzled Denis did not know what to say. Was his
father talking of murdering Michael Irons?

As though reading his son's mind, Edward a'Becket
slowly shook his head. "Taking his life is not enough. I
want him to suffer. He must be punished and punished
severely. There are men here in London for what we need.
They exist in the rookeries and the devil himself fears
them."

Denis nodded. His father was talking of London's hellish slums—those breeding grounds of murderers, footpads, cutpurses, child prostitutes, thieves—neighborhoods
of such seething violence and danger that police refused to
enter them. Lord a'Becket was talking of slums such as

'The Devil's Acre' in Westminster, or 'Seven Dials' and
'The Holy Land' in the center of London.

"I will need only one such man," said a'Beckett. "Just
one. And he must be reliable. Find him for me, Denis.
Find my demon, so that I can turn the remainder of
Michael Irons' days into a living hell."

Eight weeks later Michael, with Camilla in his arms,
slept in the master bedroom of his clipper ship, now only
hours away from Sydney harbor. Under full sail and pushed
by strong winds, the swift vessel was ahead of schedule. It
was within sight of Australian land, having just entered
Bass Strait, the stretch of water between the colony of
Victoria and the island of Tasmania. Already the ship was
preparing a swing to the left, to head north towards Sydney.

But Michael was feeling no elation at the nearness of
home. He had pulled away from Camilla; his face was
contorted and despite a cool night and open cabin window,
his forehead was beaded with sweat. He was having a
nightmare.

In his horrible dream he again saw Lord a'Becket dis-
owning Camilla, which he had actually done in a curt note
to her before she and Michael had left London. As the dream
ground on, a'Becket grinned hideously at Irons, covered
his eyes with both hands, and laughed uncontrollably. Then
he was gone, replaced by Johnny-Johnny, Michael's trusted
Aborigine mate. Michael's nightmare world was filled with
foreboding and an impending horror that he could not
comprehend, and Johnny-Johnny was attempting to warn
him. "Warrior, warrior, arise and fight. Arise and fight,"
he kept repeating.

It was when the mocking a'Beckett appeared once more,
his hands covering both eyes, that Johnny-Johnny's voice
grew louder and a sweating, terrified Irons, his body slick
with sweat, awoke, instantly sensing real danger. He twisted
away from the hook seeking to gouge out his remaining
eye. The hook was the right hand of a stocky, bearded
intruder who smelled of sea salt and tar, and who had

entered the open window by a rope dangling from a top side railing. Naked, Michael lashed out with both feet, driving the attacker back. Camilla screamed. Crouched, the attacker, his face darkened by lamp black, kept the hook in front of him, feinting, then leaping forward as though fencing.

Hurling the quilt at his attacker, Irons came off the bed. He spun the man around, throwing him face down on a bearskin rug; the hook dug into the cabin's floor. Irons could see the lump under the quilt that was the man's head and he drove his elbow twice into the temple, then stepped on the attacker's right wrist, grabbed the hook with both hands and yanked up sharply. From under the quilt the man screamed as the hook came loose in Michael's grip and blood spurted onto the quilt and floor. Crazed with agony, the attacker writhed left and right, further entangling himself in the quilt and flooding it with his blood. There was a pounding on the door and a crew member shouted, "Mr. Irons, sir. What's going on in there? Are you alright?"

Michael, his chest rising and falling with his breathing, dropped the blood-stained hook on the floor. His eyes were on the quilt and the figure beneath it. "Get dressed, Camilla. Quickly. This night has not yet ended."

The attacker was a seaman who had been taken aboard the clipper at Southampton. His papers carried the name Ben Giles. In an attempt to save his life Michael had the stub of Giles' right hand cauterized, but the attacker died of shock and bleeding anyway. But not before he talked.

Friends had put Giles in touch with a "Mr. Ridgely," a portly, balding Australian, who spoke with a slight lisp. Michael recognized Denis a'Becket at once. He had paid Giles a thousand in gold to get himself signed on Irons' clipper and promised him a thousand more once the job was completed. And the job itself? To pick a day when the ship was near Victoria, sneak into Irons' cabin and blind him in his one good eye. How he chose to do this without getting caught was his lookout.

Giles had drawn others on board into his scheme, telling them only that he planned a robbery of the owners' quarters. He induced two crew members to lower a row boat over the side—in the confusion following his mutilation of Irons, Giles would climb down to the boat, where the two were waiting. Together the three would row to Victoria, which was only hours away.

It was easy to learn the identity of the two crew members; when they heard the noise on board and saw lamps being lit in Irons' quarters, they attempted to row away. They did not get far. Plucked from the sea, they were brought on board, and Michael ordered them hanged immediately, with the ship's full company in attendance.

In his cabin, with dawn coming up, he told Camilla of her father's plan to mutilate him.

"Michael, remember he is my father. What will you do to him? I am to blame for this for having married you." She covered her face with her hands and that's when Michael knew that if he killed either Lord a'Becket or Denis the highly strung Camilla would forever hold herself responsible for their deaths.

But revenge would not be denied him. There was one thing he could do.

A week later in Melbourne a package was delivered to Lord a'Becket at his office. When he opened it the hook that had served as Ben Giles' right hand tumbled onto his desk. There was no message, no note.

Lord a'Beckett turned his head quickly, but failed to find the waste basket before vomiting.

Michael's second marriage had its effect on friends and enemies alike. Lou Heller, angry and hurt, refused to see him and ignored his telephone calls, messages, flowers, gifts. Her displeasure over the nuptials was no secret to stagehands and others within hearing distance of her dressing room. A case of champagne from Michael was disposed of within minutes; bottles were heaved into dressing room mirrors, walls and windows, filling the air backstage with alcoholic fumes for weeks. Lou Heller didn't want conciliatory gestures; she wanted revenge and got it.

In the prestigious Autumn races at Randwick Racecourse a shocked Michael, to whom racing was a serious matter, watched as one of his best horses was defeated by "Dancehall Girl," a swift mare owned by Lou. The mare had been a gift to her from a new admirer, Blue Dan Costello, a muscular Irishman who was a power in Sydney's underworld. It was a jealous Michael who watched Lou, on Blue Dan's arm, saunter into the winner's circle after her racing victories.

The obese and unscrupulous Redmond Glass, editor and publisher of the scandal sheet *Opus Dei*, used Michael's new marriage as the basis for a sordid attempt at blackmail. He threatened to publish a story claiming that on the return voyage from England, a drunken and jealous Michael had had three seamen put to death for presuming to address the second Mrs. Irons. It was Glass's approach to show his potential victims an advance copy of a scurrilous story about themselves, to be destroyed with the purchase of 'advertizing.'

"There have been rumors of a future knighthood for you," said a leering Glass to Michael. "You are most prominent in the affairs of New South Wales and you are under close scrutiny by the British Crown, particularly in the matter of Australian federation. Would it not be best to retain the appearance of being as clean as a hound's tooth? Would it not be wise to silence negative accounts of your private life before such accounts see the light of day and do their worst? Our publication is the people's voice and a primary organ of national independence for Australia—"

"Your publication is a pox-ridden rag," said Michael. "It has the moral stature of a child molester and your appeal, sir, is not to my reason but to my purse."

Before Glass could muster his anger and retort, Irons leaned forward on his black oak desk, his one eye aimed at the journalist. "I do not like you, I do not fear you. But disgrace my wife or foul her name in any way and you would be wise to fear me.''

Irons' voice dropped to a lethal hiss. "Harm her and I will come for you when you least expect me, and you will not hear or see me until it is too late. I will make you envy the dead. My word on that, sir.''

Glass did not publish that story. But he did publish others designed to be harmful to Irons. He accused 'The Iron Pirate' of fathering the Aborigine Johnny-Johnny, of losing horrendous amounts at gambling, of cheating his business associates and competitors and of being disgracefully drunk and brawling in public places. None of these stories were true; *Opus Dei*, in the classic style of all yellow journalism, cared more about selling newspapers than it did truth. No one, however, thought to ask Redmond Glass why he never mentioned Camilla Irons in any of his stories on her husband.

Heath Irons, older than his shy stepmother, was uncomfortable around her. He enjoyed the company of attractive women, but this one was obviously out of bounds to him. Like his brother, Dai Irons was polite to her, but did not come close to treating her like a member of the family. It was Morag who came to the young bride's rescue when she needed help the most.

Six months older than Camilla, Morag was lean and dark, with a sharp nose, pointed chin and green eyes filled with fire and a quiet confidence. Her spirit, intelligence and mocking humor, a highly prized Australian trait, drew men to her with unfailing regularity. On the day she saw an easily offended Camilla weep when cowed by an insolent servant, Morag took her young stepmother aside and said, "You are mistress of this house now and must assume the responsibilities that go with the position. Listen to me. There is something you must do, something quite important.''

Camilla waited to be told.

"You must sack that servant.''

Visibly upset, Camilla shook her head. "I cannot."

"You have no choice. He was disrespectful to you in front of others, who saw him go unpunished. Now all will treat you that way. Mark my words: to survive in this house, you must get rid of him."

While she knew Morag was right, Camilla could not bring herself to do it. In the end, it was Morag who fired the servant and refused to give him a reference. Thereafter, Camilla leaned on Irons' daughter, choosing her as closest friend and intimate confidante. Morag enjoyed Camilla's charm and impulsive high spirits, but was distressed by her young stepmother's intermittent fits of depression. Camilla was at a loss outside the only world she had ever known, a world where every detail of every day had been prescribed by her domineering father. Nothing in her experience prepared her for the many responsibilities that went with being the wife of Michael Irons, one of the most important men in New South Wales.

She needed Morag's help to function and preside over dinners and other gatherings held in the Elizabeth Bay mansion. But at other people's parties, dances and teas Camilla blossomed. She became gay and frolicsome and likeable as a fawn. But Morag could not help but wonder if her father noticed that his new wife's moments of elation were more than matched by periods of depression and despair.

Davy Pease, more content than ever with his house-keeper Georgina, called Camilla, "a darling little kitten," but did not tell Michael that he might have done better to have chosen a lioness, such as Lou Heller.

Pride in the past. Confidence in the future. Australians clung to these attitudes with the tenacity shown by their convict ancestors a century ago in scratching a living out of barren soil. In that one hundred years the outside world had poured over a quarter of a billion pounds into the country, a strong vote of confidence for a people who had begun life under the lash and in chains. But in the 1880's there were signs that a crisis was on the way, one that would push Australia to the wall. A drop in prices world-wide reached "the lucky country" and to a people who had lived in "splendid isolation," the results were shattering.

Wool, all important, dropped twenty-five percent; wheat slumped forty percent. Money became scarce and the Australian businessman reacted. He cut wages. The unions resisted, but with limited success, being neither strong nor organized enough to affect economic policy in all six states. For employers, it became cheaper to turn to the huge pool of non-union labor, always available and willing to accept any work no matter how low the wage. At this point union and employer clashed over the employer's right to hire as he wished.

Michael Irons led the opposition to organized labor. "I will not be told who and who not to hire, not by these scum, not by any man. I did not fight forty years and lose my damned eye to let some eight shilling a day bastard step on my face. If they want war, I shall bring it to them with both hands and a willing heart."

Because the businessmen of Sydney supported him to a man, the union leaders, with the Australian tendency to cut the mighty down to size, decided to single him out. In one night they mounted a concerted campaign to cripple the Irons & Pease company. Boxcars of their wool, waiting at the railway station to be loaded onto wagons and carried to the docks, were burned. Most damaging of all, a prized clipper ship berthed in the harbor was set on fire and destroyed. Non-union labor loading other Irons & Pease ships were attacked and severely beaten. It was a night of labor violence unlike anything Sydney had ever witnessed.

Davy Pease rode out to Michael's home to bring the news to Michael in person. But when he arrived, he learned that his partner was totally consumed with another problem. Camilla, pregnant with their first child, was about to give birth. She had already been told to expect a difficult delivery; she was narrow in the hip, of fragile health and prone to coughs and fatigue. Nor was she as mentally sound as she might be.

A worried Michael hovered at Camilla's bedside, wiping her brow, holding her hand and using words in an attempt to soothe her agony, until the doctor gently pushed him aside. A sympathetic Davy could not bring himself to disturb his partner. Leaving a message for Michael to contact him when he could, Pease left the mansion and headed for Sydney harbor to remove cash from a safe in the company's waterfront office. Perhaps the rumor was false, perhaps not. Davy, however, would take no chances. He was almost sixty, with dimming eyes and shaky hands, but he could still take care of some matters on his own. Word had reached him that the unionists might attempt a robbery of that waterfront office, another blow against Irons & Pease & Company. Well, Davy would beat the bastards at their own game.

Alone in a trap pulled by a docile mare, Davy wondered if he shouldn't stop and get some men to accompany him to the docks. Or perhaps wait until morning when surely Michael would be able to go with him. But then he thought of the devastation the unionists had visited upon them tonight. If a thing is worth doing, then it is worth doing at once. Furthermore, Davy had no fear of rascals and hooligans. It was night and therefore he should be able to conclude his business quietly and unobserved. Tomorrow he would also pass on to Michael his suspicions about Nat Gane; there were things not quite right regarding some of Gane's financial transactions on their behalf.

Davy adjusted his glasses and tapped the mare's rear gently with the reins and smiled when the aging animal refused to quicken the pace.

Long after the doctor had gone, a hollow-eyed and drained Michael sat at the bedside of his drugged and sleeping wife, her hand in his. The child, a son, was stillborn, but Camilla was alive, thank God.

Camilla moaned and he leaned forward. But then she turned her head away from him and lay still, her breathing slow and even. Irons reached over to smooth her hair, then snapped his head towards the door. Someone had just knocked, in strict violation of his orders to be left undisturbed. Again the knock, soft but insistent, and Irons stood up, ready to tear a strip off the bloke too stupid to follow directions. Incensed, he strode across the room and opened the door to see a weeping Morag, her body shaking as though standing in snow. Only with a great effort could she finally bring herself to speak.

"Davy is dead."

Irons gripped the doorjamb with both hands until his knuckles were white. He shook his head, refusing to believe.

Trembling, Morag forced herself to continue. "On the waterfront, less than an hour ago. Unionists tried to break into the main warehouse, perhaps to get to the safe or to fire the building. No one knows for certain. Davy was there. They killed him and two nightwatchmen."

"Not Davy," whispered a disbelieving Irons. "Not Davy."

Morag threw herself into his arms. "Servants say he was here early on, then left, not wishing to take you from Camilla's side."

"Not Davy," Irons said again, pushing her away. "Davy is not dead." He shoved her aside and hurried along the corridor, rushing down the winding staircase as though possessed. "I am coming Davy!" he shouted, "I am coming!"

Outside in the night, he called to the stables. A saddled horse was brought to him at once and he rode off, lashing the animal furiously with his whip. From a second floor window Morag opened her mouth to cry out, then stopped. In his crazed grief her father, by calling to Davy Pease, had sought to keep the little Englishman alive a bit longer. God in heaven, she thought, I bless you for granting my father these few moments of merciful madness.

3

Melbourne
October 1890

IT was severe and imperial, a reflection of the man
himself.

The chair in which Edward a'Becket sat had once belonged
to Thomas Cromwell, Lord Chamberlain to Henry VIII.
Adjusting his spectacles on his veined nose, a'Becket
dipped his pen into a thick brass inkwell and continued
writing to Redmond Glass in a small, exact hand, forming
his letters with icy precision as he detailed the attack to be
published on Michael Irons. Halfway through, a'Becket
paused to sip port and read what he had composed so far.
Satisfied, he resumed writing.

As a journalist Glass would, of course, transpose
a'Becket's thoughts into his own lurid and damaging prose.
The pig-like Glass lacked class, manners and refinement,
but he had his uses, which was why a'Becket employed
him as spy and informant on matters in Sydney. The
sealed envelope from the journalist had arrived in Melbourne by messenger this morning at dawn. Glass's mis-
sive told of Nat Gane's failed attempt to murder Michael

Irons and his son; of Gane's embezzling from Irons and the partners in the new bank; of Gane's sudden flight from Sydney on a French clipper. The letter contained other news as well: social gossip on the recent Sydney reception for American author Mark Twain; the financial speculations indulged in by the New South Wales governor and premier and their staffs; dates on forthcoming appearances in Sydney and Melbourne by French actress Sarah Bernhardt.

There was news on federation, too, a cause opposed by a'Becket so intensely that the very sound of the word left a bitter taste in his mouth. The War Office in London was sending a high ranking officer, Major General Sir George Geoffrey Stock to examine the colonies' military preparedness. A wasted trip, as far as a'Becket was concerned, since the colonies needed neither army nor navy. They were under England's shield, an armed might that no nation in the world would dare challenge. Major-General Sir Stock would undoubtedly include Melbourne on his tour and a'Becket would see that he talked to the right people, people whose allegiance to Britain was firm and unswerving and who regarded the idea of breaking off from her as suicidal.

"Damn them all," he had said to Denis of those who supported Australian unity. "Melbourne is British. We think, talk, and act British. Can you imagine what would happen to this way of life should Australia be united under Sydney?"

Sydney, the a'Beckets knew, was tawdry and bawdy, a pestilential swamp. Melbourne, in contrast, was an oasis of public parks and gardens, elegant shops, broad boulevards shaded by leafy trees and adorned by flowers and lawns. Life in Melbourne was lived according to civilized rules—there was little of the exuberant vulgarity exhibited by Sydneysiders at the slightest provocation.

"Victoria," he said to Denis, "is ours, so long as we stay apart from the other states. By ours, I mean us and people like us. By the Lord God who made us, we must never relinquish our power to the trousered apes of Sydney!"

In Michael Irons, the bold and aggressive son of transported Irish convicts, Edward a'Becket saw all that he despised in Sydney, in all of Australia. He saw a man who did not know his place, and who presumed to determine the future of the a'Beckets and their class. For Lord a'Becket, to suffer at the hands of an obvious social inferior, was tantamount to public crucifixion. He would never forgive Irons for marrying Camilla or for leading the fight for federation, which would surely reduce the a'Beckets to paupers subject to the mercies of Irish swine.

There were those in Melbourne who favored federation and who had been in contact with Irons. a'Becket considered them traitors to their class. In particular he despised Julius Fielding, a Melburnian legislator who was particularly outspoken in favor of federation. a'Becket planned to bring the loquacious Mr. Fielding to heel one day by any means possible.

The letter to Glass was finished. After a careful rereading, a'Becket closed it with red wax, stamping the hot wax with his seal of three crowns. He smiled. Mr. Glass obviously had sources of information in Irons' household, probably servants or stablehands, who for a few shillings would betray their own mother. Leaving his desk, a'Becket walked to the fire in his study, leaned forward and let Glass's letter to him slip from his fingers. When flame had darkened its edges and curled the single sheet of paper, the banker walked to the bell pull, tugged it sharply and returnd to his desk.

"Enter," he said to the knock.

It was a servant with the messenger, a young man in a suit, tie and derby. He was fairly presentable, though unshaven and with muddy boots.

a'Becket held out the sealed letter. The wax on it was still warm. With the letter went a gold sovereign. The messenger pocketed the coin and grinned.

"Mind you," a'Becket warned him, "travel swiftly. As usual, it is to be handed directly to Mr. Glass, no one else."

"Understood sir."

a'Becket's eyes flicked to his servant. "Show him out. Then have someone remove the mud he's left behind. I shall breakfast eighteen minutes from now, precisely. Scotch broth to start, followed by ox heart, macaroni, rabbit, biscuits, plum pudding. Lady a'Becket is to be left undisturbed."

"Very good, sir."

Alone, a'Becket crossed the study to the fireplace, to stare at Camilla's photograph, one of two dozen framed and arranged along the mantlepiece. Drawing his brocaded robe around his slight frame, the banker stared at the photograph, again feeling the anguish that touched him each time he thought of her and Irons together. He did worry about Camilla from time to time and was thankful that she had not died a few weeks ago in childbirth. But a'Becket would never unbend, never change his mind, never receive her into his presence again. Denis was married, had two children and was flagrantly unfaithful to his wife, an English lass a'Becket had chosen for him. As for a'Becket's wife Elspeth, she moved about the mansion quietly pretending that no one knew she drank from bottles hidden in secret places and giving the servants orders which they ignored the second her back was turned.

Camilla had been a'Becket's hope. First the correct marriage, then the birth of a grandchild with an impeccable bloodline. That would have compensated for an increasingly addled wife and a profligate, though loyal, son. Irons had destroyed that dream. Well, a'Becket was about to get a bit of his own back. All Redmond Glass had to do was follow orders. A tear formed in the corner of a'Becket's eye and slid down along his long nose. Dearest, dearest Camilla, I do miss you. I shall never show it, nor shall I allow you to come to me, but I cannot erase you from my mind and heart.

With bowed head and closed eyes, he let his tears fall

near the dancing, orange-red flames. The heat on his face did not begin to equal the white-hot cry for vengeance in his heart, a loud and pained cry that would not cease until it had been given satisfaction.

BOOK II
Crisis and Unity
1890–1910

4

THE driver of Morag's carriage expertly reined the pair of horses to a stop in front of the Irons & Pease building, placed his whip at his feet and started to climb down to open the door for Irons' daughter. But she was already in the muddy street, one hand inching her long skirt up to the top of her boots, the other hand tightly gripping a copy of *Opus Dei*. At the building entrance, the door yanked open and her father, his face clouded and angry, glared down at her and she knew he had read the story. He pushed past her saying, "Stay here."

"Where are you going?"

"To the bank." He took over her carriage, dismissing the driver with a jerk of his head and reaching down for the whip.

"Father, I am coming with you."

Again, she dashed out into the mud and the driver held the door open for her, gently touching her elbow and helping her back into the carriage. Then she heard the whip whirl in the air before coming down with a crack on the horses' flanks and she was thrown backwards in her seat, the door still open and banging against the side of the carriage. Dear God, he *had* read Redmond Glass's wicked story, a story that was malicious and destructive, with just enough truth to be almost irrefutable.

Glass had written of Nat Gane's embezzlements, claiming that they had seriously weakened the new bank started by him, Irons and others. He hinted that Gane had been acting for Irons, stealing to provide funds to shore up other Irons & Pease investments. Glass demanded that depositors withdraw their money from the new bank and that all creditors and stockholders immediately cut themselves loose from Irons & Pease rather than sustain such losses as the bank was about to undergo. The story took up most of the front page and in typically sensational Sydney fashion, included a caricature of Irons as a one-eyed pirate forcing pleading investors to walk the plank above shark-filled waters.

The story, Morag knew, would start a run on the bank and trigger a panic that would harm all of her father's businesses, especially if creditors and stockholders heeded Glass's advice. Gane's thefts had been kept secret, save for accountants whom Irons had hired to check company books and bank records and salvage what they could from Gane's accounts and investments. However, without Davy's financial wizardry, it was an uphill task.

Morag wanted to help her father and could have, had he allowed her to. But she was young, twenty-four, and a woman, and while he praised and was pleased by her intelligence, he assigned the jobs that mattered to men. For months she had badgered and plagued her father until he finally capitulated, allowing her to join the company as its first and only female clerk. Naturally, she started at the bottom, subject to the snickers and taunts of the men; she was the lowliest of twenty-three pen pushers sitting on high stools, wearing garters on their sleeves and green eyeshades across their foreheads and dealing with invoices, due bills, accounts payable, company reports and correspondence.

It took Morag only weeks to prove herself better than any male clerk working for the company, including the chief clerk, a prissy little man with over twenty-five years experience and a way of clucking his tongue that grated on Morag's nerves. She was gifted with a quick, decisive mind and an amazingly retentive memory. Her boldness in reaching a conclusion was matched only by her father's and when the male clerks attempted to intimidate her with petty and cruel jokes, she acted as her father would. She retaliated. A clerk who habitually snuck handfuls of mud into her purse found a snake waiting for him in the bag the next time he did so. The snake was harmless, but the man's terror was real.

A bullying senior clerk, who habitually blew his cigar smoke in her face and behind her back delighted in pouring whisky on her best cloaks, found a serious shortage in his accounts. Unable to explain the discrepancy, he was fired on the spot and given no references. Days later, Morag, casually glancing over his accounts, pointed out the error in them to the chief clerk. With that, the harassment stopped. But not the drudgery and boredom of a task that Morag felt was far beneath her. Her brothers had been given more interesting tasks and neither was as smart as she. Heath, now recovered from the kidnap attempt of a few days ago, was in the Braidwood goldfields, while Dai had an office on the waterfront where he was learning to run the shipping end of Irons & Pease.

Australia was not a woman's country. But it was Morag's country and she was going to find a place in it no matter what. Marriage and babies were not for her yet, not until she found a man who could match her strength and brains. So far, only her father could. The rest of the Australian men she found crude, uneducated and insensitive, men who mistook their own selfishness for strength of character. Morag knew of one Australian woman who, early in the century, had gone on to become wealthy and influential. She was Mary Reiby, a widow with seven children, who had been transported from England at the age of thirteen for horse stealing and had gone to make a fortune in shipping. Well, Morag was going to do better. She was going to work with her father and make both him and herself richer than they had ever been. In Australia, commerce was a calling, an art, a sport, the ultimate challenge and Morag wanted nothing less than that.

At the bank on Market Street, Morag's worst fears were realized. A mob, howling, threatening, smashing window panes in the bank and in nearby stores, was demanding its money. The bank, of course, had barred its doors. The guards were inside and a handful of police outside had already proven ineffective. Reining the horses to a stop, Irons leaped from the carriage and yelled to Morag, "Stay here! It's too dangerous!"

But she followed him, both fearful and exhilarated. She was drawn by the excitement, the danger. She was out of the carriage, one hand keeping her hat in place on her head as she ran after her father.

The mob saw him and a roar went up, sending chills through Morag. Perhaps she had made a mistake following him into the midst of this rabble.

The voices around her were hostile, insistent, offensive.

"Bloody, bleedin' Irons himself. Where's our fuckin' money?"

"We ain't leaving mate 'til we collects whats ours."

"Give us the lolly, mate, else we burns your little buildin' down to the ground."

"We ain't worked hard to enrich the likes of you, you bloody Irish sod. We wants what we wants now."

A voice behind her said, "Lookee here, it's his little daughter. Come to get hers out before he steals that, too." And the horrible laughter—Morag would never forget it.

She felt hands on her, hands tearing at her purse.

"Let's see what she's got in there. Maybe we can collect ours now without goin' inside and troublin' them fine gentlemen."

And then she was on the ground, in the mud and screaming and clinging to her purse and her father was just above her, slamming the barrel of his pistol into the face of one of her tormentors, crushing his nose, then striking another man in the temple and firing two shots in the air, magically clearing a circle around them. Silence. Her father waited, his eyes sweeping the crowd.

When he spoke, he did not raise his voice. "These men laid hands on my daughter."

He said nothing more. The crowd remained quiet as he helped a frightened Morag to her feet, and placed his lips to her ear. "If you ever disobey me again I shall flog you myself. I ordered you to remain in the carriage. Now go—"

"Beggin' your pardon, mate," said a bearded, squat, hunchback man with a miner's ruined hands, "but with all respect to your daughter, we are here to collect our money. This here newspaper Mr. Redmond Glass says that you have been thieven' and that we should beware of leavin' our money with you." There were rumbles of agreement.

Irons tucked his pistol into his belt. "Mr. Glass is a liar."

"Can you pay us?"

"Yes."

"Will you pay us?"

"Yes."

"On with it, then." And from the crowd came a roar that reverberated along the street and out into the next thoroughfare.

"We be hearin' stories," said the hunchback, "that all banks are havin' difficulties, that the ordinary man might be wiser to bury his money in his back yard under a tree."

Irons bit the end off a cigar, took a wooden match from his vest pocket and with a thumbnail flicked it into flame. After inhaling deeply he said, "I once hid some cash money under a tree. Left it there throughout the winter. Came the spring and I searched for it and it was nowhere to be found. Turned out a bunch of bleedin' squirrels had eaten it."

Some of the crowd laughed. Others only watched silently. Morag knew they were remembering what had happened a month ago at Circular Quay, when her father, in retaliation for the murder of Davy Pease, had led ten wagonloads of wool from Sydney railway station through the city's streets, where crowds cheered him and the other drivers on. The drivers were among the city's richest and most important men; the unionists had to be stopped and it had to be shown that the city was against them. It was. From the mayor down to common shopgirls the streets of Sydney were filled with men and women cheering on the convoy of wagons as it rolled on to a conflict with the strikers at the docks. Heath and Dai had accompanied their father and been with him at the docks when the unionists had attacked the wagons.

Irons and the others, including police, troops and constables, all guarding the wagons, had struck back savagely. Remembering Davy, Irons had used his whip on strikers attempting to pull him from the wagon. He had fought like a demon and in the end the strikers had been defeated, their strike crushed. Some of the unionists had even been sentenced to prison. Dai had regretted taking part in the events of that day and a terrible argument had arisen between him and his father. Morag had worked hard to bring her brother and father together again, but even she felt that the repression of the strike had been brutal. The wool had been loaded without further incident and no more strikers had appeared on the docks.

But the unions were still eager for confrontation, still determined to raise wages and improve working conditions and what had happened at Circular Quay in September was only the first battle in what promised to be a long war.

Now at the bank a woman in the crowd said with mock politeness, "If you would be so kind, Mr. Irons, sir, as to open them front doors, I would like to be serviced by you."

An Australian male next to her said, "I bet you would. You ain't been properly serviced since the old man died." The crowd howled. The tension was broken, but not by much. Morag saw her father frown and knew he was wondering how to deal with the crisis, wondering what Davy Pease might have done. And then it came to her;

drawing her father near she whispered in his ear. He listened, frowned, then said in a loud voice, "The bank will open in precisely one hour. It will remain open until all claims and deposits have been paid." He paused before adding, "In gold."

The crowd hesitated before cheering and calling his name over and over. Men and women stepped forward to pat him on the back and shake his hand. Morag had never been so intoxicated in her life. In the crush of the crowd she and her father pushed their way into the bank, to be greeted by Simon Larkin, the nervous, perspiring bank president.

In a voice made high by tension Larkin said, "Mr. Irons, I am afraid we face peril, for we do not have much gold on hand. Not enough to deal with all depositors. This is an evil day for us. Mr. Gane—"

"Do not speak that name to me ever again, Mr. Larkin." Irons turned to Morag. "My daughter has suggested the idea of gold payment and she has foreseen our shortage. I am reminded that there are gold ingots on one of our ships, currently preparing to sail in a few hours. I shall see that they are converted into gold sovereigns. After that, let us take each moment as it comes. To work, gentlemen. As my daughter has noted, today we pay not in paper, not in promises, but in gold."

With the gold from the ship and a wool crop and choice land placed as collateral for short term loans from two Sydney banks, Irons not only covered Gane's thefts but paid all depositors and creditors who wanted to be paid. Were it not for Morag's suggestion to shift the gold from the ship, the bank would have failed and Irons' credit taken a substantial beating. Both Morag and Dai worked all day with their father and the bank officers. It was Morag who learned that word of the gold payment had circulated throughout the city and some depositors, who had intended to withdraw, now decided to leave their money where it was.

Dai, who agreed with his father on the need for federation,

said, "One Australia would put an end to the machinations
we have endured today." He was stocky, with dark curly
hair, clean shaven and handsome like his father, with
Irons' square chin and a much shorter temper. Commerce
had little appeal for him; he had entered business only to
please his father. Morag would have given anything to
trade places with Dai, to learn the running of a major
shipping line, to have the power that came with manipulating men and money.

"We are in agreement on that," said Irons. "I suspect
there is more to Glass's vile deed than we can see at
present. I say he is some man's churl in this matter. I
smell it, I feel it. He has acted too deliberately, too exactly
for one so gross as he. Glass prefers the scatter shot. What
he has aimed at me is quite thought out and concentrated.
Had the bank failed, our house would have collapsed.
Money is easily panicked, easily frightened."

Dai said, "Did you know that the unionists also prefer
one Australia?"

He saw his father's face harden and he regretted having
spoken those words. The unionists had killed Davy Pease.
Irons would never feel anything but enmity towards them
until he died.

Morag attempted to stave off the argument she knew
would come if either man allowed his temper to get the
better of him. "Father, Dai means that federation is an
idea many men support. It will help bankers and—"

"Murdering swine."

The spell was broken. The triumphant mood which they
all shared suddenly disappeared. Making an obvious effort
to control himself Dai said, "If you will excuse me, sir, I
must return to the dock. Two ships from Europe will dock
in Sydney by nightfall. Morag."

When he had gone, leaving them alone in the bank
president's office, Irons dropped his head to his chest and
asked her, "Am I too hard on the lad?"

She shook her head. "No, father. There are changes to
be lived through in Australia these days and I fear that the

changes will bring us all as much trouble as happiness. He loves you, you love each other. Let that be the one thing you both remember."

He touched her face with a large, rough hand. "I remember me da' sayin' that years ago about me mum."

She took his hand in hers. There was a glow about her, and she said almost exultantly, "Father, today has been the most wonderful of my life."

He recoiled in mock horror. "Her father tottering on the brink of ruin and she thinks it's bloody wonderful. Go on with you, now."

She clung to him. "You know what I mean. I was alive, I was at your side and we faced down the world together. Isn't that what you and Davy used to say?"

He sighed, remembering Davy. "Yes, girl. 'Tis a wonderful thing to have someone like that at your back, watchin' out for you against the knives of this world. Never again will I have such a friend."

She looked up at him. He was tired and showed it. His face was lined and his breathing slow and deep. She wanted to protect him, to stand at his back as Davy Pease once had.

"Father look at me."

He did.

"Only you can give me the chance to be more than any woman in Australia has ever become. I beg you, do this for me. Let me learn from you. I'm as clever as any man and in your heart you know it. Let me work for you. Not as a clerk, but—"

He touched her lips with the tips of his fingers. "Morag, luv, I have two sons. How would it look if I favored you over them? It is in the natural order of things that a man sit at the head of the table."

"Mary Reiby," she said, her gaze holding his.

"True, lass. She did quite well for herself in this wide, brown land of ours. And you are bright as a penny and I see no man taking you without your permission, that's for sure. But—"

She was clever. And proved it. "Father, let me learn. I ask nothing more. Put me where I can learn, where I need not spend my day scrubbing black ink from my fingers. It will appear to be a job that you give me, nothing more."

He, too, was clever. "With you, lass there is no such thing as 'nothin' more'. So you're saying you wish to learn and need not offend my two boyos by doing so. Is that it?"

She smiled, not at all embarrassed at having been found out.

The day following the bank panic, Morag became the third of Irons' personal secretaries, the only one of the trio with her own office and keys to match her father's, though the matter of keys was not announced. Neither of her brothers gave the appointment a second thought.

5

Queensland.

IN a cold dawn Fallon Taylor, owner of a 100,000 acre sugar plantation, sat on horseback, a rifle across his saddle pommel. He watched as *kanakas*, Polynesian workers from the South Sea islands, were herded at gunpoint onto wagons that were to take them to the cane fields. Once or twice, he looked over his shoulder as though expecting someone to come along the crude road leading to his property. The natives in front of Taylor were dark-skinned, ill-clad, shivering; the owner had abused and overworked them since their arrival in Australia.

Few of the Polynesians had come to the continent willingly. Some had been lured aboard slave ships by trinkets or false contracts promising good paying jobs in Queensland, Australia's second largest state. Most, however, had been kidnapped by *blackbirders*, sea-going slave traders who made good money dealing in human misery; Queensland desperately needed labor to work its sugar cane plantations.

Whites, claimed the planters, were unfit for this sort of labor; planters, claimed the unions, prefered slave labor because whites would not work for low wages and under

abominable conditions. As proof, the unions noted that the
death rate among *kanakas* was five times as high as
that of the rest of the Australian population. Supporting
the unions were those Australians who saw the importation
of *kanakas* as leading to the kind of violent and bloody
conflict that had arisen over slaves in America. The reaction of Queensland plantation owners was to talk secession,
the formation of a nation independent from Britain and all
Australian colonies.

As for Fallon Taylor, no union was going to tell him
who to hire. They had tried, but he and his men had driven
them off his plantation with gun butts and whips. He paid
the *kanakas* next to nothing, worked them seven days a
week and when they died simply contracted with a
blackbirder for more. And that was all there was to it.
Some called blackbirding barbaric, but Taylor didn't
give a fiddler's fuck for anyone's opinion save his own.
Without *kanakas* he was ruined. It was as simple as
that.

The unions had threatened violence. Well, let them come.
Taylor had a dozen armed men riding with him to the cane
fields this morning and if the unionists wanted a breakfast
of bullets, they could have it.

When the wagons were loaded Taylor gave the signal to
move out. Whips snapped and horses strained against traces
and the wagons lurched forward. The road ahead was
clear. Taylor snorted. The unions could go to hell.

A half mile from the main house was a small bridge and
several kilometers beyond that lay the start of the cane
fields. By the time the convoy reached the bridge the sun
was higher and the sullen *kanakas* were gazing into it and
drawing from its warmth. Taylor relaxed, joking with one
of his riders and passing him a chunk of chewing tobacco.
It was going to be a peaceful day, by Jesus. The darkies
would cut cane or feel the lash.

Reining his horse close to Taylor's, the rider held out
his hand with the tobacco, then snapped backwards in the

saddle, a bullet hole in his forehead. Armed unionists, firing, shouting, cursing, raced from under the bridge. They leaped from behind bushes and low ridges and out of nearby gulleys, shooting at Taylor, his riders, the *kanakas*. A wagon overturned, crushing natives and spilling others into the dirt. Men screamed, horses panicked. A riderless horse clattered across the wooden bridge, then collapsed to its knees, blood pouring from its long neck and front legs.

Taylor's seventeen-year old son fired wildly, his horse rearing and spinning and eventually throwing him off. Down in the dirt road, the boy struggled to get to his feet but someone grabbed his long hair and jerked him backwards, again throwing him on his back. He looked up to see a bearded unionist aiming a revolver at his head. Ignoring the boy's pleas for mercy, the unionist emptied the revolver into him. Then the murderer himself fell across the boy, the back of his skull shattered by rifle fire.

When the shooting ended, ten *kanakas* were dead, along with five of Taylor's men and six unionists. Within hours some of the wounded on both sides would also be dead. When he had loaded the bodies of his son and dead on a wagon for burial back at the main house a bitter Taylor looked at the wounded unionists left behind by their comrades. "Kill them," he said and walked away.

Western Australia.

A monsoonal rain teemed down, pelting the rooftop and veranda of the ranch house where a lone woman peered out into the night. She quickly looked first over her shoulder at the bed where her husband slept, then out of the window at the wooden pen near the small shack where the hired help slept. Today her husband and the two hands had driven hundreds of rabbits into the pen and clubbed them to death, leaving their blood-stained, furred bodies there until tomorrow when the *rabbios*, men who made their living skinning and selling rabbits, would come.

The rabbits were a curse. There were millions of them across Australia, eating grass badly needed for sheep and cattle. Tonight's rain, the first in five months, had come too late to help her husband. Drought and decimated grazing lands had played havoc with their sheep herds. Her husband had been forced to let go a dozen workers, keeping only a father and son. Spending all their savings, her husband had purchased barbed wire, which replaced riders and shepherds, and new machinery that did more shearing than several men.

The union hadn't liked the idea of wire and metal replacing men, but her husband was adamant, his mind made up. Out of work, the union's shearers would suffer badly, and the woman knew it. Her husband was a good man, but what could he do? Her husband was desperate, as desperate as the union.

At the window, she froze. It wasn't her imagination. There was definitely someone near the dead rabbits. She couldn't see faces, but she knew who they were. Starving unionists, ready to risk being shot to death over the rain-soaked dead rabbits, in a desperate effort to feed their families. The anxious woman looked at her husband. Dear God, do not let him awaken just now. He was a hard man in matters of theft, one who believed that you did not steal no matter how badly you needed something. The dead rabbits, she knew, could furnish money to help meet payments on the barbed wire and shearing machinery.

But she thought of starving women and children, of men whom she knew would not find work in this part of Western Australia, not in these hellish days of destructive rabbits and no rain. And she could not bring herself to sound the alarm. God, she told herself, has sent the rain to protect them this night. He has decreed that the rabbits are theirs. I bow to your will, oh Lord.

And when the unionists had slipped into the darkness carrying their only food, the woman, her eyes shimmering behind tears, bowed her head in reverence and devotion. A hand touched her arm and she almost cried out.

"They've gone," whispered her husband. "They'll eat this night. Come back to bed, my love."

With a fingertip he took a tear from her eye and brought it to his lips and she collapsed into his arms with a love that made her tremble.

Tasmania

On this heart-shaped island of rolling grasslands, forested mountains and alpine lakes that was Australia's second oldest colony, a bank president in the capital city of Hobart sat behind his desk and watched his bank manager place two cablegrams in front of him. Minutes after the manager had left the president alone in his office, the cables remained untouched, unread. The president's hands, palms down on the desk, were damp with nervous sweat and there was a tingling sensation in the center of his chest, a vague feeling of foreboding that came to him each time he faced a crisis.

Until recently the bank had been prosperous. In its two years of existence money had poured in from mining and from exporting fruit. Under the ambitious president a policy of expansion and investment had been instituted, with branches opened in Launceston and in Queenstown, site of gold and copper mining. A surplus quickly developed which the Hobart bank almost found difficult to dispose of. More loans were made, to businessmen, Tasmanian banks, and even to a bank in Melbourne. This last was especially gratifying to the Hobart banker, who made certain that all local newspapers carried the story.

Trouble began with a drought that destroyed much of the island's fruit crop, forcing a good number of growers to default on loans and others to be granted indefinite extensions. Then the mines, in which the bank had an interest, began to yield less and less high grade ore. A desperate gamble—the purchase of expensive drilling machinery—failed to pay off and the mines were finally sealed shut, with the miners drifting away. Finally, the Launceston and Queenstown branches began to run at a loss and were eventually closed down.

With is back against the wall, the banker made two appeals. The loan to the Melbourne bank was overdue. As a courtesy, he had allowed the Victorian financiers extra time to repay him, but now he could wait no longer. He must have the money immediately. His other appeal had been to a contact at the Bank of England on London's Threadneedle Street, a man who in the past had been impressed by the banker, by Australia's future, and had promised help if it were ever needed.

The Hobart banker's future lay in the two cables in front of him. With trembling hands he picked up the nearest one, sliced open the envelope with a letter opener made of whalebone and read. It was from Melbourne. The bank he had loaned money to had failed, permanently closing its doors yesterday morning. It was unlikely that any of its depositors would ever be paid, let alone bank creditors. The bank deeply regretted any inconvenience to its Hobart counterpart.

He closed his eyes. The tingling feeling in his chest had become more painful, as though a tiny animal were attempting to gnaw its way through his flesh. With what remained of his courage he quickly reached out and snatched the second cablegram from a spotlessly clean blotter and with fumbling fingers ripped it open. And read. The man on whom he had depended at the Bank of England was no longer employed there, having retired some months ago to the south of France.

After reading both cablegrams once more, the Hobart banker sighed and leaned back in his chair.

Hours later he was found in that same position, dead from a heart attack. Both cablegrams were clutched in a fist now stiff with rigor mortis.

*   *   *

Across Australia, the shadows grew longer, casting a darkness that for the next decade would stain the land and chill the lives of its people. From these perilous times would come a fixed truth: Australian survival depended on Australian unity. Continued enmity and opposition among the six colonies could only lead ultimately and inexorably to the destruction of all.

6 _____

IN Melbourne's Chinese quarter, located on Little Bourke Street, Denis a'Becket motioned a small Cantonese woman aside and placed his eye to the peephole that allowed him to see into the next room. Tonight he had been hurriedly summoned from the opera to this brothel run by the old woman, who had teeth blackened by opium and carried a steel edged fan which she used on the breasts and faces of those girls who displeased her. The tableau which Denis had expressed an interest in viewing was about to unfold. He had paid the old woman plenty to be allowed to watch Julius Fielding at his vices, something that Lord a'Becket felt would be of future use.

Tonight the fat, white-haired Fielding lay on a wide bed, with a slim Chinese boy lying on either side of him. All three were naked, smoking opium and drinking. Denis smiled at the old woman, who returned his smile and bowed. The old hag will certainly have her hand out when I leave, he thought, but it will be worth it. He watched Fielding shudder with pleasure as one of the Chinese boys nuzzled his ear. Sickening, thought Denis, but nonetheless convenient that one of Melbourne's leading politicians and proponents of federation would be so accommodating as to engage in a practice that was illegal. Buggery, dear Julius, carries a prison sentence with it.

As if on cue, Fielding mounted one of the boys from the rear, as the other began licking his anus. At that moment Denis hated the politician, not for what he was doing, but because Denis himself was becoming sexually aroused. He turned from the peephole, his face flushed, his back to the old woman. When he had caught his breath he looked at her again and motioned her away from the wall. Silently, the two left and went across the hall to another room, closing the door behind them.

Denis handed her more gold sovereigns. "I wish to be informed each time he comes here. Either I or someone else will come to watch."

She placed her hands inside the wide sleeves of her robe and bowed. And as if understanding him too well, she said, "Mister care to stay awhile in our nice little home?"

Her voice was hideously dry, reminding Denis of a lizard slithering across a rock and he wished that his father had not insisted that he come here. They had hired an investigator, a former military man who knew the seamy side of Melbourne better than Denis ever would, and it was he who had learned of Julius Fielding's perverse inclinations. Lord a'Becket, however, had preferred that Denis look in on Fielding himself. Proof positive, his father called it.

Denis held the old woman's gaze, making no effort to hide his contempt. "I have no wish to stay awhile in your nice little home, as you put it. At the moment, madame, I prefer fresh air, followed by the remainder of 'Tosca' and a light supper."

He pushed past her, aware that she knew exactly what he wanted, and he could have killed her for it.

7

IN Australia, Christmas arrived when the weather was at its hottest. Here at the bottom of the world the seasons were reversed: summer ran from December to February, March to May was fall, June to August winter and September to November spring.

A week before the Christmas of 1890, in extremely warm weather, the Governor of New South Wales hosted a party at Government House for prominent Sydney politicians and businessmen, and leaders from other colonies and their wives. It was the Governor's wish that his guests hear a brief version of the report on Australia's defense which Major General Sir George Geoffrey Stock planned to deliver to the War Office in London. Michael Irons, who was to attend the party, thought he knew what Stock would say and over dinner with his three children gave his version.

"He'll tell us that we're six men standing on a scaffold with a bloody noose around our necks. Ready to hang separately, because in the American phrase, we won't hang together."

"Stock doesn't give a tinker's damn about Australia," said Heath. "London sent him out here to keep us quiet

Give Stock his gin and brandy, I hear, and he is a most happy man.''

Morag put down her knife and fork. ''Father, if as you say, Stock feels we are unable to defend ourselves, will that not make our leaders work harder for federation?''

''It is to be hoped. But you must remember that federation has been talked about for years, thirty years that I can recall, and it has gotten no further than the tips of our tongues. Colonies, politicians, businessmen, we hold onto what we have until our fingers bleed and our knuckles crack. We do not want to forego possessions or position. We talk and we stand dead in place without so much as a twitch. And yet if we are to be more than a geographical expression, someone in this land must open his hand and reach out for the rest of us. And we who see that hand must respond in kind.''

At the Christmas party, away from the women and in a meeting held in the billiard room, Stock said all of this and more. He was a small, proud man in his late sixties, balding with an enormous, drooping, walrus-like mustache, which he continually caressed with the back of his forefinger while speaking. He wore his dark blue dress uniform, with four rows of medals and a red sash. At his side was a sword said to have been taken from a Russian archduke after a lethal close encounter in the Crimean War which left the Duke and three of his body-guards dead and Stock with twelve saber wounds.

Addressing the packed room in a strong voice, the little military man stood with his back to the fireplace, a glass of brandy in one hand, the other on the hilt of his sword.

''Gentlemen, I have spent nearly two months in this area and my conclusions are as follows. I should say this represents a précis, a summation of my formal report to be presented to the War Office next year. In brief, you could be invaded tomorrow by any power that chooses to do so and by sundown of that exact same day, you would go down to ignominious defeat.''

He let the buzz of reaction run on just long enough

before resuming. "You have no forces to put into the field. As I see it, your various and sundry militias are not worthy of the name. Some colonies have a handful of men passing as a military force, while others lack even that. I believe that an army of beardless cadets from any first class military school in the world could march from one end of this continent to the other, without encountering any opposition worthy of the name."

This time there was more obvious hostility directed at Stock, who didn't seem to mind. On the contrary, it was as if he expected it and welcomed the confrontation. A little man who always had to act tall, thought an admiring Irons. He had met Stock at a reception some weeks ago and seen him in Sydney and Melbourne, but the two did no more than nod and touch their hats. In any case, little Mr. Stock was no man's toady and Irons wondered if Lord a'Becket had been displeased to learn that bit of news. a'Becket's wooing of Stock was no secret; it remained to be seen if the Melbourne banker's efforts would yield results. Stock, thought Irons, had more steel than cream in his backbone.

In a tone used to command junior officers and lower ranks Stock said, "Gentlemen, I am not here to placate you or to hum lullabies that will soothe your fevered brows. You face peril, more so than you know."

Irons leaned forward. Instinct said that Stock, whether oiled by liquor or anxious to meet a challenge from a roomful of people who basically disliked him, was about to reveal more than expected, perhaps more than he should.

The room began to buzz again. Now Sir Henry Parkes rose to his feet, both hands raised in a calming gesture. Several times the premier of New South Wales, but now out of office, he still was not without power. He was the colony's best known politician, if not the best known poitician in all Australia. A hard worker, effective speaker and capable of grand idealistic passions, he was not without his faults. He was vain and a womaniser, never out of debt and forever boring the public with his bad poetry. But

Irons knew that he had fervently supported Australian federation for more than forty years, often travelling to England to argue its cause there. At seventy-four, Parkes had been slowed by age and overwork. Tonight, however, he majestically turned his huge head, with its glistening mass of silver hair and beard, from one end of the room to the other and when it was quiet once more he said in a deep, sad voice, "Let Major General Stock speak. Why should we waste his time with womanish dithering and chatter? Sir Stock, if you please."

The room quieted, and Sir Stock nodded. "I was speaking of peril. I have heard rumors that France intends to resume transporting convicts to New Caledonia."

The room erupted in earnest now and it took Parkes, Irons and a couple of other men to restore order. New Caledonia, the island to the east of Queensland, had been annexed by France almost forty years ago and used as a penal colony. Some of its convicts had escaped and made their way to Australia, where they had caused trouble. Complaints by Australians and England had eventually stopped the practice of shipping convicts to the island. But now. . . .

"And this," said Stock. "There are Germans who wish to swallow the whole of New Guinea. Such a plan is being talked of even at this moment."

Irons hung his head. Christ on a cross. New Guinea, an island only one thousand miles off Australia's northern coast, was divided between the Dutch, Germans and the English. England could have taken over most of the island, but had hesitated, allowing Germany to move in. Only the most intense pressure by Australians, who lacked the military force themselves, convinced Britain to act. But if the Germans should decide to swallow the entire island, a powerful and aggressive enemy would be on Australia's doorstep.

"How true is that rumor?" asked Irons.

Stock finished his brandy before answering. "As true as any. But what is false this year could be true the next and vice versa. The point is you must now depend on the mercy of those around you, for you are in no position to defend yourselves. England shall, of course, do whatever is necessary, should there be any confrontation.''

''England might well decide that some confrontations are more important than others,'' said Irons. ''I see no guarantee that we will always remain uppermost on the Crown's list of those who must be protected at all costs.''

He looked around the room. He was not alone in holding that thought. The place was packed with powerful and important men who were all uncomfortable with the thought that Australia was ripe for the taking by an aggressive power.

If there were any in the room against federation, they remained silent.

The meeting did not last long. Stock answered questions for almost an hour before begging off. It was time for dinner and he had begun to repeat himself. The point had been made and only a fool would ignore it.

As Parkes himself said, before the group left the room to join the ladies at table, ''We know the disease, meaning we are half cured. Separatism is our illness. Me must not allow it to become our death.''

In true Victorian fashion, the three long Christmas dinner tables in the white-pillared ballroom were each buried under a sea of food. All seven courses were on the table at once. More than one hundred people, each attended by two or three servants, feasted on tureens of kangaroo, turtle and oxtail soup; on mutton, beef, shark meat, calves and boar's head with aspic jelly; on lobsters, duck, cold fowl, tongue, black swan à la Flamande, meat pies; on toast, muffins, rolls; on plum puddings, hokey-pokey—ice cream, puffs, jellies and tarts.

All of it was washed down with beer, local wines, rum, brandy, gin and steaming punch. Australians, like all Victorians, made time to enjoy their food and drink; mammoth appetites were accepted and encouraged and the idea of overindulgence received condemnation only from the poor, whose opinions were received with scant enthusiasm and less interest.

Camilla had been too ill to accompany Irons and Morag. And the daughter was glad that her young step-mother could not see how at this moment her father was eyeing Genista Corder, the beautiful wife of Sir Darcy Corder, the man who had come from London to replace Nat Gane. Genista was tall, in her late twenties, with blue eyes and blonde hair the color of spun gold. Tonight she wore a gown of blue and white silk that left her shoulders bare and drew every man's eyes to her shapely bosom. She was gay, witty, and a brilliant conversationalist; she had quickly established herself as a reigning hostess in Sydney. She was, naturally, an asset to her husband, a slim, politely arrogant man with hair and mustache as blonde as his wife's and a way of looking at the world as though it was something to be scraped from the bottom of his shoe. Morag knew that her father was interested in Genista. And without knowing why she strongly sensed that this elegant Englishwoman was more dangerous to him than any other woman he had ever set his eye on.

Genista Corder sat across the table from Irons and Morag and almost managed to hide her interest in the Irishman. Almost. Morag, however, caught the quick flick of an eye, a surreptitious gaze held too long, a too deliberate effort at not staring. You bitch, she thought. I could pull the hair from your head until it resembles a peeled egg. Not this one, she whispered silently, fervently to her father. There was no point hiding from the fact that Camilla was not the right woman for Irons. Their relationship was unfailingly kind and correct—and utterly bloodless as well. Lou Heller is your kind, our kind. The two of you are together once more and I am glad. Do not risk yourself on this English-woman. She is not for you— *I know it*.

Casually, too casually Genista Corder placed a finger under her chin and addressed Irons in a half mocking tone. "Tell me, Mr. Irons, is there substance to the romor that you are to receive a knighthood? If true, it would only add luster to your already glowing stature.''

Irons leaned back to let a servant remove his plate, then said, ''There has been talk of it. Lord Norris Held—''

Genista raised her eyebrows. ''Lord Held? I was not aware that Sir Held had upped his station.''

''I received a letter from him this morning, bearing Christmas greetings. The honor was bestowed upon him by Her Majesty some weeks ago.''

Morag watched Genista's eyes narrow with increasing interest as she said, ''Lord Held is rather prominent in the City. Before we left London some two months ago he arranged for a group of banks to float a one hundred million pound loan for the Italian government. Darcy and I, among others, felt that the loan would not go through, but go through it did. Lord Held has a beautiful London home, with a marvelous art collection or so I am told.''

Morag spooned a bit of jellied eel into her mouth and reached for a schooner of beer. You grasping little nit, she thought, her eyes on Genista Corder. Obviously a social cut below Lord Held, obviously never at his home and obviously, desperately wanting to be invited; the woman enjoyed warming her hands at the fires of power. Not only had Irons been to Held's London home more than once, since their meeting two years ago but to his club and his country estate in Chelsea, that London suburb which was home to artists and writers.

Dancy Corder turned from the woman on his right to his wife, then to Irons. There was a coolness between the two men, which had nothing to do with Corder's wife. When the Englishman had arrived in Sydney to assume Nat Gane's position he had all but called Irons a thief, strongly hinting that the Irishman and Gane had been in league together. He had asked to look at the books of Irons & Pease, a request which the angry Irons had denied. It had taken intervention by third parties to prevent a serious eruption and to remind Corder that in Australia calling a man like Irons a liar was a dangerous thing to do. When

Corder had learned that Irons, too, had lost money to Gane's financial chicanery, he eventually apologized. But he and Irons had not warmed to each other and it was unlikely that they ever would. Corder was a spoiled snot, conscious of being upper class English and openly unhappy at being in Australia. His father had pulled strings to get him his present position. If Darcy performed well here, then in a few years he could return to London where his future in finance, banking and perhaps politics would be unlimited.

Darcy had agreed to Australia because he wanted power and influence as quickly as possible. At thrity-five, he was cool, as elegant as his wife in his dress and appearance, Cambridge educated and heir to the golden future England held out to those of correct birth and position. Tonight the thin faced Corder wore a pink shirt and blue silk vest, along with a long, white cravat. The young men and women present found him exquisitely fashionable. Morag was unmoved.

Sir Darcy already had his knighthood, courtesy of his father's influential friends. The thought of Irons being similarly honored disgusted him, but now was not the time to dwell on that. He pointed towards the billard room with his fork and addressed Irons.

"Is the world a better place for the lot of you having closeted yourselves in that room for the better part of two hours? A united Australia." He shrugged. "Sorry, but it is not an idea that stirs my blood. No offense, sir, you understand, but aren't you really best served by maintaining strong ties to England? Wherever I go, I find no discontent among the locals, no burning desire to be set free, no fanatical praying for a Moses to lead Australians out of Egypt and to a promised land. If I might make so bold, sir, what did you encounter in that room?"

Irons sipped punch from a silver mug, then smiled at Morag. "I found, sir, that I was overcome with a desire for—" he paused and looked at Corder, "fresh air."

Morag covered her mouth, hiding a triumphant smile.

Genista's smile was there for anyone to see. And it was aimed at Irons.

Sir Corder pursed his lips, his eyes on the fork, which he now used to gouge a tear in the tablecloth. "Fresh air. Indeed. In future, perhaps, that distress can be alleviated by bathing."

He dropped the fork. "Do tell the others." His smile was the edge of a knife. Standing, he took his wife's hand. Outside on the lawn the orchestra had begun to play. "My dear, fresh air seems to be the order of the day. Shall we find some?"

When they had gone Morag whispered behind the back of her hand, "That man is a snake. He is weak and the weak can be cruel. And she is to be avoided at all costs, father, at all costs."

Irons looked at her for long seconds. So Morag knew. But then she knew so much. Too much, at times. Irons smiled. "When we leave tonight, Johnny-Johnny will see you home. I must play Father Christmas to—"

"To Lou. Do give her my love. I have a present for her in the carriage. Please take it with you."

He kissed her cheek, which did nothing to ease her feeling that Genista Corder was so menacing to her father that perhaps all would be better off if she were dead.

8

Lou Heller slept soundly, the flickering flame of a bedside candle sending small shadows dancing across her bare back. She was naked, except for Irons' Christmas gift to her, an emerald and diamond bracelet on her left wrist. At the hotel window Irons tightened a robe around him and looked down at the wooden street three stories below. A steam tram—five horsedrawn double decker cars—slid past in the night, warning lanterns swaying on all sides. A prostitute loitered near a gas light, a rolled parasol resting on one shoulder and her face hidden by a large brim hat.

Somewhere in the recesses of Irons' mind he remembered snow at Christmas, but that had been in Dublin, when he was a lad and his gifts had been toys hand carved by his father, along with fruits and hand-me-down trinkets from his mother. In all his years in Australia, he had never seen snow on Christmas. The continent did have snow, in the north and on its mountain ranges, but Irons had not seen it on Christmas in more years than he cared to remember. As usual, he too often thought of those things he did not have, which is why his mind again turned to Genista Corder.

She was as bright an ornament as ever hung on anyone's Christmas tree, the focus of all eyes in Sydney, a magnet for male adulation and female envy. Sydney's own goddess. No woman in recent years had made quite the same impression—not even Lou Heller.

Genista was a thoroughbred, possessed of a silk stocking exterior and breathtaking beauty that was nothing less than divine.

She was woman, too, Irons was sure of that. Fire and ice, offering a polished and mysterious sensuality that had taunted and haunted Irons since their first meeting. She was not common; she did not smell of penny perfume and she spoke the Queen's English with crystalline precision, a sound as delicate as tiny bells and as alluring as wind chimes. Yes, Irons wanted to bed her and unless he was mistaken, the same idea had occurred to her, too.

Genista Corder was as far above most men as heaven was above earth and for that reason alone, Irons wanted her. He was Australian and nothing was to be denied him. Hadn't his convict ancestors created a wealthy society out of a penal colony, a battle which by all odds should have been lost a hundred years ago? To an Australian, anything was possible and a man could aspire as high as his hopes could reach. Hadn't Irons done this all his life?

Another world to conquer, Davy Pease would have said of her. You could be right, old friend, but I know of no other way to live. It's fate that has brought her into my life at this time. A fate which has decreed me the best of everything—money, power, a title and Genista Corder. The best that Sydney has to offer. The best the world has to offer. Have I not earned it?

Genista Corder would think so. He knew it.

Irons looked at Lou. Dearest Lou. As warm as Australian sun and honest and giving and God knows, a maelstrom in bed. With the death of Davy she had come back into Irons' life, offering comfort and once more, her love. The hurt over his marriage to Camilla had eased; Lou would take him on his own terms, something she had never done with any man. This time he was careful to point out that no promises would be made and none would be expected from her. Still, she, who could only love with her whole heart, would not withhold any part of herself from him.

"No one can love and be wise," she said.

"That is for all of us, thick headed Irishmen included."

"Perhaps you should not have given me those poems of Elizabeth Barrett Browning's. She now preys on my mind."

"Why so?"

"She writes: *Whoso loves/Believes the impossible.*"

He took her face between his hands. "And what do you believe is possible?"

"That one day you will love me as I love you."

And tonight, as he turned from the hotel window to stare at her sleeping form, he again wondered why he could never be content. To have Lou would, for so many men, be all that they would ever need. To be content with her would mean complete happiness and yet he could not find it in himself to be so satisfied. It was no secret in Sydney that Blue Dan Costello, the Irish underworld leader, was not pleased at seeing Lou return to Michael Irons. Costello could be a dangerous man; like Irons, for whom he had a grudging respect, he did not take defeat well. Men who had not known this about him had been found in Sydney's alleys and harbor with their throats cut.

At the bed Irons bent over, kissed Lou's bare shoulder and stroked her hair. Morag is right: you are my kind. But he saw Genista's face before him, felt her, for an instant, writhing under him in bed, calling his name over and over and lifting him to heights of pleasure that few men even reached.

Lou. Camilla. Genista. Irons closed his eyes, seeing himself cursed by the fever of eternal dissatisfaction.

Downstairs in the street, the man in the dark blue carriage looked up at Lou Heller's window in the hotel and drew deeply on his cigar. In the backseat the cigar's light was a tiny, red coal in the darkness. Blue Dan Costello, called Blue with Australian irreverence because of his red hair, had found that the coals of jealousy still burned strongly within him. He wanted Lou Heller. He, who could have any one of a hundred women, wanted this laughing, strong, sensual American.

He carried her within like a sickness for which there was no cure. And so tonight, he had decided to take her away from Michael Irons, the one man in Sydney whom Blue Dan both respected and feared. The underworld leader tapped the carriage ceiling with his cane and in response the driver flicked his whip at the team and the carriage pulled away.

9

ON a gray fall day near the end of April 1891, Lord Edward a'Becket sat in his carriage and watched workmen dig up a cemetery near the edge of town. Coffins were removed from graves and loaded on nearby wagons, to be hauled away by teams of oxen and bullocks. While some workmen hastily filled the empty grave sites, other toppled tombstones or used sledge hammers to batter mausoleums into piles of rubble. Standing outside an iron fence ringing the cemetery were relatives and friends of the dead; some wept, while others shouted angrily at the desecration they were being forced to witness. Just in front of them, on the other side of the fence, were armed troops from the Victoria militia, along with police and constables.

Taking a snuff box from his vest pocket, a'Becket sprinkled a bit of the brown powder on the back of his hand and brought it to his nose, inhaling quickly in two loud snorts. Then he sneezed into a handkerchief. His head was clear now.

Using his silver-headed cane he pointed to his right. "The city is expanding and there is a strong need for a railway to connect the suburbs to Melbourne. When that cemetery is cleared, it will become the most valuable piece of land in or around Melbourne and the key to the railroad which the city plans to build."

"You are certain of your facts?"

"Indeed, sir. The railroad will definitely run through here, then continue along for at least ten miles."

"And you now own this cemetery land."

"I arranged for the city to appropriate the property, then made certain that I was the sole bidder on it. As a major land developer—"

"Speculator is a better word, wouldn't you say?" The man was politely arrogant.

a'Becket, who needed him, refused to be goaded. "I prefer 'developer'. Sounds less ambivalent and irresolute."

"But there is much speculation involving Melbourne land, is there not? It appears to be the primary commercial interest of the gentry and monied classes."

"One could say so, yes. Land has made 'Marvelous Melbourne' what she is today."

Removing a lacy handkerchief from the sleeve of his black frock coat, the other man inhaled its fragrance. There was so much money to be made in Australia, more than he had ever imagined and everyone was doing it. This primitive, uncultured land was a gold mine for a clever fellow. Why should he not profit by his position? He could risk a few ventures, grow rich in the twinkling of an eye, then take that money and flee this accursed continent for somewhere more civilized. Money was the key. With it he could leave Australia sooner rather than later and he would not need anyone's permission to do so. a'Becket, a social climber with a Jew's nose for a fast coin, was offering him that opportunity and he would be a fool not to take it.

The man looked at a weeping woman in black. There was no pity in his gaze as he watched her hysterically cry out to the workmen not to disturb her husband's final resting place. A clergyman put his arms around her in a vain attempt to ease her pain. The man brought his perfumed handkerchief to his nose and smirked. "Stupid, stupid woman. Carrying on over her dear husband being jostled about in his eternal sleep. Doesn't she realize that the poor bugger would have had to arise on judgement day in any case?''

When he looked at Lord a'Becket, the man's eyes were bright slits of self interest. "Sir, I deem it an honor to join you and your son in your, shall we say, development syndicate.''

They smiled and shook hands. "There is one thing, however," said the man. "My participation must remain our little and most confidential secret. My position, you understand.''

a'Becket understood. Nodding, he said, "I understand, sir. Rely on me to remain the soul of discretion. And please convey my regards to your lovely wife, Lady Corder, and remind her how much we enjoyed her company when the two of you last visited Melbourne.''

And riddle me this, thought a'Becket: how can we three— Sir Darcy, Lady Corder and I—best use each other in future? For that, Sir Darcy Peacock-popinjay, is what has brought us together.

Morag could not have been more hurt than if her father had slapped her face. He had just brushed by her, ignoring the report she held in her hand, a report she had carefully worked on for weeks and eagerly wanted to hand to him. He had promised her a private meeting in his office this evening, just the two of them. Instead he had rushed out, breaking their appointment without a word, leaving her standing in the doorway of his office, embarrassed and on the edge of tears. Of course the other secretaries saw it happen, which made it worse. How could he do this to her?

A junior executive hovered nearby, on the verge of asking her to join him for dinner and a late evening sail. But the look on her face told him to postpone the invitation and select a better time. Running into her own office, Morag slammed the door and leaned against it, her face hot with tears. Damn him!

Through the door she heard the sounds of men and women preparing to leave for the day. Damn them, too. If they wanted to laugh at her, let them. She walked to her desk, sat down and placed her head on the blotter. Why hadn't he remembered? Why hadn't he taken the time to at least take the report from her and just promise to read it later? She had put so much effort into it.

In her report she noted that there had been strikes all last year and in each of the five months of this year, 1891. Strikes were expensive; they caused a delay in repaying bank loans and in general hurt a company's cash flow. It was Morag's feeling that Irons & Pease should close or sell its mines, all of them. There had been miner's strikes at other claims in New South Wales and sooner or later the same would happen at her father's claims. In addition, the mines were not producing as well as they had in the past. Sell them and sell them now.

Neither the repayment of loans nor a continuing flow of bank deposits could be depended on in the event of continuing strikes and it was Morag's feeling that the strikes the colonies were now suffering would be occurring for some time to come. Neither side was willing to compromise. What's more, labor was talking of more than strikes; they were talking of political power, of starting a political party. The more strikes, the sooner labor would seek a solution not limited to economics. Too many old men ran Australia's politics; Morag was young enough to see the hard changes that were going to come. These changes, she knew, were pushing federation closer, but meanwhile someone would get hurt and she didn't want it to be her father.

But he had hurried by her this evening and she did not like it. What's more, she was going to tell him so. First, she would leave the report on his desk. Maybe he would read it the first thing tomorrow morning.

In his office she lay the neatly typed pages on his desk and was about to leave when she noticed a sheet of paper with a list of names on it. The name that caught her eye was at the top: Lady Genista Corder. Coldly, Morag studied the sheet. It was an investment prospectus, inviting Michael Irons to join a group of people investing in a vineyard. At the bottom of the sheet was today's date, along with the place and time of a meeting for potential investors. Lady Corder would be one of the hosts.

Enraged, Morag ripped the invitation to shreds, opened the window and threw the pieces down on Pitt Street. She shouted at the top of her voice, "I hate you! I hate you!"

She sank to a chair, repeating over and over, "I hate you, I hate you."

The words were aimed at her father, but could have easily applied to Genista Corder.

In the Braidwood goldfields Heath Irons stroked his blond beard as he confronted the striking miners in front of him. Heath had hardened considerably since the kidnapping incident of last year. He wore a gun everywhere, and surrounded himself with hardened men who did the same. Less and less gold was being produced at a higher cost and Michael Irons, feeling that better production methods would make a difference, had assigned Heath to run the mines, giving him free rein. The son, anxious to prove himself, ran a tight ship.

But in 1891, all of Australia was being hit by strikes and the Irons & Pease gold claims were no exception. Heath, who had a legendary father to please, was not going to be pushed around by unionists, an attitude he knew his father would appreciate.

"My father has ordered the mines closed," he said, "so you can bloody well take your signs and parade up and down elsewhere. I say you're trespassing, the lot of you, and I want you off my property."

"Your father always treated us like men," said the strikers' leader.

"That was before you murdered his partner. Now remove your stinkin' arses off this land before I lose my patience."

"We regret the killin' of Davy Pease. Wasn't a decent

thing, that, and ain't a man here who had a thing to do with it or doesn't condemn it."

Heath looked down at his hand, the one missing the forefinger, then at the strike leader. Irons' son spat tobacco juice in the man's face.

The striker's eyes widened in rage and he tossed his picket sign aside. But before he could get to Heath, the men behind Irons' son charged, wielding axe handles. The strikers rushed to support their leader and more of Heath's men joined the melee. Minutes later it was over; the strike was crushed and its leader lay on the ground with a fractured skull. An elated Heath, his pistol in his hand, yelled, "Clear this scum away. I am going to telegraph my father and tell him that it has been a glorious day for us in Braidwood. A most glorious day."

The yacht, called "Lucifer On The Waves," cruised along the Sydney coast and towards the sunset. On deck men in black clothing and women in gaily colored long dresses sipped champagne and ate a light supper from a generously laden table. These were the investors in the vineyard proposal, people of means who had concluded their business and were now enjoying a pleasant, albeit brief cruise. Shares had been offered, accepted and payment agreed upon. The venture, in fact, had received more than the money needed and a few people had to settle for smaller participation. An Australian vineyard, particularly one involving Lady Corder, had cachet to spare.

The yacht now headed back to Sydney, where it would arrive shortly after nightfall. Meanwhile the talk continued about money, for it was a topic of never ending interest to Sydneysiders. And, of course, the matter of federation came up again and again—it was more widely spoken of then ever before.

Amid the conversational hubbub, no one noticed that two people had quietly disappeared. Michael Irons and Lady Corder, whose husband was in Melbourne on business, were no longer on deck. It was inevitable that the months of polite, but highly charged conversation between the two would lead to a moment such as the one now taking place in a cabin below deck. The boat, the property of a prosperous Sydney insurance broker, was large and there were at least two dozen people and as many crew on board. In addition dusk had fallen, making it difficult to see beyond a few feet in any direction. An added diversion was a banjo player, who in candelight and with an enthusiastic presentation, was soon the center of all eyes.

Below in a darkened cabin, Irons and Genista kissed with a fierce and undeniable hunger. They had not left the deck together, but had each wandered off separately and in different directions. But as lightning will find the tree it wants to fire, so they found one another. Conversation had been brief and cursory. In the half light of the waning sun coming through the open porthole, Lady Corder had appeared feline, predatory and irresistable.

"You are most impressive," she had whispered. "There were a dozen men on deck, all with money and power, and you towered above them all. I understand you even control members of your colony's parliament."

"I have men who are beholden to me, yes." The New South Wales parliament did not pay its members, thus leaving most, if not all, open to bribes that were freely offered and gratefully accepted. Irons, as a major property owner, was also allowed to elect members of the Legislative Council, Parliament's upper house. Members of the legislative Assembly, the lower house, were elected. Even here, however, the advantage belonged to the wealthy, for men like Irons could legally vote more than once.

"We should not be here," she whispered, taking a step towards him. She wore a straw hat that was almost oriental in design and a yellow silk dress, minus a bustle, the coming fashion for women. "Powerful men excite me," she said. She was close enough to touch him. "Powerful men—"

Her mouth closed on his and he embraced her eagerly. It

was he who said, "I have no wish to disgrace you. Perhaps we should stop while we still can."

Her eye shone with lust. More than lust. Suddenly, he didn't know her. She was a different woman, wanton, daring, almost frightening. What had come over her?

"I enjoy the unexpected," she said. "I find it more stimulating than the predictable." Her hand massaged his groin, bringing his phallus into a hard, hot life of its own. "I find the danger of discovery intriguing, don't you?"

He, however, was nervous and fearful of discovery. Yes, he wanted to make love to her, but not here, not with so many people so close. What had he expected when he had followed her below deck? Not this. Not just yet.

Her voice was heavy with animal sexual energy and it was obvious that she was in charge. Irons felt uneasy, but he could not move.

"I want to serve you," she whispered huskily. "I want the first time to be for you."

And then she was on her knees like a dockside whore, clawing at his pants and he wanted to stop her, to say it must not be like this but she fought him and then she had his phallus in her mouth and so quickly and expertly did she perform that Irons almost fainted from pleasure. He bit his tongue until the blood came to keep from moaning aloud. She was wanton and commanding and when he had spent himself she still clung to him, her mouth hard against him, but she was hurting him and he pushed her away.

She lay at his feet, stroking his boots with a gloved hand, making small sounds of pleasure. A weakened Irons was both shocked and intoxicated. She was less and more than he had imagined.

Then as though nothing had happened she rose to her feet, straightened her dress and walked to the bathroom, where she used her fingers to arrange her hair. Then walking past him she said, "We must rejoin the others. I shall go first. Please allow a suitable time before leaving the cabin."

And without a further word she left him alone in the now almost totally darkened room.

God in heaven, thought Irons. Who is this woman?

When he again appeared on deck she was animatedly talking to a group of women who were admiring her bustleless dress. For the remainder of the voyage she neither looked at Irons nor spoke to him.

10 _____

NEAR one of Sydney's most beautiful beaches Camilla swam in a tranquil ocean, the sun warming her and turning the water around her into a polished mirror. The child swam beside her, smooth strokes matching hers. It was the child who first noticed that they had swum too far. "I want to go back now," he said. Angrily, Camilla turned on him. "No, just a little further. I want you to spend some more time with me. We never have time together, you and I. Stay with me."

The boy stopped swimming and began treading water. "No, I must go back now. I am beginning to get tired."

Camilla's wrath was intense. "You wretched little boy, you cruel, cruel little boy. You will not go back. You will stay with me and swim for as long as I want you to."

The boy shouted "No!" and turned towards shore, racing to get away from her. Screaming Camilla raced after him, but no matter how fast she swam, the boy got further and further ahead and suddenly he was gone. She was alone in the ocean!

She called out to him again and again. . . .

And then she was awake, in her own bed and her husband was at her side, calming her as best he could.

Morag was beside him and behind her a servant held a candle high to illuminate the room.

The same nightmare. Ever since the stillbirth this nightmare had tormented her and was getting worse. She could never catch the boy. Perhaps if she did, then the nightmare would go away.

She said to her husband, "I shall try harder next time. I will do my best to catch him. You'll see."

Irons and Morag looked at one another and back at Camilla. But she was asleep now, her face peaceful and relaxed. Until the next time, thought a worried Irons. Until the next time.

11 ─────────────────────────────

A helpless and terrified Dai Irons, held tightly by three
men, could only watch as a forth man passed a long-bladed
knife back and forth in front of his eyes, before laying the
flat of the blade against Dai's nose. "First, I plans to slice
your *hooter*," said the knife holder. "Ain't no woman ever
gonna want to look at that face agin. After that, I be takin'
away one of yer stinkin' eyes. Look like your fuckin'
father, you will. We'll teach you to come creepin' about
and spyin' on honest men."

"Turn him loose and be quick about it." The voice came
from the darkened entrance to the union hall.

"Who says?" The knife holder was in no hurry to obey.

"If you do not take your hands from him, all of you, I
meself will put the boot to what is laughingly called your
faces."

He stepped from the darkness, a lean, red-headed man
in his early thirties, with a red-blond mustache and an
easy, confident manner.

"Oh, it's you," said the knife holder. "Sorry, I did not
know—"

"Mr. Irons is a friend," said the red-headed Alan
Costello, a leader of the dock workers union. "He sup-

ports us wholeheartedly despite his father's objections and
the risk such support brings to himself. My apologies, Dai.
We do have trouble with spies from time to time and these
yobbos here were just letting their caution run away with
them. Come inside. The meeting has already started.''

He offered his hand and Dai, who had been rubbing a
sore throat, took it. Alan was his closest friend in the labor
movement, the man he admired the most and who had
gotten him increasingly involved with the workers' cause
this year. Dai's father remained immovable in his opposition to organized Australian labor, saying he would support it only when Davy Pease returned alive to this earth.
Nor did Michael Irons care for labor's sometimes violent
tactics, no matter that they were more than matched by the
repressive tactics of Australian businessmen. Though Dai
and Alan both regretted Davy's death, Alan made no
apology for using violence to achieve union goals.

''You cannot make an omelette without breaking eggs,''
he said to Dai. ''When kindness is in vain, violence is
both just and necessary. It is very English to defend property at all costs. The English army and the London police
force were formed to protect property and that attitude was
carried to Australia. When we oppose the property owners we
also oppose their bully boys. Which means we must flex our
own muscles or go under. Birth is always accompanied by
pain and by blood. Those of us who want a new Australia,
an Australia where a man has a guaranteed living wage
and decent life, must be prepared to give pain and take it
as well. There can be no other way.''

Dai believed him. It was time for a new Australia, one
people, one nation and above all, one society that was
founded on decency, fairness and a complete lack of
privilege. What had moved him to seek out the unionists
had been the harsh methods businessmen had used to break
strikes. Dai could not accept that twisted justice that saw
violence and prison meted out to strikers and their leaders
merely for seeking a fair wage and better working conditions.
He had tried to make his father see this, to see that

crushing the unionists was no different than the English abuse of the Irish, a thing Michael Irons had opposed all his life.

Unfortunately, father and son could never agree on this most sensitive of subjects and Dai felt that the wisest course was to keep his labor sympathies away from the Irons household. Heath, straining to prove his manhood and his right to be Michael Irons' son, supported his father without reservation. If called on to do so, Dai knew that Heath would kill unionists and be proud of it. And although Morag was at least approachable on the subject, she would do nothing that constituted even the slightest would not challenge to her father. Her devotion to Michael Irons was absolute.

Tonight in a waterfront hiring hall, representatives of all New South Wales labor unions were meeting to discuss the effects of recent strikes throughout the colonies and labor's role in "The Coming Event" of federation. Inside the large, bare room, thirty men sat on wooden benches facing a desk, behind which sat several speakers. After guiding Dai to a chair not far from the desk, Alan Costello joined the speakers.

"Damn federation to hell, I say!" shouted a short, fat man pounding the table with a hairy fist. "Unity will not help the working man and I do not think that we should waste precious time in discussing this nefarious topic. When strikers were fired upon in Melbourne, when workers were ridden down and clubbed in Sydney, who, may I ask, did that dirty work? The armies and police of the rich, by God. I say to you that a united Australia means a single and powerful army, a single and powerful police, both controlled by the wealthy, the bankers, the mine owners and ship owners and acting as servants to their interest, *their* interests, not ours."

He paused in the highly charged room, then jabbed the air with a forefinger. "To a single state, I say a single word—never!"

He sat down to applause, mopping his reddened face with a handkerchief.

As a fascinated Dai watched, other speakers followed, arguing hotly both for and against federation, for that issue was seen as the clue to labor's future. Some did indeed see the state as an organization for the suppression of labor; others saw unity as the only way to up the workers' standard of living. But it remained for Alan to give the most electrifying speech of the evening, to say the words that would serve as inspiration and guideline for all of labor, in all of the colonies for days to come.

He was confident, witty and utterly committed to his cause. And as Dai he listened to him, he was swept away by the force of his friend's conviction. This is where I belong, he told himself. This is the future, the right future for me and for all of Australia.

"As some of you may have heard earlier on in the evening," Alan was saying, "I am indeed Irish—"

The room erupted in laughter, clearing the air.

"And we Irish do love our little tales. I recall the one about a thief, who learned of various amounts of gold hidden in half a dozen homes in this little village. Well, our sticky-fingered boyo concoted a scheme, he did. He pretended to be a constable and he went about the village warning the good people about thieves and robbers and such. He suggested, our bogus constable, that all the gold be gathered together in one spot where he could guard it night and day. Everyone thought this was a fine idea, and brought him their gold for safe keeping. Needless to say, very shortly thereafter both the gold and the constable disappeared."

When the laughter had died down Alan said, " 'Tis a lot easier, lads, to grab it all when it's in one pile than to go about pickin' up a coin at a time here, there and everywhere. We have been talkin' about our troubles and about federation and the two are intertwined, like O'Grady over there and some of the whores at Madame Rodale's."

O'Grady smiled and waved a hand in pleasant admission.

"Boyos," said Alan, "if this country unites, when federation becomes a fact, there will be one Parliament, not six. And companions of my heart, there is just one thing for all of us to do: we, who wish to change Australia into something approachin' a workin' man's heaven, must not tear down that Parliament. No lads, we most certainly do not tear it down."

He leaned forward, both hands on the table. "*We capture it.*"

At that moment, Dai felt the hairs on the back of his neck rise.

"To feed and nourish the body," said Alan, "a man does not take a bit of beef and rub it first on his hand, then his leg, then his behind. What does he do? He eats it. Feeds his mouth, he does and it follows as the night the day that his whole body gets the benefit. We unionists can best feed our future, not just by marchin' up and down on these docks here, or in front of some gold mine or on some damn sheep ranch. We concentrate on makin' the rules by which the game is played and one does that by runnin' for Parliament."

He stopped and sipped water from a glass. No one said a word. Dai was on the edge of his chair, eyes glued to Alan.

The union leader said, "We strikers aren't doin' well, lads. We are losin' more than we are winning. Of course we will continue to strike, continue to raise our voices. But to get the foot off our throats now and forever means power and power means politics. Do not let the idea frighten you. You learned to piss without dampening your shoes and you learned which end of a horse eats oats and you can learn the ins and outs of politics.

"Listen to me: changing the laws in one part of Australia is not enough. Our brothers are suffering all over this land and we have to make sure that this stops. I say federation is the answer. Increasing the shillings in our pockets is not enough. Changing society is what must be done and that will happen only when there is a single

Parliament to fight, a single Parliament to control, yes control.''

His voice dropped to a whisper. ''And we, brothers, must be the ones to make that one set of laws to protect every workin' man in every colony.''

Each man in the room, including Dai, jumped to his feet and cheered, applauded, shouted until the noise carried from the hall and out onto the quiet night-shrouded docks. Costello was pounded on the back until he choked and his hand was pumped again and again. Dai could not make his way through the crowd that surrounded him and had to wait almost an hour before they could leave together and go for a drink. After talking for another hour, they left and began walking, continuing their discussion about labor and Australian unity.

''Alan, my father wants unity, too. Yet, you and he are on opposite sides.''

''Laddie, say a storm's brewing and you and I have no shelter. But we decide to team up and build us a cabin so's the weather won't take our lives. We do just that, but after it's built there's an argument over who's cabin it is and just how it will be used. Now it was right and proper that we pool our efforts to survive. There was nothin' else for us to do. It's just that we have reached that point where there is to be a partin' of the ways, a necessary partin' of the ways. Federation is goin' to take all the help forthcomin'. What happens after that will depend on who is the strongest. Us or them.''

Dai said, ''So to bring about this unity will require strange bedfellows.''

''Most assuredly.''

They were in the heart of town, walking past the Royale Theatre as the crowd was letting out. Dai heard his name called and turned to see his sister waving at him. She was with a minor French diplomat attached to his country's embassy, a man she had met at a cricket match. Dai introduced Morag to Alan Costello, who said, ''I have heard of you, Miss Irons. I'm told you are among the brightest of the young lights working for your father.''

"I try to keep my ambition veiled, Mr. Costello," she said. "It does not become women in Australia to aspire too highly or so I am told."

" 'A man's worth is no greater than the worth of his ambitions.' "

"I see you read Marcus Aurelius."

"And I see you are educated beyond my expectations."

Morag's smile disappeared. "Only the uninformed are ever surprised, Mr. Costello. Do not judge me until you no longer disappoint yourself in anything. Dai."

And then she was gone, on the arm of the Frenchman and into the throng of theatre patrons around them. Alan Costello put his hands on his hips, threw back his head and laughed. "Damn me, for being a right pompous ass. She was correct to leave me here wounded and dash off without offering a bandage."

Cupping his hands to his mouth Alan shouted in the direction of Morag, "I hope our children grow up to be just like you!"

At the corner, Morag hesitated, smiled without turning, then continued walking.

Near the theatre entrance and out of sight of Alan and Dai, Redmond Glass stroked his thick, red beard and made a mental note of what he had just seen and heard.

12

AT the Darling Point mansion of Sir Darcy and Lady Corder, Irons handed over the invitation inviting him and a guest to a reception for French actress Sarah Bernhardt, called 'The Divine One', and 'The Eighth Wonder Of The World'. Lou Heller would have loved to have met Bernhardt, but was in Melbourne, in the midst of a two week engagement that could possibly be extended. Just as well. Lou and Genista in the same room would have been less than soothing to Irons' stomach and nerves. Instead Irons was again escorting Morag; Camilla was at the seashore on doctor's orders, enjoying needed sun and sea air.

Since the episode on the yacht, Genista had teased and tortured him, refusing to be alone with him except for one impulsive moment.

She had shown up at one of his dockside warehouses, having learned in advance that he was there, and together they had walked among the bales of wool and grain and rows of mining machinery, talking about their mutual investment in the vineyard. And then they were alone, in a dark corner of the warehouse and it was almost as it had been on the yacht, except that this time he made love to her, the two of them lying on an opened bale of raw

Chinese silk. She had wanted him then and there and he, who had dreamed of her and thought obsessively of that evening on the yacht, could only give in to her demands. They made love with the fear of discovery never far away and within sight of a caged python, used to destroy the large sized rats which infested the waterfront.

She lifted up her skirt, drew him down and then into her and the sensation was so thrilling that Irons gasped for breath, feeling the pleasure race along his spine to his head. She was wet, ready for him and climaxed exactly when he did, digging her lacquered nails into his shirted back and drawing blood.

"My life is too planned," she whispered. "But with you, with you. . . ."

Later, they walked slowly back to the warehouse entrance, she twirling her pink parasol and speaking of wines and bottling and the cost of shipping the vineyard's yield to other countries. After that day, he neither saw nor heard from her until the arrival in Sydney of the illustrious Miss Bernhardt.

Now at the crowded reception Irons and Morag stood in line to be introduced to the most famous actress of their time. For Morag, it was Christmas morning and she was a child once again, about to open wonderous presents. Eagerly, she stood on tiptoe to whisper details of Bernhardt's life to her father.

"She was born in Paris out of wedlock to a very successful prostitute, a Dutch Jewess. She writes, paints, sculpts and she will not go onstage until she is paid in advance, in gold. It is said that she has had more than a thousand lovers. The press says she arrived in Sydney with over a hundred pieces of luggage and a dozen animals."

"Do not forget her coffin," said Irons, who knew a little about the actress himself.

"It is made of rosewood," said Morag, "and lined with letters from past lovers. She carries it everywhere and even makes love in it, I hear."

Perhaps 'The Divine One' and Genista Corder have

more in common than we know, thought Irons. But there was more serious news to ponder, some of it not to his liking. The unionists had formed a labor political party, with candidates successfully standing for office. A handful had won election to the Legislative Assembly. There was talk that similar political maneuvering by unionists was occuring in all six colonies. If so, then federation was going to be a matter of who would sit on the throne once it was built. Another Sydney bank had failed and there were rumors that two Melbourne banks were about to do the same. The two cities were Australia's richest and most powerful, heated rivals who set the tone for the entire continent and if they were having financial troubles, the rest of the cities in the remaining colonies would surely suffer the same fate. Irons wondered if Morag was not correct when she suggested that he eliminate his interest in the bank. He had read her report and disagreed with a great deal of it. True, he had closed the mines, which she had suggested, but that would have happened in any case, since the venture was no longer profitable. There were times when he wished that Morag was a man; it would have been easier to promote her, to give her her due and place her over both of his sons, neither of whom had a patch on her.

But things were not done that way in Australia. It was a man's land here and women were to remain quiet and do as they were told. Morag alone of all the women he knew refused to accept that role. So in the end, Irons had to accept her as she was, for she was his daughter and he did love her. When he had a chance he was going to go over that report of hers once more and study it carefully.

They met Sarah Bernhardt, a striking 47-year old red headed woman with the regal bearing of a Chinese mandarin and a floor length robe trimmed in lynx, ermine and polar bear fur. At her feet sat what Irons hoped was a trained and docile cheetah. Both he and Morag moved carefully around the jungle animal.

Tomorrow Irons had tickets to see Miss Bernhardt at the

Victoria Theatre in Dumas's "La Dame Aux Camelias." If
Camilla returns in time, he thought somewhat absently, I'll
take her. The two no longer lived as man and wife. The
stillbirth of their child had all but put an end to that side of
their marriage. Camilla remained seriously depressed over
the death of that baby; she was also filled with feelings of
failure and fear. She'd had a brush with death herself
during her cruelly pointless labor—sex, to her, had proved
futile and nearly fatal.

A tap on his shoulder made Irons swivel around. It was
fat, balding, many-chinned George Reid, the canny politician of whom it was said that he never slept long in public,
being quickly snapped awake by his own snoring. Reid,
however, merely looked slothful. In reality he was shrewd,
tough, witty, and tolerant of human foibles. He could also
dig in his heels on matters of importance to him. On
federation he was said to both waver on the question and
to secretly oppose it. His nickname was "Yes-No" Reid,
a tribute to his ability to avoid being pinned down on any
topic.

"Mr. Almighty Irons, we request the pleasure of your
company for some private and serious drinking, at which
time we shall discuss recent matters of pressing urgency.
We consist of Sir Henry Parkes, Mr. Edmund Barton, our
esteemed premier Mr. Dibbs and others of note. Specifically,
we wish to deal with the past election and how that bodes
well or ill for New South Wales."

"It bodes well or ill for all of Australia."

Reid smiled, saying nothing. *Yes-No* was not going to
be pinned down on the wrong side of any question.

Irons excused himself from Morag, leaving her to wan-
der through the luxuriously decorated mansion until the
crush of people became too great and the cheetah roared
once too loud and too often. And then she was outside on
the lawn, inhaling the sea air from the nearby harbor and
fanning her face with a gloved hand.

Behind her a voice said, "If every fool wore a crown,

then we would all be kings. I want to apologize for my foolishness."

It was Alan Costello.

Surprised and mildly shocked, she said, "What are you doing here? I'd hardly expect to find your sort at the Corders."

"They themselves would expect it even less than you, I'm sure. Fortunately, my presence is not known. Are you planning to give me away?"

"I am planning to leave you where I found you. I am going inside—"

"Please don't. First, allow me to make amends for insulting your intelligence the other evening."

"Accepted. Now if you wish to gaze upon Miss Bernhardt, she is in the large reception room to your right."

"I did not come here to see her. I came to see you."

Which is exactly what Morag knew he would say. Silently she cursed that part of herself that longed to hear those words from him.

"You know I cannot call at your home," said Alan, "nor can I contact you at work. Your father—"

"I know. Your brother is Blue Dan, is he not?"

"The hooligan? Yes, that is he. My brother is a most successful, and shall we say, unorthodox businessman."

"Brothels, smuggling, illegal prize fights, gambling dens and bad alcohol, along with the ownership of saloons and I even hear coining," she said indignantly. "Unorthodox is hardly the word I'd use."

A grinning Alan said, "A busy little bee, our Blue Dan. Incidentally he has renounced coining. The economy is so unstable that counterfeiting is no longer the appealing enterprise it once was. Some of his money comes from quite legitimate investments, such as the sort of businesses your father has."

"If my father knew you were here he would thrash you."

"Well, we won't tell him, will we. When can I see you?"

"I—"

"You know, I'm not entirely disreputable, Miss Irons. I am one of the first labor candidates to win a seat in the New South Wales Parliament." He was teasing her, but at the same time there was pride in his voice. Alan Costello was no man for her—not with how her father felt about his kind—but he was a man with a dream, who faced challenges as her father once had. He was no fop, nor was he the crude animal she detested in so many of the Australian men she saw. He was cultured, committed to something and he excited her.

"You must go before my father sees you."

Costello was near her, hands on her shoulders, warming her in ways that the sun never had. "When," he said.

"Can you find a telephone?"

"What good would it do me?"

"Do not use your name. Use another."

He grinned. "Of course. Morgan. I am Mr. Morgan. It is close to your name."

He kissed her, quickly, and her heart fluttered and suddenly she felt hopelessly vulnerable. When she opened her eyes he was gone.

Minutes later, in a ground floor study, with bay windows of stained glass, Irons casually looked towards the sea and saw Alan Costello hurry by. At first he thought his one eye was playing tricks. But it was Costello, the laborite who had just gotten into Parliament. What in God's name was he doing where he was not wanted and had not been invited?

". . . come to some sort of arrangement with them," Henry Parkes was saying of the new labor delegates in Parliament.

Irons shook his head. "I see no reason to stoop that low. They are without numbers, without power and without principle, as far as I am concerned. They will never figure in Australia's future, I can assure you."

13_____

IN Melbourne, Lord a'Becket felt his parked carriage dip and sway as the very large Julius Fielding stepped inside and let his bulk flop back on a leather seat across from a'Becket and his son. A tap on the ceiling from Denis's cane and the driver sitting outside pulled away from Parliament House on the corner of Spring and Bourke Streets. Fielding's fleshy pink face was watchful, alert; he and the a'Beckets had little in common, for they stood on opposite sides of the federation issue and Fielding would soon introduce a bill in Parliament that would displease the a'Beckets greatly.

As things now stood, Victoria had no liability laws making banks accountable for their actions; bankers operated with the freedom and scruples of bushrangers, doing as they pleased and never having to answer for it. Fielding was drafting a law that would hold bankers, like the a'Beckets, responsible for all monies placed in their trust. In this bill there would be criminal penalties for the underhanded practices that had made banking a dice game played in private by so-called gentlemen.

Four banks had failed in Melbourne this year and the year had not yet ended. Several more had gone out of business in other Victoria cities. Bank closings meant suffering and hardships for all, particularly those of modest means. Federation, with one strong, central government, could stabilize banking throughout the continent, protecting the less affluent, the middle class, the poor. But until that happened, Fielding would do all he could to see that Victoria protected all its citizens, rich and poor alike.

He guessed that the a'Beckets planned to bribe him, as they had done with other legislators in the past. Better to save their pounds and pence; Fielding was no saint, but he had never voted less than his conscience and would not change his ways now.

The carriage rolled along a tree-lined bank of the Yarra River, where in the late afternoon couples strolled arm in arm and a group of men in white shirts and matching flannel pants huddled on a cricket pitch, bats over their shoulders as they shared a joke.

"We shall go back in session and remain so until late into the evening," said Fielding, "so I must return at a reasonable hour."

"We will detain you no longer than necessary, sir." a'Becket stroked his long nose with a forefinger, his habitual gesture prior to leaping in for the kill. "We wish to talk to you about your banking bill, the one you propose to lay before Parliament prior to year's end."

Fielding smiled. So he had guessed correctly after all. The a'Beckets, to enrich themselves, first planned to enrich Fielding. "Gentlemen, this carriage ride will not prove as dear to you as planned. I will accept no bribes, no remunerations, no stocks in your ventures. My bill will proceed on schedule and if it hurts your interests, so be it."

"I think," said a'Becket, "that you are about to see that it is your interests, not ours, that are at stake here. You will not submit your bill and we will give you nothing."

A warning went off in Fielding's brain. "What did you say?"

"My father speaks distinctly," said Denis. "You heard every word. No bill. And no bribes."

a'Becket said, "We know of your preference for celestials, particularly *boys*." The last word was spat out.

Fielding's large hands became fists; his face reddened and his breathing grew louder.

"Buggery is a crime punishable by long years of agonizing and distressful incarceration," said Denis. "In New South Wales, it carries a term of life imprisonment. However, we here in Victoria are more civilized and it is unlikely that you would be put away for more than twenty years."

"Your word," whispered Fielding. "Your word against mine."

a'Becket leaned forward. "Do you take me for a fool, man? I can and will produce an eye witness who has observed you at your games. You have been seen in the Chinese quarter by others and that is merely the beginning. Can your reputation withstand court testimony by those yellow skinned youths on whom you have spent your lust?"

The banker leaned back, hands resting on the head of his cane. "You have made trips to other cities in the colony in order to secure information pertaining to your proposed banking bill. On at least a half dozen occasions, which can be documented chapter and verse, you again satisfied your particular vice in the Chinese quarter."

"You had me followed?" Fielding was appalled.

"You are married with a family," said Denis. "Your shame will be theirs."

Shaken and subdued, Fielding looked out of the carriage window at the sailboats floating along the Yarra. "It is nothing of which I am proud. But I am plagued by this urge and it will not leave me. I have tried to be a good husband and father and I fear God, as does any sensible man. I love this land, this Australia and I want to shape its future."

He looked at the a'Beckets. "And you swine would take that from me."

Lord a'Becket studied him contemptuously. "Your answer, sir."

"I suppose you have a bill of your own you would like proposed in place of mine?"

"We are neither cretins nor addled. Such a move coming from you would appear most suspicious. We simply wish you to cease work on your banking proposal. How you present your change of heart is entirely up to you. But since we are planning to open another bank in Melbourne next week, we would like your answer now."

Fielding shook his head. He was sickened with himself and with the men now facing him. "Another bank. Another opportunity for you two bastards to cheat—"

"That," a'Becket snapped, "is no concern of yours. You have a mighty cause, the cause of federation and you serve it well. You can continue to serve it only if you are in Parliament, where your voice can be heard, where you can support Deakin." The charismatic Alfred Deakin was Victoria's most effective political leader.

Again the warning went off in in Fielding's brain; the a'Beckets had something else in mind, but what? "Are you going to interfere with my support of federation?"

a'Becket said, "Sir, we are here to talk about your banking concept, nothing more. To secure our silence, all you need do is bury your proposal."

"Why do you fear my bill? The fact that I lay it before Parliament in no way guarantees its success. Australians are slow to act on progressive matters and in the main, prefer life as it is, without change."

Denis said, "Recent bank failures may make some see merit in your plan. It is best that you not sound the alarm. Let sleeping dogs lie, I say."

In that moment a plan occured to Fielding. "Very well, I shall do as you say, so long as I do not have to support you publicly in any way."

"Your word," said a'Beckett. "Your word that you

will neither offer the plan nor in any way personally alert one single member of that august body to any portion of your proposal.''

"You have it. Now stop the carriage. The stench in here is more than I can stand and I much prefer walking.''

When Fielding had gone, Denis said to his father, ''You said you would not interfere with his federation sympathies. Did you mean it?''

''I said what he wanted to hear. It is never wise to laden a man with too much at one time. Had we attempted to secure his cooperation on more than one issue, in this our first confrontation, he might have proven more recalcitrant. The best approach is a gradual one. First, he accepts this task, and then we assign him others.''

Denis smiled. ''I see. Step by step.''

''By step.''

''And should Fielding break his word to us?''

''Unlikely. For a loathsome sodomite with a love of 'the Slap-Bum Polka', Mr. Fielding retains a certain code of honor. His word is and always has been his bond. If, however, he betrays us, we shall resort to sterner measures.''

Michael Irons walked up the gangplank and onto the deck of the small schooner. The unloading of cargo and passengers slowed him down in his quest to find cabin three, which was below deck and aft. In front of number three he looked left and right. Then, satisfied that no one was observing him, he knocked.

''Yes?'' The voice inside was cautious.

''Irons.''

''And whom do you expect to meet, Mr. Irons?''

''Sean Cleary.''

The cabin door opened and Irons stepped into the small, dark room. He waited, and then a match was struck and an oil lamp lit.

Irons shook hands with Julius Fielding.

*   *   *

A week later Lord a'Becket waited in a corridor of Melbourne's Parliament House and when he saw Julius Fielding, a vein twitched high on his temple. He wrung his cane as though it were Fielding's neck; the fat legislator's treachery had left the banker speechless. A warning from a legislator in a'Becket's pay had hastily brought the banker to Parliament House in time to sit in the gallery and watch as Fielding's plan to control banking was presented, discussed and applauded by many.

In the corridor, Fielding, surrounded by fellow parliamentarians, came abreast of a'Becket. Excusing himself, he strolled over to the banker, showing neither fear nor remorse. On the contrary, he seemed almost pleased to see a'Becket.

"I had your word," the banker almost hissed.

"I kept my word. Alfred Deakin delivered the proposal, as you no doubt observed from your seat in the gallery. I did not give it to him."

Deakin, tall, dignified and black-bearded, was Victoria's most charismatic politician. He was a commanding orator, and a consummate politician. He was his colony's strongest proponent of federation, and Fielding fervently supported him.

"To whom did you give your proposal?" asked a'Becket.

"You had my word, sir, and I kept it. I refrained from all contact with Parliament on this issue."

"I shall ruin you."

"You will undoubtedly try. Do your worst. I am prepared."

"Deakin—"

"Knows of my indiscretions. I told him."

"*You told him?*"

"Yes. I admitted my weakness and threw myself upon his mercy and discretion. Oh, he was suitably shocked. But my past services and my position on federation have made me valuable to him. He needs all of the allies he can muster, so he has agreed to stand by me in case of scandal or blackmail. I believe, sir, that this removes your fangs or at least blunts them. And regarding Madame Wu and her nephews, do not look for them. They are no longer in Melbourne. They departed suddenly—for Western Australia, I believe. Or was it Queensland? Oh dear, memory fades. In any case, they will not be available as witnesses for you. And I would say, their absence minimizes any accounts you care to offer regarding my 'adventures' elsewhere.''

Fielding drew himself up. "And now, I have business to attend to. Do not approach me again on this matter. I am your sworn enemy and if you ever attempt to blackmail me again, I shall do you grievous bodily harm and with a willing heart. Good day.''

Fielding bowed, then moved his bulk down the empty hall. a'Becket stared at the receding figure, then stroked his long nose, turned on his heel and walked in the opposite direction. He walked erect, stiffly, ignoring those who greeted him and he stopped only when he realized that in his rage he was walking in circles, going from one passage to another and never reaching the entrance.

By the time he did reach the entrance and stepped outside, he had decided that when the time was right, he would kill Julius Fielding.

14

THE heatwave which had settled upon Sydney had made Heath Irons irritable and he dealt with it the only way he knew how. He drank. And became more irritable. With a tumbler of brandy in his hand, he stood at a corner window of his office in the Irons & Pease building and shaded his eyes against a white-hot sun. All of New South Wales was suffering a year end drought, the worst of 1891. It hadn't rained for weeks, scorching the earth, turning rivers to beds of dried, cracked mud. Worse, the drought had killed badly needed grass for sheep. What grass remained had been eaten by rabbits, who plagued Australia by the millions and were as destructive to the land as droughts and brushfires.

Sheep. Since coming to work in Sydney, in an office where he had to dress like a "silver-tail", a gentleman, Heath had made bad decisions and sheep had been one of the worst. He had desperately wanted to re-open the mies and had fought his father against keeping them closed. He'd lost. No one argued with "The Iron Pirate" and came out on top, especially in matters of money.

"I know how to earn money," Irons had said to his son. "I will not learn from you the losing of it. The mines are a liability. They remain closed."

As for the sheep, Heath had advised his father to buy more and this time his father had listened. Morag, his meddling sister, had her own opinion. Heath had seen her report on his sheep buying proposal, a snippy bit of nonsense advising against it while the market was *soft*, as she put it. Didn't she realize that Australia had come to riches on the sheep's back and would always regard that animal as a four-legged goldmine?

Heath had his way; the sheep had been purchased by the thousands, to roam on Irons & Pease grazing land, of which there was plenty. Again, Morag had spat in Heath's soup; plant some of the sheep land with wheat, she said. Heath had argued with her in the office, in front of clerks, executives and secretaries and didn't give a damn about hurting her feelings.

"This is man's business, Morag," he told her. "And if you were more of a woman you'd know that."

She had wept and he had felt good about that. Bloody good.

Then more bad luck descended on him. The drought came, killing grass, drying up water holes and making him look as though he wasn't smart enough to hold onto his hat in a high wind. Other decisions had not turned out so well, either. Heath had insisted that some of his gun-carrying cronies from the mining camp, his "bully boys", as the unionists called them, be given jobs here in Sydney. Unfortunately they, like Heath, were men born to the saddle and open air, more at home in the bush than in Sydney. The bully boys were square pegs in round holes, causing trouble on the docks, onboard ships, in warehouses, in stables. A few ended up in difficulty with Sydney constables. Eventually, all were sacked.

Dear God, why did it not rain and end Heath's troubles? He was what his father called an executive, with an office, secretary, and fat wage packet. But he was miserable. Everything he touched in Sydney turned to ashes and he dreaded each day, each sunrise, seeing himself as trapped in quicksand, sinking deeper into a morass not of his making. More and more time was spent drinking, gambling, whoring. These were the moments that gave him the illusion of being free and in command of his life.

He swallowed the rest of his brandy and returned to his desk. In his chair, he pushed the heels of his hands into his temples. *The heat*. Out of the chair once more, he rushed across the room, snatched his hat and coat from a closet and left his office. It was time for him to be with his own kind, with men who smelled of sweat and beer and whose hands were raw from holding the reins or a whip.

Minutes later when his secretary received the telegram addressed to Heath, she placed it on his desk unopened. It was Morag who, knowing that her brother had left the office to get drunk and would not return, opened it, read it twice then raced to a telegraph. It was urgent that her father, in Melbourne, be contacted at once. Damn Heath and his weakness. She ran faster, faster . . .

Camilla sat in her father's study in Melbourne, cup and saucer in her hand, smiling at Lord a'Becket, who rebuked her gently with a wagging forefinger. Both sipped tea from exquisite china cups. She felt wonderful, at peace, secure. Michael Irons was not her father; the man in front of her was. She was happy with him in this house, for she was treated well and had everything done for her. She had no worries, no responsibilities. Her father did everything for her. She was healthy again; there was no pain, no dizzy spells. Her life outside this enfolding security was no more than a bad dream.

She was awake. And she was not home, where she dearly longed to be. She was in her husband's mansion in Sydney, where servants mocked her and she was expected to plan dinner parties and see that important men had enough brandy and cigars. This was not the life for her. Why had she ever left Melbourne and her father? She felt sick again. Guilt washed over her and she wished with all her heart that she was home once more with her father, and regretted ever having disobeyed him or thought him cruel.

She would give anything to be home again.

In his room over a stable dreams also came to Johnny-Johnny. His dream was a warning from his *totem*, the Aborigine link with the spirit world and a protector. A *totem* was an animal and Johnny-Johnny's was a dingo, the wolf-like wild dog that was fast, cunning, strong. In the dream the dingo howled, a warning to Johnny-Johnny to step back and away from a beautiful Arabian horse and a small man on crutches. They were a danger to him and to someone else, a man whose face could not be seen in the mists of the dream.

To survive, however, Johnny-Johnny, according to Aborigine ritual, had to throw a bit of the cripple's hair into a fire. Should he risk going near the cripple or should he listen to the *totem*, to the tawny yellow dingo who continued to howl and warn him? The Aborigine was frightened and struggled awake before learning whether or not he was to die soon.

15 _____

MICHAEL Irons looked at the books lining the walls of Alfred Deakin's study in the politician's suburban Melbourne home. In a land where few people allowed time for mental pursuits Deakin had a truly awesome library, featuring a treasury of the world's greatest works of literature, science and history. He also had books on the occult and mysticism, which along with the piercing strength of his gaze gave strength to the report by some that he had a "mesmerizing power."

In truth, the tall, bearded Deakin was one of the most pleasant and accomplished men in Australian public life, with great charm, an outstanding mind and a sense of fair play that caused even his enemies to call him "Affable Alfred." His belief in federation was genuine and intense, but at no time did he embarrass his cause with unscrupulous or fanatical behavior. Throughout his entire career, and he was to achieve Australia's highest honors, he remained a man of the people.

Today Irons was in Melbourne to meet Deakin to discuss new tactics for federation, an issue made ever more pressing by the growing number of bank failures and strikes throughout the six colonies. Sir Henry Parkes was not well enough to travel, so he had sent Irons to meet privately with Deakin in his place. Julius Fielding was also at the meeting, along with other Melbourne legislators known to be supporters of federation.

"Parkes," said Irons, "feels that however we unite, we must remain attached to the Crown."

"Agreed," said Deakin. "To break that tie completely would spell certain defeat for federation. England is our mother. We will not cast her out."

"Next, Parkes wants to know your feelings on drafting a constitution, a federal constitution. One that speaks for all six colonies."

Deakin stroked his beard. The other Melburnians looked at him. Irons knew that his answer would be their answer.

"Yes," said a smiling Deakin. "God knows we will have the devil's own time getting Australians to agree on what it should contain, but yes, I say. Put pen to paper on this almighty issue and be done with it."

"And then," sighed Fielding, "we begin the rather tedious task of getting Australians to vote. A referendum will certainly be necessary, though it will undoubtedly be centuries before it is arranged and carried out."

"Ever the optimist," said Deakin. "First, our constitution. Dear God, that sounds beautiful. Our constitution. What does Parkes say it should contain?"

Irons pointed at Deakin. "You can be the first to answer that question, sir. Looking ahead, I would say that we must be careful. A national constitution will give us unity, but of a necessity it must also take sovereignty away from the colonies and that will be a cold plate of mutton for some to chew. They may find the meal indigestible and wish no part of it."

"Wisdom is often knowing when to be wise," said Deakin. "It will be our task to convince Australians that the moment for sacrifice of self interest has arrived."

"One man has said that federation means cheap meat and thus he is all for it," said Fielding.

All the men laughed. Deakin said, "That may well be

our approach, to convince our fellow men that they will all grow fatter from unity.''

''And suffer from its lack,'' said Irons. He thought of the telegram he had received from Morag telling him of the brushfire that had arisen out of the drought, bringing destruction to a large portion of the new sheep herd. He had telegraphed instructions to be passed on to Heath; even if they were followed immediately, and Irons had his doubts about Heath's ability to do so, there would still be a huge financial loss. Dai had his hands full with striking dock workers, though Irons had the feeling that Dai would have prefered that someone else deal with the unionists. He seemed to favor them at times, an attitude that drove Michael wild. Only Morag thought and acted as he did. God, if she were only a man. He would have made her his number two and worried a great deal less about his empire.

''Parkes feels a conference to deal with the constitution is in order,'' said Irons. ''It will involve voters choosing representatives and as you pointed out, that will take time.''

Deakin said, ''Time is what we do not have. Our house is afire. Labor troubles and fiscal uncertainty abound. We do not have time. There are events taking place in the world that cause me to fear for Australia's future. Germany, Austria and Italy have this year renewed a twelve year alliance. France and Russia have entered into an *entente*. Singularly, all of these nations are stronger than Australia as she is today. United, as some of them now are, they form a juggernaut that could crush us as one crushes a bug. If England should ever consider these new alliances a danger to herself, then she would have to turn her back on Australia to deal with that danger, leaving us to fend for ourselves. Let us make the most of what time we have. To delay is to risk paying a fearsome price.''

''Extinction,'' said Fielding and there were murmurs of agreement.

Another Melburnian asked Irons, ''So there is to be a conclave, a gathering?''

''Yes, said the Irishman. ''All colonies should have a

voice in this, through their representatives. However, I fear that Queensland and Western Australia might drag their heels. Queensland still talks of secession.''

"The heavy rains in that part of the north have turned their brains into pudding," said Fielding.

"And Western Australia," said Irons, "already considers itself apart from all, because of its distant location, and expresses little desire to fall into step."

"Our goal is a single unit, able to defend all. Not a small unit to be held hostage to the follies of one or two. We will persist, we will persevere and will not stop until our goal is reached. One Australia, gentlemen, and nothing less."

"Hear, hear." "Well said."

Deakins placed a hand on Irons' shoulder. "It could be that in a united Australia you might well emerge as a man of some influence and prominence."

Irons shook his head. "I do not seek public office. Even the small amount of political effort I expend on federation—"

"It is far from small, my friend."

"You are kind, Mr. Deakin, but whatever I do in this matter, though worthwhile, is often quite tiring as well as trying. I fear I lack the patience required for politics. With all due respect, nor could I put up with the almost daily diet of rogues and scoundrels one must encounter in the political process."

Fielding chuckled. "Aye, Michael Irons. You'll die once, which is to say when God calls you. But enter politics and they'll find a way to kill you ten times over."

The room was loud with laughter.

Deakin said to Irons, "So now you go to purchase some of our first-class Victoria horseflesh."

"Aye." Within the hour Michael and three of his men, including Johnny-Johnny, were due at the Bourke Street horse market to bid on some of the best livestock in Australia. When he had made his choices, Irons would hurry back to Sydney to deal with problems caused by the drought, leaving Johnny-Johnny and the others to bring the horses back to New South Wales by train.

Sir Darcy and Lady Corder were in Melbourne, too, a city both preferred for its strong British character. Darcy Corder openly despised Sydney, calling it "a sewer infested by Irishmen." Unfortunately, there were Sydneysiders who eagerly embraced Darcy Corder, favoring his upper class ways and snobbishness over anything natively Australian, which was shunted aside under the epithet "colonial."

As for Genista, her bizarre sexuality had trapped Irons; it was a drug spurring him to a recklessness he had never thought himself capable of. Was Genista right? Was there a connection between a man's power and the sexual feelings he was able to arouse in women? Perhaps there was. Henry Parkes was in his seventies and tiring, yet found the energy to bed a female believer or two, and there was the gross, pig-like George Reid, who was certainly no oil painting but who still fancied himself a ladies' man.

Genista. Clearly Irons fancied her because he could never be sure of her, because she lured, then rebuffed him. It was the challenge, the uncertainty, combined with the animal lust, that kept her on Irons' mind. Until no./ he had thought Lou Heller was the best bedmate he had ever had, but Genista Corder brought a new dimension to lovemaking, one that while physically satisfying, did not always bring peace to Irons' mind. He wondered if Lou suspected anything. Morag knew. She said nothing, but she knew. And disapproved.

At the horseshow, Irons and the two white workers who had accompanied him—"coloreds" such as Johnny-Johnny were not allowed inside—sat in the first row. Behind them and to the right was Lord a'Becket, his son Denis and several of their friends and associates. No one in the two parties acknowledged one another and those sitting nearby were aware of the coolness between them. Irons and a'Becket, however, concentrated on the horses, consulting their programs, whispering to their associates and pointing to animals that pleased or impressed them.

And then what spectators at the show had been waiting for happened: Irons and a'Becket began bidding against each other. The horse was an Arabian, a beautiful gray animal with a white mane and small head, well cared for and with the look of a racing winner about him. The bidding started at five hundred pounds and when it went to two thousand, only Irons and a'Becket were left. All eyes were on the two men, who at no time acknowledged one another's presence.

"Twenty-five hundred," said Irons.

"Three thousand." a'Becket offered the figure disdainfully.

"Four."

"Five thousand."

Irons fished about in his pocket for a cigar. "Seven."

a'Becket hesitated before saying, "Seventy-five hundred."

Irons lit his cigar, then blew out the match. "Nine thousand pounds."

"Ten thousand pounds." The crowd stirred.

"Fifteen thousand," said Irons. The silence was deafening.

a'Becket hesitated. He was about to reply when a small man, an Albino, came down the aisle, leaned over and whispered in his ear and for the first time a'Becket looked at Irons, whose back remained turned to the banker. a'Becket then whispered to his son.

"Lord a'Becket," said the auctioneer. "The bid is to you, sir."

a'Becket shook his head, declining. The crowd let out its breath, relaxed and chattered nervously.

While the men around Irons joyfully congratulated him, a'Becket nodded to the Albino. a'Becket had just been told of the meeting between Deakin, Irons, Fielding and the others, and he now knew how Fielding had outwitted him in the matter of the banking bill. The nod to the Albino was Julius Fielding's death sentence.

*   *   *

The wide, tree-lined boulevards of Melbourne, its royal parks and zoological gardens, its weatld, gothic mansions and apeing of British manners, hid a dark side of slums, waterfront saloons and street crime. Of the various street gangs one of the most vicious was *The Crutchies*, a gang of cripples who robbed, maimed and killed Melburnians and unwary visitors to the beautiful port city.

Tonight Julius Fielding, his belly full of oysters, eels, mussels and cockles from an oyster shop and his head light from too many American style cocktails, the new mixed drink from the United States, made his way through the stalls and shops of the open air Queen Victoria market. There were smells of the foods of many nations and flowers and fish that had not been sold during the day. There were barrows, carts, coaches and carriages nearby, some loaded with trash, some empty and ready to go off and bring back tomorrow's goods. The market was about to close down, to rest a few hours before opening up *when swallows chirp*, which meant bright and early and long before dawn.

Fielding had friends down here, men and women who made their living selling everything from cloth to stolen goods. He enjoyed the market—felt at hime in its vulgar, down-to-earth hurly burly—and the people loved him, too. They made fun of his girth and his hearty appetite, but knew him as a good man, as one of them. He had wanted oysters and good drink, but he had also wanted to reassure himself that the common people were still in favor of federation.

"Can't let the Russkies get us," a fishmonger's wife had said. "We have got to stand together and defend our virtue against the czar's mongol hordes."

Fielding had smiled and kissed her wrinkled brow. She was so ugly and reeked so strongly of fish that it would take a most desperate mongol with a poor sense of smell to inflict his carnal appetites upon her wizened carcass.

Now it was time to go home. It had been a long day,

what with a session in Parliament, the meeting with Irons, Deakin and the others and his tour of the market. It was times like these that he wished he could afford a driver, instead of having to wield the reins himself on a trap that had seen better days. Had he been less honest there would have been money for a fine coach and pair, but Fielding, for all his unorthodox sexual appetites, would never have dreamed of betraying those who had placed their trust in him. There were enough people in Parliament ready to speak out for special interests and not enough to speak up for the little man, the poor, the widow who needed less taxes and more shillings added to her pension. That's what had drawn him to Alfred Deakin. *Affable Alfred* cared about people and could not be made to betray them and long may he live.

In a trap pulled by a large gelding, Fielding made his way from the market and into Melbourne's narrow streets. The smell of garbage, rotting food and animal dung followed him for long blocks. In the growing darkness he saw men on step-ladders light gas jets and he wondered when the city council would approve the use of the electrical light for streets. He smiled, remembering that when the electrical light was recently introduced in London streets, people were afraid to touch a lamp post, thinking it contained heat. Most were convinced that the bulb was the result of a most peculiar flame, from a fire hidden within the post.

Fielding turned to his left, onto a street of slum housing and rotting tenements, where there were no gas jets and the only light came from a cross street ahead. In the semi-darkness he saw a sprinkling of cripples on either side of the street and he reached in his pocket for coins to toss to them. One, a pitifully thin boy in dirt-encrusted rags, pushed away from the wall and swung himself forward on a single, crude crutch, a hand inside his ragged clothing, seemingly to hide another deformity. Pulling back on the reins, Fielding smiled at the lad, who smiled back, showing blackened teeth and gaps where the others

had fallen out. The rest of the cripples closed in and
Fielding leaned forward to hand them the coins.

Quickly, the small boy reached in and with the knife
hidden in his hand cut one set of traces. On the other side,
a cripple cut the others. They shouted at the horse which
fled. Fielding, suspecting nothing, was slow to react. When
he saw his horse speed away all he could say was, "Bloody
beast" and he was about to laugh when he felt a sharp pain
in his side. A crutchie had stabbed him and now a dozen
others swarmed over the large man, who sat in his trap,
attacking him with knives, broken bottles, cudgels, chains.
Like a doomed, great beast with fight still remaining in
him, Fielding lashed out with his arms and legs, cursing
and spitting, sending the cripples flying in all directions.

"Help me! I am being attacked! Help me!" His cries
echoed down the dark, quiet street as he awkwardly leaped,
tripped and fell from the carriage to the dirty cobblestone
street. On his knees he swung an arm to the side, sending
a crutchie flying. But one stabbed him high on the shoulder and another brought a crutch down on his skull. Still,
the fat man did not die. He made his way to his feet, still
crying out, running as best he could, his bulk waddling
from side to side.

A whip whistled through the air, caught his ankle, then
tightened and Fielding was down on one knee, pawing at
the air. He screamed as a hamstring was cut and a crutch
crashed into an elbow. On his back he lashed out, a heavy
leg catching a crutchie in the face, but a disheveled girl of
twelve with rheumy eyes threw herself on his back, her
sharp teeth clamping down on his ear. Fielding fell
backwards, hands reaching for the girl and two crutchies
limped closer, then brought their cudgels down on his
knees, again and again, crushing them.

Seconds later a screaming Fielding disappeared under
the mob of murderous cripples. Suddenly, his screams
ceased. The crutchies, however, had more to do. They
stripped the fat man of his wallet, watch, rings, clothing,
boots, leaving him naked, bleeding and dead on the cobbles.

A one-legged, one-armed woman, who had seen Fielding kick her lover, stood over him and balancing herself on her one leg, lifted her crutch high, bringing it down on his face.

Then gathering their wounded with crutches scraping against the cobbles, they slithered away into the night like deadly rats. Fielding lay on his back, blood flowing from multiple wounds and spreading out like dark tentacles reaching for the abandoned trap several feet away.

Inside the railway car parked in the Melbourne freight yard, Johnny-Johnny sat up suddenly, awakened from a sound sleep. The three prize horses that Irons had purchased were asleep standing up at the far end of the car. The Aborigine and the two whites with him slept on straw at the other end, pistols and rifles nearby, a precaution against thieves. Tomorrow, the car would be hooked to a train heading north. At the border, it would have to be unhooked, then connected to a different train to finish the journey to New South Wales. Each colony had a different railroad guage, making it necessary to change trains each time you reached a border. It was an inconvenience which bothered Irons more than it did Johnny-Johnny, who prefered to travel by horse or on foot anyway. He needed the open air and the sun beating down on him and not the stares and insults found when travelling on trains with white Australians.

What had awakened Johnny-Johnny was a sound outside of the boxcar. It could be thieves or the night watchman. But then the Aborigine's sixth sense warned him and he smelled the smoke and he remembered the dream, where his totem had alerted him. He kicked the man nearest him and pulled at the other.

"Bloody Abo, what the hell—"

"Get up! We must get outside quickly."

"Another one of your wierd dreams, I 'spects."

The other man was instantly alert and respectful of Johnny-Johnny's intuition. He'd seen it work in the past. "You know the 'Iron Pirate' says we was to pay attention to Johnny and you know neither one of them two talks rubbish. What you been hearin', Johnny?''

"Smell smoke. Hear sounds outside. People outside."

Both whites found their guns. "People? More than one?"

One of the horses stirred and whinnied and then the three animals were awake. Smoke was entering the car near them, flowing up through the floor and floating down from the roof. Johnny-Johnny was on his feet. "Cut the horses loose. You—" he pointed to one man—"Slide the door open, then we will mount the horses and try to escape."

"Mount? You be fuckin' crazy. Them horses ain't completely broke and we ain't got no saddles. We be ridin' bareback—"

The second white man grabbed the front of the other's shirt. "Maybe you don't like Abos, but I'll wager you like livin' as much as I do. Johnny here is wise in ways you and me ain't ever gonna understand. He says we ride, we ride. the 'Iron Pirate' didn't send him along because he's a ravin' beauty. Johnny's smart, he is. You listen and do what he says or by God, I will put me foot so far up your arse it'll come out through your ugly face.''

He shoved him away and said to the Aborigine, "You're the 'silver-tall' here, Johnny. We be followin' you, like the 'Iron Pirate' wants.''

"Good. Cut the horses free before they become more frightened."

"Who's out there mate?"

"People. Bad people."

"Be needin' the guns, I suspect."

"Yes."

"Fine. Let's get on with it, then."

Johnny-Johnny approached the Arabian, remembering his dream and, at the same time, trying not to remember it. The horse shied away, its eyes bulging. The Aborigine whispered to it, reached out to stroke it and hoped that it could not smell his fear. And then he had its rope; he cut it, quickly stepped forward, grabbed a handful of mane

and swung himself into the saddle. The second white was
already mounted and the third, at the open door, hung
back. Johnny-Johnny, his gun in his hand, tried to control
his mount with his knees. His horse, however, was becoming more and more panicked by the smoke.

"Come on!" he yelled to the man at the door. "Get
mounted!"

Defiantly, the man stood his ground, planting his feet in
the open doorway. "Ain't nothin' out there. Accidental
fire, is all. Ain't nothin'—"

Hands reached up, grabbed his ankles and yanked him
screaming off his feet. He disappeared from sight. A
crutch was raised high in the air, then came down and the
man stopped screaming. Crutchies. Sent by Lord a'Beckett
to kill the prize Arabian, rather than see Irons have it.

The white with Johnny-Johnny said, "We got to help
him!"

"No. He is dead. Ride and do not look back if you want
to live."

Slapping the Arabian's flanks with his bare heels, the
Aborigine led the way, walking to the edge of the boxcar,
then calling to the horse, pushing it with his knees and the
Arabian leaped, was airborne for seconds, then landed on
its haunches and fought its way to its feet. There was pain
in Johnny-Johnny's calf as a crutchie slashed at his Achil-
les tendon and missed, getting the calf muscle instead.
Clubs were swung at him and the horse as the crutchies
attacked screaming.

Gripping the mane with both hands, the Aborigine brought
his horse to its hind legs, letting the animal lash out with
its front legs. Two crutchies screamed, falling back with
broken bones. The Arabian touched down and Johnny-
Johnny pulled his pistol, firing twice, sending a ragged,
one-legged woman flying.

The other white had not fared as well as the Aborigine.
His horse had panicked, throwing him and he was on the
ground, kicking, punching, trying to ward off a swarm of
attackers who menaced him with knives, clubs, broken

bottles. One had the man's gun and was about to use it on him when Johnny-Johnny dropped him with a single shot. Urging the Arabian forward, the Aborigine charged the cripples, scattering them. Now the white man, bleeding and hurt, was on his knees, his pistol in his hand and firing. Johnny-Johnny fired, too. Two, three, then four crutchies fell. The rest ran, ducking under railway cars and scattering throughout the railyard.

Dismounting, the Aborigine ran to the white.

"Get me to a doctor quick, mate. Me wife ain't gonna like this new shirt she made for me gettin' mucked about."

He looked at the Aborigine. "You could have gotten away. You didn't have to come back for me, you know. Ain't too sure I'd have done the same for you."

But there was unspoken gratitude on his blood-stained face.

Still, he was badly hurt. "Johnny, lad, tell me. Am I gonna live?"

The Aborigine looked up at the sky before answering, then lied. "Yes, mate. You will live."

Minutes later the man died in Johnny-Johnny's arms.

16

FROM a peephole in his office wall, Blue Dan Costello looked down on the large gaming room below, where tables were packed with men and women playing "Two-Up", craps, keno, American and French roulette, poker and hazard. The Spring Street casino was elegant down to the last detail, and staffed by beautiful waitresses in knee-boots and togas designed to show bare thighs and well groomed male dealers in white tie and tails. It was an honest club, foregoing marked cards, shaved dice and off-limits to *broadsmen*, cardsharps, *dippers*, pickpockets and *bug hunters*, those who specialized in robbing drunks. Which is why Blue Dan was annoyed at finding a *smasher*, a passer of false money, at one of his "Two-Up" tables.

The muscular, red-headed Irishman looked away from the peephole to the pound notes in his left hand. They were a good job of counterfeiting, featuring an excellent likeness of the Queen and better quality paper than anything Blue Dan had ever used when he was coining. But the lettering was a bit wobbly and the biggest mistake of all was the numbering. Each note contained the same numbers, which was inevitable with a single set of plates. The ruddy bastard who was passing the notes tonight didn't seem upset at losing. He would have been, had he known what Blue Dan had in mind for him.

Closing the Judas-slit, Blue Dan turned to smile at his brother, Alan. "So now. In love with the 'Iron Pirate's' darling daughter, are you?"

Alan, a leaner version of his older brother, sat on a corner of a desk, thumbs hooked in the pockets of a checkered vest. "I've never met a woman like her. Bright as a new penny, with a mind of her own. Stands up to her father, which her brothers are havin' trouble doing and she *reads*, dear God, that woman reads."

"Then she's for you. Your nose has been in a book since you crawled out of the womb."

"Time speeds by when I'm with her, Dan. Goes by too fast, I'm thinkin'. I'm thirty-three and she can make me feel like a schoolboy who's wet his pants."

"Taken her to bed, yet?"

Alan blushed.

Blue Dan grinned. "I see. You haven't."

"Had my share of tumblin' judy after judy, but with Morag, that doesn't seem to matter. It's somethin' special between us, was from the first and we both knew it. The rest of what belongs between a man and a woman will come in time. Have no fear of that."

Blue Dan poured two glasses of rum and handed one to his brother. "Irons knows nothing, still?"

Alan looked into his glass and sighed. "I'm still 'Mr. Morgan' when I telephone and I have yet to call at her home. We sneak about like footpads and thieves, afraid to be seen together. I don't like it one bit."

He tossed down all of the rum, made a face and held out his empty glass. Blue Dan refilled it and tried to make the next question sound unimportant. "Irons still givin' the very social Lady Corder a poke?"

"Morag thinks so, though it's not what you call your accepted love affair with regular hours and such. Irons, she says, doesn't see that much of the aristocratic Genista and sometimes it puts him off his feed. But he's not upset enough to throw himself into the harbor, unfortunately. He's got a big business to run, which is one reason he's dashing about pushing federation. Wants to protect that business, he does, and feels a strong, central government just might do the trick.''

"Give the devil his due," said Blue Dan. "Irons is also worried about Australia. Feels we should be strong enough to defend ourselves and the bastard's right. Been a fighter all my life and I've learned this much: when you can take care of yourself, the world walks around you. Doesn't give you a bit of trouble. Irons wants that for Australia and I can't blame him. I'm a gambler and I wouldn't give you two bob for this country's chances of winnin' a war, any bloody war. Least not the way we're shapin' up now.''

Alan got off the desk and stretched. "Strange that me and Irons are fightin' for the same thing, each in our way, and we cannot shake hands and fight together. Morag says he's a wonderful man, that if he and I got to know one another we'd be mates.''

Blue Dan looked at a painting of 'Dancing Girl', the price race horse he had given to Lou Heller. "Mr. Irons has a way of ingratiating himself with the best of us.'' He wondered if Lou Heller knew of Irons' affair with Genista Corder.

Blue Dan spun around to face Alan. "Well, you are in need of funds for this labor politicking of yours." He walked to a huge safe, a square block of iron and steel that stood taller than he, and began to dial the combination.

"Money is the oil that greases the wheels of any machine hopin' to move forward," said Alan. "Dai Irons gives a bit now and then, though he has to keep his father in the dark about it. On my birthday, Morag gave me ten quid. Says buy a new suit and look pretty on your first day in Parliament. The rich of Sydney resents us being in Parliament, but we're there to stay. For certain, our numbers will grow and one blessed day, may it come soon, our voices will drown out those of the rich, and their bloody lackeys.''

Using two hands, Blue Dan pulled open the thick door to his safe. "So, it is to be your hand on the whip, then, is it? And whose back will taste the lash on that fine day? Someone always bleeds, mate, no matter who is master. 'Tis the way of the world."

He removed a sheaf of pound notes, closed the safe and spun the tumblers before handing the money to his brother. "When you trade unionists rule over us mortals, what can we expect—a new day or more of the same?"

Alan pocketed the money. "It's our turn, Dan, and we mean to have it. Change is all that's permanent in this world, so let it be change in our favor and we'll see what comes of that. Our mother and father didn't live to see me sittin' on a bench in Parliament, waitin' to be called the right honorable Alan Costello. But I bet they would have been in favor, wouldn't you say?"

He put a hand on his brother's shoulder. "We were alone in the world, you and I, eatin' garbage to stay alive in these streets and shiverin' in doorways when the rains came 'cause we had no clothes, no place to lay our heads. Well, we survived, with you doin' the fightin' with your fists. Now, it's time for a different kind of fightin'. It's me now, sittin' in Parliament and makin' new laws."

"Still room for the old kind of fightin'," said Blue Dan. "Some of you unionists play tough, knockin' heads and even killin' a few people. I heard about forcin' the shearers to join under threats of beatings or worse."

Alan looked away. "Not proud of that, but it had to be done. There was no other way of persuadin'."

"And what of the day when you have to use that form of persuadin' against Michael Irons or his kin. Will his daughter still stand beside you?"

Alan's jaw tightened.

Blue Dan's voice softened. "You're me brother and you're a man with his heart set on the daughter of someone who could make a great deal of trouble for you if you hurt her in any way. To add to the problem, you've also made a friend of that same man's son and I ask you what happens when the son is asked to do more than give money and applaud your speeches.''

"Dai and I have spoken of this. I will respect his decision, whatever it is. In truth, I feel I can count on him. He grows stronger for our cause every day. Soon, he tells me, he may leave his father's business and come with us publically.''

"May, he says. Brother of mine, 'tis said that no man can chase two rabbits at the same time. This Dai, he'll have to choose his rabbit and there'll be no maybe about it. As for Irons, he seems to have at least figured a way to have as many women as he pleases, when he pleases.''

Blue Dan's voice hardened. "I'd like him to choose.

"It's still Lou, isn't it?''

Dan held his brother's gaze. "I've never been so alive as I was with her. It's not been the same without her. Heart's on me sleeve and she knows it, but it does me no good. While Irons lives she won't even look in me direction.''

"You can't kill him, you know that.''

"Yes. It would blacken me in her eyes forever. Someone else would have to do me that small service, but you know me well enough to realize I'd never set a man to do that kind of chore. Either I do it meself or it remains undone.''

Alan smiled. "I love you, brother of mine. You bend the law and you have the largest swagstore in Sydney and you've done a few men in your time, who more or less deserved it. But you're not scum and you have some idea of right and wrong.''

"Like I said, Irons won't go to his eternal rest at my hand, tho' in truth if it happened I wouldn't be too downhearted. You ought to look in on my swagstore, by the way. Never know what you might find. Drop by when you feel the need or do you still have a conscience about such things?''

A swagstore was a warehouse of stolen goods and Blue

Dan's swagstore was the talk of Sydney. It contained everything from antiques to carriages and oriental rugs and owed its existence to police corruption.

"I still have a conscience about such things," said Alan with a grin. "I'll just sit in Parliament and pass laws and take from the rich in that fashion."

"My way's better. You don't need a quorum."

Blue Dan did have his idea of right and wrong; when it came to cheating him, it was wrong to do so and right for him to stop it any way he saw fit. And so the *smasher*, the passer of counterfeit money, was brought into his office, gagged and tied to a chair, with both arms roped to the chair's arms. "You're bad for business," said Blue Dan to the perspiring, squirming man. "The players will think I take their good money and give them bad and the police will think even worse of me. I've done some time in prison and believe me, jocko, it is no bed of roses in there. So, what I am about to do to you is a warnin'. Don't come back to my club anymore. And if you have friends, tell them I don't appreciate cheats pickin' me pocket in any way, shape or form."

Blue Dan nodded. And a large man standing beside the trussed-up *smasher* brought an iron bar down on first one hand, then the other, breaking both. The *smasher* tried to scream; veins jumped out on his neck and his eyes bulged. His sphincter muscles loosened and he fouled himself.

"Take him out and drop him a ways from here. Put a pound note in his pocket. Real money this time. Never leave a man with empty pockets."

The *smasher's* feet dragged along the carpet as Blue Dan's men carried him out of the office and through a passage in the wall that led down to a back alley. Violence excited the gambler; it had been a part of his life since he was a boy and now, as a 40 year-old hardened underworld leader it was still a necessary tool of the trade. Alan's relationship with Dai and Morag Irons could mean trouble for him, meaning trouble with Irons himself. That could mean more violence, pitting Irons and Blue Dane against each other in open conflict. If anything happened to Alan, Blue Dan wouldn't hesitate to kill the man responsible. Even if it was Irons. *Especially if it was Irons.*

17

1892. Bank failures in the six colonies had become an epidemic, with every indication that this disastrous trend would continue for some time to come. Unable to get loans, a growing number of Australian businessmen were ruined or sought to survive by hiring non-union labor, a practice that met with stiff trade union resistance. Power, however, remained with business, for it controlled Parliament, police, militia and the economic structure, the elements that could and did crush almost every strike. Strike breaking was accepted and often highly praised, as were the fines and jail terms levied against some union leaders.

Why the bank failures?

"We bloody borrowed too much," said Alfred Deakin to Michael Irons. "Spend, spend, spend. That's what we did, seeing this great land as a golden goose with an inexhaustible supply of golden eggs. Land, gold, wool, shipping, wheat. They would make us all rich, we thought. But now the world has an abundance of these items and we who traded in them, to the exclusion of all else, including faith in God, must now pay the penalty for our short sightedness."

"England helped us dig this hole," said Irons. "They gave us enough rope—"

"Enough pounds, you mean."

"They overfed us and now we are sick and England turns its back on us. There will be little money from them in months to come."

"Do not blame England, my friend. Blame Australia's love of money. The people in Sydney and Melbourne talk of little else."

It was true. The making of money, particularly for those in these two cities, had become all that mattered. If a vote were taken today in New South Wales on federation, in Irons' opinion the proposition could go down to defeat. George Reid, a growing political power in the colony and a man whom Deakin despised and did not trust, irked Irons with his lukewarm support for Australian unity.

"It means separation from Britain and I do not like that," said Reid. "Why do you not assign the Crown a larger role in Australian unity?"

"Because Australia is for Australians," said Irons.

"Ah yes." Reid spoke in a drawl slow enough for anyone listening to understand his every word. "The new slogan. On the lips of one and all. This year's catch phrase."

"It says what is in our hearts."

" 'The heart has its reason/which reason does not know'."

"I, too, have read Pascal, but he is long dead and his country, France, could well be a future enemy of Australia."

The fat politician grinned slyly. "You are an Irishman and so your desire to be free of England is understandable. But most Australians have strong ties to the Crown and I fear that does not mean a unanimous show of hands for the business of federation. My regards to the 'Melbourne Mystic', Mr. Deakin, when you see him. Tell him not to waste time attempting to levitate. He already stands head and shoulders above the rest of us without any aid from the teachings of the unholy Hindu."

* * *

"Fat, selfish pig," said Deakin of Reid. "That is why I prefer dealing with you to dealing with him or his sychophants. Mr. Yes-No has already begun to court the labor parliamentarians in your colony."

"I've heard he has, yes. To what end?"

"You should know. He wants to be your colony's premier in the not too distant future. Should labor continue to grow in political power, brother Reid will thus have a wider political base and more support for his ambition."

Deakin eyed Irons before saying, "Labor will grow, my friend. There is no stopping this idea, whose time has come."

"I can neither forgive nor forget that it was trade unionists who killed Davy Pease."

"And all over Australia today trade unionists themselves are being killed or jailed. No one wants to change, not Australia's rich, not the British who regard us as ugly step-children, not your average Australian, who wishes to lose none of his privileges in a united country and not even you, my friend. But I will not press you upon this point. How fares your bank?"

Irons grinned. "Perhaps I should have listened to my daughter, who some time ago advised me to liquidate that part of my business. It stands on quicksand, sir. Oh, it appears solvent for short periods of time, but we seem to lurch from one crisis to another, barely surviving. Morag is responsible for the only good economic news I have enjoyed in some time. Bicycles, as you know, are the rage in our two colonies and fast becoming so throughout Australia. It was Morag who saw their coming popularity and convinced me to open a half dozen bicycle shops in Sydney. All are profitable. We cannot sell bicycles fast enough."

Bicycles, however, had their detractors. Irons told Deakin that farmers often shot at them, believing bicycles frightened cattle. In a complaint to Sydney authorities farmers insisted that all cyclists be preceded by a buglar on foot or continuously ring bells as they rode. Morag struck back.

She organized a protest of hundreds of cyclists, and had them ride through Sydney streets en masse, ringing cowbells, hand bells, toy bells and blowing bugles. The city council immediately dropped the bell proposal.

Deakin laughed. "God bless us, Michael. Morag supports federation. If she did not, we would have great cause to worry. I heard that you had trouble with your sheep. The drought—"

"Cost me dearly. Again, to be honest, Morag was against my buying them, but I went ahead because my son Heath thought differently. The drought and rabbits doomed my new flocks. I ended up killing all but breeding ewes and studs. The rest I boiled down."

Boiling down meant slaughtering the sheep, then sealing them in metal containers and boiling down the animal until meat, bones, wool disappeared and nothing remained but fat, which was then turned into tallow.

"Sheep sells for a shilling an animal these days," said Irons. "Same price as forty years ago. Not good. Not good at all."

"Morag appears to be a clever little thing. You should rely on her more. I assume this drought means that I will not get any wine from your vineyard, the one so dear to the heart of Sir Darcy Corder and his wife."

Irons sighed. "Utter failure, that. Vines dried up, the earth turned sour, the grapes shriveled like a witch's tit. Cost me a few thousand quid, it did."

Genista. Irons had come to Melbourne to seek Deakin, true, but also to see Genista, who not surprisingly continued to prefer this pseudo-British city to Sydney. She had promised to meet him here and his loins ached at the thought of being with her. But when he arrived, she had left; on impulse she had decided to sail to London and Paris to have new clothes and boots made. It was a rotten thing to do and Irons had no idea what he would say to her when next they met.

"Michael," said Deakin, "promise me something."

Deakin's eyes bored into Irons as though painting pictures of his soul.

"Promise me," said the Melbourne politician, "that you will be one of the delegates at next year's conference." Next year representatives to be appointed by voters in all six colonies were to meet in Corowa on the Murray River and draft a constitution for a united Australia.

"Alfred, the voters must decide."

"Let them decide on you. We need good men, not straws in the wind like Reid. And how much longer will men like Parkes live? I will feel better having you there. Stand for the position, Michael. The voters will choose you as a delegate if you run."

"Is that the mystic or the politician talking?"

"It is the friend talking, one who prefers having at least one other friend at his back in what Dickens wrote of in another connection as 'the best of times and the worst of times'."

It was then that Irons mentioned Julius Fielding.

"I admit he was on my mind," said Deakin. "When I mentioned your attending the conference. Do not ask me if I have looked into the future and seen danger." He chuckled. "I am not the mystic I am painted. I read certain books, entertain particular beliefs, but my feet are on the ground, never fear. The police have gotten no further than the crutchies in placing responsibility for his death. By an unfortunate coincidence it appears that your Aborigine friend killed the crutchies' leader and there was no one to answer questions."

"The attack on my horse leads me to believe it was a'Becket behind both black deeds. Could not a'Becket have been vexed enough with Fielding over the matter of the banking report to have ordered his death?"

"That report was offered some time back."

"a'Becket can be patient when needs be. And has not the report been shunted aside since Fielding's death?"

"In truth, yes. Without him to push it there has been a slackening off of interest in regulating Victoria's banks.

We are paying a price for that now. Our excessive interest in land speculation has come back to haunt us as well. The land business becomes more and more precarious each hour and I fear that when it collapses, Melbourne will be the worse for it.''

Deakin closed his eyes. ''Dear Fielding. His heart was as big as the man. It's monstrous that he died in such brutal fashion. And your man fared no better. Also dead at the hands of the crutchies.'' He opened his eyes. ''Lord a'Becket has not lessened his opposition to federation. I wonder how far he would go to prevent it?''

''We both know that he attempted to blackmail Fielding and now Fielding is dead. a'Becket has gone *that* far, my friend.''

The two men were silent. Then Irons said, ''You may count on me to do my best to be a delegate at next year's conference. At fifty years of age, I should be sitting on my arse a bit more and if the sitting on it in conference brings good to Australia, so much the better.''

When the moon slipped behind a cloud, the slim, cloaked figure moved from a tree and hurried across the lawn, stopping when restless horses in a nearby stable whinnied nervously. In the harbor to the left seagulls circled low over the water in search of food, calling to each other in shrill cries. When the horses were silent the figure continued to the huge gothic mansion that was the a'Becket home, crossing a patio that led to a set of French doors. A twist of a knife between the doors and the flimsy lock gave way and the doors parted. Inside, the figure stopped, listened carefully and looked around, recognizing familiar sights, smells, hearing clocks chime the hours in various parts of the house.

Joyfully, the intruder hurried towards the living room, remembering the caged canaries that had been there for a long time. There was no need to turn on gas jets or electricity. The house was an old friend and held no secrets. The pleasure at being here once more was so strong that the intruder almost cried out with joy, but kept silent. Tonight's visit was a planned impulse, a dream that on the spur of the moment the intruder had decided to live out, to bring to life. The plan was to keep silent and move about the house, drawing strength from it once more, along with the sheer pleasure of once more being near things so dear and precious.

At the living room the intruder reached out to touch the thick brass handles on the redwood door, then dropped to the ground with sickening speed as a servant brought a cudgel down on the cloaked figure's skull. "Alarm!" cried the servant, bringing the cudgel down on the intruder's head again and again. "Thief! Thief!"

Gas jets were lit and servants raced to the scene, pulling on robes and carrying weapons, pistols, clubs, knives, chains. Surrounded by several men and women, the cloaked figure lay unmoving in front of the living room door. The knife used to pry open the side doors had fallen from a small hand and the servant who had brought the intruder down pointed to it without saying a word. The weapon was enough to indicate that the servant who had clubbed the intruder into unconsciousness or death had acted correctly.

When Lord a'Becket joined the group, it parted to let him near the prone body. a'Becket wore a white nightcap and a brocade robe and there was no pity in him for the man who had tried to rob him tonight. Woe to anyone who attempted to take what was his. He picked up the slim arm, felt its pulse and nodded. Dead. "Well done," he said to the servant who had killed the thief.

a'Becket pulled back the intruder's hood and almost fainted. Behind him he heard gasps and groans and to his left an Irish maid crossed herself and began to weep. Camilla lay on her side, her face peaceful at last, long dark hair matted with her own blood.

a'Becket took her in his arms and the sound from the banker, a keening that held all the sadness of all time, was so heartbreaking that the strongest of the men watching wept with him.

18

THE Melbourne brothel specialized in girl prostitutes between the ages of eight and twelve, all with blonde hair and wearing a golden ring in a pierced left breast. Only recommended gentlemen of the most elite social class were accepted as patrons; hence, the presence there tonight of Denis a'Becket and Sir Darcy Corder. Known as "Miss Chapel's Private School", the brothel was in the south of the city, near the Princess Bridge and faced the huge Flinders Street rail station which stood at the top of St. Kilda Road, Melbourne's most majestic boulevard. In a room covered in Art Nouveau wallpaper, with its winding, luxuriant lines of climbing flowers, serpents and elongated nudes, Denis and Corder sat on a purple velvet couch and drank champagne. Behind them, a lean German woman with an impassive face played Liszt on a harp as the two men watched naked girl children parade before them.

Neither man was in a hurry to make a choice. First, there was business to take care of. It was the middle of 1893 and Corder had lost thousands of pounds in a land speculation scheme of the a'Beckets. He had also suffered personal losses in New South Wales and was currently saddled with an expensive racing stable there, which had yet to produce enough winners to pay for itself. Denis had asked for this meeting, promising to show Corder how to make money without investing a penny. Like his predecessor Nat Gane, Corder had also begun embezzling from Ferdinand Brothers in order to take risks in Australian commerce. Now he was desperately looking for a way to replace that money before his losses mounted or were discovered. And there was still the dream of growing rich in this cultural desert of a country and returning to London independent of his father.

"Heath Irons has secretly come to you for money," said Denis.

"Quite. He wishes to re-open his father's mines, this time working for himself. Silly sod. Doesn't want his father to know, of course. On behalf of Ferdinand Brothers I refused him a loan, naturally."

"So you mentioned. I've just received a cable from my father in France. He wishes you to change your mind."

"Are you mad? Every fool over the age of two knows those mines are played out. There's not an ounce of gold to be found there."

"You mentioned something else, I believe. Heath Irons plans to bring in Chinese laborers to work the mines."

"He did say that, yes. Not exactly the height of wisdom, if you ask me. Your labor unions won't sit still for that bit of business. Not when they rise in Parliament these days and talk of a 'White Australia' and threaten death to niggers, wogs, and may I add, to Kanakas as well, to any colored worker who sets foot on these accursed shores. 'Australia for Australians' is, in effect, another way of saying whites only. Not that I blame the unionists, of course. Keep the niggers and such in their place, which is far away from civilized whites."

Denis nodded his balding head, eyes on a ten year-old girl, who posed lasciviously in front of him, brazen in her nakedness. "I quite agree with you, old fruit. Let us not become contaminated by lesser stock. And one could certainly expect trouble for any man foolish enough to import Chinese workers in such chaotic times as these.''

Darcy pointed to a twelve-year-old, whose breasts were more developed than the rest of the girls. ''I say, she's beginning to blossom forth, isn't she. By the by, how is your father?''

''Coming along nicely, thank you. Expects to return to Melbourne before year's end.''

Shocked by the death of Camilla in his home, a'Becket had taken a six month leave of absence from Australia. He had travelled first to England and was now completing a tour of the European continent. During that time he had kept in touch with Denis regarding their companies; no major decision was taken without his approval. The instant Denis had learned from Corder that Heath Irons had approached him for a business loan, he knew the news would be of interest to his father. He was right. Lord a'Becket had devised a scheme to revenge himself on the Irons family and aiding Heath was the first step.

At Camilla's funeral, held in Melbourne, neither the a'Beckets nor Michael Irons had acknowledged each other. Irons, of course, had ignored the telegram from Camilla's family asking him not to show up. He had appeared at the church services and followed the hearse to the cemetary in a carriage, where he had been accompanied by Alfred Deakin and other Melbourne friends. There was nothing the a'Beckets could do about Irons' presence, but it was no secret that they held him responsible for her death. It was he, they believed, who made her so unhappy that she was compelled to make the desperate trip to Melbourne on that fateful night. Someone else had clubbed her to death, but it was Michael Irons who had all but put the weapon in his hand.

The a'Beckets wanted their own back and knowingly or not, Sir Darcy Corder was going to help them get it. Meanwhile, 'Marvelous Melbourne', once a beautiful, prosperous and proud city, had fallen upon hard times. The business of dealing in land had turned disastrous for all concerned. Thousands had lost all they had. Even the a'Beckets had seen some of their real estate money disappear, though thanks to some last minute finagling by Denis, their losses had been minimized.

And then there were the bank failures. The situation had become so bad that there were rumors saying all Victoria banks would close some time in May, for at least five days. And the number of Melbourne politicians who were being implicated in these bank failures was growing. Criminal charges had been filed against some of the politicians who had sat on the board of certain banks. Denis wondered if it might not have been prudent to have adopted the banking controls Julius Fielding had proposed last year.

The good times for Australians seemed to have gone; it was strikes and bankruptcies now and in the background, the incessant cry for federation, for unity. Bugger unity. Denis and his father would profit by this chaos and there would be no need to submit to the authority of Sydney and its convict scum, which is what a unified Australia meant.

Corder, becoming increasingly drunk in "Miss Chapel's Private School," kicked off his boots. "Damn Michael bloody Irons. Fellow doesn't know his place. What I despise about him is the way he carries himself, as if he were Lord High Priest or some such. Rotten Irish scum. Had the nerve to threaten me, not long ago. Said that it might be a good idea if someone were to check on Ferdinand Brothers' finances these days."

"And if that happens," said Denis. "If someone does check?"

Corder chuckled. "They'll find a bit of fiddling's been going on."

"Suspected as much. So here's your chance. Advance the money to Heath."

"Can't, old fruit. Poor credit risk, that one."

"My father and I will give you the money. Which, of course, will be our little secret. We will also assume your debt to the land syndicate here in Melbourne."

Corder raised his eyebrows. "Dear me. Seems Father Christmas has come early this year. And he has a slight lisp."

Denis smiled. "Of course, if you would rather have Irons press for an investigation of your company . . ."

"Bugger Irons. Bugger you, too." He paused, then muttered, "Actually, I prefer to bugger that pretty little thing who just entered the room, the one with the blue ribbon in her hair and sassy way of moving her bum. I do believe I have made my choice."

Denis took his arm in a firm grip. "First, sir, you will choose to do as my father wishes. Pass on our money to Heath Irons and encourage him in his plans to re-open the mine. And use Chinese workers."

"Why should I help you and your bloody father?"

"Because, you drunken sod, it is the only way to keep Irons from tearing down your house of cards. If you do not do as we ask, Irons shall learn of your thieving ways. Now—your answer."

Corder grinned. "My answer is," he bowed, "I am at your service." He looked at the child prostitute he had selected, "Now, let that little dear draw closer. I wish her to be at my service. I most certainly wish that."

The Corowa conference, at which Michael Irons was a delegate, did not produce a constitution; it did, however, decide that the voters in all six colonies should have a more direct say in who was to draw up that constitution. Thus it was obvious to Irons that it would be years before such a document saw the light of day and more years before it was voted on. During that time, the depression which had seized the colonies, could continue unchecked. What tried Irons' patience at the conference was the dislike colony leaders had for one another.

"Jesus God," he said to Deakin, "most of our grand and glorious governors and premiers despise each other and make no secret of it. How can they expect the people of their colonies to act differently? At times like these the whole business seems hopeless. I fear you and I are on a fool's errand.''

''Remember, Michael, the old leaders such as Parkes and Grey of New Zealand, have been cock of the walk in their respective colonies for a long time. Each is well into his seventies and cannot possibly change. Neither wants to leave the stage to the other. Grey, I fear, will stick to his position of keeping New Zealand out of any federation, which he sees as a threat to its sovereignty.''

''Some of our New South Wales delegates are making similar noises. They feel we are the oldest colony and should not bow to any one under any circumstances. Is there a date for the next conference?''

''Sometime within the next two years. It's been agreed that we meet in Hobart, amidst Tasmania's fruit trees and within sight of its snow-capped mountains. More and more of us feel that our constitution should take the best of the American constitution and combine it with the best of Britain's.''

''Not too much from Britain, I trust.''

''Spoken like a true Irishman.''

As usual, Deakin was right. In fighting for Australian federation, Michael was waging a battle on behalf of his beloved father. Conor Irons and 'Young Ireland' had failed to free themselves of England, but Michael would not fail. Australia was going to be united and independent no matter how long it took. This time, Britain would not win. *Up the Iris'! Australia forever*.

''Your father would be proud,'' said Deakin, fixing his dark gaze on Michael as though seeing his thoughts.

Irons grinned, ''I still say you see more than we do and I am not refering to what one sees with his eyes.''

''I see a united Australia.''

''Then it will be so.''

''But not without great effort and I am afraid, some bloodshed.''

His words caused Irons to look at Deakin carefully. *What did the man see? Was the remark about bloodshed a reference to Irons himself or to Australia in general?*

"When it looks blackest for you, for us," said Deakin, "and you doubt the truth of what we are fighting for, remember your father, Micahel. Remember him."

19 _____

AT the knock on her dressing room door, Lou Heller eagerly turned from her makeup table. "Yes?"

"Flowers, Miss Heller."

Her shoulders dropped with disappointment. It was her birthday and she was hoping that Michael would drop by. She saw little of him these days; the "Iron Pirate" was busy with federation, with meetings here in Sydney and travelling to different colonies for conferences. And when he wasn't caught up in all that he was trying to keep his company's losses down at a time when all of Australia was facing economic disaster. So he had sent flowers. Well, at least he had remembered.

Lou slipped into a robe, belted it around her waist and walked to the door. Josey, the stage manager, could not be seen for the flowers surrounding him. The American singer smiled with pleasure, her eyes dazzled by the display of roses, orchids and at least ten different kinds of wildflowers. Their perfume was sweet and heady. She had never seen so many flowers at one time.

"If I was a bloody bee," said Josey. "I could die happy in all this lot. The man what sent 'em is a gent of the first order."

He handed her the card. "Fifteen minutes to curtain."

Lou held the card against her heart without reading it. *Michael had remembered.* She was wrong; there was no other woman. She had thought there might be, sensing it as women do. And if there were, what could she do about it? Hadn't they agreed? No promises—meaning Michael was free to love whom he pleased. Camilla was dead and Michael could even remarry if he chose. Lou would marry him in an instant, but that was a dream she kept to herself. With each day she had begun to see that he increasingly belonged to Australia, to the land he was trying to unify. Newspapers wrote of the "Iron Pirate" and federation, as though they were one and the same. The convict past that others hid or denied, Michael proudly spoke of. If the reason for federation was to strengthen Australia, it was also Michael's last debt to his beloved convict parents.

Lou looked at the card—and was devastated. The flowers were not from Michael; they were from Blue Dan Costello. She leaned back against the door and wept. Then to hide her tears, she ran into her dressing room; alone in front of the mirror she looked at herself and saw the years beginning to creep into her face. And at last she resolved to face the truth: Michael had found someone else.

In bed with Morag for the first time, Alan felt such tenderness and love that he wept, holding her close so that she could not see his tears. But his silence spoke volumes and she said, "I love you, too." They kissed gently, hands caressing each other's body and then the kissing became more insistent and the caresses stronger and Morag wanted him, but he whispered, "Wait."

She froze.

"It is a special time, lass. What I feel for you, I have only dreamed of in the past and I want you to know that. I give myself to you totally, Morag, my darling."

"I give myself to you, Alan. I am a little frightened, for I fear that one day the love we share may exact an awful price. But for now, I do not care. I am with you and my heart is full and I have never known such joy.''

He drew her close again and she surrendered to him as she had to no man before him. He was the first. The years of self denial, even the long secret courtship between her and Alan were to be worth the wait, for Morag would only give herself when she could do it without reservation. And she did so now, surprising Alan with her passion.

Later, he feigned exhaustion. "Morag, love, you have shortened my life, but I thank you for it.''

With her head on his chest, she listened to his heart. "And you have filled mine with unimaginable happiness.'' Lifting up her head, she smiled seductively. "And now that you have opened the floodgates, boyo, beware of those torrents of lust you have unleashed.''

"Praise God, are these torrents about to come down on my poor, tired body once more?''

Her hand went to his crotch. "I would say so, yes.''

He sighed in mock resignation. "Ah well. Never shirk your given task, me da' always said. We Costellos are as capable of lying down on the job, so to speak, as any other man.''

They both laughed as he covered her body with his.

Shortly before noon, from his warehouse office facing the docks, Dai Irons heard the pistol shots clearly. They came from one of his father's refrigeration ships. In seconds Dai and several of his workmen had rushed from the warehouse to the ship and stood at the bottom of its gangplank.

At the railing, a watchman leaned over and yelled through cupped hands. "We got the bastards. Three of them. Killed one of ours, though, and wounded a couple more. Bringin' them down to you, Mr. Irons.''

Minutes later the three captured men, hands tied behind their backs and walking ahead of gun carrying deckhands from the ship, stumbled down the gangplank. Dai's worst fears were realized. The three were trade unionists from

Alan Costello's dock workers union and Dai recognized each man. The youngest was barely sixteen and was the most terrified of the trio. As labor concentrated more on getting into Parliament, strikes were slackening, but some unionists were still frustrated enough to take direct action against their enemies. These three had taken action against Michael Irons.

"Damaged the freezin' compartments, they did," said the first mate. "Got two of the frost motors and if we can't repair them, some of the food we got in there's gonna spoil. Won't be able to sail until its put right. Killed Frank Pace. Fuckin' unionists." He punched the bound boy in the kidney, dropping him to his knees and making him cry out.

The unionists bound leader attempted to get to the first mate, but was held back. "We didn't mean to kill nobody," said the leader. "He fired first and we only tried to stay alive."

A clerk who worked with Dai said, "You destroy property and you kill a man and you think you should stay alive? You'll all be topped, that's for certain. Hanged until your bloody necks are as long as a giraffe's."

Someone behind Dai chuckled, but Dai, his eyes on the sixteen-year-old struggling to get to his feet, was looking into the future. He saw the boy walking up the stairs to the scaffold.

"Back to the warehouse with them," said Dai. "Someone go for the constable."

"I'll take care of that," said the clerk, who had talked of hanging. "Have him at the warehouse as soon as possible."

Dai's heart was pounding. How was he going to save the three unionists? Then, "Bring them along. We'll keep them in my office until someone comes for them." None of the unionists looked at Dai or said a word to him. But then he managed to catch the eye of their leader and hold his gaze for a few seconds. Then Dai looked away.

In Dai's office, the three sat on the floor in a corner,

subdued but alert as the first mate told a constable what had happened on board the refrigeration ship.

"Well they're mine now," said the constable. "Get these lovelies on their feet and we'll march them out to the wagon. Won't be seein' too many more sunrises, this lot. Of course, they hang a man at sunrise, so I guess that's the last thing they'll see. Come along, me beauties."

Dai helped the unionists' leader to his feet, standing behind him and lifting him around the waist. With a shaking hand, he slipped his penknife to the man. The unionist squeezed it tightly, covering the knife with both of his hands.

"Tell me, did you help the unionists to escape?"

Dai remained silent.

Irons was insistent. "Damn you, did you help them to escape? They had a knife, man, and they used it. They cut themselves loose, then stabbed the constable riding with them in the wagon. The wagon driver was beaten and lies in hospital. So now these bloody unionists who killed one of my men and damaged one of my ships are free. I want to know your role in this."

Deeply shaken, Dai said, "One was only sixteen. They were going to hang a sixteen-year-old boy."

Irons hung his head. "Leave this house. Leave tonight. I do not wish to hear any more. I knew you were in sympathy with them. I know, too, that you have been in contact from time to time with Alan Costello."

Morag tensed and looked down at the rug.

"But," said Irons, "I did not think that you would betray me in so vile a manner as this. Go to Costello. I have no wish to see you again."

Morag hurried to her father. "Please. Dai had no idea—" Irons pushed her hand from him and wearily walked from the study.

Morag looked at Dai, who said, "I swear I did not know they planned to hurt the guards. I swear it."

She took him in her arms and felt his body shake with sobs.

*   *   *

In an abandoned Braidwood mine shaft, Heath held a rock close to the lantern resting on a boulder. With a shaking finger he traced the vein of gold in the rock. He breathed faster, the excitement speeding the rhythm of his heart until he couldn't stand it anymore and he let out a whoop that echoed and re-echoed in the musty darkness. *Color*. By God, there was color here. According to this vein, it was not a bonanza, but there was gold. And he had the money to re-open the mines. He yelled again.

This looked to be a modest strike, one best exploited by the Chinee, who worked diligently, patiently and cheaply. The lower the wages, the higher the profits and Heath was determined to make as much profit as possible. He was going to prove something to his father. Prove that Heath had been right all along about the mines. This time, however, Heath would be his own boss. He would purchase the mines without his father's knowledge or help and work them himself. Him and his Chinee, his yellow-skinned celestials, who with great oriental patience could pick the eyes out of any goldfield in Australia.

No unionists in this goldfield, mate. Not with their bloody rules and demands for high wages and their exaggerated concern with mine safety. The whites working here would be only a handful and trusted friends at that, with whips, ax handles and guns to keep the Chinee applying himself to the task. The celestials were being brought in on the sly, smuggled in by a friendly sea captain, who was being paid plenty to keep his mouth shut. Before anyone knew it, Heath would have his gold and the world be damned.

His laughter filled the mine shaft and he felt the urge to dance, yes dance, and he did.

"Heath Irons and the Ferdinand Brothers!" he cried. "Bugger everybody else!"

Because Genista Corder remained just out of reach, Michael Irons never stopped wanting her. The contrast between her highborn mien and private licentiousness obsessed him, like a narcotic he had come to depend on, sometimes blinding him to all else about her, such as her selfishness and the way she toyed with him without mercy. It bothered him to hurt Lou Heller as he had, forgetting her birthday and abandoning her whenever Genista Corder beckoned. But Irons was a proud man, too proud to refuse the challenge of matching Genista's sexual energy. No man could let a woman get the best of him, not in Australia, least of all Michael Irons. Yet, what could one make of a woman who was so unkind to her husband?

"He had failed me in ways," she said. "There were so many promises, so many, many promises. That is why I married him, you know. He was to achieve much and I was to be at his side, to be as important as he. It would appear that we have both fallen short of our goal."

"What did he promise?" asked Irons.

"That he would sit in the House of Lords before his thirtieth birthday, that he would be an officer at the Bank of England within two years after our marriage. We were also to maintain a home in France, a country most dear to my heart. Even our English residence is less than I expected. Who can take pride in living on less than a thousand acres these days? We were forced to make do with one London townhouse and two minor estates totalling less than eight hundred acres. Disappointing, really."

"You live well in Australia. You have three homes in Sydney, a domicile in Melbourne, excellent horses—"

"Which do not win races and which are costly."

"And you travel. Trips to London, Paris, Rome."

"I am bored if I stay too long in one place. Besides, one absolutely cannot get decent clothes outside of the continent. A good dressmaker is a godsend, believe me. This business of federation appears to concern you muchly. Is it merely to protect your personal holdings or do you really care for Australia?"

"Both."

"Darcy says you are an Irish upstart born with an urge

to strike out at England. Your parents did that in Ireland and you are doing it here.''

''He is correct. England has no business in Australia. We convicts and sons of convicts built this country and it belongs to us, not to come white-wigged, bloody Lord-how-are-you, who jerks us around as though we were cheap puppets at a 'Punch and Judy' show.''

''The 'Iron Pirate' has spoken. Your likeness is in all the newspapers. 'The Apostle of Federation', they call you.''

''I'm easy to write about. I am the son of convict scum, Irish scum at that and I stand taller than your average horse and have but one eye and all of this makes me notorious, if not colorful.''

She gently touched his eye patch. ''And when you become prime minister of your united Australia?''

''I do not wish such an honor. I do not seek it and won't take it if it's offered. I have land, sheep, cattle, ships and other investments to concern myself with. Leave government to those who fancy such carryings on. Allow me to occupy myself with commerce.''

''Even Darcy feels you seek the position.''

''Darcy is a fool.''

''Agreed.'' She moved closer to him in bed, her thigh gently sliding up and down his. ''But if you were prime minister of the newest nation on earth, your wife would be a most prominent woman, would she not?''

''One might assume so. But I have no wife and no desire to occupy any governmental chair.''

Genista licked his ear. ''Michael, if you were prime minister, I would marry you.''

He turned to look at her.

''Yes,'' she whispered. ''I would enjoy being the wife of such a man. He would have more than national acclaim, would he not? World acclaim, perhaps.''

He continued to stare at her.

''We could be together all the time,'' she said. ''You

and I, with you as the most prominent man in this new country. Would you want to be with me, Michael?''

''Yes. I would want that.''

''Good.'' She seemed satisfied, as though they had agreed on their future together. ''I do so like men of ambition. Your son Heath is such a man.''

''How so?'' Heath had recently asked to be relieved of his duties at the company, in order to travel and visit old mates from his mining camp days. This did not seem very ambitious to Irons.

''His purchase of the mines,'' said Genista. ''Oh dear, Darcy said you were not to know. Oh well. What good is it to know a secret if you cannot repeat it.''

Irons grabbed her wrist.

''Michael, are you mad? You're hurting me.''

''The mines. Explain.''

''You're hurting me. Heath owns those Braidwood mines that were once yours.''

''You are wrong. I sold those mines to a group of men—''

''Heath hired them to do his bidding. My poor wrist. My skin is quite delicate, you know. Pain has its place in love, *mon cher*, but only when we agree on the game. My husband arranged for the financing, though why he should do so is beyond me. More than once he has told me that your son had a credit rating only slightly lower than that of a turnip. Seems your offspring plans to use Chinese labor.''

Irons sat up in bed. ''Dear God.'' He was across the room and pulling on his clothes. ''The unionists will destroy him.''

''Where are you going?''

''To save my son's life before it's too late.''

''Darcy feels the entire business is some sort of joke. The a'Beckets are the ones who put him up to it. Dear Darcy is always in need of money, but I wonder if the a'Beckets aren't rather bizarre themselves, giving him all that money for a mere joke. Australia is such a difficult country to understand.''

She knelt in bed, a finger casually stroking one nipple as she talked. "You really would make a fine prime minister, Michael. And I will so love standing beside you at receptions and on state occasions. It will be such jolly fun."

He turned and the fury in his face shocked her. "If the unionists harm Heath, your husband will not find me such jolly fun. Good day, woman."

At the door of the small cottage where Alan Costello lived, Irons looked around at the carriages and horses tied to trees and a hitching rack. From within the cottage came the sounds of men and women laughing and enjoying themselves. When Irons banged on the door with his fist, a male voice inside called out, "You're too late, mate. The beer's gone."

A smiling Alan Costello opened the door, but when he saw who had knocked, the smile disappeared.

"I need your help to save my son's life," said Irons. "You must stop the unionists from—"

Irons suddenly went silent. Behind Costello he saw Blue Dan and Lou, the two side by side at a table piled high with food and drink. Dai sat beside them. There were other men and women present, as well, and the cottage had the air of celebration and festivity. At the head of the table sat Morag, attractive and nervous in a white gown and looking like—*a bride.*

"You had best step inside," said Alan somberly.

Irons' eyes were on Morag, who despite a growing fear, forced herself to hold his gaze. Behind Irons, Alan said gently, "We were wed an hour ago."

Spinning around quickly, Irons punched Alan in the face, sending him back through the open cottage door and into the dirt outside. Blue Dan leaped to his brother's defense, rushing Irons and driving him into a wall. Other men hurried to separate the two as Morag shouted, "Stop it! Stop it!"

It took six men to hold the enraged Irons who said, "I will kill him. I will kill the bloody bastard!"

"Why?" asked an angry Lou. "For falling in love? For wanting to marry? Who in hell do you think you are? You love as you please, whom you please and now you want to deny Morag and Alan that same right. Damn you! Damn you!"

"You may own Australia or a good portion of it," said Blue Dan, "but you don't own all of the people. I want your word: if we turn you loose, no fighting. It is to be a happy day, at least for your daughter and my brother. We cannot hold you in this position forever. Your word."

"You have it. Now take your bloody hands off me."

Alan reentered the cottage. Blood trickled from a corner of his mouth and he used his tongue to probe for loose teeth. Morag ran past her father and threw herself in Alan's arms.

"Behind my back," whispered Irons to the two of them.

Morag looked at her father. "You gave me no choice. As much as I love you, you gave me no choice. Am I to live without love for all of my life? I have never betrayed you. I would die before doing so. I do believe in what Alan wants for Australia and I believe in you, too. But Alan understands that I will take no part in his activities."

"True," said Alan. "We often disagree on what the trade unions propose. 'Tis possible that your daughter believes more in you than in me. Despite that, we love each other."

Irons looked at Morag, then Dai. He said to Alan, "You have my son and now my daughter. Will you be stealin' my dogs next?"

Alan held his gaze, but said nothing.

Irons said, "I came here to ask you to call off *your* dogs, your unions dogs. My son Heath is opening the old Braidwood goldfields and plans to use Chinese workers."

"I know," said Alan.

There was shock on Morag's face. "You knew? And kept it from me?"

He sighed. "We cannot allow him to use coloreds. You

know how workers feel about cheap labor, particularly colored labor. We plan to deal with the Chinese and leave Heath alone. Just deal with the Chinese, that's all.''

"And how," said Irons, "do you tell your murderin' friends to shoot at the heathen and leave the white man be? Answer me that, union man.''

Irons took a step forward and so did Blue Dan and the other men. It was Blue Dan who said, "I think you had best depart, Mr. Irons. Go in peace. While you can.''

"I wish I could help you," said Alan, "but I will not lift a finger against my brothers. I do not expect you to understand that.''

"I have no wish to understand it. I am leaving for Braidwood immediately and if any of your *brothers* harms my son, you can start digging graves, for I shall fill them, with your *brothers*.''

He looked at Morag and there was such pain on his face, that she wept and reached out to him. But he turned his back to her and left the cottage. In silence, all inside stood and listened to the hoofbeats of his horse as he rode away.

Lou took Morag in her arms. "Lordy," said the American, "what the hell would that one-eyed bastard have done had he known you were carrying Alan's child?''

Dai's horse stumbled, but didn't go down. The animal was not given to speed, but speed is what Dai needed most of all. He had left the Costello cottage just minutes behind his father, but on a different route and a different mission. He planned to get to Braidwood ahead of Michael Irons and talk the unionist out of harming Heath. Dai, too, was shocked at the idea of Heath's re-opening the mines with Chinese labor. Alan had said nothing to him about the plans to "deal" with the Chinese, but since the Chinese were "coloreds," dealing with them could only mean one thing. And that was violence.

If nothing else, Dai owed his father this one bit of help. Hadn't Dai aided the unionists with everything from jobs to money to a penknife when it was most needed? Didn't he know most of the unionists in New South Wales and some from other colonies as well? Hadn't he helped Alan to obtain his seat in Parliament?

Still, it was wise not to mention his plan to Alan. Some of the men at the wedding were staunchly for trade unions and might not have cared one way or another about Heath. Dai could help. All he had to do was get there in time, before his father arrived, before the unionists struck. He owed it to Heath. And to the "Iron Pirate".

Dai spurred his horse and the animal snorted. Speed. That's what Dai needed most of all. Speed and some small amount of luck.

20 _____

THE train slowed down, wheels sending sparks flying into the night as it inched its way up the steep hill. As steam trailed from its engine, the train's whistle echoed across the bush, the sound disappearing into the thick woods that formed an impenetrable blackness on either side of the track. Heath Irons, who with one of his men rode in the cab with the engineer, furiously shoveled coal into the fire that fed the engine. The sooner the train reached Braidwood with its cargo of illegal Chinese, the better.

Each of the four cars behind the engine were crammed with the smuggled workers and it was just now that Heath was beginning to feel apprehensive about what he had done. He was dragging around four carloads of trouble. All he could do was move fast, get them working in the goldfields, and then out again. The only whites were trusted mates, "bully boys" some called them. Heath was paying well for their silence, with promises of a bonus when the job was done, when enough "color" had been torn from the earth. Until then, nobody left the mines. Not whites, not Chinese.

The celestials had arrived by night, by ship, and moved inland in darkness to this special train and were still travelling by night. Heath's mates would have to watch them carefully, to see that none of them escaped and made their way to the nearest town. If a unionist saw so much as one Chinee, there would be hell to pay. The past three years, with their strikes, had only hardened the trade unions' position about cheap labor. Heath would have to be very careful.

The train was almost at the top of the hill when the first explosion ripped out the track behind it, sending chunks of metal, trees and earth flying towards the sky. The second explosion, also dynamite, destroyed track in front of the engine. Desperately, the engineer pulled back on the brake with both hands. "Can't hold her! She's sliding off the track! We're heading into the trees. Jesus God!"

Slowly turning over like some great beast about to die, the engine angled off the track. With a loud wrench, the track under it came loose, the metal curving up to point at the moon. The cars followed the engine off the track and into the dirt and trees. Two cars turned over, landing on their sides. Inside all of the cars, both Chinese and whites screamed and cursed and fought each other to escape.

From the trees, the unionists lit flaming torches then threw them at the train, lighting up the night and firing the wooden train. Their leader, a burly man in a checkered shirt and leather hat, shouted, "Shoot to kill! Kill them all! The bloody whites and the heathen Chinee! Kill them all!"

Less than half a mile away Irons, on horseback and at the head of twenty armed men, heard the explosions. And then the gunfire.

He spurred his horse, saying nothing. Johnny-Johnny, his tracker, followed close behind. The Aborigine could not bring himself to tell of the sorrow his friend would face this night.

Irons' men rode in shooting, using long guns—rifles and shotguns—and concentrating their fire away from the train.

If the unionists were determined, Irons' men were hardened and practiced with the use of guns. Taken by surprise and from the rear, the unionists panicked and ran for their horses. The horses, however, were gone. Johnny-Johnny had killed the two men left to guard them and quietly driven the horses off.

Irons led the way, firing until his pistol was empty, then tossing it aside and pulling another from his belt. As the unionists scattered in the woods, Irons yelled, "Track them down and dispose of every man jack of them!"

Leaping from his horse he looked for Heath. And found him sitting against the hissing engine. Irons' heart was in his mouth as he bent over his son.

"I am alright, father."

"You're sure?" Irons gripped him by the shoulders.

"Yes. Bit of a sore shoulder. Thrown from the cab. But I am—"

He broke down and wept. Irons held him. "Foolish thing you did, lad. Quite foolish. You should have come to me."

There were scattered shots as Irons' men cleaned up, pushing into the woods and seeking out the unionists as he had ordered.

"You're alive, boy. That's all that matters."

Someone called Irons' name and he looked up. Everywhere around him men were moaning and in the darkness, there were more shots. Irons stood up in time to see Johnny-Johnny walking towards him carrying a body. On either side of the Aborigine, men silently stepped aside. Holding the body out to Irons, Johnny-Johnny said, "Found him near the horses. Two bullets in the back of the head."

It was Dai.

"Unionists say he come to them to stop the attack. Come to them to save his brother. But unionist do not listen. They want to make attack. He die trying to save Heath."

Irons took the body of his youngest son from the Aborigine, turned and walked away. From the darkness came the sound of more gunshots. Nearby, a weeping Chinese crouched on the ground and rocked back and forth, clutching a corpse that could have been his son.

21 _____

FOR more than an hour a drunken Darcy Corder sat in his
study staring at a broadsword hanging over the mantle.
The 300-year-old weapon had belonged to an ancestor,
Rombaud of Calais, a sixteenth century swordsman and
professional executioner. It was Rombaud who had beheaded
Anne Boleyn, second wife of Henry VIII. Because she had
a lifelong fear of axes it was as a favor to his queen that
Henry imported the French headsman. Corder, who was
now in fear of his life, lifted his half-filled glass of brandy
in a toast to the sword. Ancestor, would that you were
here today, to stand between me and Michael Irons.

The study door opened and his wife entered. She wore
black; the veil hiding her face made her appear both
alluring and intimidating. Without a word she crossed the
room, poured brandy for herself and swallowed most of
the glass. When she had refilled it she said, "Funerals are
a bloody bore. Faces as long as broom handles and everyone whispering as though they were in a library. Seems the
whole of ruddy Sydney turned out to see Dai Irons laid to
his eternal rest. I need a hot bath, but first there is something I think we should discuss, you and I."

"And pray tell, what might that be?"

"I am leaving you. I wish a divorce."

Corder flopped back against his leather chair and slung a leg over its arm. "Methinks we have discussed this subject before and if memory serves, I told you that divorce is unthinkable in my family. Who had you set your cap on that time? Ah yes. Lord Barsdale, the one who appears to be doing extremely well in the Foreign Office these days. May well end up prime minister, I hear."

"I want a divorce, Darcy. And this time, you will comply."

He laughed, swinging his arm and spilling brandy on the rug. " 'This time you will comply'. You're bloody mad, you are. Listen, you stupid bitch: I did not come here to the back of beyond to blacken my name. I am here to elevate myself, to rise to my rightful place in that elegant zoo known as London society and a divorce does not fit into my plans. I have an idea about who you're having it off with this time. Tell the blighter that I am retaining my wife and he can fuck off and die. We are talking about Michael Bloody Irons, are we not?"

Genista removed the pins which kept her hair in place and shook her head, setting her hair free. "Dear Darcy, your problem has always been your inability to look ahead. For example: Michael Irons' grief over his son's death and his disappointment in his daughter's marriage to a hated trade unionist, have utterly preoccupied him all this past week. But now Dai has been planted and the matter of Morag's marriage is a *fait accompli*. Which leaves him free to deal with you. Darling, you did have your fingers in the rather sticky pie backed by the a'Beckets and given to Heath Irons."

"I did not know Dai Irons would be killed."

"Let us say that you did not care. Dai, Heath, what did it matter? You wanted money and you played the a'Becket's game. Darcy, dear one, unless I stop him, Michael will kill you. This, after all, is Australia and not Westminster Abbey. A brutish lot, these diggers. Unrefined and unforgiving. An eye for an eye, a tooth for a tooth, that sort of rot."

She finished her drink, sat the empty glass down on the table and began walking away. Then she stopped, turned and smiled. "I was discreet with him, was I not?"

"Quite. This time you almost managed to hide your whoring from me. You are improving." He lifted his glass in a mock toast to her.

"I'm so glad. One should improve where one can. You will attend to the matter of the divorce soonest, won't you? Michael is not the most patient of men and if I am to save your life, I had best do it within the next twenty-four hours, wouldn't you say?"

Standing in her dressing room, Lou Heller said to Michael Irons, "Thank you for coming. I was not sure—"

"I have no quarrel with you. If anything, it is I who should beg your pardon. I have not treated you with the respect and consideration which you deserve and the shame is mine. I make no excuses for what I am and what I have done. But you were ever dear to me. I wish you to know that."

She looked down at her hands, which were folded in her lap. "What I have to say involves Morag and I wish you to hear me out. I will not interfere between you two, so have no fear. In truth, you have given her neither the respect nor the consideration she deserves. But I am learning that when it comes to women, all women, Australian men can be hard cases."

She looked at him. "Morag is with child."

Irons frowned. "Is she—"

"She's fine. Healthy and looking forward to the boyo, as she calls it. Misses working with you. Misses you."

Irons said, "Her brother is murdered the day after her wedding and by men who follow her husband. How can she expect me—"

"Michael, Alan did not kill Dai. They were friends. He was devastated by his death and threatened to kill the men responsible himself. That it, until he learned you had already relieved him of that little chore. He even threatened to leave the labor party over it. They had to work hard to get him to change his mind.''

"All the unionists had to do was hold a pistol to his head, as they do with all who disagree with them.''

"You're forgetting something, aren't you? Alan is Blue Dan's brother. Nobody is going to harm him, believe me. Whether you like it or not, Alan was angered by Dai's death. He wept, Michael. The man wept.''

"His tears will not bring my son back to life.''

"You seem to overlook Heath's role in all of this. Forgive me, but had he not been so, so—''

"Greedy?''

"Greedy, anxious and just plain dumb, none of this would have happened. Heath had more to do with Dai's death than did Alan Costello.''

He snorted. "As usual, you are mouth almighty and tongue everlasting.'' He looked away. "However, you speak the truth. Heath did play a most unfortunate role in this business. I want to thank you for coming to the funeral.''

"Morag was there as well.''

"I saw her.''

"But did not speak to her. Christ, you Australians are stubborn and hardhearted.''

He looked at Lou. "Did she ask you to plead for Alan's life?''

"She doesn't know a thing about it.''

Irons nodded. "I must leave now. I respect Alan's affection for my son. I saw him at the funeral. He . . . he did weep. There is someone else who used Heath and Corder and it is that man I shall deal with. Lou, there is one more thing.'' He hesitated.

Lou turned her back to him and said, "I have heard of your forthcoming marriage to Lady Corder. She is quite beautiful.''

Irons reached for her, but she stepped away. "Dearest Lou,'' he said. A longing for her returned, along with a rush of guilt.

She covered her face with her hands and wept silently.

Taking his top hat and stick from a chair Irons said, "Please let me know if Morag should ever need anything. I would be most grateful. Of course she is not to know . . ."

The sentence went unfinished.

Lou nodded. But kept her back to him.

Even after Irons left, gently closing the door behind him, she remained standing where she was.

Irons stepped into Alfred Deakin's book-lined study in Melbourne and received the shock of his life. Sitting on a worn leather couch were the two men whom Deakin, without mentioning names, had insisted that Michael come to Melbourne and meet: *Lord a'Becket and his son Denis.*

Speechless, Irons could only stare at the two until his rage bordered on the uncontrollable. It was then that he turned to Deakin. "You played me false, mate. You lied—"

"I did not lie, Michael. I said it was imperative that you meet two men who could prove indispensible to Australian federation. That is the truth."

"This pair would steal the pennies from a dead man's eyes. I am their sworn enemy and will have nothing to do with them."

"Michael, look—"

"*I have looked, damn you.* And what I see are a pair of snakes who had a hand in my son's death."

Deakin's mesmerizing eyes held the angry Irishman's gaze. "You will listen to me. You, Michael, hold the future of a united Australia in your hands."

Struggling to calm himself, Irons looked from Deakin to the a'Beckets. "Alfred, you do not know these men as I do."

"Michael, please sit down. Please."

Reluctantly, Irons took a chair. Then Deakins said, "It goes so slowly, this unity business. I am convinced it will take nothing less than a miracle to bring it about. In your New South Wales, I hear more men now oppose it. They fear the colony will lose its sovereignty, that it will be dominated by Victoria. No one wants to bow to anyone else.

"And there is George Reid," continued Deakin. "Sir Yea-and-Nay is now your premier and federation is not a matter he clasps to his bosom."

"He speaks well," said Michael. "He can also make himself the butt of a joke and the crowds are pleased by this. A fat buffoon, but a cunning one."

"Now, Michael, I shall tell you why you are here. Of the six colonies, two are giving the matter of federation very little chance with their voters. One, of course, is Queensland, ever ready to secede over the matter of black labor. It will take some doing to get her on our side. The other is Western Australia."

Michael nodded. Western Australia was perhaps more of a troublemaker than Queensland. That colony, where he had spent his youth, often chose to be deliberately out of step, seeing itself as so far away from the influential eastern colonies that it might as well act solely on its own behalf. Western Australians were as obstinate as mules. Bloodyminded to the nth degree. They had laid down a condition for supporting federation: all of the other colonies would have to agree on linking Western Australia to the east, via a trans-continental railroad. Such a project would be so costly as to stagger the imagination, but at the moment it was the price for Western Australia's participation in the dream of men such as Alfred Deakin and Michael Irons.

Deakin pointed to the a'Beckets. "These men say that they will see this railroad built. Do you know what that means?"

"It means," said Michael, "that you got me here in order to arrange some sort of truce between me and this pair."

Lord a'Becket rose from the couch. "I warned you, Mr. Deakin. Mr. Irons is not a reasonable man."

"You killed my son. As surely as if you'd held the gun yourself," Michael said with quiet savagery.

"And my daughter is dead because of you, sir."

"Gentlemen, please." Deakin stepped between them. "You have each suffered greatly. I deeply sympathize with you both. Would it not be a fitting tribute to the memory of your dead children for you both to join in creating a new Australia?"

Irons pointed at a'Becket. "This man has no honor, no integrity, no decency."

"Michael," said Deakin, and this time he raised his voice. "You are in my home."

Irons stood up. "I can remedy that, sir." He started for the door, but Deakin blocked his path. "Australia deserves better from you," he said.

Michael stopped. It took all the self control he possessed, but he stopped.

Deakin said, "At times my courage wavers and I feel we cannot do this thing and then I find that I can go on, I can try, I can take another step towards the dream of one Australia in my lifetime. In my lifetime. It's your dream, too, Michael."

Irons looked at the a'Beckets. "Is it theirs as well?"

Denis said, "We can make it ours, if left in peace. That railroad will certainly tip Western Australia into the federation camp. Isn't that all you care about?"

Irons looked at Deakin. "Has he told you how he plans to bring about this miracle?"

Lord a'Becket inhaled snuff, sneezed, then blew his nose. "We intend to put together the biggest investment syndicate this country has ever seen. Banking has improved somewhat in recent months. The nightmare of the past three years had receded. Our syndicate will encompass banks and investment houses from America, England and Europe. A trans-continental railway could be extraordinarily profitable."

"One of the things which makes such a railway attractive to potential investors," said Denis, "is the recent gold strikes in Western Australia. Naturally, we are consorting with only important financial houses. I can assure you that all concerned feel the project is a viable one.''

"Michael," said Deakin. "Your word. Your word that you will not bother the a'Beckets until after federation is achieved.''

"No." And then he smiled. "But you have my word that I will consider that a truce exists between us until this pair proves treacherous once more.''

a'Becket said, "I came in peace to Mr. Deakin. He welcomed us. It is you, sir, who offer treachery. I can see that we shall find no fair play in this house. Denis.''

Deakin, however, stopped the a'Beckets from leaving. In the end, his charm and persuasiveness won out; Michael's promise was accepted. So long as the a'Beckets honorably served the cause of federation all animosity between them and Irons was to remain, in Deakin's word, inactive.

When the two bankers had left Irons said, "A month ago I buried my son. This day I buried my honor.''

"You are wrong," said Deakin. "Your honor shines more brightly than ever. It serves Australia. And because of that, you are a man worth honoring.''

"I assume that the a'Beckets denied manipulating Heath?''

"Lord a'Beckett claims that Heath dealt only with Sir Corder, who secured financial backing for the project. The facts seem to support this explanation. The a'Beckets say you are unbalanced by your grief.''

"Does this mean you have absolved them for having murdered Julius Fielding?''

"No links have been found between the a'Beckets and the murderous crutchies. Just as our police have yet to connect the a'Beckets to those who attacked your men in the rail car. Alas, no police force in Australia suffers from excessive efficiency.''

The Melbourne politician hesitated before saying, "May I congratulate you on your forthcoming marriage to Lady Corder?''

"You have long ears, my friend. We have as yet made

no official announcement. First, there is the matter of Lady Corder's divorce. Her husband is agreeable, but we must go through courts here and in England. The Church of England, too, must play its part in the dissolution of Lady Corder's current union. So I fear the nuptials will not take place until next year, perhaps near the end of '95. You will attend, of course.''

"Of course. It would be my honor." Deakin almost mentioned Sir Darcy Corder's hasty ''recall'' to London by his investment firm, but decided it would have been in poor taste.

Irons grinned. "Genista talks of my becoming prime minister of a united Australia. She will not accept my lack of interest in such a position.''

Deakin studied his friend carefully. "Power can be most seductive, I fear." *Especially for those who admire the ones to whom it may come*.

"Not for me," said Irons. "I shall leave that prize to those with the stomach for it. Genista is a woman and women live on dreams. It will be enough for me that Australia faces the world as a single nation.''

But will it be enough for Genista, thought Deakin.

In the carriage taking them away from Deakin's home a'Becket said to his son, "We have done much to enrich ourselves this day. With the blessings of federation leaders, we shall profit beyond our wildest dreams. And destroy Michael Irons. Nor shall his children be exempt from my vengeance. A most relentless vengeance.''

His voice dropped to a chilling whisper. "For you, Camilla. For you.''

He smiled and patted Denis's knee. "Patience. Above all, patience.''

22 _____

New South Wales. 1896

"LOOKEE here. Not the bank of England, but it's something worth swinging a pick for," Heath Irons muttered. Behind him, two men leaned closer. They stood in a Braidwood mine shaft, and Heath had just come upon a thin vein of gold embedded in a wall of dark rock.

In the eighteen months since the attack by unionists, Heath had worked the mines with a fair degree of success. There was only a modest amount of gold, but it turned a steady profit. He was where he worked best, outdoors and with men and away from the crowded city of Sydney, where the population was almost an astounding half million. It had pleased him greatly when his father admitted that Heath was right, that the mines were worth re-opening. A handshake and clap on the back from the "Iron Pirate" was high praise indeed.

Of course the mines now used union labor. Morag's husband had seen to that. But at least there was peace in the camp; the only trouble was the Saturday night punch-ups between drunken miners battling over the favors of whores.

Heath passed his lantern to one of the men with him,

signalling him to hold it closer to the wall. "Here's where the vein starts. Might do better using a small charge first—"

A hand covered his mouth. Then a bowie knife was against his throat, followed by a hideous pain and Heath could not believe this was happening to him. More pain followed quickly. In his back, side, chest. Now he was on the ground, seeing shadows cast on the wall by the lantern, shadows of the two men stabbing him. Suddenly he felt cold and he wished his father were here to hold him. There was the stickiness of his own blood and a desperate wish to wake up soon, to end this shocking dream.

He looked up to see one man holding the dynamite charge and the other lighting it, before setting it down near the wall. And then they ran.

In agony and losing blood rapidly, a weakened Heath could hardly move. Nor could he cry out, not that anyone would have heard him so far beneath the earth. So it took him minutes to turn over on his side and crawl towards the dynamite. When he was only feet away he stretched out his arm for the sputtering fuse and then there was a light more brilliant than a million suns and he was swallowed by roaring flames.

In the mining camp men in tents and shacks, by the river and in the whores' tents, heard the explosion and immediately raced towards the mine shaft. In the crowd converging on the shaft were the two who had killed Heath Irons.

Two days later, the pair of killers reined their horses in a clump of woods near a deserted section of the New South Wales coast. Dismounting, they greeted a small man who had white hair and skin almost as colorless. He was their paymaster, an albino called Jack Straw, who was about to reward them for a job well done.

"Ruddy good accident," said one killer. "Pieces of the bugger spread from here to China. Nobody doubts that it was an unfortunate accident. Be no questions asked about Mr. Heath Irons' departure from this earth.''

''No loose ends,'' said the albino, right before he killed them. ''That's what me boss said.''

He brought a sawn-off shotgun from behind his back and blew away their faces. Despite his small size, Jack Straw was strong. He lifted each man, carried him down to the water's edge and placed the bodies in a battered rowboat. Then taking a small shovel from his own horse, Straw scooped up the bits of skull, flesh and blood-soaked ground and carried them down to the boat.

Next, he rowed out into the cove, where he slit the belly of each corpse, so that it would sink, and pushed it overboard. He whistled while he used an ax to chop holes in the craft's bottom. And as it slowly sank, Jack Straw carefully removed his bloody clothing and boots, using his belt to tie them in a bundle. Minutes later he was expertly swimming back to shore, where he removed dry clothes from a saddlebag, dressed himself once more and tied the dead men's horses to the tail of his own mount.

In the saddle, Straw, one hand pushing half of a meat pie into his mouth, wheeled his horse about and headed back to Melbourne. With the money taken from the dead killers and the money he would get from selling their horses, Jack Straw's work would yield him a pretty penny this day. It was, however, only a pittance compared to what Denis a'Becket had paid him to arrange Heath Irons' murder and dispose of those who had committed it.

23 _____

IN her father's Sydney mansion, a disgusted and angry Morag looked down at a copy of *Opus Dei*, which was damp with spilled liquor and lay on Irons' desk, just out of reach of his hand. Behind her, Alfred Deakin and Johnny-Johnny sadly looked at Irons, who was on the floor. Unconscious and reeking of alcohol, he had slipped from his chair and now leaned against his desk, one arm pointing towards Glass's offensive front page cartoon. It was a black and white drawing, showing Morag's father in his familiar 'Iron Pirate' guise, this time alone and weeping on a childlike pirate ship as his wife Genista circled in the air above him.

Third Mate Abandons Captain, Frequently, read the caption. A balloon near Genista's mouth read, ''Melbourne, Paris, London, Timbuktu. Any old place but Sydney will do.''

It was 1897. Irons' two year-old marriage to Genista had been a horrible mistake. The third Mrs. Irons was a spendthrift and shallow, making no secret of her distaste for Sydney and her husband's friends. Her time was spent in travelling, attending parties, buying enormous amounts of new clothes, shoes and boots and cultivating aristocratic friends. Her hold on Irons, Morag knew, was one of the flesh. And degrading to her father. He was fifty-six now, fleshier and with more lines on his face. His remaining eye was weak, but still he refused to wear the pair of spectacles recommended to him by a doctor. One lens was prescription, the other painted black and Irons felt he looked foolish wearing them.

To please Genista he had attempted to wear a monocle, but his friends had laughed that idea into oblivion. Irons was a tired, lonely man. Both sons were dead and he still refused to see Morag. But, she noticed, he did have her photograph and that of her two infant sons on his desk, which brought a tear to Morag's eye.

"He has given so much," she said, "and received so little."

"We need him," said Deakin. "We need him more than ever."

She whirled around to angrily confront him. "You don't need him. You wish to kill him. You and that trollop he married. You ruin his body with your damned federation and she crushes his soul with her absence."

"No one in New South Wales can carry federation forward as can your father. Parkes is dead. Reid cannot give a straight answer to any question and Barton, who leads the federation movement since Parkes' death, is a dull man. He is educated, handsome and courteous, but 'Toby Tosspot' cannot fire the spirit. Irons can. I fear federation is becoming harder to achieve in this colony than it ever was and that's why we need him."

"I do not care," said Morag. "I care about my father."

"The new lady has hired English servants," said Johnny-Johnny, "and they do not care for the master. They shame him, but he dare not discharge them for fear of displeasing her. I did not want to bother you but—"

"I thank you, Johnny-Johnny," said Morag. "You are my father's one true friend." She stooped to pick up a letter on the floor near Irons. It was from Lou Heller, who had moved back to America. Morag glanced at it quickly, then folded the letter and placed it on the desk. The two had been corresponding. Thank God for that. Lou was the woman he should have married, the woman who would have stood by her father instead of tormenting him.

"His spirit is not what it once was," said Deakin. "The loss of both sons, the unhappy marriage, the seemingly impossible business of bringing about federation—"

"Six colonies who despise one another," said Morag, "and leaders who do not wish to lose their place in the sun to a central government. Promises made to my father by these men, then broken. Do you wonder at his frustration?"

She took one step toward Deakin. "And something else. He is being eaten up by the promise he made to you, the promise to leave the a'Beckets unharmed so long as you need them."

"Australia needs them."

"You need them, Mr. Deakin. And you have no idea what a price my father has paid in giving you his word to let them live. They killed Dai and I, for one, feel strongly that they killed Heath as well. If I had the opportunity, I would destroy the a'Beckets and rejoice over it."

Deakin smiled. "I believe you. Your father is a proud man and has dealt with his enemies in prompt fashion all of his life. For him not to do so in the matter of his sons, well, I understand."

"You cannot, sir. When you have lost two sons, then you can understand. Johnny-Johnny, where is Mrs. Irons?"

"Melbourne, Miss Morag."

"I am Morag to you and have been since we were children together. I know you are supposed to show respect in front of whites, but Mr. Deakin, I'm sure, will understand. If he does not understand, then he can go to hell."

"Mr. Deakin understands," said the Melbourne politician. "And respects what he understands."

"Good. I would be grateful, Mr. Deakin, if you were to help Johnny-Johnny lift my father from the floor and place

him in his chair. Johnny, when you have done that, please
go outside and bring me your coach whip.''

"Yes, Morag.''

She smoothed her father's hair. Dear God, she could
weep. How exhausted he looked. How beaten. How
abandoned. She had seen him over the past three years,
but only from a distance. His pride had been an insurmount-
able obstacle and so had her fear. Fear of what he might
do to Alan, should they meet and argue, and fear of what
he might say to her. Weeks slid into months but the love
she felt for her father never waned.

For the most part her marriage to Alan was a satisfying
one. But he had the ego of an Australian male and could
not always deal with her intelligence and outspokeness. In
an argument he had once struck her; she had then slashed
him across the hands with a kitchen knife, threatening to
do worse should he ever strike her again. It only made him
love her the more. And not lift his hand to her again. Their
sons—Michael Alan and Daniel O'Connell were healthy and
the joy of both husband and wife.

"Praise God,'' said Alan. "They have your brains and
my looks. They are bound to make their way in this pig
iron world.''

She did not care for Blue Dan. He was a thug, a
larrikin, who had found profit in crime and immorality.
His fingers were in quite a few dirty pies, and even the
new labor party as well. More than one man who sat in
Parliament was obligated to Blue Dan. The New South
Wales Parliament had little in the way of organized political parties; members banded together as self interest decreed.
Most fell into two groups—on the one hand, protectionists,
who favored high tarifs and *free traders*, who favored none,
on the other. Blue Dan had corrupted men in both groups.

Nor was he above fixing prize fights, cycle, dog and
horse races. His charm hid a ruthlessness that made Morag
uneasy. Through him and Alan, however, she had learned
much about the underworld, Parliament and political parties.
The three, it seemed, were intertwined.

The children kept her busy, but she needed more to occupy her mind than baby formulas. She watched the labor party's money, kept its accounts and advised it on expenditures. No man had her brains and ability to deal with figures. In Australia, few men and almost no women, had Morag's education; many still signed their names with an X and had trouble reading.

She dearly wished to be working with her father again. Rumor had it that because of his frequent travels on behalf of federation, his company was being mismanaged and slowly ruined. She could make a difference; it was a company she knew well and still followed closely. He needed someone he could trust, who cared for the company, who could make hard decisions and see them through. He needed Morag.

Johnny-Johnny returned with the coach whip.

"Announce to the servants," she said, "that my father wishes to see them in his study immediately."

When they were in the study, man and maid servants, Morag said, "Is this all? Johnny-Johnny please lock the door."

An English butler said, "Some are occupied at present, madam and so could not see their way to be here. But I shall pass on your message. I assume it is you who will speak." He looked disdainfully at the still unconscious Irons.

"Very well," she said. "Here is my message. And do pass it on."

She brought the whip down on him, sending the butler screaming to the floor. Except for a shocked Deakin, and Johnny-Johnny, who laughed, the room panicked. Her arm rose and fell as the terrified servants sought to escape. Johnny-Johnny and Deakin ducked into the empty fireplace and watched as men and women ran into each other and yelled and cried out when the whip landed. Morag's anger was cold, deliberate and she lashed out at men and women indiscriminately. There was the sound of breaking glass as someone smashed a window and leaped through it.

Suddenly, she stopped. Her chest rose and fell with her breathing. "I want all of the servants in this study and I want them here now. Johnny-Johnny, open the door."

Minutes later, a ragged group of weeping or frightened men and women, some with welts on their arms, faces and hands and with torn clothes, listened silently as Morag said, "The Master and Servant Act of 1828 is still in force. It says that an employee may be jailed for leaving an employer or for not working to the employer's satisfaction. As of now and until further notice, you will work to my satisfaction. Is that clear?"

"Yes mum."

"If any of you ever again shows disrespect to my father, I will make you wish you had never seen this house. Or me. Now go to your stations. In thirty minutes I shall tour the house and inspect it. It would be to your advantage if I am satisfied with what I see. Now get out of my sight, all of you."

She turned to Johnny-Johnny. "I want a doctor here immediately. I want my father examined and treated."

To Deakin she said, "You will have to do without him for a time. He needs rest and care."

"There is a conference to be held in Adelaide and then it is to be moved here to Sydney for three weeks in September. Next, that same conference will move to Melbourne. Michael is one of seventy-nine delegates who will attend. We're closer now than we have ever been. We will select a date for a referendum, for a vote on the constitution and federation. It's Irons and not Barton or Reid who holds together the New South Wales delegation. Without him, they will fold. Queensland still threatens to break away and Western Australia—"

Morag said, "You traded my father's peace of mind for Western Australia. That colony is your problem, you and the a'Beckets. And what has become of their grand railroad, may I ask?"

"It is a huge project and cannot be done overnight. They are meeting with important men and surveying land—"

"And growing rich. Yes, I know of their windfall."

"It is only fair. They are the guiding force behind this venture and are entitled to a profit."

"Not without producing a railroad. Yes, I know. You are going to tell me about bonds, advance money and stock issues and such. I am no fool, sir. I fully understand the world of finance. But I share my father's hatreds and suspicions, and I believe, Mr. Deakin, that you will not see a transcontinental railway from the a'Beckets."

"That remains to be seen, Mrs. Costello."

Irons stirred in his chair, but continued unconscious. Morag said, "His wife is saying that he has disappointed her, as did her first husband. She expected federation to have been accomplished by now and my father to be a prominent man, so that she could bask in his glory. That is another reason why he pushes himself, to please her, she who does not care."

"When Michael feels better—"

"He won't feel better, Mr. Deakin."

"I don't understand."

"I shall see to it that he does not feel better. I shall see to it that he spends an indefinite time recovering. That is, unless you cut a deal with me."

Deakin smiled. "By God, you are his daughter. Very well, let's hear your terms."

"You need him and undoubtedly he will do his best for you. But his company suffers and he faces ruin. You know men in all colonies of great legal skill, lawyers, legislators, men such as these."

"I know such men in Sydney, if that is what you wish me to say."

"What I wish, sir, is for you to have a competent lawyer draw up a paper for me, one that will survive in any court in the land, if needs be. I wish it drawn up as soon as possible. Today would suit me well. Do this and I shall not stand in the way of my father's killing himself on behalf of you and Australia."

Deakin looked at the bloodied whip on Irons' desk and

smiled. "You can be most persuasive at times. Do you mind if I accompany you as you inspect this house? I am most curious to see the results of your ultimatum. Afterwards we shall attend to the matter of the attorney. And please, may we dispense with the whip this time? I believe you have made your point. With them and with me as well."

The next morning in her father's office Morag, in the one and only good dress she owned, faced the officers and chief clerks of the Irons & Pease Company. In her hand were the papers drawn up by the attorney provided for her by Alfred Deakin. Intrigued by what Morag planned, Deakin himself had offered his own legal expertise. The document was legal, ironclad and irrefutable. And the biggest gamble of Morag's life.

To hide her fear, she spoke slowly, deliberately. "Gentlemen, it is a proper document, signed by my father and duly witnessed by no one less than the eminent Alfred Deakin and the chief judge of the highest court in New South Wales. I have my father's power of attorney and can act on his behalf in any capacity I choose."

"He must have been bloody drunk when he signed that," said a director.

Morag smiled. "You know who I am. I am my father's daughter and not your common sheila, so take no liberties with me. Let me add: I am the wife of Alan Costello and the sister-in-law of Blue Dan. I can close this company down with a half dozen strikes, hitting at your profits and jobs or I can order Blue Dan to cut your throats."

There was a new air in the room—uncertainty on the part of some, disbelief on the part of others and a growing apprehension on the part of the rest.

"As of now," said Morag, "the top three men in the company are to report to me each morning and an hour before leaving each afternoon. I shall use my father's office. I wish to see the books and all outstanding accounts. Nothing is to happen without my approval."

One man raised his hand. "Beg pardon, but just how long is this unusual state of affairs to persist?"

"Until my father returns, which may be in a few days or a few weeks. I suggest you return to your departments and your desks and prepare to tell me exactly what you have been doing."

"I do not care what that paper says," said a top officer. "I am not taking orders from any woman. I am going to see your father."

He turned and walked to the door. When he pulled it open, three large men stood in his way. The men were on loan from Blue Dan.

"Tell them to get out of my way," said the officer.

Morag folded her arms. "You're a man. You tell them. I'm just a woman."

The officer, his face red with shame, turned around to stare at her.

"My father," she said, "is not to be disturbed. Should anyone appear unannounced at his Elizabeth Bay mansion, he will be greeted by such men as are now standing behind you." It was a bluff. Irons lay sleeping in his mansion, attended only by Johnny-Johnny and servants now terrified of Morag, who tried not to think of what her father would do when he learned he had been tricked into giving her power of attorney.

"Gentlemen," said Morag. "I believe you have work to do."

When they had left, she leaned against the door, hands on her pounding heart and breathed through her mouth. Dear God, what have I done? Alan knew nothing about it; he thought she was with her father. Blue Dan must have told him by now. Alan would be furious. She closed her eyes and prayed to God for right understanding and the strength to follow that in practice.

24

Sydney
June 3, 1898

THEY had worked for this day, prayed for it and at times doubted that it would ever arrive. Today in New South Wales, Tasmania, Victoria and South Australia, people were voting on federation. Western Australia and Queensland would not vote; the two continued to march to their own drummer. But for the other four colonies, the conferences and conventions were over. No more meetings and arguments, no more long sittings, no more heated discussions of resolutions. Thanks to men like Deakin, Irons and others, there was a constitution to vote on, a question to be answered: was there to be a commonwealth of Australia?

Irons and Morag, with Alan, Blue Dan, Edmund Barton, George Reid, still the premier of New South Wales, and hundreds of others, crowded into the rooms of Government House to await the outcome, which was by no means certain. Reid, ever cautious and incapable of a straight answer, had not made it easy.

"The yes vote in New South Wales must reach eighty thousand. If not, the proposition is defeated."

Barton and Irons had argued with him in vain. The pig-like Reid remained immovable.

And now Barton, handsome, well-spoken and dignified said to Irons, "The voting in Tasmania is running strong for it and it is the same in Victoria. We cannot allow them to leave us behind. We must match them."

"Me bookies have taken money from both sides," said Blue Dan. "I figure to profit no matter how it turns out."

Morag stood on tiptoe to whisper in her father's ear. "He has told me that New South Wales will reject federation. He is certain of it."

Before Irons could answer, a roar went up from the crowd as a man, standing on a table, yelled, "Over fifty thousand for! Thirty odd thousand against!" The shouting drowned out the rest of his remarks.

Close, thought Irons. Too damn close. To have worked all these years and lose. It was unthinkable. He had closed down his company today and his warehouses to allow his employees the opportunity to vote. That had been Morag's idea; they had reconciled and she was his second. He had been a fool not to have given her the position earlier and an even bigger fool to allow his stubborn pride to keep them apart. She had saved his life. A year ago his heavy drinking and overwork had brought him to the brink of death, or so the doctor had told him.

He had needed a month of rest and during that time Morag had run his company and his household. Irons had come to depend on her more than he had on anyone since Davy Pease. Naturally, the power of attorney had been torn up, with Irons resuming control. But he had appreciated her daring and rewarded her with the position she had always wanted. He had no choice. And yet it had worked out well, for him at least. For Alan, it had meant having a wife now earning thousands of pounds a year more than he and spending a great deal of her time out of the home. Such a thing was unheard of for Australian women.

"You are my wife," said Alan, "and you belong here

in my home, carin' for my children and cooking my meals."

"My father needs me. He has no sons."

"So, I'm to feel guilty enough over the killin' of Dai to let you do as you please, is that it?"

"If you love me, you will not force me to choose. You knew the kind of woman I was before you married me. That is why you married me. I am no man's chattel, Alan, and never will be. I love you, but I will not see my father alone and abandoned."

"He has a wife."

"She has a life of her own and it rarely includes him."

"I do not want to lose you, lass."

"You will not. I have looked at no other man since we wed and I never shall. But do not ask me to see my father ruined. I cannot do anything about his wife, but I can do something about his business."

"I am told they fear you at the company."

She smiled. "It saves me the trouble of repeating myself. They listen carefully, then obey the first time."

"Would that you were as devoted to labor as you are to your father."

And as the evening wore on in Government House, the vote total ran closer, until there was but a five thousand vote difference between those in favor and those against. Genista was in Melbourne, holidaying with English friends recently arrived in Victoria. Irons tried not to imagine her with other men, but he knew that it was a strong possibility. He still hungered for her, was still strongly aroused by her. No other woman held the sexual power over him that Genista did and at times he was ashamed of himself because of it. During those times he drank too much, but never in front of Morag.

His daughter and Genista despised each other and on those rare times when their paths crossed Genista was quite careful in what she said to her.

Barton said, "If it fails, what do we do?"

An angry Irons said, "It cannot fail. I have set my heart on it and pledged my life to it. Federation cannot fail."

"Is it possible that Reid knew how strongly some in New South Wales opposed it? Is that why he insisted on eighty thousand votes as the minimum 'yes' vote?"

"We will win. We must win."

But they didn't. In the end the votes showed over seventy-one thousand in favor and over sixty-eight thousand against. A bitterly disappointed Irons watched a smiling George Reid leave Government House. The eighty thousand total had not been met and unless Irons and the other supporters of federation wanted to drop the idea, the best they could do was start again. It had passed in Tasmania and Victoria by huge majorities and won in South Australia by two to one. But in Irons' New South Wales it had fallen short. And because of that all of the colonies would have to vote again.

Irons pushed his way through the crowd and left alone. Fearful at what he might do to himself, Morag ran after him.

In Melbourne, a naked Genista obeyed the man who was her new master. He ordered her to crawl about the floor and when she had done that, he sat while she sucked his toes on command, licking each one with a darting pink tongue. Once, he leaned down and twisted her nipples painfully and she shuddered with an obscene pleasure. He, of all men, had touched her soul in a way she had only dreamed of before. He exercised power over her as she wanted a man to and she was happy to be his slave.

On command, she remained on the floor on all fours as he caressed her buttocks with his foot, then roughly pushed her down on her face.

"May I rise?" she asked.

"No. Stay where you are, bitch."

"Yes master."

Later, when they had finished he said, "It is truly power that excites you, isn't it?"

"You are a powerful man. You . . ." She began licking his body. Suddenly he grabbed her hair and yanked her head back. "Your husband has been humiliated in his own colony and now I enjoy his wife."

"Do with me what you will."

"What a fool he is. There is already talk of Melbourne one day becoming the capital of a united Australia and Irons knows nothing of this. When that happens, I shall be an important man."

"I know."

"Bitch," said Denis a'Becket, striking her across the face. "You fucking slut!"

"Please! Please!" she cried. "Not across the face. He musn't know."

Denis a'Becket immediately became solicitious. "I am sorry, my darling. Never the face. I won't forget again. Never the face."

She smiled wantonly. "Thank you master."

25

SYDNEY
June 20, 1899

ROCKETS streaked across the night sky, then exploded in showers of multi-colored sparks. On the ground, cannon roared and rifles and pistols cracked. At an hour when Sydney streets should have been deserted they were jammed with cheering, shouting men, women and children. On the lawn of Government House, where hundreds celebrated the occasion, Irons lifted Lou Heller off the ground in a bear hug and swung her around in a circle. It was the greatest day in Australia's history; by an overwhelming vote, five colonies had approved federation. With Western Australia abstaining, the vote in New South Wales, Tasmania, Victoria, Queensland and South Australia had been 519,000 in favor, with 328,000 opposed. A weeping Lou, her face pressed against Irons' neck, said, "It's not even my country, but this is the most exciting thing that's ever happened to me. I cannot stop crying."

"Neither can I, love. Neither can I."

They held each other there on the lawn and listened to

the sounds of victory, to cannon, rockets, guns and to the shouts and cheers that came from the human heart. "The Coming Event" had arrived. What Deakin called "The Final Miracle" had been achieved. But not without struggle.

Following last year's defeat Irons had left Government House with every intention of getting paralytic drunk and staying that way for a long time. Instead, Johnny-Johnny had saddled two horses and together they had ridden north along the coast, camping out and saying little. They had stayed away from Sydney for over a week and when they returned Irons felt cleansed. While Deakin and other friends had worried about him, Morag had not. "He is with his mate. No harm will come to him."

Later in Melbourne with Deakin and other supporters of the defeated referendum Irons said, "Being out in the bush was like using soap and a hard brush on my soul, my brain. Cleansed me inside and out, it did. Did a bit of thinkin'. Me da' and Daniel O'Connel and those who supported 'Young Ireland' had a go at gettin' free and failed. Some were hanged. Others like my father got transported. What they didn't get was a second chance, the chance we're goin' to get next year. I say we try again and if we fail, we try again and again."

They were all on their feet, with Deakin leading the applause.

Irons held up his hands for quiet. "My mate's an Abo. I know most of you here don't like coloreds and I shall not quarrel with how you feel. But he says to me out there in the bush, 'If my people had fought harder, this land would still be ours. It's yours now. Do not make the mistake we made. Fight for Australia.'

"One more thing: In New South Wales, we lost, not merely because of George Reid, but because a lot of people just didn't bother to vote. They abstained. This time, we work on them. Not just in New South Wales, but in every colony. Get the abstainers out of the house and to the polls and victory will be ours."

The cheers, whistling and stomping of booted feet rattled Deakin's bookshelves and the panes of glass in his study windows. "The last miracle," he said. "With the 'Iron Pirate' and his mate on our side, it has to come. God, let it come."

After one year of hard campaigning it did, winning the approval of over seventy percent of the voters.

On the lawn at Government House, Irons walked through the crowd with Lou on his arm, stopping to shake hands, accept congratulations and drink from several bottles offered in victory toasts. Genista was in London to visit her family, attend the races at Ascot and tennis at Wimbledon. How long she would remain there was anybody's guess. More than once Irons had decided he was through with her. But when she was near him, it was a case of moth to flame and he had no will. He could despise her, even accuse her of infidelity, which she denied, and still when her flesh was against his, he was her prisoner. He forgot his aging body, the more than twenty years difference in their ages and he made love to her as she wanted, sometimes doing things to her that later he would be ashamed of. He wanted to leave Genista, but he could not.

And then there was Lou, back in Australia and his life after an absence of almost five years. The slight signs of age in her face only made her more appealing. She was as warm as ever and still in love with him. They had corresponded and she, claiming to miss Australia, had returned. Morag had been so delighted to see Lou that she had wept. The city of Sydney had been delighted, too. A crowd met her at the docks, unhitched the horses on the carriage waiting for her and pulled the carriage through the streets to her hotel.

Blue Dan had also been waiting. And was furious when he saw that it was Irons she had come back to be with. Irons and Australia. Lou also had bonds which she could not break.

Tonight she clung to him and never felt happier. "What happens now?" she asked.

"It begins," said Irons. "There will be the usual fight

over the spoils of victory. Some of us want Sydney as capital, others want Melbourne.''

''Much as I love Australia, it's a desert, with a few coastal cities. Sydney and Melbourne are the only two you can really call cities, if you ask me.''

''We have grown a bit all over, since you've left.''

''I know. I've seen your waistline.'' She poked it in fun.

''Stop that, you wicked woman. Talkin' about Australian cities. Perth, Hobart, Adelaide, Brisbane. All big towns. Had to show my face in all of 'em for this federation, which we now have. Blessed Lord, it's come. But it's still not official.''

''I don't understand.''

Irons snorted. ''England, damn them. Her Majesty's government and Parliament have to approve. Until that happens . . .''

''And *will* they approve?''

''They have to. We have one hold on them. Britain's still fighting the Boer War in South Africa and right now they're losin' over there as often as they're winnin'. Wouldn't be wise of them to stand in our way. Might give us serious ideas about breakin' away. Unfortunately, too many Australians see Britain as the mother country and don't want to break away too far. I'm not one of them.''

Lou threw back her head and laughed. ''I gathered as much. Will I see you tomorrow?''

''Probably not. I must go to Melbourne and meet with Deakin. He feels certain that the esteemed British prime minister—'' Irons spat out the words, ''Robert Arthur Talbot Gascoyne-Cecil, the third Marquess of Salisbury, will now want to meet with a group of us colonials.''

''And so you'll be going to England.'' Genista, thought Lou.

''In a few months, yes.''

He lifted her chin with a hand. ''But we have tonight, that is if you don't mind bein' with an aging, one-eyed digger, whose girth is expanding too rapidly.''

"To be with you on such a night is worth travelling for weeks on a ship that had more leaks than Australia has kangaroos."

"Next time, love, travel on one of my ships. Has no leaks, but it does serve kangaroo meat to passengers and crew. Let's walk a bit before retiring. I want to savor this night, this lovely, lovely night, before closin' me one eye for the evening."

In Melbourne Deakin said, "I cannot tell you, Michael, how glad I am that you have agreed to do this thing."

"We have won and that is all that matters. If Lord a'Becket is willing, then so am I. Let matters between us stand as they now are. Let us live in peace, he and I. I'm getting on in years and so is he and we should spend what is left of our days puttin' our house in order for the great journey. A man should get ready for death. I have enough blood on my hands. I wish no more if it can be avoided."

"I shall speak to him and Denis. I feel strongly that they, too, want peace."

I have my doubts, mystic friend, thought Irons. He said, "How goes their railroad?"

"Most slowly. Some money has been raised but there is talk that eventually our new federal government will have to step in."

"Meanwhile, the a'Beckets have collected money from six nations and more than a few stockholders. Thanks to the battle for federation they have had time enough to steal half the world blind."

"In their own way, they contributed to federation. If nothing else, by keeping a truce of sorts with you."

Irons grinned. "Well, I am a grandfather with two handsome grandsons and I do not wish to bring trouble down on them. For that reason alone, I am willing to let things stand as they now are." He would not have put it past the a'Beckets to harm the boys. So let it be done with, this rivalry.

He and Deakin toasted each other with brandy. "One

Australia," said the tall, bearded Melburnian, "and peace between my dear friend Michael and the a'Beckets. God is indeed kind sometimes."

May God never sleep while the a'Beckets breathe, thought Michael.

Alone in his study Lord a'Becket, looking older and thinner because of the pain, spooned the medicine into brandy, then drank half of the small tankard. Less than two more years of life, the doctor had given him. And after that the cancer that was eating at him would have completed its task. He winced, closing his eyes. Damn painkiller. Far from thorough, far from complete. Better the brandy alone. At least it left a decent taste in a man's mouth, unlike the doctor's witch potion.

He slowly walked to the mantle, where he gazed at Camilla's picture. She had been cheated out of life and he had been cheated out of her and all because of one man. a'Becket's wife was now dead as well, but he had ceased to care for her even while she lived. Camilla, however, had always been dear to him, even after her betrayal. He would cherish her memory even into the next world and never forget her. Nor would he forget Michael Irons. Patience. Gradual tactics were the most effective. Had that not been proven with the death of Irons' son? No one suspected that it had been murder. a'Becket had now waited long enough to strike again at Irons and his family.

With the time remaining to him, a'Becket would continue to amass wealth, for that game kept him alive. In that time he would also kill Michael Bourke Irons. For good measure the lives of Irons' daughter and grandsons were also forfeit. Jack Straw would see to it. The banker stiffened, clutching his stomach. Stricken by time, not merely by the cruelty of cancer. Time destroyed everything—love, family, health. Unforgiving time, sweeping all from its path and turning dreams into elusive shadows.

Still, a man had to fight time, as a'Becket was doing. He doubled over with pain and the bottle of medicine slipped from his grasp, shattering on the brick hearth. In a sudden panic he dropped to his knees, to carefully pick at the shards of wet glass as he desperately sought a portion that contained enough of the painkiller to pour into another glass of brandy.

Johnny-Johnny said, "There was a white man in my dream. His hair was white and his skin was same. He walked in your shadow and when you turn to look at him, he disappear. Then you walk and he follow. Very white hair, very white, white skin. Means to harm you. Maybe harm grandchildren."

Irons looked at the sky. "We know of one such white, white skin."

"Jack Straw. Works for Denis a'Becket."

"Nasty piece of work, Mr. Straw. Does the dirty for Denis and on occasion acts as his bodyguard and coachmen to boot. And he appeared in your dream, did he?"

The two men were on a Sydney dock and still sitting in the carriage which had brought Irons to the ship that was to take him and several New South Wales delegates to London for a meeting with the British prime minister regarding Australia's new constitution. It was January 1900, the beginning of a new century and for Australia, the beginning of a new role in the world. Lou and Morag were off to one side, along with Irons' blond-haired grandsons, four and six years old, who hunkered down over two spinning tops. Each of the boys wore fake eye patches, a childish tribute to the grandfather they adored.

"Your dream makes me fear leavin' the boyos," said Irons. "Perhaps Blue Dan can put some men—"

The Aborigine shook his head. "White-white see guards, he disappear and come back another time. Best white-white die. Save boys. Maybe save you."

"a'Becket. They say he is wasting away of the cancer. I'm not sure if that is true. Damn his eyes!"

A seaman onboard called out, "All ashore that's goin' ashore!"

Irons stepped from the carriage. "Jack Straw has had a wicked life. It had to end sometime."

He started to walk away, then stopped. "Say nothing to Morag. Leave quietly, return the same way." He removed his wallet, took out some pounds and gave them to the Aborigine. "Should someone ask, you happen to be travelling south to buy horses for me. That is, should someone ask."

Johnny-Johnny shook his head, refusing the money. "No one will ask. No one will see me."

Irons put a hand on his shoulder. "Take care, mate." He drew the Aborigine to him and they embraced. For a second, Irons thought that Johnny-Johnny had gripped him too tight, as though this were the last time they would see one another. He pulled back, looked at his friend's dark face.

Johnny-Johnny smiled. "Lon-don. Do well in Lon-don, 'Iron Pirate'. You have been a good mate."

"And you too, you bloody Abo."

They grinned, touched each other on the arm and then Irons walked over to embrace his grandchildren. Saddened at their final parting and knowing that he himself was to die soon, Johnny-Johnny blinked tears from his eyes.

26 _____

LORD a'Becket had long kept a one-story country home
on the slope of a mountain in the "Blue Dandenongs," a
range of rolling hills and wooded valleys seventy miles
from Melbourne. Up close the landscape's blue color was
actually the gray-green of giant eucalyptus, Australia's
tallest tree. Hills and valleys were aflame with gladioli,
daffodils and tulips, but it was the variety of bird life, to
be enjoyed on walks along forest trails, that pleased the
ailing banker the most. His favorite bird was the *lyre*, an
uncanny mimic with the ability to accurately imitate any
sound it heard. a'Becket had heard it reproduce the sound
of ship's whistles, meshing gears and gunfire.

The cancer-ridden banker spent as much time away from
Melbourne as possible. In "the Blues," there was time for
quiet, restful walks and the mountain air proved invigorating.
In a study, with a magnificent view of the countryside, he
worked on private correspondence and those business pro-
posals that required much thought and concentration. One
servant was sufficient to cook, clean and shop in the
market gardens and orchards which dotted the slopes.

This afternoon a'Becket felt better than he had in some
time and so he walked longer, spending almost an hour

alone in the forest. Back in the resort home, he found himself with an appetite and ate a larger lunch than usual, with extra wine. Now it was time for a nap and after that, a little work. The coming of federation had brought talk of a Commonwealth Bank, which would undoubtedly be the largest in Australia and strong competition for private bankers like himself.

Opposing such a bank was out of the question. Too many powerful forces, including the states' premiers and private individuals such as Michael Irons, were in favor of it. Therefore, the wise thing was to join them and find a way to turn the Commonwealth Bank to the advantage of the a'Beckets, father and son. If nothing else, a way had to be found for Denis to become directly involved. The new central government would now rule the economy with an iron fist and like it or not, one had to accept that very harsh truth. Better to blend with the powers that be, than be a fool on the outside looking in.

Alone in his ground floor bedroom a'Becket inhaled the scent of flowers coming through his open windows and wondered what Michael Irons would do when he returned from England to find his daughter and grandchildren dead. a'Becket had charged Denis with seeing to it. Denis' bully boy, Jack Straw, was reliable in such matters. Straw had promised to find a way to dispose of mother and children, a way that would appear as accidental as the murder of Heath Irons. Only his desire to see Irons howling with torment was keeping a'Becket, daily being eaten away by cancer, alive.

Thinking was too tiring; a'Becket lay down on the bed, covering himself with a winter quilt. No matter how warm the day, the cancer always managed to chill his body. Drowsy with wine and good food, he closed his eyes, then panicked. *He couldn't breathe.* The pillow now covering his face was being pressed down by arms strong with corded muscles; the small, cancer-stricken banker was no match for his killer. a'Becket's legs lashed out and the quilt slipped halfway to the floor. He pulled at the pillow, then at the wrists of the man using it to murder him, but his efforts to cling to the little life he had remaining were in vain. His arms flopped to either side of his body and seconds later he was still.

Johnny-Johnny continued to press down with all his strength. To kill a snake, one removed the head. Between father and son, the old one was the most evil, for in the Aborigine's dream he had seen the father telling Jack Straw to kill Irons' daughter and grandchildren. Straw was still in Melbourne, but would leave soon to do as the old one had ordered.

Removing the pillow from a'Becket's now discolored face, Johnny-Johnny placed it gently beneath the dead man's head, then pulled the quilt up to the banker's chin. To the world, it would seem as though the old one had died naturally, taken away in his sleep by the sickness that destroyed from within.

At the edge of the forest Johnny-Johnny turned to look once more at the house. The servant, busy in the kitchen, had heard nothing. The ground floor bedroom windows, through which Johnny-Johnny had entered and left, were still open and there was peace in the woods. The Aborigine moved deeper into the forest, avoiding the trails and keeping to dense underbrush and clumps of trees. His thoughts were on Jack Straw, the albino, the white-white man.

And he thought, too, of his own death soon to come. He was half-white, but in Australia that made him colored and so he had been forced to cling to his Aborigine ways of thinking. Death meant going to your spirit-home. And it meant being reborn, for the spirit never died and kept its power throughout a lifetime. A part of him feared dying, but he was the one person who could deal with Jack Straw. Irons was on his way to London and had asked that his daughter not be told of the danger. Irons had already lost two sons. That was enough. Johnny-Johnny would give his life to make sure that it was enough. Irons was a true mate and for a mate, a man must be willing to do anything.

The Aborigine found his horse where he had hidden it, mounted and headed towards Melbourne. His had been a good life. The next one would be better.

Whistling through his teeth, Jack Straw combed and curried his horse. Alone in a Collins Street stable and working at night by the light of a lantern hanging from a stall, the albino methodically cleaned and pampered the animal, showing it a tenderness that he rarely displayed to anyone human. Tomorrow he would leave Melbourne for Sydney, where he would do the a'Becket's bidding and perform what he called "a removal". He had killed women before, but not children. Nevertheless, it should not be a problem. The a'Beckets wanted it to appear accidental or in the natural order of things and Straw had a thought or two on how to go about that. He would leave at dawn, riding his mount and avoiding trains. Being an albino made a man twice as likely to be noticed, so it was necessary to move about most carefully.

As the small, powerfully built Straw combed his horse's mane and whistled a bawdy song taught to him by a whore, a hand dropped to his waist where a pistol was tucked in his belt. He let the hand rest on the gun butt. Suddenly he whirled and the gun was in his hand and he fired twice. In that same instant he felt hot pain across his chest and he stumbled back against his horse and fought to right himself. The gun slipped from his hand, as he stared down at the pitchfork driven into his chest by Johnny-Johnny. Jesus wept. Ain't that a laugh and a holler, thought the albino. I heard the bastard, but I turned a wee bit too late.

Straw's heart was pierced; to him it felt as though that most vital organ was in a cruel vise, squeezed by icy fingers that were determined to do him much harm. He dropped to his knees; his mind willed his hands to pull out the pitchfork, but darkness was moving closer and the albino surrendered to it. The pitchfork prevented him from falling forward, so he fell to the side. With a booted foot

Johnny-Johnny shoved the albino onto his back, then pushed down on the pitchfork, driving it deeper.

The Aborigine coughed blood and staggered, fighting to keep his balance. He had taken Straw's two bullets in the chest. But he did not want to die here, not in a stable and not in a city. He would find a forest, and die there, with the sky looking down and the moon shining on leaves and the trees talking to him. Come back soon, Irons. I will be in the spirit world and your daughter will need you. She is still in danger. And so are you. Hurry home to Australia, where you belong and where I. . . .

He coughed again, bringing up more blood. Had to get to his horse, before . . .

In the saddle, he nudged the animal with his knees and it moved, leaving the stable and travelling through dark streets until it was out of the city and heading towards a clump of gum trees. Once amongst the trees, it stopped as though knowing and a dead Johnny-Johnny slipped from the saddle and fell to the ground where he stared unseeing up at the night sky.

27

London
March 1900

THE approval of the new constitution and the Australian Commonwwealth by Her Majesty's government was necessary, but with the round of meetings at Parliament, Westminster and Downing Street came parties, balls, dances, soirees, hunt breakfasts and fêtes, all in honor of the colorful Australians, citizens of the newest nation on earth. Alfred Deakin and Michael Irons remained indifferent to London society; Deakin saw it as empty and vain, while Irons, remembering his years of rejection by the English here and in Australia, saw it as treacherous and false.

The other delegates—Western Australia had joined at the last minute—enjoyed the attention that came with being men of the hour. The Australian twang was heard in the aristocractic clubs of St. James Street and Pall Mall, in the drawing rooms of Belgravia and at the chicest of Mayfair parties. With courtesy, however, came condescension. "They see us as dogs prancing on our hind legs," said Irons. "We chase away their boredom for a time and then, like tradesmen, we are ushered out the back door and other entertainment is quickly sought after.''

From the beginning the features in the constitution most pleasing to the British government were those based on English institutions. There were a few aspects of the American constitution written in, but there was no doubt that the Australian constitution had been framed to show an unquestioning loyalty to throne and empire. As Deakin said, ''To be loyal to Australia is to be loyal to England. Our people would have it no other way.''

''I would have it a different way,'' said Irons. ''I would have Australia united *and* free. At the moment, we have one and no one seems to want the other.''

''No one but the most stubborn of Irishmen. You seem to forget that many Australians consider themselves Britons at heart, that some even one day dream of leaving Australia and returning to—''

''Damn it all, man!'' Irons cried impatiently. ''These same people live like kings in Australia. Here in England, they would be lucky to be rag pickers. Attending this conference has taught me something: I see Australian nationalism as one thing and British empire building as another. Mark my words, mate. The empire will demand that we bow our head and bend our knee and serve her before we serve ourselves.''

''I disagree. I see no difference between serving Australia and serving England.''

Irons touched his eyepatch. ''I only have one eye. You have two. But this is one time, my mystic friend, when I may well have seen more than you.''

The euphoria over federation, however, and the long-standing loyalty to the empire, left no room for questions such as those posed by Irons. The new Australian Commonwealth was to be under the rule of a Governor-General appointed by the British monarch as representative of the Crown. He would have the power to veto legislation, dissolve the Australian Parliament and was Commander-in-Chief of the army and navy. Australia's prime minister and members of the cabinet would be appointed by him, albeit from the majority party in Parliament. Australia's defense and foreign affairs would be handled by England.

"Australia wants this, Michael," said Deakin. "If you attempt to turn us against England, you stand alone."

"Ah. So in fighting for federation I was free to be against whom I pleased. But now that we are all one, I must have my enemies hand picked for me. Is that it?"

"England can never be an enemy to Australia. She is its mother."

"Listen, mate. I am a bit long in the tooth to tear me heart out over the Queen's empire, so I will simply say that Australia wants one thing today, and may well want something else tomorrow. That is the way of the world. For some federation is the final step. For me, it is only a beginning. Important, but only a beginning. I tell you, mystic man, there will be a second fight concerning our new country and that fight will be over who is to run our lives."

In London, Irons more or less freed himself of Genista. Drawn by the attention being paid him, she appeared one evening at his hotel. In her late thirties and fashionably dressed, she was still remarkably lovely. Automatically she drew Irons into bed, but for the first time, her extraordinary sexual skills did not drug him as they had in the past. Lou Heller was in his heart to stay. It was with a sense of joy that he realized this; he would never again bed Genista after tonight.

"There is much talk of you throughout London," she said. "The Iron Pirate. The Apostle of Federation. You are being made as much of as any man in society. I knew it would happen. I am so proud of you. It is all the talk that you and Deakin will be knighted. Oh dearest . . ."

"Deakin and I have refused the honor."

She sat up. "You are joking."

He got out of bed and put on his robe. "We sent our

regrets to the Queen yesterday. Speaking for myself, my father would not want a title around my neck.''

"You're a bloody fool," she hissed. "Do you know what you've done?"

He sat in a chair and stared at her for a long time before saying, "I am leaving you, Genista. I wish a divorce."

Her mouth dropped open.

"I shall give you a more than generous allowance, but I wish to be free."

"I see. Well, Michael, I have no wish to be free of you. Not at this particular moment."

"I am not surprised. You always did run with the pack. So now you think I am a man of note in my country and you wish to run along side of me."

She leaned back in bed. "You will change your mind. About me, about the knighthood. You can go far in Australia, especially since you are, I guess one can say, a founding father."

"I want a divorce, Genista."

"The answer is no, my darling. You tell Lou Heller to find herself another digger. Is that what they call them?"

"And you can tell Denis a'Becket he is welcome to you."

Her eyes narrowed, then she smiled. "Michael, why must we talk about such minor matters? Come to bed."

"I think you should get dressed and leave."

"Denis tells me that you have expanded your shipping to include steamers and the latest turbine engines. You gain in wealth daily."

"The day of the clipper is past. Credit Morag with that conclusion. She has done wonders for my company. No man could have served me better or more faithfully."

"Odd little creature, she is. No offense. She and I never quite managed to pair off. Dear Michael, I could not possible agree to a divorce at this time. Two divorces do not benefit a lady's reputation these days, especially when the second involves—''

"An Australian born of transported Irish parents? What if you were to drop me instead?"

Genista laughed. "We are in lock step, you and I. At present I gain by remaining attached to you. As Mrs. Michael Irons, I too, have come in for my share of acclaim these days. Some even assume that I played a role in Australia's unity. An amusing thought."

"I will see that you live most comfortably."

"The answer is no."

"Very well."

His calmness was a surprise, a tactic she had not expected. Determined to deny him even a partial victory, she controlled herself, showing no reaction.

He stood up. "As I said, you shall be provided for. But in future, you shall not be allowed the extravagances you have so recently enjoyed. Perhaps you shall be the one to change your mind. The battle for federation appeared hopeless, too, but victory—"

"The battle for divorce will remain hopeless and unchanged. I am no longer a girl—"

"You are still quite beautiful."

"Thank you, kind sir. However, the years are passing in quick succession and I must give an eye to the future. I have a husband and would like to keep him, thank you. I have seen what happens to women who desperately seek a mate at an age when they are no longer able to compete with younger members of their sex. No, Michael, that will not happen to me."

He continued dressing. "Tonight I am to dine with the maker of the finest ship's engines in England. Forgive me if I allow you to find your own way out."

"If you felt this way, why did you make love to me?"

He paused, thought, then said, "Call it a needed confirmation of what I have long suspected about the two of us. Call it a reflex or remembrance of days past. Questions were answered tonight and there will be no need to consort with you in future. Not that you will be lonely. Your sort never is."

Kicking back the covers she threw herself across the bed, found one of her shoes on the floor and hurled it at him.

He ducked and came up grinning. "You will never bowl cricket for England, love. Get Denis a'Becket to show you the proper way to make a toss."

At Crockford's, London's most famous gambling club, Sir Darcy Corder pulled piles of *plaques*, the square chips used in baccarat, towards him. Excellent run of luck tonight. An exceptional week, in fact, with winnings at dog races and at the prize fights. What spoiled his pleasure tonight was the group of laughing and drinking Australians in the club, a bunch of drunken sods fawned over by Englishmen who should have known better. Bloody Aussies reminded him of Michael Irons, who had given Darcy the fright of his life. Ran him out of Australia with his damn tail between his legs, a humiliation that Corder had never forgotten. The Irishman had taken Genista as well, making Darcy look quite the fool among his London friends. And now here he was in London, acting like Lord God Almighty.

Gossip had Genista whoring with one man or another, which served Irons right. Let him wear the horns and see how it feels. Even thinking of Genista put Darcy in heat; he had yet to find a woman to match her in bed. His second wife, a lovely enough woman with the correct bloodline and appropriate dowry, did her best underneath the sheets but she was not a patch on Genista. Darcy would not mind bedding that bitch once more. She had no shame, no inhibitions, and a man could handle her in any fashion he chose. There were other women you could do those things to but none enjoyed them as much as Genista did.

Meanwhile the swinish Australians were fouling the air at Crockford's with their godawful twang and their boasting about their so-called country, which had been in existence for two hot minutes. Even Londoners who should have known better were throwing themselves at the muddy boots of *diggers*.

"Splendid, splendid chap, Irons," said a familiar voice behind Corder, who turned to see the banker Lord Norris Held holding court, addressing English aristocrats and Australians. "The Apostle of Federation. Well named. Well named indeed. First class businessman and a brilliant mind. If you ever get a chance to do a deal with him, take it. Made a few quid for me in my day and there may be more to come."

Held called Darcy's name. "Corder here knows Irons, don't you?"

"Indeed."

"Irons and Crafford are meeting tonight. Arranged it myself. Crafford's ship motors are the most advanced of any on the face of the globe. The best of Britain, by God. And soon to be the best of Australia, if Irons has his way."

Darcy didn't need an old fart like Lord Norris to tell him about the Crafford motor works. On Darcy's sudden return from Sydney, his father had stopped being angry long enough to find him a post in Whitehall, in the ministry of defense, one of the most important of government departments. One of the ministry's jobs was to sell British arms to the world, not a difficult job since Britain made the best weapons available. With the demise of the clipper ship, to all intents and purposes, the Crafford motor for ocean going vessels was very much in demand. A certain amount of bribery, political pressure and corruption followed all arms sales, but that was the nature of the beast. Darcy had warmed to the task and in the process, made money for himself as well.

Crafford motors. Efficient, up to the minute designs, which Crafford was constantly improving. No wonder Irons wanted them. Sitting at the baccarat table, it occured to Darcy that if he wanted to get back at Irons, and take him down a peg or two, Crafford motors just might be the way.

"Lord Held, please join me for a drink," said Darcy. "By the way, in what short of ship does Irons plan to use the motors?"

SYDNEY
January 1, 1901

On a humid Tuesday morning more than 200,000 people jammed Centennial Park to cheer and witness the birth of the Commonwealth of Australia. While Melbourne, with its more central location, was to be the interim capital, Sydney was given the honor of being the inauguration site. Bands and banners led a parade of trade unionists, city officials, dignitaries from the six states and foreign countries, city officials, clergy, lancers in scarlet tunics and troopers in khaki. Finally there was the carriage containing the Earl of Hopetown, who was to be sworn in as the new commonwealth's first Governor-General. To Edmund Barton, "Toby Tosspot", had gone the honor of being the first Prime Minister, pending the first national elections.

An ornate stone pavilion had been constructed for the occasion and Irons, with Lou and Morag, stood there along with all high officials and watched the Earl take his oath of office and repeat his oath of allegiance. Barton was then sworn in, along with Alfred Deakin and the premiers of the six states, all of whom would constitute an interim cabinet.

"A team of captains," Irons whispered to his daughter. "Each used to commanding and being obeyed, which means, that with the exception of Alfred, they'll all be at each other's throats before sundown."

Morag, who had been searching the crowd with her eyes, reluctantly turned to her father. "Sorry. You were saying?"

"How does it go with you and Alan?"

The answer was in her face. She dropped her eyes and pressed her lips together.

"It goes like that does it," said Irons. "He does not care to have a wife who can match, perhaps outdo him. Your success with me is unacceptable to him." He sighed. "I have come to depend on you as I would a son. It may be a long while before a woman of your stripe comes along in this country."

She looked up. "And if may be even longer before a man such as you comes along to give a woman the opportunity I have had."

"In truth, I can take little credit. There was no choice left to me. You proved yourself to be most able."

"Even when I sacked some of your oldest executives and replaced them with men of my choice?"

He smiled and nodded.

"And," she continued, "when I sold the mines without telling you and recommended that we grow more wheat and less sheep?"

"We profited, lass. As we did in this horrendous drought, thanks to you."

Australia was in the midst of a drought that had lasted for almost six years. Water was worth its weight in gold and without it, sheep died and crops failed. Morag, however, had purchased expensive drilling equipment and dug deep, producing artesian wells on Irons' land. In return for sharing the water with farmers and land owners who could not afford to drill on their own land or who lacked the necessary soil for such a well, Morag extracted payment in kind. She accepted services performed for the Irons & Pease Company, as well as sheep, land, wool and wheat.

She was her own cause. There were no women to equal her and few men and so it was men whom she hired and fired, being quicker than her father to discharge employees and executives for imcompetence or insubordination. Behind her back she was called "Lady MacBeth" and "The Medusa"; men were still reluctant to do business with her, but given no choice, were forced to. A few admired her, especially when she proved to be as ruthless as they.

Her chief problem was Alan's pride. Despite his love for her he could not accept her achievements in business. Morag's power, respect and money were more than anything he had been able to accomplish. They now argued more, with Alan ending up spending an increasing amount of time away from home. Today at the inauguration he marched with the trade unionists, proud to be among those who had been among the first to envision a new and united Australia. Morag loved him for his dream and wished that he could love her for her dream as well.

They had moved to a larger house with servants, all of it paid for by Morag. And all of it upsetting to Alan.

"What the bleedin' hell am I, a ponce? Some sort of fancy man livin' off a woman's earnings?"

"Alan, it's our money, yours and mine."

"Mine, is it? And when did that come about? I go to sleep a poor man and wake up stinkin' rich, it seems. Australia is truly a golden land."

"Your damn pride—"

"Listen Mary Bloody Reiby or whoever you are. You have as much pride as me and don't you forget it. Now if you don't mind, I think I'll take myself away from this here enchanted castle and spend a few hours with my mates. Their wives are not as brilliant as mine, the lucky buggers."

She had seen little of him recently. She missed him, and wished right now that he were by her side at the inauguration. But the cool politeness between him and her father, combined with past tensions between her and Alan, made that impossible. On what should have been a wonderful day, she was heartbroken, sad, confused. For the first time she seriously doubted whether she had done the right thing in going to work for her father.

Irons knew what she was thinking and while he selfishly wanted to hold on to her, he wanted her to be happy. Since Johnny-Johnny's death Morag, in effect, was his closest mate, the one person he knew he could depend on at all times. It was upsetting to see her sad. Looking at the crowd he spotted Alan, who had gone unnoticed by a subdued Morag. Costello was staring at her and from the look on his face wanted to come over. Did he think Irons still wanted him at arms' length? The two men had been civil to one another these past few years, but were far from close.

Johnny-Johnny on the other hand was a mate for all time. He had disposed of Jack Straw and sent Lord a'Becket on to the next world, something Irons had not told Morag. A good mate, Johnny-Johnny. Denis a'Becket was here today, with his hatch-faced wife and three toothy daughters. The few times he and Irons locked eyes confirmed Irons' suspicion that Denis still despised him and was to be considered a most treacherous man. Federation had changed nothing between the two.

But by the Lord God above, it was still a glorious day. Which was why Irons signalled Lou to say nothing to Morag, then left the two women to walk over to Alan Costello. Both men stared silently at one another, with Alan the more uncomfortable. He would never admit it, but Alan was awed by Irons. "The Iron Pirate" had achieved much, with a deserved reputation for manliness and courage. He was indeed worth of respect, even if you disagreed with him.

With trade unionists watching, Irons offered his hand to Alan. "It is a great day for Australia, a day for shakin' hands and startin' anew. Haven't always agreed you and I, but you do have my respect as a man."

Alan took the hand eagerly and pumped it with both of his. "And you mine, sir."

"You also have the respect and love of my daughter. If you respect me, I would ask that you go to her this day. She needs you. Never forget that. Do your best by her."

Alan looked at Morag, who was now staring at him and her father with tear-filled eyes. Irons' eyes sparkled with good natured firmness. "You might remember, Costello,

that my daughter is the cream of the crop and I'd be
obliged to see her treated that way. You knew what she
was when you took her to wife. If your luck holds, man,
she just might manage to bring out the best in you as she
has in me."

Irons leaned forward, his one eye hard on Alan's face.
"Would you be humorin' an old man and go along now to
your wife?" It was a mock threat and Alan could only
smile. And quickly hurry to Morag, who took him in her
arms.

Around Irons the trade unionists stepped forward to
shake his hand and clap him on the back. "*Australia!*"
one shouted and the chant was picked up until it raced
throughout the crowded park like a brush fire.

28 _____

IN Melbourne's Parliament House, Michael Irons watched from the visitors' gallery as Alfred Deakin spoke of the war between Russia and Japan, which had broken out in March 1904, just a month ago. This time parliament was packed; the half-hearted interest in the political process, which often saw many legislators absent and others occupied in the billiard room, bar, on the cricket pitch or bowling green, was missing today. Instead every bench on the floor was filled, as was every chair in the gallery. Deakin, now prime minister, spoke of a war taking place thousands of miles away, a war that could have its effect on Australia.

The charismatic Deakin did not mince words. "This hellish war, the largest in history, is being fought with weapons of a frightening complexity. Armored battleships, land mines, rapid firing artillery, modern machine guns and self propelled torpedoes are being used for the first time. The resultant carnage will be awesome to both victor and vanquished alike."

"Russia is England's enemy and therefore, ours. Already, Britain's forces are in a state of alert regarding this conflict and it is not inconceivable that she could well be dragged into it on the side of Japan, her ally. Which means, my friends, that Australia, lacking defense forces and depending entirely on Britain, loses her sole protection. No man can challenge my loyalty to the crown and yet I do not believe that we can continue for very much longer in such a state of vulnerable dependency. Relationships between the great European powers worsen daily, resulting in an armaments race of horrendous proportions, one which condemns the world to live in fear. Australia needs her own defense force.

"Britain and France are once again allies and should Europe explode into war, a growing possibility, it follows that Britain will be a participant. Again, where does this leave Australia? In a word: helpless. Hear me when I say, *helpless*. And I say this cannot be, it must not be, it will not be. Let us pledge ourselves to protect ourselves and let us do it soon."

He sat down to great applause. And then it was Alan Costello's turn to speak. The Laborites, of all political groupings in parliament, were the strongest supporters of an Australian defense force, seeing the country's isolation and great distance from possible allies as good reasons for self reliance. Alan had less hair and more weight but he was still an effective speaker. "Wars are rarely won. They are, however, frequently lost. Meaning that the vanquished is more often than not the cause of his own defeat. For so long Australia has had the sweet advantage of distance, of being away from both friend and foe and today we still fall back on this as an excuse for continuing to stagnate—"

There were scattered catcalls.

"And continuing to keep our heads in the sand and our arses where they can be shot at."

Laughter.

Alan pointed to the gallery. "There above you sits a man who has pledged his fortune and energy to building an Australian navy. Yet, parliament slams the door in his face. I am speaking of Michael Irons, who in vain has attempted to point out the folly of relying on anyone else to fight our battles. Yes, even England.''

More catcalls, mixed with cheers, boos, applause. Alan continued, raising his voice above the din. ''What good does it do to be one nation if that nation plans to remain weak. Irons—''

''Treason!'' The voice came from the floor, from the left of the house. ''You challenge the integrity of Britain and I call that treason!''

Someone yelled for quiet and respect for the speaker. A fist fight broke out and then another. Alan continued to speak, shouting at the top of his voice over an ever increasing pandemonium. Irons removed his spectacles, placed them in his pocket and with gallery eyes following him, left and went out into the hall. Australian politics was a zoo with frock coats, top hats and enough alcohol to flood the largest desert. He patted his spectacles. At sixty-three, his one eye was dimming, but no matter. He did not have to see, he had only to hear and what he heard today was no different from what he had been hearing for the past three years.

Isolation and the promise of British protection had made Australians indifferent about their own defense. Well, the world was changing and Irons knew it. So did Deakin, so did Alan and a handful of others. One fine day, in the not too distant future, England would be involved in its own wars and on that day it would be devil take the hindmost. Australia would have to fend for itself and it had damned well better be prepared. The new century had brought with it a belligerent Germany, an ambitious Japan, an aggressive Russia and an America anxious to flex its strong, young muscles. Sooner or later, these four would knock heads and the world would feel the pain.

Federation had failed to create a rush to build a military force. Australians, it seemed, did not want to tax themselves to pay for a permanent defense force. Penny wise and pound foolish, thought Irons. So what if the British navy paid impressive visits to Australia? Australia paid good money for those visits as it did for the building of British battleships which she never saw, but which she was told would come to her aid if and when. Australians also paid to station a small British naval detachment nearby, a detachment that could sail anywhere in the world without a moment's notice. In Irons' opinion, Britain had Australia by the short and curlies.

In the hallway outside of the gallery he stopped and lit a cigar, aware that he was being stared at by passersby as thought he were some icon. What do you think of that, Davy Pease? The grey-haired, one-eyed son of Irish convicts is now the subject of gaping and wonderment. But you're famous, lad, says Davy. You build Australia's finest ships, you have men in parliament beholden to you, you are a *toff* in a major Sydney bank and your company— *our company*—is flourishing. You hobnob with Australia's rich and powerful, who hang on your every word and three times you have said no to the crown when it's offered you a knighthood. Proud of you, I am, says Davy. Proud indeed.

Inside parliament the uproar had not ceased. Hard to believe, thought Irons, that it was this so-called majestic and elevated body which had approved minimum wages, pensions and compulsory arbitration for labor disputes, established tariffs to provide federal income and given women the vote, something women did not have in Britain or nationwide in America.

In Deakin's private office Irons waited for the prime minister to join him. He was about to close his eye and sleep, for he tired easily these days, when there was a knock at the door.

"Yes?"

"The clerk, sir. Cablegram for you, Mr. Irons. From London."

Irons crossed the room, opened the door and took the yellow envelope from the clerk. Alone, he hooked the wire ends of his spectacles over his ears and excitedly opened the cable. For almost four years he had waited for Crafford in London to complete work on the motors, paying him 500,000 pounds in advance. There had been a huge back-list for the Englishman to fill before he could deal with Irons' orders, but now the motors were ready to be shipped to Australia. When Australians saw what a difference they made in a ship, when they saw how fast such a vessel could split the waves and sail the earth, then they would change their minds about a navy.

The cable spoke of trouble. It was from Lord Norris Held, who was acting as Irons' agent for the motors. *Come To London Immediately. Motors Will Not Be Shipped. You Have An Enemy Here. Held.*

Enemy? Who?

Nine weeks later in London, Lord Norris Held said, "Sir Darcy Corder."

Irons frowned.

"Defense ministry," said Held, offering Irons a brandy and soda in his study. "Corder's one of the Oxbridge set, the ones who attended Oxford and Cambridge and ruddy well rule this country. He fits in well, fiddles a bit here and there and is a member in good standing of the old boy network. Oh, did I add that he hates your guts?"

"I am well aware of that. What I'd like to know is how that bastard managed to impound both my motors and my money."

"Simple, old boy. It's called national security. Because of the Russian-Japanese war, England has decided to remain at the ready. With Corder pulling the strings, your motors are now earmarked for possible use by British forces or for resale to its ally Japan."

"And my half million pounds?"

"Well, old fruit, I can only say that getting it back will be an uphill battle at the very least. You're an Australian upstart, you realize—"

"I realize."

"And from what I can gather, the powers that be feel you should be willing to wait until the so-called emergency is lifted. In other words, know your place and trust Mother England to take good care of your money and deliver you the motors in the sweet bye and bye.''

Irons rolled his empty glass between his large hands. ''So, no motors and no money. And Corder gets his own back.''

''Legally. He's been bragging about it all over London.''

''Has he now?''

''Quite. Has you wrapped and tied and feels there's absolutely nothing you can do about it. Another drink?''

''Thank you. Tell me, old friend, would you say that the American and German navies are strong?''

Held snorted. ''Too damn strong if you ask me. Excellent ships, the both of them. Germany in particular is planning a dreadnought, a monstrous battleship that promises to be the most ferocious thing in the water.''

Irons smiled. ''Good. I want you to get someone else to act as my agent in what I propose. You shall receive your usual commission, but it is best that you not be publicly associated with what I intend to do.''

''Which is?''

''Prove to Sir Darcy Corder and the rest of the Oxbridge, old boy network that an upstart Australian is not to be mucked about. I would like you with me when Corder and I meet.''

Held shook his head. ''He boasts that he shall never see you, nor shall you be allowed to plead your case to the ministry. He'll prevent that from ever happening. Australians must be taught their place, he says.''

Irons sipped his drink, then looked up at the ceiling. ''The bugger will meet me and he'll do it within twenty four hours.''

Less than twenty four hours later a sullen Sir Darcy Corder and two high officials from the Ministry of Defense met Irons and Lord Norris Held in Whitehall.

''Serious business this,'' said the senior official. ''Dealing with foreigners in a matter of this importance. Bad form, Irons. Very bad form."

"So is robbery," said Irons evenly. "You denied me my motors and kept my money and you have the nerve to speak of bad form? You must deal with fools constantly. I see no other reason for your lack of intelligence."

The official's nostrils flared. He looked down at a piece of paper on his desk. "You have approached Germany and the United States of America about buying motors from them. Do you have such contempt for your king—"

"*Your* king, Sir Guy, proposes to take from me what is rightfully mine. I propose to see that he does not."

"So. If we do not comply with your demand to return what you claim is rightfully yours, you will deal with foreigners, is that it?"

Irons nodded. "And I will do my best to see that Australia continues to deal only with those who respect her."

"Australia, Mr. Irons, remains loyal to the crown. You do not have the power to change that."

Irons leaned forward. "I have the power to buy motors where I choose. If you force me to deal with 'foreigners', it could become a habit and if that habit is successful and profitable, other Australians might follow suit."

The official coughed, looking over his bifocals at Corder and the second official and said, "This is a subject which cannot be dealt with in such haste. Perhaps in a few days—"

Irons stood up. "This afternoon I will let the Americans or Germans know of my decision. Tomorrow morning I sail back to Sydney. You will give me your answer within the hour. Gentlemen. Lord Held."

Outside in the corridor Held took Irons arm and chuckled. "I thoroughly enjoyed myself in there. You have them in a corner. Now it remains to be seen if they'll fight or capitulate. With rats, one never knows."

*   *   *

A day later Irons stood at a railway station and watched his motors being loaded on rail cars for shipment to the port of Southampton, to be immediately placed on ships bound for Australia.

When the loading was done Crafford and his staff shook hands with Irons, as did a representative from the Ministry of Defense. Darcy Corder, however, who had been ordered to oversee the transfer of the motors to Irons, turned and walked away. He didn't have to say that the business between him and the man who had taken away his wife was not yet ended.

29

"SLUT," hissed Denis a'Becket. "I could kill you."

"I do believe you mean it. Do take your hand away. You're hurting my wrist."

"Answer me: are you sleeping with other men?"

"And since when is that a concern of yours?"

Genista and Denis were in an open carriage moving along Melbourne's Collins Street. His jealousy obsession with her had reached the point where he could not bear to have her out of his sight. He was besotted with her; time had not lessened her sexual hold on him and Denis, who had once been the master, found their roles gradually being reversed. In bed Genista would still assume the role of slave, but her appetites seemed to have grown until Denis found it almost impossible to keep up, let alone surpass her. He sensed her infidelity, was convinced of it in fact, and wanted to punish her for it. But how could he do so when Genista was so utterly in control?

"I still wish to marry you," he said. "Irons will agree to a divorce. Why do you not accept his terms?"

"And your wife?"

"Will do as I say."

Genista smiled at him with exaggerated sweetness. "And

can a divorced man enjoy high public office? What of your ambition to serve as chairman of the first Commonwealth Bank? Or your desire to be Australia's first High Commissioner, not to mention your desire for knighthood.''

Denis shook his head. ''Yes, I have a wish to achieve those things. I expect your husband to oppose me, but no matter. I have friends in high places and can give a good account of myself. I can be an important man—''

She waved him away. ''Yes, yes. I have heard it all before. In fact, I've heard it so many times over the years that I'm sick of it. And you.''

He reached for her, but she held up a hand. ''You promised to achieve certain things and you have not. I am disappointed in you, Denis. How can I marry a man who does not keep his promises?''

''I can do what I promised. Give me time. The Commonwealth Bank—''

''Deakin has asked my husband to become involved in that project.''

Denis snorted. ''Your husband. It's been years since he's bedded you. Or wanted to. He's no more your husband than, than . . .''

''Than you are.'' She twirled her parasol and gazed at the shops along Collins Street. ''I do need to do a bit of shopping.''

''If it's money you need—'' Denis reached in his jacket for his billfold.

''I have money, Denis. My husband sees to that quite nicely, thank you. I have had another proposal of marriage. From a gentleman in London. Titled, of course, and well fixed. Extremely well fixed. Owns land in four countries.''

She looked at Denis a'Beckett. ''Do you really want to marry me?''

''You know damned well I do. I'd do anything.''

''To begin with you can have the driver go by the river. This Australian sun is absolutely destructive to my complexion and I'm sure it promises ill for my hands as well. The year ends soon, Denis. A matter of weeks and 1906 will be but a memory. I wish to wed next year, the year after at the latest. I don't know how much longer my husband will continue to put up with this situation between us. I know he lives with his concubine, the extremely common Lou Heller, and for reasons which elude me, has actually come out and said he wants to marry the creature.''

''And you oppose the match?''

She twirled her parasol with gloved fingers. ''I am thinking that my husband might do something impulsive, which is to say against my interests. He is quite devoted to this Lou person and who can say if, in his dotage, he might not decide to force me into a divorce against my will? He is getting on in years. So I wish to provide for my future.''

She looked at him. ''Next year, Denis. Early the following year at the latest. I know life moves slowly in Australia, but if you wish to marry me—''

''You know I do.''

''Then bring me a reason for the marriage.''

''Power. You said you enjoyed power—that is men of power.

He closed his eyes. ''Your husband is my sworn enemy. He prevents me from getting what is mine.''

''The matter of the High Commissioner and a post with the Commonwealth Bank are still open to you.''

''The Commissioner has yet to be chosen, true. Parliament cannot agree on how to go about it.'' The post of High Commissioner was an idea pushed by Deakin, Irons and others. For years each colony had a representative in London, called an Agent-General, to represent its interests. But in 1906, the Commonwealth had no such representative; the idea had been postponed because of jealousy over who was to be selected and how.

''Is my husband more powerful than you, Denis?''

Anger made him blurt out a secret. ''My father and I killed his sons. And sooner or later I will kill Irons.''

Genista frowned, not knowing what to make of what she had just heard. But she looked at Denis with a new respect.

"Let us return to my hotel. We can talk better there." She stroked him seductively. "Did you really kill Irons' sons?" she murmured, feeling the heat rising within her.

Blue Dan leaned on the rail at Sydney's Randwick Racetrack and eyed a swift mare speeding around the empty track. It was shortly before noon and he had asked his brother for the meeting now taking place between them. It was a strained encounter and both men spoke without looking at the other, keeping their eyes on the fleet mare, owned by Blue Dan.

"You've turned against your own brother," said Blue Dan in a soft, bitter voice.

"That's not true," Alan rejoined. "I have done what is best for the Labor party, what is best for Australia."

"Done what Michael Irons has told you to do, damn his eyes!"

"The men we removed from positions of responsibility in the Labor party—"

Blue Dan turned to face him. "Were mine. Bought and paid for. Beholden to me."

Alan looked down at his folded hands. "That was the problem, Dan. Beholden to you and not to the Labor Party. 'Whose bread I take, his song I sing'. Isn't that how it goes?"

Blue Dan sneered. "Next you'll be calling me a hooligan and slappin' me face for corruptin' your beloved party."

"Dan, listen. Labor has long wanted a strong defense, in particular a strong navy. We now have Deakin on our side, thanks to Irons. He and the prime minister are close friends and it was Irons who smoothed the path between Deakin and us. So now Deakin is willing to stop paying 200,000 thousand pounds a year to Britain for its Royal Navy and use that money to create Australia's own navy, as we want, as Irons wants. A navy, with our own ships, means jobs buildin' ships, submarines, dreadnoughts."

"Taking those men away from important posts has cost

me money, Alan,'' Blue Dan said venomously. "I wanted a certain law passed about racing and a friend of mine, who has been disbarred, wants to practice law again.''

Alan shook his head. "Dan, your friend Jeremy Mason was disbarred because he swindled his clients. I know that Parliament is no collection of saints. There is much corruption and confusion there, but we have good men sitting among us as well. Mason's swindle caused a woman to kill herself. Getting rid of him was the right thing.''

Blue Dan spat. "That for doin' the right thing, little brother. And you can tell your friend Michael Irons that soon we'll be settlin' our scores with one another. I have waited long to do so and the waitin's done. Tell him for me.''

He walked away, leaving Alan alone at the rail of the empty race track, with the mare behind him racing against time.

30

LOU Heller, her arms filled with packages, waited impatiently on a Sydney street corner for the traffic to subside, so that she could get to the theatre directly across the street. As usual much of the traffic was speeding too fast, with carriage and wagon drivers laying on the whip as though competing in an ancient Roman circus. She wondered what would happen when the American automobile became more popular in Australia. Only a handful of the well to do, Michael Irons among them, owned motor cars. The majority of Sydneysiders, if not all Australians, considered the automobile a passing fad. Hadn't the horse been around for thousands of years?

The packages Lou clung to were all for Michael. He had a birthday in a few days, a fact he did not want to be reminded of. "Just another nail in me coffin," he said. Despite that, Lou always brought him presents. Today she had purchased a checkered cap and goggles for Michael to use when driving his new Pierce-Arrow motor car, one of three he owned, and all of which he preferred to drive himself. "If I am to end up in hell for riding in one of these things, let is be me own hand that takes me there."

Lou heard cries urging on horses and heard whips whistle in the air and looked to her right to see two cabs racing each other down the dusty street, the drivers, undoubtedly drunk, viciously beating their animals. There was probably a wager on the outcome as well. Dangerous as hell, thought Lou. She watched pedestrians scatter and horsemen rein up their mounts to let the cabbies pass.

Someone recognized Lou and called her name and she turned and never saw the wheel. It broke from one of the speeding cabs and hurtled towards her and when she finally acknowledged the shouts and turned, it was too late.

The wheel smashed into her, scattering the packages and knocking the singer into the air. Her screams stopped only when she crashed to the wooden sidewalk and lay unconscious, blood trickling from her nose and mouth.

There was a tear on a lens of Irons' spectacles and he gently smoothed it away with a thumb before putting the spectacles back in their case. He spoke to Morag, but his eye was on a bandaged Lou Heller lying in the hospital bed. "I should have married her. She wanted that. Never complained, never pressured me. God in heaven I should have married that woman."

"It's not too late."

"God willing," Michael said fervently.

For days Lou had lain near death, suffering from a fractured skull, crushed pelvis, two broken legs, cracked ribs and internal injuries. The best doctors in Sydney had worked around the clock to save her life, and the best they could say was that her chances of survival were now infinitesimal instead of non-existent.

A saddened Irons thought of the contentment she had brought him these past years, of her good humor and unwavering love. They shared his Elizabeth Bay mansion, indifferent to gossips and scandal mongers such as Redmond Glass. Irons' marriage to Genista was nothing but a hollow legalism; she rarely appeared in Australia and when she did her preference was for Melbourne and Denis a'Beckett, along with his circle of anglophiles.

Irons took Lou's hand. "If she lives, I will give her my name as she has silently wished. Genista will give me my divorce or live to regret her refusal. God in heaven let Lou live, I beg you. I wish to make her my wife. I demand that she live."

The ultimatum to God, however, failed to quell Irons' fears.

31 _____

ON the grounds of his Elizabeth Bay estate Michael Irons, with the aid of a cane, walked beside Alfred Deakin, whose black beard was streaked with gray and whose handsome face was becoming increasingly lined. Stopping to shade his eyes against the sun Deakin looked out at a steamship sailing into the harbor. It was 1908 and the fifty-four-year old Deakin was in his second term as prime minister, having succeeded Sir George Reid, who had held the post for less than a year, but who had found the time to recommend himself for a knighthood.

"It would be a most daring thing to do," said Deakin.

Irons grinned. "Then by all means, do it."

"It is all well and good for you to say that, since it is I who will be going behind the back of the almighty British government and not you."

"Given the chance, I would gladly do so."

"It is your idea, after all. Perhaps I should let you have the honor of causing trouble, for trouble it shall most certainly be if I follow your advice."

Irons bit the end off a cigar and spat it out. "Tell me what sort of free nation is it that lacks a navy or army of its own? Write that letter. Write it for Australia."

The letter, which was Irons' idea, would eventually end up on the desk of Theodore Roosevelt, President of the United States and England would be none too pleased. Roosevelt, who proudly proclaimed that "one should speak softly and carry a big stick", had decided to send the American Battle Fleet, sixteen of the world's most powerful battleships, on a cruise of the Pacific, with an eye towards impressing Japan, now more aggressive than ever since her victory over Russia three years ago. Deakin, ever wary of Japan, and like Irons, a fervent believer in an Australian defense force, wanted the fleet to visit Australia. He and Irons both felt that such a visit would let Britain know that Australia had other powerful friends.

Because Britain still conducted Australia's foreign affairs the request for a visit from the American navy would have to go through London's Colonial Office, which at best would be reluctant to invite the fleet. Irons had figured a way to get the Colonial Office to do as Deakin wished. "First write a letter to the American Ambassador in London and the American consul here in Australia. Request that both men advise President Roosevelt to accept the official invitation from Whitehall when it comes."

Irons grinned. "You'll have Whitehall in a vise. Make sure they hear about your letter, of course. They will have to extend the invitation."

"What a rascal you are. And what a brilliant idea."

"It's the Irish in me. The English and Scots in this country may love Britain with all their heart and souls, but me, I remember my father and mother on a prison hulk eating rancid meat and rotten vegetables. Let Britain think that the Americans are being considered a substitute protector. See how well that sets with 'the men in black.' "

Deakin said, "I shall do it. It will be a grand day for us if the Americans accept."

"They will. And know this: when Australians see those ships it will be like a child seeing a toy. They will want their own."

* * *

Inside at dinner Irons helped Lou into a chair near his, while a servant took away her crutches. Alan, Morag and their two sons, now teenagers, stood waiting until Irons and Deakin had taken their seats. The talk, not surprisingly, was of politics, with a discussion of the conflict between Australian nationalism and loyalty to Britain, the mother country. There was also talk of Australia's growing tendency to become a "welfare state", with its legislation protecting workers in all fields and its guarantee of pensions.

What Alan was most proud of was Labor's growing power. It was Deakin who effectively analyzed why labor was the strongest political grouping in the nation. "Its members support it with a religious fervor and that is its strength. It has discipline, loyalty and does not encourage disobedience or deviation from the party philosophy. Other parties have money, numbers and influence. None of these, however, can match labor's unity and belief in itself."

Alan said, "The day will come when both houses of parliament and the prime minister's chair, too, will be occupied by labor."

Deakin, who had come to power with labor's support, sighed, "I fear so."

A servant entered with a cablegram for Irons, who had been listening quietly and holding Lou's hand. She had never fully recovered from that tragic accident of a year ago. She had endured a half dozen operations and needed crutches to walk, but she was alive. That's all that mattered. Irons read the cablegram. It was from Genista, only his second contact with her in a year. She had been in Egypt and the Middle East for six months. And she still refused to grant him a divorce. Irons crumpled the cable, squeezing it tightly in his fist. Forcing a smile he looked at the gathering. If it killed him or Genista he would get that divorce.

In bed that night Morag finally sat up and gently told a restless Alan that it was time to talk about it. Reluctantly, he agreed. He said, "Blue Dan says he will oppose me.

He says that I have harmed him greatly by doing what I could to remove his men from positions of power within our party. I could not remove all of them, of course, and even now one or two remain.''

"You acted correctly. I think it is not merely you that he is against. He opposes my father as well. Obviously he feels that my father unduly influences you.''

"Your father is a great man and I was a fool not to see it sooner. We disagree, yes, but he still has my respect. More than once I have found his advice and wisdom to be of help to me. He has suggested that I run for the upper house, the senate.''

Morag hugged him. "An excellent idea. It is time for you to step higher.''

As a representative of New South Wales in the federal parliament, Alan served a three year term. As a senator—each state was entitled to six—he would serve a six year term and have more influence.

"You will win, Alan. I know you will.''

"My own brother will mount a formidable opposition.''

"At least he will not do you violence.''

He kissed her. "Have no fear. Blue Dan is still my brother. Besides, some of his hatred is still directed at your father. He has not forgiven him for Lou. Even now, after all these years.''

She smoothed his balding head. "If nothing else we Irish can give the world a lesson in how to hate. If Blue Dan should ever harm you or my father, I would show him the true meaning of hatred. There are certain men on the docks who work for my father, men who have been with him for years and are very loyal. There is nothing they would not do for him.''

Alan's shoulders slumped. "I do love Blue Dan, you know. I owe him so much.''

"You do not owe him your soul. That belongs to God and one day he will come to reclaim it. Do not let him find it in the hands of Blue Dan. Now lie down beside me and tell me a wonderous story as only you can, boyo.''

*   *   *

Backed by a handful of supporters, who held flickering torches to light the night, Alan spoke to a crowd gathered at King's Cross, one of Sydney's tougher neighborhoods. He spoke of what labor had done for Australia and would continue to do and he spoke of his role in the social programs passed by parliament, a program that had prompted some to call Australia "The Worker's Paradise." Alan had almost come to the end of his speech when suddenly from nearby rooftops lumps of coal started to rain down on the rally. The crowd began to scatter, save for one tough goldminer who drew his pistol and began firing at the rooftops.

Someone else in the crowd began firing. From the rooftops, their fire was returned and men fell bleeding to the ground.

Alan Costello was one of them.

32

MELBOURNE
1909

DENIS slapped Genista Irons across the face with all his strength. She fell back on the bed and covered her face as she wept. Brutally, the fat banker kicked her in the leg with his booted foot. She screamed and tried to get away from him, but he followed her, aiming more blows and kicks until finally her terror and hysterics forced him to stop.

Breathing heavily he said, "You stay away from me all these months, then come back expecting things to be as they were. How many men did you sleep with, you fucking harlot!"

"Don't hit me, please don't hit me!"

"Why did you come back? Was it for me?"

"Y-yes. I missed you, Denis. I did miss you."

He spat on her. He was so beside himself that he tore his own clothes, ripping his shirt front and sending studs flying. "You lie, bitch. You came here because Irons is in London and you did not want to face him."

"I could have gone to France or some place."

"Too close. Irons wants his divorce and means to have it. I think this time he will."

She huddled in a corner, red faced with tears and looked at him.

"Yes," he said. "I know something you do not know."

She touched the welt on her face. "I see Redmond Glass still manages to bribe Irons' servants."

"When Irons finishes with you, I doubt if you will be able to afford a single servant. He means to have his divorce, dear Genista. The Iron Pirate had made contact with his lawyer about changing his will. When he returns from London with Deakin, the matter will be pursued further."

She scurried to her feet. "He has left me 100,000 pounds in his will. It was his wedding gift to me."

"Count on changes, none of which you will enjoy. Either you grant him a divorce and soon, or he will cut you off without a penny."

"My allowance—"

"To be stopped entirely, I hear."

"He would not dare. No civilized man would even consider such a thing. It would embarrass him in polite society."

Denis sneered. "Irons does not always move in polite society, as you know better than anyone. And I feel he is willing to risk social disgrace in order to bring you to your knees. Irons is old and his paramour Miss Heller is not well. They wish to wed before the grim reaper carries them off. At present Irons and Deakin are in London, attempting to convince the British Admiralty to allow Australia to build its own naval fleet."

"Britain is quite angry with my husband. That business of the American ships visiting Australia did not go down too well with the Crown."

It had, however, gone down well in Australia where hundreds of thousands turned out to cheer the ships and crew, over two hundred of whom jumped ship to live in Australia. Parliament had been so impressed with the American navy that it had come out stronger than ever for an Australian defense program.

Genista looked in a mirror and used trembling fingers to comb hair from her face. "Who on earth cares about such rot as battleships?"

"More and more Australians, it seems. Do you care about your future?"

She froze, her fingers touching a cheekbone. "Would he really do it? Did Glass say—"

"Glass reports. He does not practice clairvoyance. He is neither sage nor soothsayer. I believe it is time we talked, you and I. Before he left for London, Irons managed to do me more than a small amount of harm."

He told her. The current prime minister was Andrew Fisher, a forty-seven-year old Scot and former coal miner who was cautious, shrewd and hard-working. Denis desperately wanted to be included in talks on the first Commonwealth Bank, which had been a dream of his since first hearing of it. But it was Irons who killed that dream by bringing to Fisher's attention the a'Beckets failure to provide a trans-continental railroad as promised. In all the years of trying the railroad, often promised, had never been delivered. Both a'Beckets, however, had profited greatly from the project.

"Before my father died," said Denis, "he pointed me in the direction of the Commonwealth Bank. It was to be our greatest triumph. Now thanks to Irons, once more I know the taste of ashes. He plans to make more of the railroad business, a matter which has laid quiet and undiscovered until he called attention to it. The scrupulously honest Fisher does not want me near the Federal Bank, thanks to Irons. I give you my word: soon Irons will trouble me no more."

Genista remembered what Denis had told her about killing Heath and Dai Irons. And was afraid. "Denis, love, I really did return to Melbourne to see you. You are my master, indeed you are. But this business of Irons . . ."

"He is almost seventy and the Bible says that a man need have no more years than three score and ten. There is always the chance that if he were to shuffle off this mortal coil, I might finally profit in this new commonwealth of ours. To date, he has seen that I do not."

"What can I do?"

"Protect yourself. Help me. What happens to you if he changes his will? And make no mistake about it, he plans to do just that. You are still a handsome woman, though God knows you have the soul of a viper. But without money, even your looks will not last long."

She cleared her throat. "Were I free to marry, would you still want me as your wife?"

He nodded. "God forgive me, I cannot help myself. After all these years I cannot help myself. At times I wonder which of us calls the tune and which of us does the little dance."

She crossed the room, smiled and stroked his round, perspiring face. "I shall do your bidding, master. And we shall be man and wife, as you desire. Always as you desire."

Irons stood off to the side and watched Morag lay flowers on Alan's grave. He had come directly from the docks, where he and Deakin and the others had landed with triumphant news.

In London they had convinced the Admiralty to consent to Australia having its own navy. The ships would come under British control in time of war and money to build a battlecruiser, three light cruisers, three submarines and six destroyers, would come from a loan of almost four million pounds. Irons, Deakin and the labor delegates sent by Fisher had bitterly fought the requirement that the vessels be built in England, but in the end they had lost. Australia would have its navy, but its working force would not get the job of creating it. Darcy Corder had had much to do with this part of the agreement. He had gotten some of his own back after all. Still, it was a triumph. Until Irons landed at the dock and heard about Alan's death.

"Blue Dan's men," said Morag. "I am certain. They did not mean to kill Alan. They just wanted to scare off his supporters. But matters got out of hand. Blue Dan is now in Ireland to grieve alone. No one knows how long he plans to stay there."

"I am sorry, lass. I know how much you loved him. He was a good man."

Morag touched Alan's headstone. "The nights are the worst. I expect him to come home filled with excitement, bursting with ideas. And the bed is cold without him. Without—"

She threw herself into her father's arms. "His own brother. Blue Dan—"

"He did not mean it, lass. His men acted on their own. He feels the pain as you do."

Morag looked up at her father. "He took away my husband and my sons have no father. How can he feel what I feel when he is neither wife nor mother?"

"Morag, listen—"

"When Davy Pease was murdered, what did you do? And Lord a'Becket's quiet death. What about that?"

Irons was shocked. "You knew?"

"I am nobody's fool, father. Johnny-Johnny, a man who was a brother to you, disappears for good. And at the same time Lord a'Becket passes away from seemingly natural causes. And Jack Straw dies a violent death. He fires two shots from his revolver and the bullets are never found. And Johnny-Johnny is never found, either. But then, do not Aborigines prefer to die in the open, nearer to nature and their God? Yes, father, I knew. And approved."

Irons touched her face and said nothing for a long time. Then, "When it is done, share the knowledge of it with no one. Bear the weight of it alone, no matter how heavily it lies upon you."

She nodded, understanding perfectly what he had just said to her and filled with resolve to proceed with her revenge.

33 _____

GENISTA had insisted that the meeting concerning their divorce take place in Melbourne. Sydney was not her city and never had been. If she were to capitulate, then better she do it somewhere pleasant. Irons, desperate to be rid of her, would have gone to the Sahara. Instead he had only to go to the hotel on Spencer Street, a rundown and unpainted establishment catering to whores, thieves and drunks. Not the sort of place one associated with Genista, but who knew what was going through her mind?

"She doesn't have a mind," said Lou. "She has tentacles and used them well. I really do think she'd make a nice meal for one of your eighteen-foot white sharks."

"Be of a good cheer, Apache. When I return I hope to be able to sit down with you and select a wedding date." Apache was his nickname for her; Lou had been born and raised in the Arizona territory, a very wild part of the American west, which had yet to attain statehood.

"Yesterday would suit me fine," said Lou, referring to Irons' selection of a day.

"Would you settle for tomorrow?"

"I'd settle for Genista's head on a pole. Go on, leave.

The sooner you get out of here, the sooner you can come back.''

Now in the hotel he paused before room eight and was about to knock when he heard Genista cry out, ''Please don't! Please don't!'' Irons turned the knob. Locked. Stepping back, he lifted his foot and kicked the lock, sending the door flying open. Rushing into the room he saw two men tearing at Genista's clothing. Irons lifted his stick, ready to bring it down on the nearest one but there was a searing pain in the back of his head. Genista screamed again and Irons willed himself to help her, but there was more pain, pain which filled his skull. He dropped to his knees and the man behind him struck Irons once more. The Irishman fell forward onto a threadbare, stained carpet. Irons thought he smelled smoke and he imagined himself to be floating, leaving his body and hovering in the air to stare down at himself on the floor. His mother called to him and he was a boy again, in Dublin playing with homemade toys.

Genista called his name, but everything around Michael disappeared and he himself felt nothing.

The death of Michael Irons not only made newspaper headlines in Australia, but in England as well. The parliaments of both countries read resolutions praising him as a great patriot; his dear friend Alfred Deakin, now prime minister of Australia for a third time, was so broken by the news that he had to be excused from his duties for a day. Morag, in shock, remained in total seclusion for a week, emerging only to attend her father's funeral. In January 1910 he was buried in Sydney with Deakin, his cabinet, the Governor-General, the premier of New South Wales, the British consul and representatives of all political parties in attendance.

Genista had been hurt badly. Her nose had been broken and her face badly bruised. In addition the men who had murdered and robbed her husband had also cut off her hair in brutal fashion and the experience had left her numb. In a turn around of affection, Morag had sympathized with Genista and done everything to help her. The experience had been terrifying and Genista needed all the help she could get.

The tragedy of Lou Heller, however, would always mystify Morag. Two weeks after Irons' death, Lou died quietly in her sleep, apparently the victim of a broken heart.

"She loved him so," Morag said to Genista, who nodded. "I understand."

"I will have her buried beside him. He would have liked that."

Genista wept into a handkerchief. "He was so special. Who could have done this to him?"

"Perhaps one day we'll find out. Stay here in the house for as long as you choose. If you need anything, the servants are at your disposal."

She looked at Genista. Hair hacked down to the skull and a swollen nose. She had indeed suffered quite a bit.

Alone in her room a terrified Genista trembled in the dark and wondered why Denis had betrayed her. Why had he first degraded her with the beating and loss of her hair, then almost had her killed? She had not spoken to him since Iron's death and had no way of knowing what was on his mind. Hadn't she done as he asked? Hadn't she gotten Iron's to come to the hotel? How was she to know Denis had planned to kill her husband?

Meanwhile she felt miserable and looked worse. She needed Morag's help. No one suspected a thing. Merely an unfortunate happenstance. Genista had gone to meet her husband in a rather seedy hotel and he had . . .

Too horrible to think about. She needed rest and care. One day she would ask Denis why had he done this to her, but for now she was going to stay clear of him. She didn't understand him anymore.

*   *   *

April 1910

In one of his last official acts before turning over the reins of government to Andrew Fisher, who for the second time would be a labor prime minister, Alfred Deakin stood before packed houses of parliament and read in a clear voice—"We, the undersigned, do petition the British Admiralty to assign the name Michael Bourke Irons to Australia's first battleship."

There was more but Morag, both sad and proud, did not hear it. She wanted to break down and weep and cry out for her father, but she could not. She stood between her two sons, both with the reddish-blonde hair of their father and growing taller every day. She whispered to them, "When you are grown, you will serve on that ship, the both of you."

They nodded. She was always right and she was a good mother. It was fitting that they honor their grandfather by doing as she ordered.

Alan would have loved this day, too, she thought. Deakin was making ready to turn over the government not only to a labor prime minister, but to a parliament in which labor had the majority in both the senate and representatives. Never in Australia's brief history had one party captured all of the needed governmental power. Fisher had promised to give Australia its own sea and land defense and they would all be "made in Australia."

The applause brought Morag back to reality. At Deakin's urging she and Genista came forward and each received a copy of the proclamation. Genista, well on the mend, looked beautiful. She wore a hat to cover her short hair, but she looked stunning and the tears in her eyes only added to her appeal. She took Morag's hand. "Thank you. Had it not been for you—"

She couldn't finish. Morag embraced her and the parliament, on its feet, applauded the two women.

*   *   *

On board the steam ship taking her to England, Genista relaxed in her cabin. She had a bank draft in her purse for one hundred thousand pounds and she was free of Australia, and of Denis, who had behaved so treacherously. He had told her so.

"I wanted to fix you so that no other man would ever look at you again. I wanted you so broken that you would never leave me."

She was leaving him now. For good. Leaving the gullible Morag, Sydney and all of Australia. And no one would ever know of her role in her husband's death. Only Denis and his hired thugs knew and they would never tell.

There was a knock on her door.

"Yes?"

Again the knock.

Genista walked to the door and cracked it.

Morag.

A shocked Genista could only open the door and stand aside as Morag entered. And then two men pushed their way in and closed the cabin door.

When it is done, share the knowledge of it with no one. Denis a'Becket and Blue Dan were already as good as dead. But first . . .

Morag said softly to Genista, "Now you're worth killing."